OATH OF THE SIX

Book Thirteen in the Pantracia Chronicles

OATH OF THE SIX

Amanda Muratoff & Kayla Hansen

www.Pantracia.com

Cover design by Andrei Bat.

ISBN: 978-1-990781-04-9

Second Edition: February 2024

For Adam & Dave.

We know we're a lot.

Thank you.

♥

The Pantracia Chronicles:

Visit www.Pantracia.com for our pronunciation
guide and to discover more.

Chapter 1

Autumn, 2032 R.T. (recorded time)

AMARIE'S BACK HIT THE WALL, air leaving her lungs in a rush as Kin's body pressed against hers. A whisper of a breath escaped before his mouth closed the gap between them, his tongue playing along her lips.

Shadows rippled over the wall on the other side of the small alcove. Curtains, dancing in time with the celebration outside, fluttered with each gust of sunset breeze.

Her stomach still roiled, her muscles vibrating against her will.

Queen.

Kin's hands roamed over her dress, rounding her backside as his hips rocked against her.

She reveled in the distraction from the title she never wanted but tried to accept.

"They're going to notice your absence," Amarie breathed, voice low as his teeth grazed her neck.

He growled against her skin, nipping at her as his kisses moved lower. "Let them. What can they say?" His hand, no longer as smooth as it'd been before, slid up her neck into her hair, encouraging her chin back to grant him greater access.

A whimper slipped from Amarie's throat as he tasted her collarbone. She closed her eyes, letting herself melt into a world without titles and bloodlines and assassination threats.

The citizens outside the Feyorian palace may have been celebrating, but not all were joyous for their new king.

And queen.

Shoving the thoughts from her mind, Amarie pulled Kin's mouth back to hers, only vaguely aware of the occasional set of footsteps passing through the hallway. A door separated it from the shallow alcove they'd retreated to, and that door was enough.

The medallion adorning Kin's coronation cloak thunked on the ground, muted by the rich pelt that fell around it. He kissed her harder with each minute tug at the fabric of her dress, his desire apparent as he rocked against her. Moaning against her mouth, he broke the kiss and pressed his forehead to hers. "I want you. Right now."

Amarie bit her lower lip, touching the tip of her nose to his as she laced her arms over his shoulders. "I'm not going anywhere," she whispered. "And no one is coming in here, my *king*." Lifting her chin, she bit his lip and gently pulled.

His breath caught before he opened his eyes, the steel blue of them piercing even in the dim light of their alcove. "Don't doubt Damien's uncanny ability to appear when he is least wanted." He ran his hands down her hips, gripping her ass harder before lifting her to pull her weight against his hips. "My *queen*."

A chuckle escaped her, even as her stomach flopped again. "Even our *beloved* Rahn'ka won't be able to open that door. We may not have long, but we have long enough." She pulled on her skirts, grateful for the few layers rather than the cupcake of a dress the tailor originally suggested. With Kin supporting her weight, she wrapped her legs around him. "Unless you'd like to wait for a more... convenient time." She murmured the last words against his neck, one hand buried in his hair.

"We've waited long enough." Kin reached beneath the fabric. His fingers freed the front of his pants before they teased the center of her core, sending a jolt of pleasure through her. At her gasp, he took her mouth with his again. His hand worked feverishly to clear the various fabrics out of the way before his touch found skin.

Amarie arched against the wall, tilting her head back as her chest heaved.

Kin's mouth turned molten on her skin as he eased himself into her, inch by silken inch, until fully sheathed in her warmth. His groan rumbled along her skin as he held still, letting her body adjust.

Smirking against his kiss, she tilted her hips, drawing a short gasp from him.

Kin moved, just as she needed him to, to drown out that incessant, irritating voice at the back of her mind. The voice that kept insisting on her unworthiness.

It blurred, dissipating like snow in summer as pleasure built in her core. It warmed her, spreading heat through her limbs until everywhere she touched him burned in the best way.

He leaned into her, his lips pressing fiery trails along her neck until he nuzzled at the base of her ear. His breath teased the sensitive skin, teeth grazing her. "I love you." His whisper vibrated through every part of her. Every inch. Coupled with his steady pulse inside her, she blazed like wildfire.

All those years apart. All those years asleep. All that time spent trying to hate him. Trying to forget him and trying to move on. None of it mattered anymore. They weren't just together, but married. Bound together for the rest of whatever fate would throw at them.

Amarie's legs shook as the anticipation intensified. She panted, mouth slightly agape as she gripped him tighter. And then she shattered, his mouth finding hers to stifle the cry she hadn't even tried to stop.

Using her heels, she pulled him deeper, riding out her euphoria as his body responded to hers. His breaths shortened, faltered, and he groaned into her mouth as heat flooded her.

They remained, unmoving, as they caught their breath.

"And I love you," she finally answered, kissing his jaw, his cheek, his mouth. "Always."

Kin smiled with her kiss, letting it resolve slowly. He leaned back, meeting her gaze as he ran a hand through her hair. He didn't speak, just watched her. But something in his eyes spoke to the thoughts he'd expressed moments before the coronation and countless times before that.

Amarie smiled, rolling her lips together. "I'm lucky too, you know."

Easing her back to the floor, Kin glanced at the door while fastening his pants, another anxious set of footsteps passing by. "We probably should get back. The coronation is done, but there's still places to be. Even if I'd rather just enjoy the quiet we're finally getting."

She rearranged her dress, using the unnecessary pad in her bust line as a barrier in her underwear to prevent his seed from ruining anything.

The quiet will last at least a short time.

Damien and Katrin had worked together to create wards around the palace. Not just to keep Uriel out, but Shades and Corrupted, as well. It would do little against anyone else Uriel employed, but it would have to do. Gods knew the creature was probably desperate enough to try anything, now.

"Your hair is a little..." Amarie snickered, trying to fix it. "I hope mine isn't this messy."

Kin ran a hand over the side of her head, where her long auburn hair had been pinned back with a diamond-encrusted comb. "Not too bad. I only messed it up a little. We'll just say you had to get away and go for a ride."

Amarie rolled her eyes, smoothing her hair and dress in a final check. "They may have bought that excuse twenty years ago, but..." She let her voice trail off, walking towards the door. With everything else she'd suffered... everything else they'd endured, it seemed foolish to still grieve for her horse. The desire for late night rides or fast escapes along the beach had yet to return. If they ever would.

She touched the door handle, releasing the Art she'd used to seal it from unwanted visitors. "Let's find the others. Hopefully some of them are still sober enough to have a toast with us."

Kin stooped to pick up the dense coronation cloak, shrugging it over his shoulders. "At least this whole king thing created a good excuse for all of us to be together. Do you think Damien will stay off the obvious topic until tomorrow? Pretty sure Ahria made him promise he would."

"Rae did too," Amarie pointed out as they exited the alcove. "So I think he will. At least for one night. It's nice to be all together for a *good* reason for once."

She wasn't entirely sure when she'd started considering these people friends, but somewhere along the way, it'd happened. After years of fighting solo, of trusting no one, it still felt odd. But they'd become her friends, and in some cases, even like family. All fighting together for a single purpose.

Her heart squeezed. "Do you think we'll still all be... friends, after all this is done?"

Kin took her hand as they strode together down the arched hallway. "I think after all of this is done, the bonds we have will be stronger than ever. We just have to get to that point."

Amarie smiled up at him—at her husband—and nodded. "We won't worry about that tonight, though. Tonight we celebrate."

Chapter 2

"MAYBE WE SHOULD FIGURE OUT—"

"No." Rae lifted a finger while holding her glass of whisky with the same hand. "No."

Damien scowled. "You don't even know what I was—"

"No," she repeated, meeting her husband's feigned fury with a playful smirk. "The only thing we need to figure out is if you prefer this whisky..." She clinked her glass against the one he held. "Or that one." With a tilt of her chin, she gestured to the lighter-colored amber liquor on the table.

Lifting the glass to his lips, Damien took a slow sip, still watching his wife with his single bright hazel eye. "The guests of honor aren't even here." His gaze twitched behind her to where the door to the king's private rooms met the hall.

The area reminded him of Jarrod's chambers in Helgath, with multiple living rooms, guest rooms, and dining areas. And his private bedchambers beyond those.

"But Ahria is here," Rae murmured. "And you promised."

Damien gave an exaggerated sigh as he took another swig of his whisky. "I'll behave."

"Doubtful." The neck of a decanter tapped against Damien's glass. Corin grinned down at his brother as he filled the glass to the brim, and Damien rushed to sip some as a trickle overflowed onto his hand.

Rae laughed, grinning at Corin.

"Gods, I don't need that much." Damien awkwardly leaned forward to slurp the overflowing whisky, trying to refrain from spilling it on his fine clothes. The finely crafted leather tunic fit him perfectly, tailored by the royal seamstress in Veralian. More recently, he'd asked her to craft the matching eye patch that covered the wound even the powers of the Rahn'ka couldn't heal.

"I beg to differ, little brother." Corin nudged his shoulder before turning Damien's head towards the others. "*That's* what we should *all* be doing."

On the other chaise and couch, Matthias lounged with Katrin, Jarrod, Liam, and Dani. And they laughed, gasped, and held their breath, listening to Liam tell a story.

Micah sat with Talia on a loveseat, quietly conversing, just the two of them. Coltin and Deylan occupied the chairs across from them, also engrossed in their own conversation.

Neco's tail thumped on the floor as he rolled onto his side, begging for belly rubs from Conrad and Ahria at the edge of Liam's engaged audience. Ahria leaned over to indulge the beast, who looked more the part of an attention-starved pooch, while Conrad remained protectively behind her. Her ever present bodyguard, stiff as he usually was, though a half empty whisky glass in his hand rested casually against the back of Ahria's chair.

"See?" Rae murmured, stroking Damien's arm. "It's all right to relax a little, even just for tonight. Blow off some steam. We've earned it."

"Maybe you should get a dice game going, Sis. Might even loosen up the prince over there." Corin tilted his head in Conrad's direction. "He and Damien both look like they could hold up the Dul'Idur Gate with their spines."

"Dice games are hardly becoming of a bunch of royals. Or did you forget again? That's what we've all become." Damien lifted his eyebrows at Corin, who frowned.

"Oh damn, is that what happened?" Corin rolled his eyes. "We're still people with money to be lost. Just like any poor sap. Doesn't matter if half the people in this room wear crowns."

"Half is a bit of an exaggeration..." Rae looked around the space, counting, and then cringing. "Or perhaps not."

"You plebeians will be out numbered as soon as the reasons for the celebration arrive, too." Corin grinned, topping off Rae's whisky before setting the decanter on a side table. "Good thing your big brother married up so you could—"

"Could what?" Rae straightened. "What, Corin? So he could marry a lowly thief?" She rose onto her knees on the chair, giving him a playful, threatening look. "I *will* fight you."

Corin looked her up and down, shrugging. "And win. Probably. But without your Art I'd give it a solid maybe." He touched his bicep, playfully flexing the muscles beneath his formal king's consort attire. "I'm still master of war beneath all these frills. Besides, Jarrod would be very disappointed if I let myself go."

Rae snorted. "Getting a little gray, though, aren't you, old man?" She quirked one eyebrow, taunting. "I see one... right..." Slowly extending her arm, she poked his temple. "There."

Corin opened his mouth, surely to retort, but before any words came out, the doors to the large chamber opened.

Conversations paused, and everyone stood, Rae following suit, though on the chair cushion.

Kin and Amarie stood at the threshold, looking slightly more flushed than they had at the coronation.

Rae narrowed her eyes at her friend and chuckled inwardly. Only months ago, the idea of Amarie marrying Kin would have set Rae on edge. But things had changed. Drastically. And they were happy. And she would do her best to see the best in Kin, despite the history he carried with Bellamy's namesake.

The room erupted in applause, a sharp whistle coming from someone on the other side of the room.

The freshly-crowned newlyweds entered the room, the doors shutting behind them. Conrad was quick to pour drinks for them, while Ahria hugged her mother.

Damien poked Rae in the ribs. "You look like you know something, Dice."

Rae side-eyed her husband. "Oh, I most definitely do, Lieutenant."

He hummed as he stepped away from his chair. "Should we go congratulate them? On both recent changes?"

With the preparations, neither Damien nor Rae had been able to speak to Kin or Amarie since they'd arrived. Fortunately, Matthias had been available to share the news of their wedding, rather than learning it at the same time as the rest of the kingdom during the coronation when Amarie was crowned beside him.

"Mhmm," Rae murmured. As soon as Ahria released her mother and moved to her father, the Mira'wyld launched herself over the back of the chair, holding the fabric of her thin Aueric-style skirt to avoid getting caught. She crossed the room in long strides before she engulfed the new queen in a tight embrace. "I can't believe you got married without me."

Amarie laughed, squeezing her back. "I know. I know. But this can be a celebration of both events, can it not?" She pulled away enough to look at Rae's face, the apology right under the surface of her smile.

Rae nodded, grinning. "Of course. I'm so happy for you."

Her friend raised a brow. "Are you?"

"Yep," Rae murmured. "I promise." She released her, letting her take the glass of whisky Conrad offered. She didn't even wait for Amarie to wrinkle her nose before taking it from her and gesturing to the table of refreshments. "There's wine over there."

Damien's glass clinked against Kin's before he took the new king into a rough embrace. He muttered something, but Rae turned with Amarie towards the large banquet table along the wall.

"How are you feeling, with all of this?" Rae slid the unwanted whisky onto the table, plucking up a wine bottle. "You all right?"

Amarie met her gaze, irises their usual vivid blue. "It's been... nerve-wracking." She huffed, picking up the glass of wine Rae poured for her. "But I suppose that's normal after a spontaneous wedding and unexpected induction into royalty."

Rae smirked, lifting her glass in a playful toast. "To new roles in life?" She chuckled, sipping. "It's certainly a bit of a change. Especially for women like us with our old habits."

"Are you calling me a thief?" Amarie quirked a brow, lips tight to hold back her smile.

"I'd never *dream* of it," Rae whispered.

"Plotting already?" Deylan approached beside them, smiling at his sister before embracing her. "Congratulations, Ree."

As he released her, Rae studied his arm, wondering if the skin beneath his formal attire still bore the scars from the Shade's attack like Damien's did. "Looks like Lygen did a decent job patching you up."

Deylan opened his mouth to reply, but Ahria appeared beside him and cut him off.

"Are you going to call both of us that? Won't it get confusing?"

Her uncle scowled. "What? I have to choose which of you to call Ree?"

The conversation flowed easily over the next hour, interrupted frequently by refills and people mingling through the room.

True to her nature, Rae started a dice game at one table, but abandoned it once those playing understood the rules. Neco slept in the corner by the entrance doors, ever their guardian, and as the night wore on, cigars were lit along with candles.

Wafts of aromatic smoke and a cool autumn breeze drifted in from the balcony, where Damien, Corin, Dani, and Liam sat. Micah stood with Talia near a window, and Rae narrowed her eyes at their low tones of conversation.

Something is going on with those two.

Rae poured herself a glass of water, the alcohol blurring her mind as she scanned the rest of the room. Kin sat with Amarie on the sofa, her feet bare and on his lap. The Mira'wyld smiled, taking in the solace of the room. The laughter, the smiles, the joy. It felt so overdue, so beyond earned, that she took a minute just to bask in it. She had no illusions that it would last forever, or even for long, but for now... it was perfect. This was what they all needed, and the memories of these moments would sustain them during whatever came next.

Swallowing a cool gulp of water, Rae just watched.

"Thought you'd be over there throwing dice with the others." Damien's warm voice still managed to send a shiver up her spine. His hands slipped around her waist from behind, and she leaned back into his chest. The leather strap of his eyepatch rubbed against her temple, still strange, but a small price to pay.

Turning her face towards his neck, she looked up at him, a surge of gratitude welling up within her. "I guess I'm more of a spectator tonight."

A cheer erupted from the table, where Katrin gathered winnings while Matthias groaned.

"What are you thinking?" Damien murmured into her hair.

Rae let out a long breath, the room still spinning. "Everyone is so happy." Her throat tightened, though she wasn't sure why. Perhaps there had been too much of the opposite. Too much anguish and loss. And Damien had come so close to joining Nymaera. The sound of the machine that had kept him alive still haunted her dreams.

His grip tightened, and he kissed her forehead. "I know." He rocked her slightly, kissing her again. "It's the moments like this that make it all worth it."

Turning in his embrace, Rae faced him. "It wouldn't have been worth it," she whispered, angling her face up to meet his gaze. "If I'd lost you, none of this would have been worth it."

"It was close, but we know better now. We won't make the same mistakes again." He brushed hair back from her face, tucking it behind her ears. "We're in too deep now. He knows who we all are and what we're trying to do. Tonight's only quiet because of the wards." His steady stare moved back and forth between her eyes. "Tomorrow, after we all have time to talk, we'll find a way to keep everyone safe."

Rae studied him, his face, the leather eyepatch, and breathed, "Kiss me."

Without a heartbeat of hesitation, Damien pressed his lips to hers, helping the rest of the room slip away and take her fears with it. He tasted like fire wine and smoke, and she wondered when he'd switched from drinking whisky. And where'd he'd gotten the tasty alternative she had somehow missed being introduced to the party.

As he drew away, she murmured, "Who brought Xaxos fire wine?"

He thumbed her lower lip playfully. "Leave it to you to recognize that flavor from a kiss. Such a lush..." He tutted his tongue.

Rae smiled, licking the tip of his thumb. "You didn't answer my question."

"Conrad." He squeezed her middle, as if to say he wasn't about to let her go. "A gift for the newlyweds from Ziona, I suppose. Though from what I can tell, it's Ahria who favors it."

"Perhaps he thought her mother would share the preference." Rae tilted her head. "Though there's something poetic about bringing Helgathian liquor to a Feyorian coronation as a gift from a Zionan prince."

"Times are indeed changing. Something good to come out of all of this. Perhaps Pantracia will finally have the unity it's always needed."

"Not until I get a glass of the fire wine, I'm afraid," she whispered, mouth near his. "And perhaps my husband will accompany me in joining the fun table in the room."

On cue, another cheer burst from the dice game, where Katrin again pulled winnings towards her. Playful accusations of cheating floated between the players until Jarrod laughed and gestured to Matthias. "Why don't you just go back and change it?"

The Isalican king grinned, tapping two dice on the table. "Because *that*, my friend, would actually be cheating."

Rae lifted her chin and breathed over Damien's jaw towards his ear. "Please?"

His chest rumbled. "Actions like that don't exactly encourage me to take you anywhere but our bedroom." Hands roamed down her sides, but loosened their hold. "We should enjoy the peace, right, Dice?"

"We can play a few rounds," she murmured against his skin, distracted by his scent. "And then enjoy the quiet in our bedroom until sunrise. Sound fair?"

"A few rounds." He relented, slipping his hands away. "And I'll smuggle a bottle back to the room. For just the two of us."

She lifted her eyebrows. "I'm a wonderful influence. Damien Lanoret. A thief at last."

Chapter 3

SLIPPING SILENTLY OUT OF BED, Conrad parted the curtains. The sliver of bright sunlight shot across the room, passing over Ahria's legs still tangled with their bedsheets. He dared to edge the curtain open a little further, but didn't let the light travel higher than her hips.

Regardless of his efforts, Ahria groaned and pulled the blanket over her head. "No..." she whispered. "It's the middle of the night."

He chuckled, blinking out the window at the black shape of the mountains beyond it. The navy roof shingles of the palace shone like jewels, offsetting the otherwise dark structures. "Actually, it looks to be closer to lunch time."

Ahria hissed. "Stop yelling at me."

Shaking his head, Conrad crept across the room to prevent his feet from trodding on the wooden floor too loudly. He leaned over her, blocking the sunlight as he pulled the blanket down and pressed a gentle kiss to her temple. "Someone drank too much fire wine last night," he whispered.

"You can't blame me for enjoying what *you* brought." She blinked at him, her icy-blue eyes slightly bloodshot. "Can't we sleep longer? I need my strength." Burying her face in the pillow, she sighed.

"If only, my love. But if I recall, the plan was to meet for lunch. However, rest assured, I doubt you are the only one suffering. Misery loves company, doesn't it?" He kissed her temple again, running his fingers through her hair as he cuddled up behind her. He'd grown used to the feeling of her body pressed against his, and craved every moment of it.

Suddenly, the idea of needing to leave their bedroom sounded monumentally difficult. Not only to remain near her, but because his body craved more sleep as well.

He couldn't remember a night that he'd slept soundly in the past several months, often laying awake while his mind struggled with dreams. Nightmares. But he didn't let Ahria see. She, fortunately, never seemed to notice, even amid her own troubled nights. And while he'd only gotten a few hours of solid sleep that night, he would keep it to himself.

"You're not suffering." The pillow muffled her words.

He smiled, pleased she'd slept through his awake hours again. "I may have been slightly more restrained."

Ahria turned to peek at him. "You're always more restrained," she murmured, brow twitching as she looked at his face. The corner of her mouth lifted in a ghost of a smile. "Almost always."

He lifted an eyebrow. "And, unfortunately, I will need to remain so this morning." He ran his hand down her hip, following the smooth curves of her naked body beneath the sheets. He fought against the fire, just enjoying the feel of her despite the business they would need to undertake soon. "We should get dressed and check in."

Groaning again, Ahria abandoned the pillow and buried her face in his collar. She took a deep breath, humming. "How do you smell so good right now?"

Chuckling, he kissed the top of her head. "Just to torture you, I'm afraid. But it's probably better that only one of us needs a bath this morning. Limit the possible distractions."

"Ah, distractions..." Ahria pulled away from him with exaggerated distaste and stretched her arms over her head. The sheets only covered to her waist, giving him an unobstructed view of her bare chest. She looked at him, not a hint of color staining her cheeks at her brazen nakedness. "Will you fill the tub for me, Captain?"

It took more strength than he expected to rise from the bed. "Anything for you, temptress." Pulling on some rumpled sleep pants, he watched her from the corner of his eye as he made his way to the bathing chamber's door at the far side of their bedroom. The lavish accommodations were appropriate for the new princess of Feyor, though being in such a place still felt foreign to him. But she belonged in such luxury.

The quiet of the bathing chamber disappeared as he worked the knobs to start the flow of water. Steam filled the chilled space, the large frosted windows beyond the freestanding brass bath doing little to keep out the cold of late autumn.

In the bedroom, blankets and sheets shuffled around on the bed, and he wondered if she had risen or simply made herself comfortable again to fall back asleep.

With the onset of the colder weather, memories returned to him of the weeks before he'd even met Ahria the previous year. The ship had taken damage in a storm, and they'd sailed south to warmer temperatures to deal with it. It'd been a couple months after that when Ahria had stowed away on his ship.

My ship.

He swallowed, checking the heat of the bath water.

So much has changed. How has it been less than a year?

His mind warred to comprehend it all. Suddenly being pushed into the position of crown prince hadn't been Ahria's doing, even if it had entwined their fates. And the rest of it... The Shade that had attacked her and killed her father had been after his position, not her specifically. At least with now being a part of the war against Uriel, he knew the name of the being responsible.

Even though I have no business being present in this upcoming meeting.

"Conrad?" Ahria's whisper jerked him from his thoughts.

He turned to see her sitting up in bed, dark chestnut hair tousled, with the blankets wrapped around her body under her arms.

Straightening, he shook away the thoughts. "Hmm?" He tried to look distracted by the collection of bathing soaps and oils on an iron shelf beside the tub.

She blinked those gorgeous eyes, but something haunted lay behind them. "Is something wrong?"

He hid a flinch from her expression. He didn't need to worry her. "Everything is fine." He smiled faintly, hoping it would lighten the tension still hovering inside, but she didn't return it. Thoughts of Uriel, of the monster who could have easily killed him in that underwater bunker, cast a shadow over his mind. "Eucalyptus, lavender, or jasmine today?"

Ahria only watched him for another moment, silent, until her throat bobbed, and she shrugged. "Lavender is fine." Turning from him, she got off the bed and left his field of view, but he could hear her brushing her hair.

The festivities had been undisturbed, but Conrad wondered if Katrin and Damien knew more, since they maintained the Art-crafted wards surrounding the palace. His hands found the oils without his full focus, dark amalgamations dancing through imaginary hallways. Corrupted, unstoppable with his sword, taunting him as he leaned over the tub.

The scent took a moment to register, but too late, he realized it was wrong.

"Damn it." Conrad checked the bottle in his hand, which he could have sworn was lavender, but now showed the image of jasmine.

Ahria entered the bathing chamber a moment later, running her fingers through her smooth hair. She didn't look at him as she stepped into the nearly full tub.

"I'm sorry." Conrad returned the bottle to the shelf.

"What for?" Her gaze shot to his.

"I put in the wrong oil. I... just distracted, I guess." He thought about standing. Leaving to give Ahria her privacy, but something kept his knees bent where he crouched near the head of the tub.

"Oh." Pausing, Ahria sank into the tub and shook her head. "It's fine. It smells nice." Despite her reassurance, what looked like disappointment slouched her shoulders. She slid deeper, slipping beneath the surface entirely.

He watched her, so calm under the warm water, her eyes closed and brow relaxed. She stayed under so long that he almost reached for her before she finally rose above the surface.

Wiping drips from her face, she retrieved the vanilla-scented soap from the small side table and began washing herself.

He tried again to stand. But again, his knees refused. Giving up, he sat on the cold tile. He stared at his hand on the rim of the tub, trying to imagine his sword in it. His chest ached when the image faded from his mind. "I'm..." The words caught in his throat. Looking at her, he could see the worry in her eyes. The hope that he might finally talk about everything plaguing him.

Why is it so hard? It's Ahria.

She placed a warm, wet hand on his, putting the soap down. But she said nothing, pressed for nothing, and patiently waited as she usually did.

It felt as if something squeezed his throat. Black shadow tendrils that he couldn't fight against. Closing his eyes, he pushed all the strength he could muster into his legs and stood. "I better go get dressed."

Ahria remained silent until he reached the doorway to the bedroom. "I know you don't sleep."

Her statement stopped him short, but he didn't face her as she continued.

"Do you think it's a coincidence that I hold you more those nights? Do you think I'd judge you for telling me the truth, when I suffer just as you do? I'm right here, Conrad." Her voice wavered, and he swallowed. "I'm right here. And I'll always be right here. Whenever you're ready to talk."

Though she'd phrased her words as questions, her final statement held an air of finality to it, like she expected no response from him. Because that's all he'd ever given her. No response.

He remained in the doorway, trying to shake the shadows. "I know. I just..." He tilted his head back, rolling his eyes. It felt so ridiculous. All of it.

Staring at the door from the bedchamber that would lead to the hallway and ultimately the meeting room where the others would be, he clenched his jaw. All the heroes that were fighting to free Pantracia from darkness.

I don't belong.

"Can I get you anything before the meeting?" He turned back to her, steeling his expression. She had enough on her plate without his insecurities.

Ahria stared at him, eyelashes wet. She gave a minute shake of her head before looking away.

"What do you mean he tried?" Jarrod interrupted Damien, who sighed as Conrad opened the heavy oaken doors of the meeting hall.

"I mean just that. He *tried*. I don't know what else to tell you."

Matthias tapped the table. "But he failed, obviously. That's what matters."

"But he could try again," Amarie cut in. "When you're not here."

"Which is the entire point of this meeting. So we can plan and be ready for *when* that happens."

He urged his feet to keep moving into the room, Ahria coming in behind him. She took a deep breath as she sat next to Rae, who looked over at the two of them as Ahria spoke. "We miss something?"

Conrad sat beside her, keeping quiet. They hadn't spoken more than a few words to each other since her bath, and tension grated between them.

The large hall was likely intended for intimate dinners hosted by the king of Feyor. Large windows on one side left Conrad feeling far too vulnerable, especially considering the conversation topic. But everyone else seemed unfazed, sitting along the edge of the wide table.

The unlit intricate iron chandeliers hung from the ceiling like ominous cages, though enough natural light streamed in through the uncurtained windows. Even with the sunlight, the wooden paneling and stone floors kept the room darker than he'd like.

Kin sat at the head of the table, Amarie and Matthias on either side of him, Deylan beside his sister. The doorway behind him looked oddly empty without the presence of guards.

The only guards he and Ahria had encountered had been far down the hallway from the actual hall's entrance.

Food had already been served and placed at the center of the table, and Conrad couldn't help but notice the lack of staff. But someone must have prepared the roasted meats, fresh baked rolls and cheese. A heaping bed of salad and roasted root vegetables sat near Damien, along with vegetable-stuffed sandwiches.

"Uriel tried to pass through the wards last night." Rae rubbed her temples. "He failed. That's all they're talking about." She reached for a pitcher of water, refilling her empty glass, and poured two more for Ahria and Conrad. She picked at the food on her plate, which looked mostly untouched.

Ahria chose a brown roll of bread and a few pieces of

cheese. Modest, considering how much she usually ate. Given how awful she felt this morning, he hardly blamed her.

Conrad looked down the table again, where Damien filled his plate with salad, his head turned to whisper something to Deylan while ignoring Kin and Jarrod's prodding glares.

A bird swooped by the windows behind him, and Conrad reached for a sword he didn't have. He growled at himself silently before filling his plate. "Am I the only one bothered by those big windows when they're talking about Uriel trying to get in here?"

"I like the windows." The airy voice on his other side came from Dani, who gazed towards the bright light with cloudy eyes.

"Don't worry." The man on Dani's other side leaned forward, a wry smile on his lips. "Katrin and Damien still have this place locked down tight. No Corrupted getting within a hundred yards of that window. And the dragons are flying nearby, too."

Conrad tried to take comfort in Liam's words. He hadn't had much contact with the dragon rider. White ran through the sides of his combed-back black hair, but his forearms were corded with muscle and his strong hand rested on top of Dani's beside her plate.

"All right, listen up," Amarie said as she stood from her

spot next to Kin. The room quieted after a few moments, and she waited. "Now that we're all here, there are some things everyone should know." She gestured to Kin, and a second later, the infamous bloodstone bladed dagger appeared before him. It hovered, the red tones in the metal flickering like lava.

Conrad had seen the dagger before at Kin's side, both during their wedding and at the coronation. Its presence had been out of place then, but he hadn't questioned it. Not of the man he might some day consider a father.

"This is Sephysis. Kin, Matthias, and Deylan found..." Amarie paused, looking at Corin, who held his loaded fork motionless halfway between his plate and mouth. "You can keep eating," she teased, smiling as he resumed his meal. "They found the dagger before Uriel could. And before Alana died, she told me that Uriel planned to take the dagger to someone named Melyza in Aidensar. Kiek, to be more specific. Apparently, she has information that Uriel needs, which he'd planned to trade the dagger for."

"And you trust this information from Alana? Who was loyal to Uriel." Corin shook his still full fork at her.

Ahria put her water glass down harder than it deserved. "Yes." She sat straight, shoulders back. "Alana may have served him once, but she used her last minutes to save not just my life, but my mother's and Conrad's as well. We can trust her information."

Corin lifted a hand in placation as Conrad slipped his hand over Ahria's knee beneath the table.

"So we need to find Melyza." Damien looked to Jarrod. "How are those negotiations with Aidensar going? Could we get their assistance?"

The Helgathian king huffed. "Doubtful. They've been stonewalling us pretty hard. I won't be able to get anyone in under a political guise."

"I'll go." Amarie sat, glancing at Kin as if they'd previously discussed this. "Kin will remain here, as we don't want Sephysis anywhere near Melyza."

Kin shifted, face growing taut.

Conrad could understand his hesitation to let Amarie out of his sight after what had happened the last time. He'd trusted Conrad to protect both her and his daughter in Lungaz, but he'd failed.

"Sounds like a little much for one person. Who will go with you?" Dani leaned forward, milky eyes drifting in Katrin's direction. "We were in Kiek a couple years ago. We could get you there faster."

"How's Isalica's relationship with Aidensar?" Corin spoke through a partially full mouth.

"Well enough," Katrin gave a graceful shrug. "I may be able to assist with relations there as our last visit was positive."

Matthias leaned back. "You've been interested in seeing their libraries for years. Perhaps we can use that as the basis for the visit."

"If we both go, then we can leave quickly, too." Dani clicked her tongue, then reached for her water.

Amarie held her mug without drinking. "If Katrin will be researching, it will just be me and Dani. I'd prefer another fighter with us."

"I'll go." Liam leaned forward behind Dani, but the Dtrüa put a hand on his.

"You need to go to Draxix. The dragons should be apprised of all that has been happening." Dani's calm voice only accentuated the frown on her husband's face.

Another pair forced to split up for the endeavor.

Conrad's coffee tasted bitter as he dreaded any suggestion that would force him to separate from Ahria. Of course it would go that way, with how little he could contribute.

"The dragons have been rather silent in recent months." Matthias took a deep breath. "I'll ask Micah to return to Nema's Throne to check in on the kids since we won't be returning home right away." He exchanged a quick glance with his wife, and Katrin nodded with a grateful smile. "And there's a slight issue with the prison, so I'll need our friendly Rahn'ka to accompany me there."

The tension in the room thickened.

"What's the problem with the prison?" Deylan finally spoke.

Matthias shook his head. "Unimportant right now. I'm sure Damien can fix it."

That's not ominously vague at all.

"What would you like from the faction?" Deylan looked between Matthias, Amarie, and Damien.

"Right now... nothing. They've done enough for us already." Damien looked across the table to Rae. "It's because of the faction library that we fully understand how Taeg'nok is carried out. But we'd appreciate your people being ready should something change."

Deylan nodded. "You know how to reach us should that happen. For now, we'll hold and continue our repairs."

"I'll be returning to Helgath with Jarrod and Corin," Rae chimed in, pausing when Neco yipped. "And Neco. I need to check on Sarra and see that the Ashen Hawks are running smoothly."

"When will you be explaining our individual roles in this... spell to lock Uriel up?" Kin spoke for the first time, and Sephysis, floating beside him, twitched, sunlight flicking off the bloodstone blade.

Damien frowned. "We can explain it now, but it may be better to speak of the details for each individual privately. No one will go in blind to their role."

The room quieted.

"What of us?" Conrad had tracked the plan of all their destinations, which hadn't included himself or Ahria.

Will they want me to go to Aidensar?

The idea sounded insane.

Most of the eyes in the room turned in his direction and he suddenly felt infinitely smaller.

"You will return to Ziona with Ahria," Amarie said softly, and he nearly breathed a sigh of relief. "I will be giving Ahria some lessons before you leave, as well as a piece of our power to help keep you safe. The two of you are strongest together and can meet up with us in Isalica when it's time."

Ahria glanced at Conrad and nodded.

"That's everyone," Amarie muttered. "But I still need another to come to Aidensar."

"You could go." Jarrod nudged Corin. "I can survive without *Master of War Lanoret-Martox* for a bit if I must."

The king consort's eyes widened. "Actually go out into the field? I dare say I'm a little rusty, impressive title or not."

Amarie wrinkled her nose. "If he can't fight..."

"He's being daft." Damien waved a hand in his brother's direction. "Corin hasn't gone a day without training and sparring, even if he looks old. He'll be able to protect you.

He's still one of the best fighters in Helgath, even with his *pretentious* title."

"Ah, little brother. You do still know how to talk sweetly to me." Corin touched his cheeks as if blushing, though there was no color there.

Jarrod rolled his eyes. "Aye. Can confirm he still knows which end is the pointy one."

Corin's face sobered, his hand twitching towards Jarrod's, brushing over it before interlacing their fingers. "What about the matters at home?"

A deeper question lay hidden beneath those words, Conrad was almost sure of it, but he didn't dare pry.

The Helgathian king nodded. "I'll take care of it, and Rae will be with me, too."

Corin took a swig from his mug, as if it were a response. And Jarrod seemed to acknowledge it as one.

Amarie hesitated, her gaze locking with Conrad's. The thoughts behind it... he wasn't sure, but she sought something from him. Before he could decide how to react, she looked away and nodded. "All right. Corin will come with me, Katrin, and Dani."

"Matthias and I will go to the prison after dropping Micah off in Nema's Throne. And Matthias will let me know what's going on at the sanctum on the way so I don't walk in completely blind. Rahn'ka or not." Damien smirked in the king's direction. "Liam will go to the dragons. With their silence, we need to know if they're still going to support us in our fight against Uriel. Hells, it'd be nice if they'd even give us a bit more information about him since he started out as one of them." The Rahn'ka paused. "Actually, Liam, do you think you could get me and Matthias a meeting with the dragons' leaders? We could head to Draxix after we're finished at the prison."

Liam hesitated, glancing at his wife before answering, "I don't know. I will speak to Zedren about it and see if we can get you an audience with the Primeval. But I have no idea if they'll allow it."

Damien nodded. "We need all the knowledge we can get to lure him to the prison when we're ready. We don't know anything about his new host."

"And until we can figure it out, keep sensitive information behind closed doors. He could be anywhere. Any*one*. And as soon as any of us learn something, share it." Katrin glanced between everyone.

"He'll likely take an auer, again." Matthias glanced at his wife, nodding in agreement to all she'd said. "But we can't be certain. This visit to Melyza should help us identify what it is he's trying to do, though, and that can only help."

Rae stood. "As soon as we locate Uriel, we can devise a plan to get him to the prison. So when Katrin says share it, share it as fast as you can, by whatever means necessary. We may not have long, since we have no idea what he's planning."

"Wouldn't the safest place for Sephysis be in the middle of a volcano or something then? Can we destroy it to stop Uriel from stealing it back and trading Melyza for information? She might not even want to talk to us." Corin gave a pointed look at the bloodstone dagger, still hovering behind Kin.

"Destroying Sephysis would probably kill *me*." Kin frowned. "The safest place right now is with me. And much to my disappointment, I'll be staying here. Until we're ready to meet again in Isalica." He looked at Damien and Matthias. "Which will be the final step before we move to imprison Uriel?"

Matthias nodded. "One way or another, this will all be over soon."

Chapter 4

"I KNOW YOU'RE NOT HAPPY with this situation, but you know it's the best thing right now." Matthias looked at Kin as they walked down the wide hallway back towards his chambers.

Deylan strode behind them with Coltin, quietly filling in the lower ranking faction member with the details of his continuing assignment in Feyor.

The others had all dispersed from their meeting almost an hour ago, just before Kin had been summoned to yet another mundane council meeting about the future of Feyor.

"Once you start putting the pieces in place to reform your government, things will get easier," Matthias continued, staring ahead. "And you can always reach out to me if you need advice while I'm not here." Emotion played beneath the king's tone, but the exact source was difficult to pinpoint.

"You mean when you're not busy working to take care of the real threat to our world." Kin controlled the growing frustration in his voice. It wasn't just that Matthias finally needed to leave, but everyone did.

The Isalican king gave a low chuckle. "Regardless of the higher threat, your success is still at the forefront of my mind." He glanced at Kin, and finally the former Shade noticed the threads of concern in his friend. Care.

Gods. Is he worried about me?

Matthias cleared his throat. "We have fast travel options, between our winged allies and the portals. None of us should hesitate to use them. I'll be here. For whatever you need."

It still felt strange to look at Matthias. Sometimes, he couldn't help but still see Uriel. And the guilt that came with those moments always caused Kin to look away. He controlled the instinct this time.

Matthias deserved better from him for all he offered.

Kin nodded. "Thank you. I'll be fine. You've already sacrificed enough time to help me this last month or so. Surely you have your own royal duties at home in Isalica that you need to return to, as much as the other things." They both already knew he wouldn't be going home, but the open hallways were not the place to speak of where he really needed to go.

They rounded the corner to the palace's royal chambers, and Kin opened the main door before the guard could. He paused with his hand on the door and looked back to his companions before focusing on the guard. "You're dismissed for the evening. The pair of guards at the main entrance to the royal chambers will be sufficient."

The guard nodded, giving a quick salute as Kin turned and strode inside, Matthias behind him.

When Deylan and Coltin, still talking quietly, moved to follow, Matthias halted in the doorway.

Blocking their path, the Isalican king smiled. "We've established that Coltin will remain here, in service, as Kin's personal faction guard, but was there anything else?"

Deylan paused, blinking. "Coltin needs to go over procedures with Kin to establish proper communication guidelines for reaching me and the others."

Kin held in the groan, unable to stop the flexed tension of his jaw.

Great, more meetings.

Matthias looked at Coltin. "Kin will meet with you tomorrow. Or the day after. Sound good?" The man opened his mouth, but Matthias shut the door on them both and turned to Kin. "You're welcome."

Kin's surprise faded into a smirk. "Seems I continue to owe you one." He let out a relieved sigh as he reached to the iron brooch on his shoulder, letting the thick fabric of his formal cloak fall loose. The cold outside had seeped through the massive paned windows on the far end of the living space, encouraging Kin towards the freshly stoked hearth.

Matthias followed for a few paces before stopping, a thoughtful expression on his face.

The warmth of the fire encouraged Kin to the plush grey chair beside it, gesturing to the one across from him. "Stay for a drink? Or did you need to return to your wife?"

Conceding, Matthias continued to the chairs and sat in the one next to Kin. He waited while the new king poured a modest amount of whisky into their glasses. "Probably all I can handle after last night."

Kin gave a knowing smirk. "I tried to be moderate, and I still woke up with a headache." He settled back into the chair, a heaviness resting on his shoulders despite the comfort. Meeting Matthias's eyes, he knew the Isalican king could sense it, too.

They sat in silence, which Kin heartily welcomed as he sipped the whisky. His eyes slipped to the fire in the hearth, focusing on the flames instead of the million other things outside his chamber doors.

"Did I ever tell you about when I proposed to Katrin the first time?" Matthias stared at the fire, whisky resting on the arm of his chair.

"The first time?" The implication buzzed in Kin's mind with the tinge of the alcohol. "I guess it didn't go as you expected?"

The Isalican huffed. "I had very, very poor timing. And we'd only just reunited. I laid my heart bare for her, but she declined. And me, being the fool I was, didn't give her time to think or explain before I pulled time backwards and made her forget those words had ever left my mouth." He swirled his whisky but didn't drink. "It was a mistake, to be so vulnerable and then ensure I was the only one who remembered. It caused a lot of miscommunications later, until she learned what I'd done."

Kin rubbed the rim of the glass with the pad of his thumb. "Based on what I know of your wife... She was probably furious with you. But it seems like things worked out."

"They did." Matthias looked at him. "But I vowed not to undo those moments again, even when they don't go as hoped, because no one can truly understand us if we prevent them from seeing the vulnerable side."

Kin eyed Matthias, hoping he didn't notice the flash in his gaze as the former Shade saw his master sitting in the chair beside him. Just for a moment. Lifting his whisky, he buried the image, again seeing only his friend. "Makes me only a little less envious of your ability. I certainly have a few moments in my life I wish I could take back."

"Hmm. Don't we all." Even with the agreement, Matthias's tone lacked humor. "I can see it, when you see my face, sometimes." He raised his hand when Kin opened his mouth to deny it. "It's fine, really. Believe it or not, I understand. But it's important to me that you know the truth, and I feel like perhaps we're finally close enough that I can tell you."

"Tell me what?" Kin's heart jumped. "You don't owe me anything. You've already done so much. I wouldn't be sitting here without you."

Matthias tilted his head, lips quirking in a slight smile. "But you don't understand *why* I will always do all I can for you. And it's not that I feel like I owe you. I just... I spent many, many years watching you grow into the man you are, and even though you were unaware, I saw the trials and the victories and the failure. I saw it all, and gods, a part of me saw myself in you."

Kin winced, his mouth suddenly dry. "I sometimes forget all that you would have seen. It's kind of you to say you saw yourself, but we both know the darkness I fell into during those years. The horrible, murderous things I did." Something deep in him hummed as the thoughts surfaced. It followed the slight vibration at his thigh, where Sephysis rested. Its interest in the conversation sent a shiver down Kin's spine.

Matthias shrugged with one shoulder. "Yes, but I also saw you prevail, regain your humanity. Fight against that darkness." He paused. "I know you think I've done enough to help you in recent months. I know you think I need to return to Isalica and focus on my throne, my *family*. But I need to make it clear, Kin, that to me, that includes you."

The hum turned to a foreign warmth in him, and Sephysis quieted. His tongue wanted to move, but was unable to as Matthias continued.

"I had no one in those years, and I—" He cleared his throat, the firelight glinting off his eyes. "I came to see you like a son. So there is no *enough*. I will do anything and everything I can to help you, and there is no time frame on that. Just as I will be there every second I can for my sons. And it doesn't matter to me that you don't see me the same way, for I will always bear this face, but I need you to know that."

The sound of his blood thundered in his ears, but Kin had heard every word. Felt every word. "Thank you." His eyes burned, but he forbade the emotion as he cleared his throat and sipped whisky instead. "I'm not accustomed to a father so willing to be open. And the only other man to fill those shoes for so long was Uriel." Speaking the name felt like acid on his tongue, but he reminded himself of

Damien and Katrin's wards. Meeting Matthias's steady gaze, Kin banished Sephysis's intruding presence, trying to take hold of his emotions. "I'm grateful to now have you. I hardly believe I deserve it."

Matthias smiled, shoulders easing. "You do. So when I tell you to come to me if you need anything, I truly hope you will."

He nodded, leaning forward to slide the rest of his whisky onto the low slung table between them. "I will, assuming you're accessible. I suspect things are about to get a little crazy for all of us." The idea of Amarie leaving, along with Ahria, opened another hole for Sephysis to bury itself in. This time, Kin accepted the dagger's energy mingling with his but was certain to hold it still.

It's not enough that I'm now dealing with ruling a kingdom, but Seph is always trying to wriggle free of my control, too.

The dagger's attempts to sway him towards violence had grown more insistent during times of stress. And those times were not about to lighten up.

The bloodstone vibrated lightly against the outside of his thigh in irritation.

"I suspect you're right," Matthias murmured, finally sipping his whisky. "Coltin staying in his assignment here must be fun for you, too."

Seph hummed before Kin could even fully acknowledge the annoyance. "I understand that Deylan feels it's necessary to keep a faction member implanted here, but I wish he'd have the decency to at least pretend to keep their identity secret from me. Isn't that the entire basis of the Sixth Eye?"

Matthias chuckled. "Perhaps, but I guess once you're in the know, you get to know. I've got a few in my palace, too. And they think they're sneaky. At least with Coltin, you can directly communicate with Deylan. Will help, since he will be keeping tabs on Amarie and Ahria. So you'll at least know if anything happens, right?"

"I suppose there may be upsides to being in the know with a secret faction." Kin half smiled, leaning back into his chair. "Deylan has already promised me he'd send whatever information they have on Sephysis. So at least I won't be terribly bored here by myself."

"Bored? That's your concern?" Matthias let out a short boom of a laugh. "Trust me. As a king, you'll never have to worry about that again."

He wrinkled his nose. "Temporary king. But I suppose that just means I'll be even more tied up in meetings trying to disassemble the monarchy."

"Most likely. It will take time to establish a new government and change the ruling system. Especially with all the chaos Feyor is currently suffering. I may have spared you more meetings today, but you'll have to get good at multitasking in the coming weeks and months."

Kin sighed. "And I thought the meetings my father dragged me to about the wine business were dull." He looked back at the fire, mind wandering to his childhood among the vineyards and estate. "I wonder what happened to the old estate. If my father is still alive, he'll probably hear about the new Feyorian king. He'll learn I'm alive."

Matthias's brow furrowed. "We can ask Deylan to find out. I know the viewing chambers were destroyed, but he might have someone nearby who can look into it."

"Maybe." Kin rubbed his chin, trying to imagine the look on his adoptive father's face if he saw him again. And just how old he would be now.

I keep forgetting I missed twenty years.

Burying the memories, Kin focused back on Matthias. "When are you leaving for the prison?"

"Later today." The king glanced around the quiet sitting area. "Where is Amarie? I thought you two would be spending every moment you can together before she departs."

"With Ahria. They've gone out of the city to do some training and for Amarie to pass some power to her." He considered the doorway behind Matthias, wishing Amarie would walk through it right then. "How do you do it?"

His friend quirked an eyebrow. "Do what?"

"Stay away from her. From Katrin. You're going to be separating, too, and before this you weren't with her for months because you were with me."

"Ah." Matthias nodded. "I think you just get used to it. To the knowledge that there will be a next time and the wait will be worth it. But we've also been married much longer than you and Amarie. And during much more trying circumstances. But usually, it's just the knowledge that it's temporary that gets you through. And reunions..." He huffed with a smile. "Reunions are the best."

Ahria smiled at Amarie, both of them standing beside Kin in the royal gardens while they waited for the carriage that would take Ahria and Conrad to the docks. To a ship that had arrived earlier that morning to take them home. Ziona's queen, Talia Pendaverin, had embarked on her voyage home the day before, keeping the two Zionan royals on separate vessels. The élanvital pair had offered to open a portal for them, but the two had opted to enjoy a little normalcy and take their time returning to Ziona. In the meantime, Katrin and Dani would soon open a portal that would take themselves, Amarie, and Corin to Aidensar.

"What if it wants me to take more?"

"Then you put it all back," Amarie advised, smirking at the question their daughter had already asked, with slightly different phrasing, more than once.

"And if I feel like I can take more?" Ahria looked hopeful, though a playful gleam shimmered in her gaze.

"You don't." Amarie gave her a pointed look. "You take as much as I instructed, and no more. Not until we can meet again and I can be there with you. And remember, you promised."

"Yes, yes. I promised." Ahria's smile softened. "I'll be careful not to draw too much."

Amarie had only given Ahria a portion of their shared power anyway, which aided Kin's nerves at Ahria venturing off on her own yet again.

Though, not entirely on her own. Conrad would be with her, and she'd have the protection of Ziona should anything happen.

At least something good can now come of being royalty. The people won't question their relationship.

"I wish we had more time," Ahria murmured, sensing Conrad's approach behind her and leaning back into him once he came close enough.

"We will," Amarie assured. "This is temporary. We will meet again in Isalica in a few months, and one day we'll join you in Ziona permanently." She looked at Kin, and he saw all the thoughts she'd voiced to him that morning behind her expression. Parting ways, so soon after promising to stick together, didn't sit well with either of them.

Sephysis vibrated against his upper leg, and Kin ran his thumb over the smooth stone in its hilt.

Stop trying to seize every opportunity.

The dagger seemed to sigh in response before settling, and Kin turned his focus to Conrad.

"You take care of her." He extended his hand to the Zionan prince, who maintained a stoic expression.

Taking Kin's hand, Conrad nodded curtly. "Always. As best I can." Something in his tone and in the tightness of his jaw gave Kin pause. He didn't release Conrad immediately, studying the man who might someday be his son.

"All ready?" Corin's footsteps across the garden's gravel pathway drew Conrad's gaze, and he pulled from Kin's grip.

Dani clicked her tongue in a habit Kin didn't fully understand as she followed beside the Helgathian master of war, her white leather boots barely making a sound on the path. "We know not what awaits us. I hope you have enough blades."

Amarie smiled, her short sword at her side, dagger on her thigh, and a second, new sword strapped to her back. They'd discussed her using her power as little as possible. With Uriel unaccounted for, he could be anywhere, and the last thing they needed was a surprise confrontation because he sensed her use of the Art.

"I have a few," the Berylian Key replied, winking at Kin.

She's got more hidden that I don't even know about.

With all the time she'd been spending with Rae, it was hardly a surprise.

Dani carried no weapons other than a small bone-blade at her lower back, but Corin appeared as armed as Amarie. A plain broadsword was strapped on his side and a row of knives on the other. His dense leather armor made him look the part of a soldier, lacking the embellishments of a royal. But he wasn't going as a king consort, and it'd be better to blend in.

The door to the gardens swung open once more, and Katrin joined them. She hardly looked suited for battle in a long, flowing, pale yellow dress. Her silky black hair tied in a neat bun at the top of her head provided the only indication that she was ready for any kind of action. She looked to Dani first, then her soft eyes passed over the rest of them.

The others had departed the day before, with Matthias, Damien, and Micah heading for Isalica and Liam flying for Draxix. Jarrod and Rae had walked through their friends' portal to Helgath early that morning.

With everyone leaving the palace, and Kin staying, he couldn't help the gnawing desire to be a part of one of the ventures. But he needed to remain in Feyor, surrounded by wards courtesy of their Rahn'ka.

"Everything is in place. I've double checked the wards, though Damien created plenty of contingencies throughout the palace. They should hold until we meet in Isalica." She smiled at Kin, and he couldn't help but be comforted by it.

"Which location do you want to use?" Dani asked Katrin.

And while the two discussed where to open the portal, Amarie embraced Ahria. "You be safe."

"I will," she murmured, releasing her mother.

Amarie eyed Kin. They'd said everything they'd needed to that morning, but tension weighed the air between them as she wrapped her arms around his shoulders. "You be careful, too," she whispered. "Staying here is probably the most dangerous position of all."

Kin nodded as he wrapped his arms around her, unwilling to let go. "I'll stay within the wards at all times. And I have Seph. Uriel won't be able to get to me." He kissed the side of her head as they embraced. "You make sure I'll get to see my wife again."

Her lips pressed against his neck before she pulled back enough to look at his face. "I'll be all right."

Cracking radiated through the air, and Sephysis heated at his side in response to the Art springing to life near a patch of hibernating rose bushes. Kin watched a ripple of a rainbow drawn like a line between Katrin and Dani, who stood facing each other with their palms parallel. Slowly the pair stepped apart, and with each movement, the tear grew. Like the sheen of a bubble, it wavered under an invisible breeze.

"I love you." Amarie touched his face, then angled to Ahria and touched hers, too. "And you. I'll see you both in Isalica."

Ahria came to stand beside Kin, Conrad on her other side, as Amarie joined Corin near the portal.

The circular hole in the fabric snapped into place, shimmering like the surface of a lake.

Something tugged at Kin to move towards the portal, but he knew it was Sephysis, hungry to get close to the outpouring of Katrin and Dani's power. Or perhaps the dagger knew that Melyza was somewhere within. Either way, he placed a firm hand upon the dagger, urging it to hush.

My place, for now, is here. As is yours.

An angry buzz passed up his arm, but Kin ignored it as he locked eyes with Amarie.

Her jaw flexed, throat bobbing as she glanced between him and Ahria.

Dani passed through the portal first, followed by a backpack-laden Corin, then Katrin.

Amarie blew them a kiss, but worry lined her eyes as she finally turned and crossed through the portal. A breath later, the power winked out.

Ahria let out a sigh, the sound of carriage wheels crunching over gravel reaching them from the other side of the garden's walls. "This feels so final."

Turning to his daughter, Kin shook his head and lightly touched her arm. "It's not. There's still a lot that needs to happen, but we'll all see each other again." Doubt lingered in his own mind, but speaking it aloud, Kin dared to hope. "We'll all come out of this, one way or another."

The carriage wheels came to a stop.

"That's for us, isn't it?" Ahria glanced at Conrad.

He nodded, stepping forward. "I'll see to getting our things loaded. You take all the time you need." He leaned in to kiss her on the temple before giving Kin another look. Avoiding direct eye contact, the prince gave a minute bow of the head before he walked towards the carriage, his sword tapping against his leg.

Ahria watched him go, shoulders drooping as she faced Kin. "I... I've been blessed with more fathers in my life than most." Her eyes shone as she gave him a pained smile. "But I only have one left. Please be safe."

"I promised your mother, and will promise you, too." Kin opened his arm to her, and Ahria moved into the hug.

"Uriel will know where you are as well as he does me, though. So you'll need to be ready."

Sephysis jerked in the sheath, but Kin tapped the pommel to quiet it.

"I'll be ready." She squeezed him, filling his chest with warmth. "And I'm sorry, again, for what Alana said."

Hollow grief stirred in his chest, remembering the quiet conversation he'd had with his daughter that morning. Alana had confirmed his father's death, and that even though he'd left her the estate, she'd passed it on to someone else. The vineyard thrived, but without his parents, Kin had no reason to ever return.

"It's all right, Bug. I'm grateful to know. I'm glad you told me." He didn't know where the nickname had come from, but it rolled off his tongue with such ease that he embraced it.

Ahria squeezed him and then pulled away, a faint smile on her face. Her weapons were less obvious than her mother's, but he counted at least four knives on her.

Talon did well training her.

Another pang of grief echoed, but he let it roll off.

Ahria opened the garden gate, looking back at him. "Bye, Dad."

A new jolt passed through his veins at her words. She'd never used the word for him before, at least not when speaking to him. It made his gut churn in a pleasant way.

But one that just made it harder to lift his hand in a brief wave. "Love you."

Returning the farewell gesture, Ahria nodded. "Love you, too," she whispered, and then disappeared through the gate.

Kin stood there in silence, listening to the click of the carriage door and then the crunch of gravel as it departed the palace. Everyone leaving at different times had been intentional, for the moment they left Damien's wards was their most vulnerable.

For the briefest moment, Kin considered accompanying Ahria and Conrad to the docks, Sephysis in tow to ensure no Corrupted would follow them. But that would only bring greater attention. The city, after all, was clamoring to get a peek at their new king who had barely set foot outside the palace. So Kin remained in the garden, alone.

Sephysis sent a hum through his senses to remind him that wasn't entirely true.

Well, mostly alone.

Kin reached for the dagger, freeing it from the sheath. Holding it before him, he studied the bloodstone blade as the sun shone off its dark surface. It hadn't touched blood in some time, which had caused it to darken, though the pulsing red was still visible within. "I suppose I promised if you behaved, I'd give you a little freedom."

Sephysis glimmered, vibrating in response.

"Though you did make several attempts to gain some footing. I noticed." Kin could only hope no one saw him talking to his dagger in the garden.

Seph's vibration grew deeper in displeasure. As Kin allowed the bond between them to open ever so slightly, he felt the depth of the dagger's frustration at teased freedom.

Releasing the blade, Kin urged the parts of himself connected to the dagger to awaken. It wasn't too unlike the Art when he'd controlled it as a Shade. The dagger floated in front of him, swirls of red flickering around the edges, so slight that Kin was certain only he could see them. He studied them for a moment before persuading Sephysis to move, gradually spinning.

The door from the palace to the gardens opened, and Kin instinctively reached out to grab Sephysis. But when Coltin appeared in the entrance, he eased his grip and allowed Sephysis to hover once more.

"Councilors Nyrat, Analyd, and Ashley have arrived for your briefing on the new internal administration guidelines." The man hardly even noted the floating dagger, his tone impassive. "They'll be expecting you in about fifteen minutes, your majesty."

Sephysis grumbled loudly in his mind, mingling with Kin's own groan at the formal title and news.

I know, I know.

Kin nodded to Coltin as he loosened the bonds, allowing Sephysis to move on its own as the faction spy returned inside. The dagger moved in lazy circles around him at first, but at Kin's urging, gradually sped. He focused on the direction of the dagger, determined to practice turning and spinning Sephysis in every direction possible while maintaining speed. The dagger sang in his mind, pleased to be released rather than trapped in its sheath. And Kin found a kind of euphoria in it as well, especially as Seph took to tearing through some of the partially frozen foliage. The dagger seemed happiest when destroying.

Just have to keep that destruction pointed at appropriate targets.

Kin had tried to reason with the dagger in different ways. Tried to ascertain directly from it what Uriel would possibly desire with it. But he never gleaned more than vague emotions. So now he had to hope Melyza would have the answers. And share them.

Slowing the dagger, much to its disappointment, Kin brought it to a resting position floating in front of him again. Slowly, he reached out and took the hilt once more. Stretching his thumb beyond the guard, he pressed the pad to the base of the blade, where the sharp edge sliced into him. Blood welled up, but instead of coursing down, it flowed sideways and up the center shaft of the blade. Seph gave a satisfied sigh as Kin's blood sank into the metal, granting it a brief shine of crimson before it faded back to its darker shade.

"Satisfied enough to allow me to get through this meeting in peace?" Kin questioned as he turned the dagger in his hand and returned it to its sheath. He lifted his thumb to his mouth, sucking on the wound as Seph gave an agreeable hum.

"Good." Tucking his hand into his pocket to retrieve a handkerchief, Kin walked back to the palace. Where he would need to continue to act as if nothing dire was happening beyond his own kingdom's borders. He tried to hear Matthias in his mind. The advice the Isalican king had given him. Even with everyone else out in the world preparing to fight Uriel, Kin had a different goal to focus on. It felt wrong.

Seph's power sent a calming wave over Kin's senses. As if the dagger was now trying to comfort him.

Kin grumbled, pushing his wrapped thumb against the hilt again. "Let's just get it over with."

Chapter 5

JARROD STUDIED RAE'S FACE AS she read the cryptic letter he'd kept in his pocket for the past few weeks. He'd received it right before departing for Feyor, and Corin had ordered their forces to prepare in case the letter proved as true and dangerous as it sounded.

"Read that last part again." Jarrod glanced over his shoulder as Maithalik entered his study, though the auer didn't say a word.

"The need for preparation may be here. Invoking our treaty is not a matter I take lightly. You must converse only with myself and the center seat. Shadows hover at our backs." Rae looked up from the worn parchment as she finished

reading it aloud. "*May this bring warmth to your hearth. Q.*"

"The letter Q?" Maith settled gracefully into one of the chairs in front of Jarrod's unoccupied desk, reaching for the tea set near the center. "Qualtavik is feeling extra secretive."

"He implies you should burn this." Rae waved the letter in the air as she walked behind Maith's seat.

"Aye," Jarrod muttered. "But I wanted you to read it first."

"Best to do so as soon as possible, if he is requesting such action. The threat he feels must be very close to him." Maith's expression hardened, concern in his amethyst eyes.

Jarrod gave Rae a single nod, and the Mira'wyld tossed the letter into the simmering fire within the study's hearth.

"Our armies are standing by. But we don't know who the threat is. Shadows at our backs?"

"Could be about Uriel," Rae murmured, staring out the window in thought. "But why only converse with him and Erdeaseq? That must be who he means when he says center seat."

"Qualtavik is afraid of whatever it is, but desperate enough to send you this message." Maithalik leaned forward, resting one forearm on Jarrod's desk but angling his torso towards them. "I think the *at our backs* bit is important, too. He doesn't trust the other elders in the council."

"He's suspicious enough of the elders to ask us to prepare our military? This could be something we need to take seriously." Rae met Jarrod's gaze, and he knew that look.

The Helgathian king blew out a breath. "Aye. And we are. Our army and armada will be ready to move, if need be, whenever word is given."

"This'll be a big undertaking if it ends up being unnecessary," Rae pointed out slowly. "Plus it could leave Helgath open to attack if this is a diversion."

Jarrod frowned at her, shaking his head. "That doesn't mean I need a spy."

Rae's mouth kicked up at the corners. "Doesn't it?"

"It's convenient timing, considering you're expected some time this year to return for further Mira'wyld training." Maith blew on the steaming cup of tea as he lifted it.

That part was true, since Rae had actually been due to return for training two years ago, but she'd bargained with the auer to postpone. Bellamy had started showing signs of gaining the Rahn'ka power, and she'd decided to stay with her family.

Sarra likely will soon, too.

"They won't suspect a thing. I can just go and see what's happening over there. Talk to a few people. Maybe even talk to Qualtavik if I can get a moment alone with him." Rae leaned back against the wall, her fitted leather attire so broken in it made no noise. "If this does relate to Uriel in some way, we can't afford to ignore it."

"I can accompany you, though we don't need to leave right away. I may have easier access to the Elder Council if I give them some warning of our arrival." Maith gave her a playful smile. "Though I know well enough not to get in your way."

"We could leave in a few weeks, giving us plenty of time to prepare and to let Qualtavik know we're coming," Rae agreed. "More importantly, it'll give me time to evaluate Sarra. If she's to become a Rahn'ka, her connection will form soon."

Memories of the chaotic time when Bellamy first began to experience the forces of becoming a Rahn'ka made Jarrod wish Damien could be present to potentially help build Sarra's mental barrier. He and Corin could only do so much, but his time battling the wolf in his own mind at least gave him understanding of the danger.

Though, knowing Sarra, being forced to navigate the power and learn how to shield her mind with only instruction from her mother, the young woman might learn even faster.

Jarrod still couldn't banish the churn of lingering anxiety in his gut. "Do we think this really could be Uriel? Or is it merely the auer playing their own political games?" He could already imagine the disapproving look Damien would throw his way if he allowed Rae to waltz into a situation with the master of Shades.

"I can handle either scenario, and I have the faction device from Deylan in case I need to call for help." Rae crossed her arms. She and Damien had decided to keep the gift from Deylan with her, since they were unsure if it would work in Draxix.

"Regardless of whether or not you can call for help, you can't take on Uriel."

"I won't." Rae tilted her head, tone softening. "If he's there, or I catch any hint that I could be in danger, I'll run. I promise. I'll get out of there and come straight home."

I've heard those words before.

But Jarrod was well-accustomed to Rae's methods, and rarely did they involve running.

"This does feel purposeful, the timing of it." Maith's teacup clinked lightly to the table. "You all are growing close to imprisoning him. It is a logical maneuver for Uriel to create distractions that would divide your attention. And he knows Helgath's allegiances with Isalica. He'll be growing rather desperate, I imagine."

"That doesn't mean we can afford to do nothing," Rae countered. "The auer don't deserve to fall to him, and if we can stop that from happening, we need to." She faced Jarrod. "Let me go."

Jarrod ground his teeth, but he was very aware that her request was hardly a request. Even if he said no, she'd go anyway. He nodded. "All right. You and Maith can leave for Eralas when you're ready." He pointed at Rae. "But I want you armed to the teeth, an earring in your pocket, and I want that hawk of yours consistently in the sky."

Rae gave him a serious expression and nodded. For once, her voice held no mirth as she said, "Understood."

Chapter 6

THE WIND HOWLED OUTSIDE THE cave Zelbrali had left the three of them within. Lightning flashed in the sky, highlighting the dark outline of the swaying pine trees, while thunder vibrated the stone Matthias leaned against.

He shrugged his cloak further onto his shoulders, the fur lining tickling his cheek. Thankfully, Micah put another log onto the fire they'd constructed near the cave mouth, and warmth prevailed.

Damien sat across from him, legs crossed and looking far too comfortable considering he didn't have a cloak on at all. He stared at the fire, and Matthias swore he could see the thoughts swirling around in his single hazel eye as the

Rahn'ka considered the news Micah had just shared.

"You didn't see anything?" The Rahn'ka looked at the crown elite as Micah sank back into his bedroll and blankets.

"Not a thing. But the moment I walked up to those two pillars, it was like hitting a brick wall." He kicked off his boots as another roll of thunder reverberated through the cave.

They wouldn't be going anywhere for a while.

Hopefully Zelbrali found a good place to hunker down, too.

Damien rubbed his short beard. "This doesn't make sense."

"It's the guardian, right?" Matthias watched his friend across the fire. "Has to be."

"Remind me what that is again?" Micah broke off a piece of dried bread. "And why they felt it was necessary to nearly break my nose with an invisible wall?"

"They're a collection of ká. Spirits, essentially. But assembled from a lot of different sources over thousands of years. They're like... wardens of the Rahn'ka. Trapped within the sanctums."

"And this one has evidently decided to seal off the sanctum. Certainly could have better timing." Matthias huffed and sat closer to the fire. "Zel won't come back until it's safe to fly, and judging by the lack of wind, this storm might stick around for a day or two. But I'm assuming you can't do anything about the sanctum from here?"

Damien shook his head. "No. I'll need to speak to the guardian directly. I wonder what might have set them off. They're not always the most reasonable of beings, but they should realize how important it is for us to access the prison." He rolled his shoulders, shaking his head again. "I should meditate."

Micah eyed Matthias, and the king narrowed his gaze. "What?"

The crown elite smirked. "You cooking, or am I?"

Matthias sighed. "You already know the answer to that."

Two days later, after a quick stop in Nema's Throne to drop off Micah, they landed on the outskirts of the island off the coast near Orvalinon in Isalica's northern reaches.

High, vertical bluffs surrounded the sanctum, making the island inhospitable to civilians and the perfect place to hide the prison they'd built for Uriel with the dragons' help.

Not just because of the exterior land, but because the sanctum lay *within* the island, deep underground. The surface ruins were scant, nestled in the 'v' of the massive cliffs on either side of the island. A single round structure that'd partially crumbled in the thousands of years of disuse.

"What *exactly* did Yondé say about the guardian here?" Matthias trudged through the rocky sand towards the sanctum entrance, a gust of icy air blowing his hair forward as Zelbrali returned to the sky.

"That they wouldn't be a problem." Damien had rolled up his sleeves, despite the cold, displaying the navy blue runes of his tattoo. "Though, now that I think of it, Jalescé did chuckle at that."

"That's the lizard one, right?"

"Right." Damien stepped faster to get ahead of Matthias as they reached the shadows of stone steps leading to the ruins. The overgrowth around them had shed their leaves for the winter, leaving a thick layer of orange and brown coating the stone. Though Damien didn't slip as he jogged up the steps.

Lizard, bear, deer. Matthias had a hard time keeping the animal likenesses straight.

The hum of the Art in the air grew impossibly thick against Matthias's skin as he trailed behind the Rahn'ka. "You feel that?"

Like walking through water.

Damien didn't even glance back. "Mhmm." He frowned, slowing as he approached a pair of massive monoliths positioned at the top of the steps. They were draped with dead vines, worn carvings beneath them. Matthias had walked past them what felt like hundreds of times at this point, but now they felt far more foreboding.

"Good to know they're trying to keep you out, too," the king muttered.

As Damien lifted his tattooed arm, the ink on his skin brightened to a sky blue. His entire body stiffened as something faint passed from his hand towards the monoliths. Like a snake shedding its skin, the vines fell from the rock as the ancient runes along their lengths sprang to life. They glowed the same as Damien's tattoo, and the thrum in the air changed. For a moment, it lightened, and then seemed to double down even harder than before.

"Something tells me we should have brought you here sooner." Matthias watched the power flow, his own Art dormant in his veins. But if he needed to jump, he was ready.

"Too risky." Damien remained focused on the left pillar, shifting his entire body to face it as he lifted another hand. "Though... I wish the guardian would just *tell me* why they're so upset." He spoke the second part louder, shouting into the ruins.

The force preventing them from continuing their stride pushed back against them, forcing both men to concede a few steps.

But nothing else greeted them. Just silence.

"What do we do?" Matthias faced Damien. "Wait it out?"

Damien didn't answer, staring beyond the invisible barrier towards the open courtyard beyond. His shoulders tensed before he sighed and rolled his shoulders. "For you, it'll be a lot of waiting." He sat right there on the ground, crossing his legs beneath him on the narrow stair leading up to the monoliths. He settled his hands on his knees, rolling his shoulders again. "It's a lot of meditating for me. I've got to convince the guardian to appear, and they're... being stubborn."

Matthias frowned. "Waiting feels rather useless. I'll take Zelbrali to Orvalinon for supplies, since this looks like it will take awhile."

A while had been an understatement.

In the week that passed after arriving at the sanctum, they'd seen no sign of the guardian. Damien received no response to his pestering, pleading, or, in complete desperation, when he tried to order the guardian to appear. Just dead silence, but the Rahn'ka assured Matthias the guardian *was* still there. Just being stubborn.

I'd say a bit more than stubborn.

Matthias had caught, cleaned, and cooked a rabbit for

himself, along with a meatless soup with leeks and squash. He spiced it and had to admit the vegetarian cooking aligned with his tastes just as well as the rabbit.

He and Damien had set up a full camp, with tents, firepit, and even a clothesline. Flying back and forth from Nema's Throne was too time-consuming, and probably only strengthened the guardian's resolve to keep them out.

So they stayed.

But the Rahn'ka's patience thinned, along with the king's.

"Maybe we should try something new today," Matthias suggested, nudging Damien's knee with his boot. He'd just settled in to begin his routine of closing his eyes and not moving for hours at a time. "Meditating doesn't seem to be working."

Damien opened one eye, pursing his lips. "What exactly do you propose?"

The king eyed the empty sanctum entrance. The fur around his shoulders ruffled in the slight breeze, his beard longer than he usually kept it. But it kept his face warmer, and Katrin wasn't here to complain about it.

Not that she would.

Matthias smirked, his mind lurching off in an unexpected direction.

She'd probably like the feel of it on the inside of her thigh...

"Well?" Damien's annoyance sharpened his tone.

Matthias scowled at him. "I'm thinking."

"About productive things, I hope," the Rahn'ka muttered.

The king chuckled low and deep, well aware of the man's ability to sense emotions. "Well, you've tried appeasing them, begging them, and I'm pretty sure you tried to assert your dominance once or twice." He smiled, enjoying the irritation directed his way. "Maybe you should try giving them an idea of the consequences of ignoring us."

"Like what? Throw a few monoliths around? I'm not even sure my Art works that way."

Matthias tilted his head. "Can't you manipulate objects?"

Damien shrugged, crossing his arms, the tattoo running from his collar to his left wrist glowing only slightly, visible because all he wore was a light sleeveless undershirt despite the chill. Matthias had interrupted before he'd gotten too deep into his connection with the same monolith he'd focused on time and time again.

"I can't do much. At most I can interact with the ká of something a bit, but usually I just borrow portions of energy to reweave it into something in front of me. The most I did with objects was turn some pebbles into precious gems, but I haven't done that in years. No need since my living situation has become a bit more legal."

"A bit." Matthias huffed. "But toppling monoliths might get their attention. We can't keep sitting here for weeks on end."

"What other option do we have? We need access to the prison. Otherwise it'll be like starting from square one."

"Except worse, since we can't make another prison, anyway."

"Then we're not going anywhere." Damien turned his voice towards the sanctum, raising it like he did sometimes for the guardian to hear. "Until we're able to work something out." The tattoo on his arm pulsed brighter as he tilted his palm to the monolith, the runes upon it blazing to life. The awe of it had faded slightly, considering Matthias had seen it multiple times a day for a week now.

"What if we worked together to help you break through the barrier? I could jump, while you channel your energy, and we could destroy—"

"You'll do no such thing..." A cunning voice reverberated from the stone, but nothing visualized.

Deep in the ruins, pale light flashed among the stones.

Damien tilted his head towards the top of the pillar, frowning as he shot to his feet. "Finally... Why are you blocking us from entering the sanctum?"

Matthias followed Damien's gaze, but saw nothing.

"This is *my* sanctum. You never sought permission to build anything here, Rahn'ka. You should know better.

And threatening to make a mess won't aid your cause." The voice came from the top of the pillar, bodiless, and Matthias frowned.

Oh, I see how it is.

"Yondé and Sindré of the south assured me they had reached out to you."

A cackle of a laugh echoed through the crisp air. "Yondé and Sindré. Hah!" A small snort. "I see they haven't changed one bit."

"Why can he see you, but I can't?" Matthias crossed his arms, frustration vibrating beneath his skin.

Damien lowered his hands, but the glow in the monoliths remained. "The guardian can choose who sees them." He didn't alter his focus from the top of the stone.

"Jealous?" The guardian teased. They let out another low hiss of a laugh. "Fine, fine, oh king of these frosted lands." Swirls of snow dusted around the top of the pillar until a form manifested. Perked ears, a bushy tail, and a black, pointed nose. But the body maintained an ethereal blue hue, unlike anything he'd seen before.

A fox.

Matthias withheld the chuckle. Of course it would be a fox, with how cunning and clever the voice sounded.

"I apologize, Guardian, if I was misinformed by the others." Damien bowed his head politely. "I should have visited sooner."

Matthias scowled at Damien. "I said that a week ago."

The Rahn'ka shot him an annoyed glance.

"I am Mirimé." The guardian watched Damien with narrowed eyes, ignoring Matthias's comment. "And I want to know what you've been doing in my sanctum. Nothing is how I left it. And it smells of dragons." They hissed the last word, lip curling to reveal needle-sharp teeth.

"What's wrong with dragons?" Matthias couldn't help the question.

"They shit wherever they want." The fox gave him a deadpan look, long tail curling around the monolith beneath them. "And they burn everything."

"Do you mean to tell me that Sindré and Yondé *lied* about you being all right with the prison for Taeg'nok being built here?" Damien frowned, crossing his arms. The glow in his tattoos had faded, but Matthias could still sense the Art flowing between him and the monoliths.

Mirimé glared at the Rahn'ka, baring their teeth again. "If I cannot hear their request, how am I to give consent?"

"Are you not connected to the fabric like them? I assumed you—"

The fox leapt from their perch, body shifting as they fell and landed in a crouch. Legs elongated and straightened, the thick fur around their neck spreading into a pelted cloak. Their nose, still vaguely pointed like the fox, centered between two overly large eyes. They shone with the various shades of Rahn'ka blue, looking something like a child. They stood a good half-foot shorter than Damien, but that presence... It felt anything but short or small. Several hoops pierced their left ear, with another through the center of their nose. The bright, radiant hair fell in a braid on one side, the other side shorn nearly to their scalp.

"You *assumed* wrong." Their voice came in an echo of a multitude of tones. "I've been locked within nothingness for almost *three decades*, abandoned by the others unaffected by my plight." Each word was clipped, as sharp as those teeth, and Matthias resisted the urge to step away from the furious being.

"You were... trapped?" Damien took a step back from the guardian, as if intimidated by their small form.

Matthias furrowed his brow. Almost three decades? That lined up with...

The dagger.

"The spell on Sephysis contained you as well?" he whispered, glancing at Damien.

Mirimé's lip curled, large eyes focusing on him. Something dark glimmered behind that unnerving gaze. "Trapped within our own mind. Something you couldn't begin to fathom."

"Actually," Matthias sighed, empathy washing through him. "I can."

Chapter 7

DESPITE THE CIRCUMSTANCES, AHRIA GRINNED. She stood on Dawn Chaser's rigging, gripping the rope and facing the bow. Waves crashed against the hull, spraying seawater into the air in a fine mist. The cold breeze bit her skin and numbed her fingers, but it just felt so... right.

Being back on this ship, with Conrad, sailing for Ziona.

Her chest ached with missing her birth parents, but they were safe. Happy, even as they set off on their own adventures.

A swell lifted the ship before it plunged down and broke through the rough water.

She sighed, vaguely aware of Leiura shouting orders to her crew. Power swirled in her soul, but she kept it tamped down, concealed within the shoddy hiding aura her mother had helped her craft in so little time. But it would do, even if it wasn't pretty or perfect.

It'd been surprisingly quiet since they'd left the safety of the wards around Feyor's palace. She'd half expected a dozen Corrupted to come springing out of the shadows as the carriage made its way down to the docks. They'd had guards with them, of course, all trained and ready for that kind of attack, but none had come.

Even now, as a shadow flickered beneath the rise of a wave, she caught herself studying it, expecting some grisly sea beast borne of Uriel's darkness to attack.

But there was nothing.

It temporarily suspended her lighthearted mood, reminding her this wasn't anything like the last time she'd been on this ship. Even if she wished it was.

The uncomfortable quiet settled through her bones, leaving her more on edge than if the danger had been obvious. Or real at all.

She scratched the back of her neck, tickled by the hairs that escaped her braid.

The grey shape of Lungaz hovered on the south horizon, shrouded by fog still clinging to the shores. The distant roar of the maelstrom at the center of the bay had dissipated yesterday as they sailed past, but rocky crags that looked like melted and hardened wax still felt dangerous.

A shudder clawed through her.

Even just thinking about that place, what lay further inland... The air felt thinner, panic sparking in her gut. She couldn't even see the prison outpost, but he'd taken her there. Taken her, and...

"Ahria!"

Conrad's voice rocked her from the darkness, and sorrow edged at her senses with how fast her delight had devolved into fear. She closed her eyes, breathing deeper, before looking down at him through the rigging.

"Are you going to stay up there all morning?" He shielded his eyes from the sun with his hand.

Tempted to.

Ahria shrugged and called back, "Is there somewhere else I should be?"

"Maybe." He glanced behind him towards the captain's cabin. Despite his protests, Leiura had insisted they use it for the journey. Dawn Chaser wasn't meant as a royal transport, but she wouldn't accept the crown prince sleeping in crew quarters. The matter was only further cemented when Leiura realized Ahria was now a crown princess as well.

Ahria gripped the rigging lower and swung down, finding a low foothold. She descended quickly, enjoying the burn in her shoulders that dissipated when her boots connected with the deck.

Standing from the crouch, she wiped the dark thoughts from her expression as she looked at Conrad, who wore the leather gloves she'd given him what felt like a lifetime ago. "Maybe?"

He didn't speak for a moment, just studying her. She recognized the look in his eyes. Worry. Like he saw all those fears she tried to hide. But as much as she wanted to be open with him, she couldn't. Not when he kept his suffering so close to his chest. He didn't need to bear hers as well.

"I asked for some lunch to be brought up to the cabin. You hardly touched your breakfast, so I thought you must be hungry." Conrad's concern remained. Even if she buried the thoughts, he could still see them.

Just like I can see his every time he shuts down.

It was true, though. She hadn't been very hungry at breakfast, which was more than unusual for her. But she chalked it up to nerves. After everything she'd been through, a lessened appetite made sense. Though now her stomach grumbled at the mention of lunch.

"That sounds nice," she forced out with a smile. "I should practice a little, too. Ama—Mom said to practice at least once a day."

He nodded, turning to hold out his hand towards the captain's cabin. "Should I tell the ship's Artisan to stay on the opposite side of the ship, just in case? Though, knowing Irmiz, she might not listen."

Ahria's smile felt a little more genuine at the mention of the Artisan who'd given her pointers the day before. "Honestly, if I lose control, it won't matter where she is on the ship." She paused, walking with Conrad. "But that won't happen. I'll be careful."

Amarie hadn't given her all the power, or even half of it, but she still had enough to sink this ship with a wrong breath. The pressure of that responsibility helped keep her ambition in check.

"So which is first, food or practice?" He opened the door to the cabin, holding it for her.

"Food." Ahria hoped her answer would lessen Conrad's concerns. She walked into the cabin, noting the slightest bit of tension leaving his features as she did. "I'll focus better if I'm not hungry."

As the aroma of roasted fish and baked beans hit her nose, her stomach growled louder.

Maybe my body is starting to remember how to enjoy food.

Two domed dishes rested on a tray latched to the desk to prevent it from sliding off in rough waters. She removed the dome off one, and carried the plate with a fork to the bed. Sitting, she watched him strip off his cloak and gloves, then collect his lunch and sit in one of the cushioned chairs bolted to the floor.

In the seven nights they'd spent at sea since departing Jaspa, nightmares had been relentless. And not just for her. But he'd refused to speak to her of them, even after the time he'd launched himself out of bed and vomited over the side of the ship. He hadn't been the first to lose the contents of his stomach during the night, but he'd shut down even harder after that.

It left little room for conversation as she tasted a bite of fish. It could use more spices, and perhaps some lemon, but considering the limited equipment on the ship, Orlin, the cook, had done a splendid job.

She busied herself with her meal, forgoing her desire for conversation altogether.

Things hadn't been the same between them in so long. Not since before Uriel attacked the underwater faction bunker. It dragged on her soul, and a thought flickered through her mind.

Maybe this isn't meant to work.

The dire notion constricted her throat, her fork pausing halfway to her mouth. The idea that they wouldn't make it... That they had an end date and a time would come, one day, when she no longer could call him hers.

It wouldn't be the first of her relationships to end. By whatever tiny mercy the gods had granted her, Davros had found employment on a different ship since she'd left him on Dawn Chaser. But she doubted she'd ever look at the ocean the same way again if she lost Conrad.

An icy wave of isolation washed over her, but she forced the fish into her mouth.

Conrad didn't press for conversation, either. But his eyes drifted up to her from his plate plenty of times, his worry still nagging at her. Slowly, he nestled his fork onto the half-eaten food and slid the plate back onto the tray. He paused, leaning against the desk with his eyes on the ground. He still chewed his last bite, far longer than it needed, as if it helped him process whatever wild thoughts ran through his head.

He swallowed as he finally looked up at her. "You know, you can still talk to me. Tell me what you're feeling…"

Ahria met his gaze, but bitterness rose in her throat as she quietly asked, "You want me to talk to you, but you won't talk to me?"

She wanted to close her eyes, perhaps even take back the words, because pushing him had resulted in nothing. But the double standard was horseshit, and he knew it.

He grimaced, lowering his gaze. He stared at the hard planks of the captain's cabin. A place that had once been his, but now it seemed like so long ago. She found her own eyes wandering to the familiar cracks she had studied when escorted to this room after being found as a stowaway. The number of wood planks that spanned the room between the bed and desk. The distance that lingered between her and Conrad.

"It's different. I *know* I can talk to you. I just... need more time. But that doesn't need to affect you. I'm still here for you. I still love you." He remained rigid, like he didn't know what to do with his body.

Ahria's eyes heated, and she looked away. "Sometimes, I'm not so sure." The admission weighed on her chest, her jaw flexing.

"There's nothing I said that you should doubt." Conrad moved, crossing the room quicker than she expected. He sat beside her, the soft bed causing her hip to shift into his. He paused for a moment before he gingerly took the plate from her lap and placed it somewhere behind him. "I am still here. And even if I hardly belong with someone like you, I *do* love you. More than you'll ever know."

A frown found her lips. "What does that even mean? You don't belong with someone like me?" That uneasy feeling returned, the one that whispered about their end.

His breath caught in his throat, but he touched her knee, turning his hand over to expose and offer his palm to her. "It's not fair of me to say that. I'm sorry. But please don't doubt that I would do anything for you. Anything to be with you. You are everything to me, Mouse."

She heard the words, but they didn't warm her chest the way they normally would have. But she took his hand anyway, wanting anything else. Anything other than this indescribable coldness. "Want to see what I can do now?"

"Always," he whispered.

Closing her eyes, Ahria lifted her other hand, palm up, and dove into herself. She found the place where her power dwelled, but while her mother had referred to it as an ocean, Ahria now saw a valley of embers much clearer than she had the water. While Talon's book of instructions hadn't suggested viewing the power in a different form, Amarie had assured her that if it worked better for her, it was the way to see it.

Kneeling within her mind, she picked up a glowing ember, marveling as she always did at the lack of heat on her skin. Moving away from the rest, she pulled herself back to the physical and a small orange flame danced in her palm.

Water was easiest for me, Amarie had said. *Fire might be easier for you.*

Conrad opened his mouth, but she sucked in a breath, focusing on the fire. It wiggled, twisting, shaping, until it took on the form of a single-masted boat. The sails whipped in an invisible wind, making sparks flitter off into the cabin air and disappear.

He squeezed her hand, leaning against her. He nuzzled a kiss beneath her ear, the orange glow of her flaming ship reflecting on his dark skin. "You're remarkable," he whispered, placing another slow kiss against her neck.

Her stomach rolled, even as his kiss finally warmed her chest. The back of her neck itched, and she cringed, letting go of the energy to have it rejoin the dormant power within. A foul taste lingered on her tongue as she tried to shake off the feeling, leaning into Conrad. "It was only a few months ago I was completely ordinary."

She felt his smile against her skin. "You were never ordinary."

Ahria opened her mouth to protest, but then shut it, considering how they'd met. How many blades she'd hidden among her clothing. A rush of nostalgia touched her heart, at their first conversations. At their adventure through Haven Port.

That kiss.

"I wish I were." The truth slipped out. Or, at least, how she felt in that moment. "I wish you were a captain and I was a stowaway, and that's where it ended. I wish this was our life and we didn't need to worry about losing more people we love and messing this up so the world has to suffer. I wish..." She swallowed, eyes blurring as her stomach settled. "I wish things could go back to how they were before..."

Before she'd watched her father die to a Shade.

Before she'd been tortured by Uriel.

Before Alana...

He ran his thumb over hers, holding her hand in her lap. "I know." He released her, only to turn and wrap his arms around her entirely, pulling her gently against his chest. "But that's not what the gods had in store for us, I suppose."

"Do you think we'll make it?" she whispered, daring to give life to the question that plagued her every time she looked at him.

"I have no doubts in the stubbornness of your mother. And the more I learn about Damien, I think he may be even more so than her. I don't want to believe in a future where you all don't succeed."

You all.

Ahria caught it, the words that excluded him. She furrowed her brow. "You mean *we*. A future where *we* don't succeed." At the tension overcoming his body, she sighed and quickly diverted the conversation. "But that's not what I meant. I meant *us*. You and me. If you think *we* will make it."

He pressed his lips to her head, drawing out a kiss on her hair. "I have never doubted us." He pulled back, gently lifting her chin to meet her eyes. "I will love you until the day I die, Mouse, and even beyond that into the Afterlife. There is nothing that could change that."

Tears pricked at her eyes, his words finally gracing her with a hint of hope. "Promise?"

He touched the wetness as it rolled down her cheek. "I promise." He pressed his lips to hers in a tender kiss, gentle in the way Conrad could only be with her.

Thoughts of their relationship failing drifted away beneath the brush of his lips, sending a shiver through her. Tilting her head, she opened for him, the heat of his tongue meeting hers. She pulled away, gazing at his face. "I love you, too, you know."

His eyes glimmered with emotion, the same as they usually did whenever he couldn't speak about something. When he'd wake in the middle of the night and the only thing she could think to do to warm his soul was kiss him. To pull him into affection until pleasure ripped thoughts of anything else from his mind. It worked for her, too, often easing the exhaustion that lingered in her muscles and the relentless queasiness of her anxiety.

Conrad's mouth claimed hers again, less gentle this time as he eased her backwards onto the bed.

Chapter 8

DAMIEN LIFTED HIS HANDS IN placation, the weaves of his Art still tangling with those of the sanctum. He could feel Mirimé's anger through the mingling of his ká with everything around him. It boiled and raged far worse than the small guardian let on.

Lucky Matthias, I guess.

"I am deeply sorry for the misunderstanding and for what you went through being imprisoned. But what we are doing here is immensely important. Could you perhaps allow us at least into the sanctum grounds so we might discuss how to move past all this?" Damien gestured to the rugged courtyard in front of the single structure that held the entrance to the chambers below.

Mirimé somehow managed to look down their nose at Damien, even from below him. "So *you* are Ailiena's successor," they sneered. "Yondé chose you, didn't they?"

"Sindré, actually."

The fox guardian frowned with a soft snort. "It was my turn to choose the Rahn'ka when I became trapped. I wouldn't have chosen you. I have no obligation to choose you now."

To his credit, Matthias kept his mouth shut and just watched them.

"Perhaps we should attempt to commune with the others? I'd very much like to hear their explanation for why they didn't tell me what was happening to you." Damien wished desperately he could read the guardian as he did people. But the cyclone of thousands of ká composing the being made the task impossible. He'd lock on to one emotion, only to be hit with a completely different one a moment later.

Gods, I hate talking to guardians.

Mirimé barked a laugh that sounded far from human. "I know what they'll say." And in perfect form, the fox took on the expression Damien had often seen on Sindré's face as they imitated the antlered guardian. "Barely any time has passed, and complaining about it won't change anything."

Matthias's lips tightened as he fought back a smile, and Damien glared at him.

"What can I do?" Damien bowed his head, hoping Mirimé would find it a sign of respect and guilt. "To make up for not coming to visit sooner."

Studying their pointed nails, Mirimé considered. "Kill Yondé."

The Isalican king choked.

Damien frowned. "Maybe something a bit more... doable? I don't know if that's even possible, to be honest. I thought you were all eternal."

"It's possible." Mirimé sighed and rolled their eyes. "Sort of." They turned, striding deeper into the sanctum courtyard.

Matthias glanced at Damien before speaking. "Are we to follow you?"

"Only if you'd like this conversation to continue," the fox drawled.

The pressure of Mirimé's ward around the sanctum weakened, and Damien drew back the tendril of his power connecting him to the monolith. And as he did, he half expected the fox guardian to vanish, but they remained, nonchalantly walking towards the single altar in the courtyard. A nub of a stone, broken by the centuries it lay open to the elements in this crevice between two monstrous peaks.

Mirimé paused beside the altar, lifting a hand. Stone rose from the ground, rebuilding the small structure within moments. The fox climbed onto it, sitting cross legged and facing them as they approached. "I have not chosen you, Rahn'ka. And I will not choose you until you prove yourself to *me*. And until then, you cannot enter the sanctum depths."

I'm too old for this.

Damien sighed. "What do you have in mind for this trial?"

For that's what it was. And Mirimé wasn't the first guardian to put him through one. And they were never easy. Or quick.

The fox lifted their chin, narrowing their eyes just enough that Damien and Matthias halted their approach eight feet away from the altar. "I have had some time to think about what your trial should be. And I have decided that you will repair my sanctum."

Matthias looked at Damien, brow twitching, but said nothing.

A kernel of hope sprung forth in his gut. "I can absolutely see to the sanctum's repair with the assistance of builders and architects. I just need a few days to assem—"

"No." Mirimé cocked their head in a purely fox-like gesture. "Alone. You will repair it alone."

The spark died. "Alone?" He looked to the crumbled stone monoliths around the altar area, and didn't need to look behind him at the cracked and fallen atrium. "I can't even lift a monolith by myself."

"Use your Art, Rahn'ka." The dryness of the guardian's tone grated through him.

Didn't they just hear me say I can't do that?

"I can't manipulate stone like that."

"And, see?" Mirimé gave him a deadpan look. "This is what happens when one of us is left out of your training. You fail to learn an entire aspect of your power."

Beneath a lingering annoyance at the idea of him needing to be the student—again—a strange excitement bubbled up.

"You'll teach me, then?" Damien focused on the guardian's large eyes, still twinkling with mischief. "I'll need your training to complete the trial."

One eyebrow quirked up. "I will provide instruction. Training. But you will accomplish the task without help." Their eyes darted to the empty sky. "And most importantly, without the dragons."

Chapter 9

One week later...

A LIGHT DUSTING OF SLUSHY snow had coated the palace training arena, but the open air was still far more welcoming than the empty halls of Kin's private chamber. Amarie hadn't been there for weeks, nor had anyone else, but her departure still felt raw. He distracted himself in Feyorian politics as much as his mind could bear, but it still meant returning to an empty bed at night.

"Keep the reins taut." Coltin's voice tore Kin from his self-pity.

The massive creature beneath Kin shifted, making his stomach jump. Daydreaming while on the back of a wyvern was definitely a bad idea.

"Why are you the one instructing me on this again?" Kin hadn't mastered keeping annoyance out of his tone around Coltin, even though the emotion really had no standing any more. The Delphi heir had absolutely outgrown his attraction to Amarie, considering how long it'd been for him. Yet, for Kin, the jealousy he'd felt watching Coltin and Amarie together in the gazebo of the Delphi estate was still relatively recent.

Coltin scowled, but it barely changed his stern expression. "Because I have the most experience training wyverns and their riders in this city. Would you prefer someone less qualified, your majesty?" He bit the words out, surely adding the title to further irritate him.

Kin frowned, but did as instructed, shortening his reins. The wyvern stilled, his massive head looking straight ahead. A lingering tightness in his chest made him want to procrastinate the training, but he needed to learn. By wyvern would be the best way for him to get to Nema's Throne for their rendezvous in a month. And he'd be making that journey alone, despite the protests he expected from royal advisors.

"All right, now what?" Kin looked down at Coltin, who looked perfectly relaxed standing beside the beast that could turn and chomp his head off in seconds.

Who the hells thought it would be a good idea to train these things?

"Repeat what you did before, nudging *gently* with your heels and squeezing with your calves." At least Coltin looked equally displeased to be here, though Kin wasn't entirely sure why the heir had a problem with *him*. "When Xykos starts moving—"

The wyvern interrupted him, turning his horned head towards Coltin. Kin's heart leapt, and he tried to tighten his hold on the reins further, but the creature ignored his direction. Rather than opening his jaw, though, he snuffed a few quick breaths right in the Delphi's face.

Coltin pushed him away with a click of his tongue. "You can have treats after." He looked at Kin again, utterly unfazed. "When he starts moving, keep tension on the reins but give him enough slack to swing his head."

"And this is keeping us on the ground, right?" Kin didn't even want to consider what would happen if he accidentally ended up in the air.

It had been different on a dragon. A dragon, who could speak and understand verbal directions. A wyvern was just a giant, deadly, flying horse.

"Yes, you will remain on the ground." Coltin's tone flattened at the question he'd answered several times already. "To launch, you give lots of rein while leaning forward and tapping quickly with your heels."

Kin made a mental note not to do any accidental tapping. He did as Coltin instructed and Xykos took a lumbering step forward with his left wing, the right following a moment later as they began walking to the far end of the training arena.

"Good," Coltin praised, even though his tone didn't match the sentiment as he walked alongside their trajectory. "Squeeze a little harder."

Kin did as Coltin asked, and the wyvern picked up his pace, the ride smoothing out.

"You *want* to fly?" the heir called out, walking smaller circles in the center of the arena as Kin and the wyvern tracked the perimeter.

If it was as simple as flying, Kin would have said yes. He missed the sky, having been teased with it once more when riding the dragons with Matthias. It was the only thing that still made him crave the power he used to hold.

"Not yet." Kin eased his pressure on the wyvern, the draconi slowing to a standstill.

Coltin sighed and then evened his expression. "If you're planning on flying to Isalica, you need to get into the air sooner rather than later. The ground is the easy part."

"I have a month." Kin loosened the straps securing him to the saddle.

"No, you *think* you have a month." Coltin strode towards them, pulling a scrap of something out of his pocket that had Xykos eating out of his hand a second later. "But what if something happens? What if plans change?"

"Then I'll figure it out." Kin hopped down from the saddle, hand instinctively going to his hip to steady Sephysis as the dagger bounced in its sheath. Even the slight touch sent a spark up Kin's arm.

"We'll train again tomorrow," Coltin said while collecting the wyvern's reins. "I want you in the air within a week, and if you disagree, you can find another trainer." He led the draconi towards the arena gate.

Kin couldn't help but quirk a brow. "Getting frustrated with me already?" He considered letting Coltin go without further word, but the man was the only person Kin had to talk to in the palace that understood everything that was happening beyond Feyor's borders.

Coltin paused, looking back at him. "You procrastinate. You refuse to give it your all. If this is an indicator of future lessons, then I fear when the time comes and you *must* fly, you won't be prepared."

"That's hardly fair for you to say. I am giving this my all, but my all happens to be rather spread out at the moment." Kin tried to control the rising frustration. Sephysis buzzed against his thigh as if it recognized the change.

The man's eyes darkened. "If the Key falls into danger, I will do what I have to do, even if it means leaving you behind."

"I believe you're talking about *my wife* and *my daughter*." Kin's expression darkened.

"Exactly, which is why I thought you'd be more dedicated to learning how to get to them."

"I was told I needed to stay here. We agreed I needed to stay here, or you damn well know I'd be out there with them right now. I'm supposed to be here for at least another month. I'll learn how to ride the damn wyvern."

A muscle in Coltin's jaw worked. For a few moments, Kin thought he'd say more, but he turned in silence and led the wyvern out of the arena towards the roosts.

Sephysis burned at Kin's hip. The blade all but vibrated in its sheath as Kin fought to rein in his anger. He debated going after Coltin, but to what end? There was little more that could come out of the conversation with them both angry. Sighing, Kin paced and focused on the dagger that wrestled to take advantage.

Blood.

The thing craved it as Kin's own veins continued to heat. He had to get control of whatever was happening or he would never keep Sephysis contained. The lingering fear of being on the wyvern certainly hadn't helped things.

He gripped the dagger's hilt, squeezing as if to strangle the weapon. The force helped ebb the emotion from his body, and he sucked in a deep breath.

I'm in control. Not you.

Sephysis quieted, the energy turning to a low rumble within the stone at the end of the hilt. It seemed to blink at

Kin as he looked down. Reminding him that it was always watching. Always waiting for an opportunity to wrest more control.

The dagger had chosen him, yes, but it still had its own priorities. Its own desires of what they could accomplish together.

Kin walked at a leisurely pace back towards the palace, exiting the arena and only glancing towards the roost where Coltin had taken the wyvern.

The man was unbuckling the saddle, hauling it off and dropping it on a horizontal post. With his back turned to the beast, he didn't see the attack.

The draconi sprung on the Delphi heir, taking him out in one fluid motion to the ground as the man shouted.

Kin moved before he could fully comprehend what he might do. Rushing to the gate leading into the roosts, he threw it open and stepped into the muddy enclosure. Sephysis begged to be withdrawn, but even with the danger, Kin hesitated. Especially when he didn't see any blood.

As he hurried closer, expecting to hear flesh tearing, his steps faltered at the sound of muffled laughter.

"You're too big for this, Xyk!" Coltin laid in the mud on his back, the wyvern's snout pressed to his chest. A rare smile adorned his face, even as the beast huffed a hot breath into it.

Kin blinked, trying to reconcile how Coltin could be laughing while being mauled. The wyvern chuffed, playfully jumping away with the help of his wings, and lowered to the ground like a puppy in play. The action looked ridiculous from such a large, foreboding creature.

Coltin rose, curling his lip at the mud all over his uniform in what ended up being a mock distraction before he charged at Xykos. Grabbing a horn, he swung himself over the draconi's neck, and they both tumbled to the ground with the tackle even though the beast could have easily tossed him twenty feet.

Xykos stood and shook, studying Coltin, who lay still as death in the mud.

Kin narrowed his eyes.

The wyvern took a cautious step closer before Coltin barked a shout to surprise his apparent playmate. The draconi screeched and bounded off, flying a few yards before landing a distance away.

Coltin stood once more, not bothering to brush off his clothing, before Kin caught his eye. His expression sobered, but light lingered in his eyes. "What are you doing in here?"

"I thought you were being mauled." Kin looked towards the wyvern, who looked curiously at him now.

The corner of Coltin's mouth twitched up. "So you came to save me?"

Kin frowned, crossing his arms. "Maybe." He watched

Xykos, who seemed to be evaluating whether Kin was also there to play.

The wyvern crept closer to the king, earning a sidelong look from his trainer. "Xyk was the first wyvern I trained. Playing and blowing off steam is good for their bond with their riders."

Kin wasn't sure where this newfound openness from Coltin had come from, but he wouldn't complain. He eyed Xykos and held up a hand. "I don't think we're quite at that point, yet, boy." The familiar fear of the wyvern's teeth still lay coiled in him, though now it felt more dormant than mere moments ago.

Xykos needed no further invitation, leaping into the air and landing a breath later right in front of Kin, sniffing his hand as if expecting a treat.

His heart thundered, his feet instinctively taking a step back. Sephysis gave a comforting vibration, as if reminding him it stood ready to defend him if he needed, but Kin pushed the connection down. He wanted to believe he wasn't in danger as he kept his hand extended, letting the wyvern nudge it around. "I don't have anything. Sorry, Xyk."

Coltin appeared next to him, subtly slipping a large strip of dried meat into his other palm.

Xykos immediately changed focus to Kin's other hand, and a whine erupted from his throat. He didn't snatch the treat, surprisingly, but a purr rumbled in his chest as he tilted his head.

Kin thumbed the treat, debating what commands the wyvern would know. "What was that word for crouch down, again?"

"Dak," Coltin muttered, and the wyvern plopped to his belly with a thud. He scowled affectionately at the creature and said with dry sarcasm, "That was graceful."

Kin offered the strip of meat, casually moving close enough for the wyvern to extend his neck far enough to grab it.

"Fah," Coltin warned Xykos.

The motion of his mouth was gentle, as if the animal knew the damage he could accomplish, and he took the treat. Once clear of Kin's fingers, he chomped the food down with barely a chew.

"I have to be hard on you." Coltin's softer tone came as a surprise. "Amarie and Ahria may be your family, but I've dedicated nearly twenty-two years to protecting them and their power. With everything coming to a precipice, I don't want there to be anything left on the table."

"I do understand." Kin watched the wyvern for a moment before he turned to Coltin. "I think I'm in a pretty good place to understand *exactly* the danger that Uriel is to all of us. And what is at stake. But I hope you can understand me, too. My life is a system of balances right now. And I will become more confident with Xykos, but I need a little *time*."

Coltin huffed. "I do admire your desire to reform Feyor. This country is a mess, and I can't imagine the work involved. And I realize Sephysis complicates matters, too." He stiffened for a breath before pulling his faction device from his pocket. Opening it, he stared at the dials whirled around, spelling out their message. He snapped it closed once it stopped, returning it to his pocket.

Kin watched him for a moment, waiting to see if he would volunteer whatever information he had received, but Coltin's face remained impossible to read. "News from Deylan?"

Coltin hesitated for a moment, then sighed. "Nothing good," he muttered, half-smiling when Xykos pushed his nose into the man's chest in what looked like an attempt to comfort him. "The attack this summer crippled most of the faction's resources. Aside from weapons and communicators, we're basically useless." Resentment dripped from his voice, along with something else. Something almost... sad.

Kin cringed. The attack on the faction's headquarters had been because of their mistakes. Uriel might have had awareness of the Sixth Eye, even made attempts before to smoke them out from their hiding places. But it was their traveling party from the royal estate in Ziona that he'd been tracking when they led him straight to the bunker. "I guess the construction of a new headquarters isn't going well?"

Coltin patted the wyvern's head before turning to return to the palace, waiting for Kin to fall into step beside him before he answered. "They're trying to relocate the viewing chambers, but the technology is complicated and not borne of faction hands. It will take time, a lot of time, if we are successful at all."

Realization flowed through Kin. Coltin's only purpose now was him. Training him, preparing him, because all other goals were now sidelined. He wasn't even sure what Coltin's life would look like once Kin left for Isalica. Would he remain in Feyor? Continue to play the part of a royal advisor while being an inactive faction agent?

But when Feyor's government restructured, there would be no royalty, let alone advisors.

Maybe he'll join the senate in some way?

Though, politicians would need to be elected.

Suddenly, Kin empathized with a man who surely had no idea what his future held. If all he'd worked for would end up being for nothing.

"The Sixth Eye will rebuild. And we will finish this with Uriel." Kin didn't know what else he could say to comfort him. "You've already made a difference in your monitoring of Uriel here in Feyor, and the faction provided the knowledge on how to seal the prison, not to mention they saved Damien's life."

"Trying to console me?" Coltin quirked a brow at him. "You're as transparent as Xyk. But I appreciate the effort. It's better than the whole deadly-thief act you put on the first time we met."

Kin couldn't help the grin. "I may have been a Shade, but I'm not completely heartless." Admitting the truth of it out loud seemed odd. He avoided talking about his former life as much as possible, but had accepted Damien's title of 'Shade redeemed' whenever he spoke about the part Kin would play in all of this. And the others had kindly stopped mentioning it.

"Yes, a Shade." Coltin hummed. "A phantom who drains the life of everything around him. Yet, you were still more desirable than the heir to a fortune."

"In her defense, Amarie had no idea what I was at the time." A strange guilt bubbled up, accompanied by old musings about whether or not Amarie would have been better off staying and becoming a Delphi. He'd regretted taking her from that life for a time, but looking back on it now... that life was never one she would have wanted, anyway.

"Well, that helps a little." Coltin smirked.

"Things got... infinitely more complicated after that, too." Kin glanced at Coltin. "Did you know that Killian was reporting to Jarac and not just your family?"

"I did. Killian was a mercenary who worked for our family, appointed by the royal family. We both recognized your face, and he made the call to involve Jarac. He told me after that you'd used the Art to borrow our prince's face, but I learned the truth after Deylan recruited me."

"The Art certainly seems like an easier explanation than the truth." Kin grimaced at the thought of his brother. He'd really only interacted with Jarac in extreme situations. He'd find himself wondering, sometimes, if a relationship with his real family would have ever been possible, but Jarac's choice to become a Shade had ruined that. And now he was dead.

Not that I can fault him, really, for making the same choice I did.

Sephysis purred against his hip at the memory of Jarac's death. At the blood on its blade.

Kin sighed. "That encounter in your family's collection room seems so mundane now, with everything else." He paused at the doorway into the palace, looking to the east edge of the grounds where the invisible barrier Damien and Katrin had put in place remained. His eyes lingered on the shadows of the black mountain beyond, imagining them shifting with power.

"Tell me about it," Coltin drawled, then huffed and looked at his muddy clothing. "I need a change. And then an ale, I think."

Kin opened his mouth, ready with the offer to buy, but chuckled at himself instead. "I guess I'm buying, since you're probably going to be grabbing it from the royal kitchens. Mind company?"

Coltin turned surprised eyes at him, hesitating before answering, "Sure. Why not."

Chapter 10

MATTHIAS WATCHED THE SKY AS Zelbrali soared into the clouds. His friend, the dragon. Sometimes, it was still surreal.

A large pack lay at his feet on the rocky beach, another slung over his shoulder. Supplies for the next week.

The king stood there well after the dragon had disappeared, letting his mind wander to where his wife might be at that moment. They'd taken a portal to Belgarath, since she and Dani hadn't both known a closer location. Traveling through Ziona was favorable to traversing the dangerous forest floor of Aidensar. They'd have to cross grygurr territory to reach Kiek, which only worsened his tension.

But Katrin could handle herself, and he trusted Dani's ability to fight. The Dtrüa would protect Isalica's queen with nothing less than her life.

Amarie and Corin are also with her.

While the Berylian Key was a target capable of drawing the attention of the worst foes, she could also decimate most enemies with little effort. And Corin had well-earned his position as master of war for Helgath.

Still, Matthias swallowed.

Katrin will be fine.

Taking a deep breath, he heaved the second pack off the beach and strode towards his camp with Damien. They'd been here for two weeks now, and fortunately, the second week boasted far more progress than the first.

Under the guardian's orders, Matthias couldn't aid Damien in the repair of the sanctum. Not that he'd be able to imbue stone the way the Rahn'ka could, anyway.

So he occupied himself by helping in other ways. His repertoire of meatless meals had grown exponentially, and he'd even given up entirely on bringing meat in for himself unless it was dried and required no preparation before eating. He dropped the packs by their tent. It stood taller than him, with basic cots inside covered by thick blankets.

He'd improved upon their firepit, adding a grill above the flames to serve as a makeshift stove. With the winter chill approaching, they stoked the fire high enough that it would last through the night with only minor tending, keeping them from freezing beyond the sanctum's warmth.

For that warmth, he was eternally grateful.

Whether the guardian had done it, or Damien himself, he hadn't asked. But the barrier that had once kept them out, now held in enough heat that he could remove his furred cloak while inside.

Abandoning the supplies, Matthias strode into the sanctum's courtyard, and the pressure of the barrier swelled against him before giving way. The late-autumn cold vanished, easing the tension in his shoulders. Once Damien finished repairing the exterior, Mirimé had promised they could move their camp within the heated area.

Damien stood by the atrium entrance that would also lead him within the underground section of the sanctum. His uncovered eye was shut as he worked, seemingly unaware of Matthias's presence, but the king knew better.

Matthias shrugged off his cloak, draping it over a freshly-repaired courtyard bench. The pillars were now pristine, carved with runes like they'd only been constructed days ago.

I guess they sort of were.

He continued to his friend, watching each stone weld into the next, threads of light-blue energy seeping into the rock. Stuffing his hands in his pockets, he didn't interrupt as Mirimé gave instructions from their perch on top of the archway.

In fox form, the guardian's ears twitched. "Use more energy as you place these. It is a key component in the structure."

In contrast to how the relationship had started, Mirimé proved a good teacher. And according to Damien, the fox had been extremely, unexpectedly, transparent about how to accomplish things.

"You can't build this half-assed like you did the steps," Mirimé sighed.

Well, they aren't without their moments.

"Going well, I take it?" Matthias eyed the fox before settling onto the nearby courtyard steps Mirimé had referenced. At the top was a small raised gazebo that Damien had rebuilt from the very foundation. It felt unnaturally solid, more so than just stone.

"So well." Matthias could sense the eye roll behind Damien's closed lid. Sweat gleamed on his bare chest and his hair stuck to the leather strap of his eyepatch. In the week of work, the manipulation of energies had sharpened the Rahn'ka's muscle definition despite the lack of physical movement. Barely any indication of Damien's coma remained, his body strong once more.

That must feel damn good.

They'd refrained from talking about how long the entire trial would take. A week in, and Damien had only almost finished the exterior work. He hadn't even set foot inside to start the interior, and the damage within was much more extensive. Yet, Mirimé had made him repeat his work in the courtyard several times, insisting on perfection, and he figured Damien's skill would eventually reach a point when he'd get it to an acceptable level on the first repair.

Two more weeks at least.

But with everyone else occupied by their own tasks and goals, the time hardly seemed to matter. They needed access to the prison first and foremost. The rest could wait.

"Any requests for lunch?" Matthias rested his arms across his knees. "Got all the supplies here. Or should I work on getting our camp out of the cold?" He directed the second question towards the fox, who blinked at him.

"He's not done with this section yet. And based on how it's currently going…"

"Better wait until late afternoon." Damien opened his eye and glanced at the cloudy sky above. "Hopefully before sundown." His tone wasn't convincing.

"I'll get started making some food, then." Matthias rose, gathering his cloak as he walked towards the camp.

Mirimé muttered, the words barely reaching his ears, "I could teach two Rahn'ka with the same effort as teaching one, you know."

Matthias's steps slowed, boot dragging over stone for a breath before he resumed his pace.

Two Rahn'ka?

He furrowed his brow, resisting the urge to glance back and ask what Mirimé meant. He swore Damien's one-eyed gaze burned into his back as he reached the barrier.

The cold snapped around him, and he hurried to drape his cloak over his shoulders. The mottled black fur on the mantle tickled his neck, but it kept the freezing ocean breeze at bay.

Unpacking only the necessities, since he'd be relocating their camp soon, anyway, Matthias set about cooking lunch. He'd brought flatbread from the nearby city, and it would pair nicely with the spiced pumpkin curry. Thoughts of Katrin and her journey to Aidensar had inspired him to pick up the more exotic spices in the Orvalinon marketplace. And cooking would give him time to consider what Mirimé might have hinted at.

An hour later, he filled two bowls, laying a large piece of bread over each one before carrying them to the sanctum. He noted Damien's progress on the archway, but the fox wasn't in sight.

"Pumpkin and chickpea curry with flatbread, if you're hungry." Matthias smirked, knowing what the Rahn'ka would say.

"I hope there's still more back at camp." Damien took the bowl before stepping up the stairs towards the gazebo. "Thank you."

"When has there ever *not* been more back at camp?" The king chuckled, following. "Oh, and there's a jar of walnuts and pecans for you in the supplies. Thought you might want something different to snack on between meals. Though I did bring more apples."

Mundane talk of food, but Matthias watched Damien's face for any indication of the truth. Trying to read what secrets he might be hiding and the look of discomfort still lingering in his expression. His avoidance of eye contact.

If there is another Rahn'ka, and Damien has been hiding them from everyone...

Damien settled onto the bench that encircled the inside of the gazebo, lifting the bowl of curry to his nose as he gave a grateful smile to the king. "You almost take better care of me than my wife."

Matthias laughed. "I enjoy cooking. Rae not into it?"

He made a face. "Not at all. And thankfully. She's not exactly a good cook. Knows it, too, so I can say it."

"Fair enough." Matthias dipped his bread into the curry and bit it, humming in approval. "My mother taught me from a young age, said it would be the most useful skill I'd have, aside from fighting. She wasn't wrong."

"Seems an odd skill for a queen to teach her son, though. Not like you'd need to know how."

"And yet, I *have* needed to know how. It's like she knew. My mother was... different. She wanted me to be self-sufficient, even if I didn't need to be." Matthias smiled, enjoying the warmth of the sanctum almost as much as the curry.

"Well, I'm rather grateful to her right now." Damien lifted his bowl slightly in salute before taking another large bite. "And that you're here to help keep me sustained. Otherwise, I'd probably be eating a lot of nuts and dried fruit. And this would be going a lot slower."

"I'll be here until you're finished. Micah is having a great time with my kids, anyway. Though I wonder if I'll lose him soon." Matthias chewed a bit, thinking of the friend who'd spent his entire life serving him. He deserved any and all happiness that found him, even if it took him away from Isalica.

The Rahn'ka's face grew more serious. "I am sorry that you're losing out on time with the kids. I know how important that is." He took a large bite of bread as Matthias nodded, only half chewing it before speaking again. "But why would Micah leave?"

"He's in love, I'm pretty sure." Matthias smiled, imagining Micah with little ones of his own, but his friend had no plans for children. Never had. At Damien's quirked brow, he clarified, "With the queen of Ziona. It's rather ironic that he spent most of his adult life impersonating me only to become royalty himself. Assuming it works out, that is."

"Huh." Damien chewed more slowly for a moment. "I hadn't noticed." He shrugged. "Guess I was too busy thinking about other things, but now I feel bad that I didn't."

"They've been keeping it quiet, so don't be hard on yourself." Matthias took another bite, hardly missing the ground turkey he usually added to the dish.

Silence settled for a few breaths, and once Matthias was certain the Rahn'ka wasn't about to offer up the information that weighed on the back of his mind, he asked with as much sincere curiosity as he could, "Do you trust me?"

Damien stiffened, his spoon frozen in front of his mouth just before his bite. "That's an ominous question."

Matthias shrugged, keeping his tone casual. "Uriel inhabited my body for two decades. I'm used to the subconscious stigma that comes along with that. But I'd like to think I've proven myself an ally to this cause, no?"

"Of course you have." Damien put the full spoon back in his bowl. "I know you're not Uriel, and that he's long gone from you. You probably want him imprisoned even more than the rest of us."

"Can I ask you a question, then?"

Damien grimaced, likely already sensing what was coming. "Sure."

"I heard what Mirimé said, about teaching two instead of one." Matthias held his friend's gaze. "Is there another Rahn'ka?"

Damien cupped the bowl in both hands, lowering it into his lap. He averted his gaze to the ground, and Matthias wondered for a moment if he'd lie. If he'd try to deny what Mirimé had given away. The Rahn'ka pursed his lips and looked up, meeting Matthias's eyes, but didn't speak.

I know that hesitation.

Realization dawned in the king, and he blew out a slow breath, any tension he'd held onto melting away. "Oh," he murmured, nodding. "Is it Bellamy or Sarra?" He understood. He'd felt that same reluctance when Zael had shown an aptitude for the Art.

Damien's eye dropped again. "Bellamy." He chewed his lower lip for a moment. "Sarra is almost the age where she'll start showing signs... if she's one, too. We don't know for sure yet, but I think..." He didn't finish the thought as he moved to set the nearly empty bowl on the bench beside him. "I hope you can understand why I've chosen to keep him out of this."

"I do." Matthias sighed. "Of course I do. I won't tell a soul." He paused. "Was it him who brought you back, after the bunker?"

A hint of a smile came, then vanished as quickly as it'd appeared. "Yes. Rae sent for him when it became clear I wasn't getting better with only the faction's care, as advanced as it was. But that's the limit of his involvement. I don't want Uriel even getting the barest whiff of his existence in case..." He stopped himself from saying it.

In case we fail.

"I understand." Matthias put a hand on Damien's shoulder. "As a father, I would do the same."

Chapter 11

WARMTH FILLED CONRAD'S CHEST, THE first comfort his surroundings had provided in weeks, as he took in the familiar private dining hall of his mother's chambers. Talia stood by the back doorway that led to the staff-run kitchen serving only this room. Even if it was only the three of them and the single server, his mum looked perfectly put together, as always. Her coarse dark hair had been braided close to her head, the gold circlet of her crown woven within it.

That part is still a little strange.

The door behind him and Ahria clicked shut as the guard on the other side pulled it closed, drawing Talia's eyes to them. She smiled, and another wave of relief passed through him. With a minute bow, the server departed, allowing them the privacy Conrad cherished.

"I know it hasn't been long, but I'm still happy to see you." Talia crossed the room to them. She reached for Ahria first, extending welcoming arms to take her into a brief hug before moving to her son.

He'd gone so long without her hugs, Conrad had never realized how much he missed them after he'd run away. But now, he couldn't imagine giving them up again.

"The kitchens know it's only three of us, right?" Conrad gestured his chin to the overloaded table, filled with various sandwiches and side dishes.

Talia waved a hand at it. "You know how Kepper is. I swear he can't help himself if there's any opportunity. My first mistake was saying the word *celebration*. I was only excited to have you home, at last. Don't worry, the leftovers won't go to waste."

They walked together to the table, Talia pausing to pick up a bottle of wine that she took back to her seat at the head of the table.

Conrad released Ahria's hand to pull a chair out for her. Her expression looked focused as she sat—her stomach had been bothering her most of the morning. He'd taken on all he could in their departure from the ship at the royal dock, allowing her time to rest in bed. It was the least he could do after waking her up in the middle of the night with more nightmares.

He blocked the return of images that had plagued him as he sat at his mother's table.

None of it was real, and now I'm home.

It was odd how comforting the thought of the palace being home was.

Something he swore he'd never get used to.

He loaded his plate with a variety of different flavors, all specifically made to avoid the things he didn't like. He'd be a fool to complain.

Out of the corner of his eye, he watched Ahria choose just a few things for her plate. He didn't want to say anything again. She hadn't eaten breakfast, and her lack of appetite was a stark contrast to the woman he first met who could out-eat him any day. Even his mother's eyes flickered to Ahria's plate for a heartbeat.

"How have things been here since your return from the coronation? We were told you only arrived a few days before us." Ahria's throat bobbed, and instead of reaching for her fork, she picked up her water glass yet again. "Has it been hectic catching up?"

"It's been relatively peaceful. I think I may finally be getting accustomed to this queen business." Talia smiled as she lifted her own glass. "Security is in place and we haven't had any reports of disturbances related to Shades anywhere within the city, save for the one who attempted to investigate the death of Talon's murderer. But Micah and his soldiers stopped them before they even made it a block into the city. And with Feyor finally finding some stability, far less refugees are seeking to cross the border."

Ahria's hand briefly shook as she set down her glass, and Conrad suddenly wondered if this place offered her comfort, like it did him... or the opposite.

Her father was murdered here...

He tried to catch her gaze, but she refused to look at him.

Which wasn't shocking, given how their conversation had gone after he woke in the middle of the night.

"Hey, it's all right. You're all right. I'm here, it's safe here," she'd murmured to him in the darkness of the ship's captain's quarters, rubbing his back. "It was just a nightmare."

The pools of black, swirled with gold flecks, flashed in his mind. The sinister laugh as blood spread around Uriel's feet, Amarie's lifeless body beneath his boot. Then the body changed to his mother, to Kin. To Ahria. Her eyes open, staring at him without any of the light they'd once had. They brought more shadows. Corrupted growled outside of his vision, lost somewhere behind.

He tried to remember that it was only a bulkhead, only the rocky shores of the Astarian River as they made their way to New Kingston's port. But his body heaved for breath, sweat coating his skin.

Ahria's arms had wrapped around him. "Conrad?" she whispered. "Do you want to tell me what you saw?" Patience radiated from her, even as her body sagged with exhaustion.

He stared across the dim cabin, taking in every familiar detail that had been his life for so many years. When he'd been no more than a ship's captain. But now every shadow seemed to shift unnaturally, causing a chill to roll up his spine and lock his tongue in place. He felt Ahria's arms, urged himself to find comfort in them, but they felt impossibly warm and he struggled to breathe.

"I just need a minute." Conrad needed to stand. Needed to get away from the bed and look into the shadows to be certain. He moved, hoping it would help his body realize it was no longer in the dream. He nearly slipped on the cold, polished wooden floor, but he steadied himself on the bed post. His face felt wet, and he wasn't sure if it was all sweat or if the tears he'd shed in the dream hadn't been confined to that realm.

Ahria wrapped the sheet around her torso, moonlight glimmering off her eyes. "Talk to me. It will help, I pro—"

"I can't!" He hated the tone of his own voice, and the flinch that rippled through her. "Stop asking me to, and stop... stop *looking* at me like that."

Without another word, Ahria had dressed and left. And damn him, but he hadn't stopped her.

I can't blame her for being angry.

Apology after apology had streamed out of his mouth the next morning, but the words failed to penetrate her icy stare, even as she nodded. Even as she still let him hold her hand.

He reached beneath the lunch table, touching her knee gingerly as he looked at her nearly untouched plate.

I'm sorry. You've been so patient.

A knock echoed through the space, followed by a guard opening the door to the dining chamber. He bowed to the queen. "Your majesty, I apologize for interrupting, but Councilor Yinik needs a quick signature from you."

His mother nodded, glancing at Conrad and Ahria. "Excuse me just a moment." She rose and walked to the doors, but didn't exit the room.

Ahria stared at her water, giving no reaction to his touch beneath the table.

Voices murmured from the doors while Talia and the councilor spoke, but Conrad paid no attention to them.

"I'm sorry." It felt futile to whisper it again, but he did anyway. "I'm going to keep saying it until you can look at me again. You didn't deserve that last night."

Frustration tightened the skin around Ahria's mouth. "No, I didn't," she muttered, her voice lacking strength. Or perhaps keeping low because his mother was well within earshot. "But your apology means nothing when nothing is changing. When you're making no effort to even *try*."

He gritted his teeth, the familiar anger bubbling up within him. "I *am* trying." Even as he said it, he could feel his jaw locking down at the mere thought of explaining. The thought of telling her everything he saw in those dark dreams. Everything he felt. Thinking about it only made the metal hallways of the faction headquarters close around him.

"Trying to shut me out, maybe. Trying to keep it to yourself. Trying to be *strong* for me." Her whisper soured with sarcasm.

"You haven't felt well for *weeks*. You're going to be expected to fight against an impossible foe in some ruin in Isalica in a few weeks. Where you might very well see people we care about *die*." Conrad tried to control his volume, but his mother's eyes darted in their direction. He schooled his voice. "You don't need more."

"That's not your choice to make," she hissed, abandoning the quiet tone. "Maybe I'd feel better if I had someone I could openly talk to. Maybe I'd feel less like a *freak* if the only other person who went through it too didn't act like there's nothing going on." She finally looked at him, eyes bright with swirls of amethyst, even with the shadowed circles beneath them. "Maybe then I'd feel less *fucking* alone."

Conrad opened his mouth, but paused when he realized Talia had returned to the table, standing silently beside her seat. Concern etched all over her face.

"I'm sorry," Ahria whispered, rising as she addressed his mother. "I'm not feeling well. Excuse me."

He wanted to reach for her, to stop her. To tell her... anything. But he didn't, watching her leave and the doors shut behind her.

Talia silently observed as Ahria left, settling into her chair. She eyed him as the doors closed. "You should go after her, you know."

"It won't help." Conrad pushed his plate away, suddenly disappointed by everything in front of him. "I've already fucked it up enough."

Talia lifted an eyebrow as she sipped her wine. "That's unlike my careful son. What has happened?"

The familiar sensation of his tongue getting stuck to the roof of his mouth returned. He glowered at the table, his mother's subtle movements in his peripheral vision. She only sat there, still idly munching on her meal, and it somehow allowed Conrad to relax, at least slightly.

"You said Ahria hasn't been feeling well for weeks?" Talia still didn't look directly at him. "Nauseous?"

"Mostly. She's always tired, too. Hardly eating. Which is *very* unusual for her." Speaking about her was far easier, and he was grateful for the change in subject. Though, knowing his mother, it would come back to him.

She won't judge you. She's your mum.

"Has she had her cycle?"

The question made Conrad's spine go rigid, crumbling all attempts for him to remain calm. "Her... what? Why?"

"Her cycle, dove. And you know why."

His chest felt impossibly heavy. "Not in..." He tried to count the weeks.

How long has it been since we found her in Lungaz?

Two months. It'd been nearly two months.

Talia rested her wine glass in her hand, elbow on the table. "We can send for a healer to be certain."

Oh, gods.

"Why..." Conrad's head spun. "Why wouldn't she... tell me?" His throat dried, forcing him to take a gulp of water.

"She likely doesn't know for certain herself. I assume she's never carried a child before. And... if I dare point out the obvious... your conversation a moment ago doesn't sound like the two of you are communicating well."

The cyclone of emotion in him only made it more difficult to find words. The absolute fear tangled with an odd sense of joy buried beneath it. Excitement, yet utter terror at the timing.

If she is... and with the upcoming battle with Uriel...

"We should send for a healer." Conrad finally looked at his mother. "If you're right, we need to know."

"You should probably confer with her about that decision first." Talia studied him, seeing right through him. "But that might require you to give something as well." She stood, gliding around the table towards him. Her hand settled on his shoulder as another wave of possible happiness turned into shame. "I know how you are. You've always been this way since you were a child, always trying to protect me."

Conrad sucked in a breath, putting his hand over hers. "I felt like I needed to. Without Dad..." He stopped, squeezing her hand. They never talked about him. She'd always avoided the subject, but now speaking about him felt so very important.

I might be becoming one, too.

"It's all right, Son." Talia took Ahria's seat, but angled it towards him. "I understand that growing up without your dad changed a lot of your behavior. And I know it's been difficult to bring him up. And that's my fault. Grief is..." She sighed. "What's important is that I finally tell you more about him."

"Why now? The obvious aside." He studied her. "You couldn't speak of him at all before."

Talia gave a barely noticeable shrug. "When the heart begins to move on, speaking of those we've lost becomes a little more bearable." Before he could latch onto that statement, she continued. "Your father was many things, and many kinds of wonderful, but one of the things that made him strong, made *us* strong, was that we kept nothing from each other." Her tone was as gentle as the hand sliding down his arm.

"I don't remember him at all." The admission left his chest hollow. "Not even the slightest image or memory. Only what I painted of him in my own imagination." He pursed his lips, urging the words never spoken before to continue. "I know he was alcan. That's all I know for sure because of my blood. But I imagined him as this tall, imposing figure. Stern, always serious. Strong and stoic."

Much to his surprise, a laugh burst from Talia's lips. "Oh, your father was strong, all right. But he was also a lot of *fun* and definitely not stern. We had a dog, for a while, before you. He loved her so much that when she passed, he could hardly handle it. He wept while we buried her, and I always admired his capacity for love. And of course, whatever he felt for the dog was multiplied infinitely for you. Gods, you were the center of his whole world. But at his heart, he was always a warrior, and when his people called him for aid in a conflict between two alcan clans, he couldn't turn away from them. And before he left, he was afraid. Afraid of not returning to us. Hells, we were both terrified. But we supported each other through it up to the day he had to leave."

She took his hand, squeezing it. "We may not have had a happy ending, but we never shut each other out. With that or any struggles before it. When we hurt, we did it together, and instead of doubling the pain onto another person, it lessened it. When you choose to spend your life with someone, you share *all* of yourself. Not just the bits you're proud of. And if Ahria is that person..."

"She *is* that person." Conrad turned more to his mother, trying to comprehend all she'd said. The image of his father had always been so set in his mind, but now it warped, reforming. "I'm glad you finally feel you're able to talk about him. I have a lot of questions that I plan to ask you later. But for now, I'm just glad you're able to love someone new." He squeezed her back again.

"Oh, I don't know about *love*, yet." Talia's cheeks flushed in a way he hadn't expected, and she shook her head.

He gave her a teasing smile. "Every time he's around, he's only ever with you."

His mother's gaze shot to his. "What do you mean? You have no idea who I'm talking about."

"You're not nearly as sly as you think you are, Mum. I'm pretty sure everyone has noticed how you and Micah are around each other. Matthias certainly has."

The blush on her cheeks deepened. "He has not."

"You forget how friendly I am with all these other kings, now. He has. And it's nothing to be embarrassed about. You two have every right to be happy. Even if he is Isalican. And old." He gave a teasing frown.

Talia tilted her head with a mock scowl. "He's..." Her tone shifted from denial to something softer. "He's so kind to me, and yes, Son, I know he's *older*, but age matters little to the heart." She cleared her throat. "But we aren't talking about me. Because while my... *affection* for Micah is relatively new, he's still been very open with me. He's been through some awful things, and sometimes, they still haunt his sleep."

"So you've slept with him." Conrad wasn't certain he wanted to pursue the line of questioning, but anything was better than where she was heading.

Talia choked on a sip of wine. "That is *not* what I intended for you to get out of that. But if you must know, he *told* me about his nightmares long before I was ever *with* him. They're rare now, but his willingness to share that vulnerability with me was..." Conrad opened his mouth to insert the first negative word he could think of, but Talia raised her eyebrows and finished, "Romantic."

"I don't think sharing my nightmares with Ahria could ever be considered romantic. You don't know what they're even about." Conrad glowered, turning his gaze away.

"So you do have nightmares, then." His mother nodded, not waiting for his confirmation, since he'd already stupidly given it. "It doesn't matter what they're about. You're suffering. She's trying to help you, and you won't let her. Why? Because of some misplaced sense of protecting her?" She scoffed. "This may surprise you, my dove, but from what I can tell, she can protect herself."

"I know she can. But telling her won't help anything. She can't do anything to change it. No one can. It is what it is."

Talia squeezed his hand so hard it hurt. "Is there even a small part of you that can admit that maybe... just maybe... that's where you're wrong?" She narrowed her eyes, lines appearing between her brow.

"How? How could I be wrong?"

"Look at it this way. Is keeping her at a distance helping? Not just you, but your relationship? Because it doesn't look like it. It looks like you need to change tactics or risk losing her. And I know you don't want that. You can tell her you love her, but it won't mean anything if you don't show it, too."

Conrad's chest seized. "What if I can't?"

"You can. Because being strong isn't about keeping it inside. Being strong means giving voice to those thoughts and fears. It means talking about it, even when it's terrifying to be vulnerable. And I know you're strong enough to do that."

He tried to imagine himself finally telling Ahria what brooded in his mind, but it still left his chest aching, his stomach roiling. But he'd fought through these kinds of fears plenty of times, though it usually had entailed a storm and some broken rigging. This felt far more raw. Far more dangerous.

In the silence, his mother reached up to rub the back of his head and it sent a calming wave through his body. The familiar action, one she had used on him hundreds of times in his youth, still worked. The cloud of anxieties and nightmares gradually cleared, allowing him to see Uriel at the center of it all.

This is all just giving him power over me.

He scowled.

As if he needs more.

"Thanks, Mum," Conrad murmured, his expression softening.

She smiled gently and lowered her hand. "I'll send for the healer?"

"Please. I'll go talk with Ahria about it so she's not surprised. But I think we're far overdue for a healer with how she's been feeling, regardless of what suspicions anyone might have." Conrad looked at the table, still laden with food they hadn't touched. But his mother would see that none of it was wasted. "I'll take a couple plates, just in case her appetite comes back."

The doors to the dining hall burst open without a precursor knock, drawing their attention to the guard— No, not a guard.

A familiar healer stood in the threshold, garbed in white, a disgruntled guard directly behind her rushing to catch the door. "Your majesty," she rushed, hastily bowing as Talia stood. "I came as soon as I could. Princess Ahria has been taken to the royal infirmary."

Conrad jumped to his feet, rounding the table towards the woman as his stomach knotted. "What happened?"

I should have been with her.

Talia followed close behind.

"She lost consciousness on the way to her chambers." The woman backed up as Conrad approached, motioning for him to go with her. "Follow me, please."

Conrad cast a quick look at his mother, the anxiety of Ahria's possible pregnancy returning to the forefront of his mind. They'd never even discussed children.

His mother paused in the doorway, the guards flanking her. She gave him a quick nod. "Send me an update later?"

He returned the gesture before refocusing on the woman he walked behind. "Is she still unconscious?" They nearly jogged through the hallways, taking a route he wasn't familiar with. The side halls were more narrow and plain, but one wall had windows open to view the Astaria River below. The cold chill blowing in from the mountains rustled the ivy leaves, still clinging to their summer green.

The woman made a sound that was either a laugh or a snort or a cough. "No. She's *very* conscious now."

"Am I to then assume... unhappy about her location?" Conrad could imagine the fight she was probably giving the royal healers.

The woman glanced at him, a bit of color rising to her cheeks with her sheepish smile. "Quite."

When they approached the doorway to the royal infirmary, he half expected to see Ahria marching out of it, but only her voice reached him. "I don't need observation, and I don't need an escort. I can return to my chambers by myself."

"If you would just be patient another few moments..." Another healer spoke, an older-sounding woman.

Ahria paused. "Why? Why another few... You sent for Conrad, didn't you? I told you—"

The healer who'd led him stepped aside, standing next to the open door with her head bowed, exposing Conrad.

"Too late." He lifted his brow, hoping to show her amusement rather than just concern. It might soften her reaction.

As soon as Ahria's gaze met his, she pinched the bridge of her nose and closed her eyes. "This is ridiculous. I'm fine." She stood next to a twin bed and sighed as she looked at Conrad again. "I'm *fine*."

The older healer eyed her before turning her attention to the prince. "Princess Ahria fainted in the hallway, so we brought her here, your highness, for examination."

"I'm right here," Ahria said between clenched teeth. "And I don't need you to call me *princess*."

Conrad gave a gentle smile to the healer before he walked across the brightly lit room to her. "Trust me, it's hard to get them to stop." He reached a hand towards her face, and when she didn't scowl at him for the action, he gently brushed her hair behind her ear. "I was just about to come talk to you about speaking to a healer, but you always find ways of beating me to the punch."

Ahria frowned, but the corners of her mouth twitched. "I want to go back to our rooms now."

"Can we talk first?" He only had to gesture with his gaze towards the older healer before she bowed her head and shuffled towards the door, ushering the others out with her.

The door clicked closed behind them, leaving them alone.

"I'm fine," Ahria repeated, tone softer as she pulled his hand from her cheek. "I got a little light-headed, is all."

"We both know you aren't fine. You've hardly eaten for weeks, and that alone is cause for all my concern. We both know you'd rather be emptying out the kitchens on a daily basis." Conrad slipped around her, sitting on the edge of the bed. He patted the spot beside him, watching her.

Ahria didn't smile as he'd hoped, facing him but not sitting. "I mentioned my symptoms to the healer, and she recommended I rest and drink lots of fluids."

"Ahria." The spot in his chest tightened. "My mother pointed out another possible cause for your symptoms."

Something dark flickered beneath her expression. "She's wrong."

"Do you even know what she thought?" He stood, realizing she would never join him. "I know the timing isn't ideal, but I want you to know that I'd be happy. Excited, even. If it were the case."

Her brows twitched upward in the middle, her shoulders drooping. "I'm not pregnant, Conrad."

He opened his mouth to question if the healer had confirmed it, a sharp pin of disappointment now stabbing where the tightness in his chest had been. He took her hand, holding it to that spot as he studied her. "You're sure?"

Ahria nodded, and whether she held the same disappointment, or if she'd had the same suspicion, she didn't let on. "The healer confirmed it."

He lifted the back of her hand to his lips, kissing it. "Then the healers think this is going to pass soon? Just a temporary sickness?"

She stared at him, eyes hard. "Probably."

The disappointment bloomed further, turning back into concern. The healers had years of experience, but this still felt different from a minor chill like he used to catch as a child. "Then we can send for tea and soup to our rooms." He released her, turning towards the closed door. "Maybe get some sleep."

Just a stomach sickness, maybe.

Conrad swallowed, taking her hand.

Hopefully.

Chapter 12

WISPS OF LUSH REDS AND oranges drifted past Dani's face, bringing the spicy scents of cumin and cardamom. The food in Aidensar had surprised her, with all the bright flavors and the burn of heat on her tongue. Though, it would be easier to enjoy if she didn't need to be paranoid about falling a hundred feet to her death.

Whoever thought it would be a good idea to build a city within the treetops...

But as much as she disliked the elevation, the danger on the ground made the local population's choice to be above it make sense. Thieves, grygurr, dire creatures. The wilds of Aidensar were unmatched.

Except, perhaps, by Feyor's war beast training grounds. But those barely existed anymore, and what remained would be barred up under Kin's rule. She didn't want to think about what might happen to the beasts Feyor still held captive.

Kin will be merciful to those innocent.

"You look comfortable," Amarie said from somewhere to her left. On one of the solid pathways built between city districts. "You've been there for over an hour."

Dani sat on a massive branch, feet dangling in front of her. "If I pick a spot and needn't move, then I cannot fall, can I?"

Amarie, Katrin, and Corin had all been overly protective of her inability to see among the endless opportunities for her to step off a platform. And for once, she didn't mind.

"Have you heard from Katrin? I haven't seen her since they finally allowed her in to speak to the royal council. Don't know where Corin is, either." She muttered the last part in an afterthought.

"Hitting more taverns, I think." Dani lifted herself to her feet, clicking her tongue before joining Amarie on the wider path. "I've been listening to everyone I've walked past this morning, and I've not heard mention of Melyza. Maybe he's had better luck."

"I hope so." The ropes along the edge of the platform creaked as Amarie leaned against the banister. "We've been here a week and we know nothing." Doubt lingered in the

Key's tone, and Dani understood her hesitation in believing the auer who'd once followed Uriel.

The unspoken worry hung in the air.

What if we're chasing a ghost?

Or worse yet.

What if it's a trap?

But there'd been no sign of Shades or Corrupted. Only rowdy tavern patrons and a grumpy innkeeper who didn't seem to care that they traveled with foreign royalty.

Dani tilted her head, picking up the faint stride of their friend. "Corin approaches."

His boots echoed along the wobbling bridge as he crossed onto the garden platform with Amarie and Dani. "This the new spot, then? I swear I didn't mean to scare the gardener at the last one."

Amarie chuckled. "He probably thinks Helgath plans to invade Aidensar now."

"Did you get any information?" Dani turned to Corin, but a little voice in the back of her mind told her he would have led with it if he had.

"I'm starting to believe Melyza doesn't exist." The ropes groaned louder than they had for Amarie when Corin leaned. "No one has heard of her, let alone how to find her."

"Fantastic," Amarie breathed, but Dani fell silent.

They'd asked countless people. In the streets, in taverns,

the inn, and at markets. No one had heard of anyone by that name.

"Maybe she's using a different name," Dani murmured. "Or maybe we're asking the wrong people."

"Or everyone in this damn place has decided I'm a Reaper and are just protecting her." Corin's leather bracers rubbed at his chest piece as he crossed his arms. "No point in bothering to tell them Jarrod dismantled those bands twenty years ago. Sarians still believe Helgath is corrupt and kidnapping Artisans."

Amarie grunted her agreement. "Then maybe we change tactics."

Dani tilted her head but kept quiet.

"Maybe we should get Melyza to come to us. Seek *us* out."

"How?" Dani blinked through her blurry vision, picking up the bright yellow scent of turmeric drifting on the breeze from the nearby tavern district. "Can't exactly place posters around."

Amarie paused. "If Melyza is old enough to know about Seph, and has potentially cooperated with Uriel, then it stands to reason she has the Art. Which means she would sense it if I—"

"No, no way." Corin interrupted seconds before Dani could. "Far too dangerous with us still not knowing who Uriel is in. And we've dodged his kind of trouble so far."

"You got a better idea, then?" Amarie challenged, though her voice lacked hostility.

"Katrin's our best chance. She's finally in with the royal council. Maybe she'll get something out of them. At least Aidensar seems willing to talk to a representative of Isalica."

"Where is she meeting us?" Amarie directed the question at Dani.

The Dtrüa shrugged. "She'll tell me when she's ready. Why?"

"I'm hungry." Amarie walked a few paces towards the city before stopping. "Anyone else?"

"Always. The curry at this place I was at earlier smelled amazing." Corin's footsteps started towards the bridge that led from the garden platform. "Might as well fill the time while we wait for the queen."

"Fill your stomachs, you mean." Dani followed, clicking her tongue. "Not that I'm arguing."

In her new typical means, Dani held Amarie's elbow as they maneuvered through the city. It lessened her fear of walking off a ledge unprotected by a railing or rope. When Katrin had given Dani a view of the city through her eyes, it'd only made the feeling worse. Possibilities for an accident existed on almost every platform.

Corin entered the building he'd led them to, holding the door for the women. The scent of a sweet, rich curry hit her senses, making her mouth water. The spices, the sauces, and the fire-roasted flatbread dappled with garlic and butter made her reconsider living in Isalica. The food at home was good, but... She couldn't wait to bring Liam here one day.

Shortly after sitting, their table filled with shared plates of different dishes and breads. Dani dug in, scooping sauce-laden chicken into her mouth with the thin, chewy bread. The taste danced over her tongue, and she silently vowed to eat as much of the food as possible before leaving Aidensar.

"This is the best food we've eaten since arriving here." Amarie's surprised tone came between bites. "I vote we have *all* our remaining meals here."

"Seconded," Dani said around a mouthful of bread.

Mmmm, what smells so good?

Katrin's voice made Dani smile. "Garlic flatbread and some kind of tomato-cream spiced chicken." The others paused when she spoke, understanding. "We're at Lramandoo's Tavern. Want to come taste it?"

I'll be there in a few minutes. I'm starving.

"We should order more flatbread." Dani smiled. "Katrin's hungry, too."

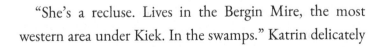

"She's a recluse. Lives in the Bergin Mire, the most western area under Kiek. In the swamps." Katrin delicately chewed on a piece of bread, not at all fazed by being the last person eating.

"Not exactly a hospitable location for a house." Corin leaned back in his chair, the back legs creaking as he rocked on them. "Everything I've heard suggests no one lives in the mire, not even grygurr."

"Which is probably why she likes it. She's a rejanai, and avoids the public."

"So Eralas banished her," Corin murmured. "Wonder what for..."

"Shit," Amarie muttered, sipping an ale. "Auer. She could have been alive long before Seph was entombed, then. Who knows what she knows."

"Can we just... go to her?" Dani tilted her head, drinking water.

"Well..."

Corin interrupted Katrin. "Don't tell me. First, we need to fight a great beast of the forest to find a key into her dwelling, where we will then disarm multiple traps—"

"Not exactly." Katrin's voice was stoic, but a playful lilt lingered beneath it. "But close, actually. Whenever the council seeks advice from her, they bring a relic as a peace offering. They suggested if we're set on speaking to her, that we do the same."

"What kind of relic?" Amarie sounded less optimistic than the others.

Katrin shifted, finishing a bite before replying. "There are ancient ruins in the mountains just east of here. They're abandoned, but some still contain knick knacks from a long lost time. If we can retrieve something from those ruins, we can offer it to her."

A brief wave of fear scented off Amarie, quickly dissipating.

"And you know why those knick knacks are still there instead of being picked clean? Grygurr and whatever other manner of beasties are on the forest floor. No one's stupid enough to go looking." Corin rocked forward, his chair slamming back to the ground.

"Maybe you weren't so far off when you mentioned fighting a great beast in the forest." Dani smirked at Corin.

He grumbled. "Pretty sure I'd rather fight Corrupted than risk whatever's down there. There isn't another way to get to this Melyza person?"

"Trust me, I asked the same thing. It's the only honest way." Katrin's wine glass tinked against the table as she set it down.

"She may not be on our side." Amarie lowered her voice. "She may even be on *his* side. But we can't assume anything, and any wrong approach could swing this in a way we don't want it to go. If we have a chance of swaying her to our side, we need to take it."

Chapter 13

LOOKING OVER THE SOUTHERN HORIZON, Kin lavished in the feel of the wind on his face and the ground far below. It wasn't the same as it'd been before, with the pressure of the air against his own feathers, but the steady drum beat of the wyvern's wings brought a different kind of comfort. Of freedom.

He squeezed the wyvern's left flank to encourage him to bank, and Xykos obeyed. Taking to a steep angle, they glided down through a thin cloud, revealing more of the wooded terrain below them.

This was only his second flight, but already the joy eased all nerves from his body.

Coltin had convinced him to take to the sky the day before, and the man had seemed genuinely pleased with Kin's progress. Things between them had been less tense since Kin had found the faction spy playing in the mud with Xykos.

You're a natural in the sky, Coltin had said. Which came as a shock, given Kin's ineptitude with horses. Turned out, once his mount was airborne, some of his old instincts with flying kicked in.

Flying on a separate wyvern this time, Coltin soared alongside him. The day before, he'd ridden behind him on Xykos, but this was preferable.

"Pick a spot soon to land!" Coltin shouted over the wind. He'd prepared Kin for today's lesson—take offs and landings—the two things he needed to work on most.

Looking down beyond the umber scales of Xykos's neck, Kin surveyed the wilderness. The tree line broke apart as the forest encroached the rugged black Dykul Mountains. Old rock slides had created several clearings, but few looked flat enough to land on. It was better if they stayed further from the populated areas, too, now that they were beyond the wards. It was still possible an agent of Uriel's somehow followed them, watching from the shadows outside the palace for the right opportunity. A distant anxiety lay buried in his chest beneath the elation of the flight, a knowledge that even now they were in danger.

If something was out there, wouldn't it have already made an attempt, though?

Perhaps the presence of two wyverns discouraged whatever lurked. He'd kept his eyes open for any black birds following, but nothing dotted the sky behind them.

He spied a flat patch of ground beneath, a long fissure cutting from the base of the mountain out into the tree line. It left a large enough section of exposed meadow for their two wyverns to fit. The shadows lingering within the fissure made him look away, but there was nowhere else that would accommodate them.

There's nothing following us. Seph would have sensed it.

The dagger, secured as it always was against his left thigh, gave a buzz of agreement. Though something still felt odd as Sephysis's energy mingled with his own, as if the dagger was keeping a secret.

Stop overthinking it.

Tapping Xykos's flank like he'd been trained, Kin loosened his grip on the reins. He aimed the wyvern's nose down to the clearing, watching as the ground grew rapidly closer. "Fah!" He hoped he'd gauged the proper distance as the wyvern suddenly extended his wings to slow their descent.

Xykos flapped with extra force to maintain the right distance, causing Kin to lean forward in his saddle as the wyvern's back legs contacted the ground before falling forward onto folded wings. The jerky motion nearly made Kin tumble out of his saddle, barely catching himself before his face slammed into the wyvern's neck.

Coltin's wyvern landed beside him in near silence, the man's eyes trained on Kin. "You leaned forward too much. That's why you almost broke your nose."

"I thought I was going to fall off the back if I didn't." Kin grumbled, straightening himself as Xykos settled.

"Gotta trust yourself. When you lean back, you'll actually feel more stable in the saddle. Try it next time. Otherwise, you did well." Coltin relaxed in his seat. "I'll stay here. I want to see your take-off and landing again."

"Now?" Kin quirked a brow.

Coltin smirked. "Now."

He sighed, knowing that Coltin was only trying to help by making him practice the worst parts of flying a wyvern. He turned the creature away from Coltin. "Vah."

Xykos trotted a few steps away to give them space from Coltin and his wyvern.

Kin urged his stomach to stay in place as he prepared his body for the coming motion. "Vah'kro."

The draconi took only a slight hop forward before launching from the ground. He managed to keep himself upright out of sheer will, knowing Coltin would critique his form if he didn't. Gravity compacted his spine, but as soon as Xykos leveled, gliding downward before catching the wind blasting from the mountains, Kin felt light again.

They banked at Kin's command, and he watched the tip of Xykos's wing cut through a looming cloud bank near the mountain. He couldn't see the rocky cliffs, and relinquished some control to the wyvern, knowing his senses far out powered his own.

He looked back to the woods, the dense trees only growing taller in the far south. Memories of flying over Aidensar in search of Amarie and Talon panged in his chest. Thoughts of his friend flooded him and the lessons Talon had put him through when he suddenly had the Art with no understanding of how to use it. He'd been a brother to Kin, then became a father to Ahria. The loss of Talon still felt raw, and Kin fought to gain control of his rampant thoughts as Sephysis hummed as if to comfort him.

Gods, I wish I could have seen him again.

Their final interaction had come shortly after Amarie's death in the ruins of Aidensar. And Kin had placed the burden of watching over her on him. The auer had made mistakes, but also far surpassed what Kin had asked of him.

Movement far below caught his eye, where Coltin and his wyvern waited, yanking Kin from his memories. The man had dismounted, attention on the trees rather than on Kin and his wyvern like it usually would be. Unease tingled over Kin's skin, and he guided Xykos back around to come in for a landing.

Coltin drew his sword, the copper catching the midday light like warm flame.

Kin urged Xykos faster. Down and down towards the clearing, where Coltin finally looked up at them.

"Fah!" Kin shouted the command for the wyvern to slow. To land, but the Delphi heir's voice boomed from below.

"Vah'kro!"

The wyvern didn't even hesitate in obeying his trainer, banking and returning to the sky.

Kin's heart leapt, annoyance rippling through him. He shifted in his saddle, turning Xykos until he could see below.

Several dark shapes darted from the tree line, aiming for Coltin. The sun gleamed against onyx scales and fur, their sleek bodies sending a rip of terror into Kin. Sephysis responded, heating at his thigh with a thrill of excitement coursing into Kin's soul. It eased the fear rumbling in his gut, and he gratefully embraced the feeling. And with it, the solidified connection to the blade.

He pulled hard on Xykos's reins, the wyvern letting out a screech of protest as he whirled back towards the clearing at Kin's command.

As Kin neared again, Coltin swung his sword and decapitated a lunging Corrupted before taking his eyes off the fight to look at the king. *"Get back to the palace!"* His attention tore to another misshapen beast, his wyvern handling a swarm of them on his own. Jaws snapped on the mutant Corrupted, lifeless broken bodies striking the ground, only to be crushed by the wyvern's claws.

Black blood coated the flattened grass of the meadow, the wyvern howling as she tore her head back from the body of a Corrupted beneath her. Leaping over his mount's lashing tail, Coltin barely avoided joining several Corrupted hurtled towards the trees. The leaves shook at the impact of their bodies, wood splintering.

"Fah! And don't you dare listen to him again." Kin reached down to the latches of his harness, despite the stupidity of loosening them pre-landing.

Sephysis all but screamed at him, still secured to his thigh. Flecks of red danced into the corners of Kin's vision, the vibration running through every inch of his body.

But before Coltin could issue another command to Xykos to get Feyor's king to safety, a large bear-bull Corrupted flattened him onto the grass. Horns nearly gutted him while clawed paws swiped at his legs.

Lurching forward as Xykos landed, Kin used the momentum to fling himself from the wyvern's saddle. He hit the ground in a crouch, his muscles singing with the impact. His fingertips buzzed as they finally freed Sephysis. Before he could even stand, the dagger launched into the air. A streak of red darted in front of Kin, aimed at its first target.

The bear-bull roared as Sephysis sliced a line across the back of its neck, strange mutilated bone protruding up through the lesion. It lifted back on to its hind legs, rising from Coltin and swatting its massive paws at the air as if fending off a mosquito as Sephysis whipped around.

Coltin took his opportunity and slashed his sword through the bear-bull's neck, blade severing bone with unnerving ease. He rolled. The head toppled, smacking the ground where Coltin's chest had been moments before.

Rising to his feet with black blood coating his skin, he snarled at Kin, "Get back on that wyvern and within those wards!" Emotion laced his words. True fear beneath it. But he spun to face another advancing creature, his wyvern roaring.

"You first!" Kin extended his hand, old habits of his Art still present as it summoned Sephysis back to him. The blade blurred in the air, encircling Kin just as a snake-cat lunged from a crack in the stones behind him. Spinning, Kin watched the bloodstone blade sever the cat's head with deadly accuracy before it resumed its cyclone around him. Fear had vanished, replaced by elation as Sephysis obeyed his command to assist Coltin's wyvern.

Xykos had joined the fray as well, large claws at the end of its wing gutting Corrupted that dared lunge at it.

"It's my *job* to protect you!" Coltin feinted left and brought his blade down on a Corrupted's spine, mid-back, cutting the thing in two.

They both had effective weapons. The wyverns took out just as many. But the Corrupted streamed out of that cavern behind them in an unending wave. Dark wings flapped as several took to the air. No longer could they fight one at a time, as the numbers grew to surround them all.

Coltin's wyvern launched into the air, focused on the threats above. Xykos screeched again, plowing over at least a dozen with a wide swing of his horned tail.

Sephysis soared through the air, lashing through neck after neck, severing spines and cracking through skulls with mere thoughts from Kin. The destruction brought an odd wave of joy, but he understood it was the dagger and not him who felt it. Yet the emotion was infallible, tangled with his own. He fought against the sheer excitement to rationally examine their situation.

"This is too many for a single summoner." Kin had worked his way through the gore coating the ground towards Coltin, Sephysis weaving his path. His boots stuck in the black-stained grass. "I don't think Seph can keep them off us long enough for us to mount." Even as he said it, another swarm of various sizes lunged at Xykos, forcing the wyvern closer to the trees. He beat his wings, forced into the air with the other wyvern, suddenly leaving them on the ground alone.

A huge claw or tooth stuck out of Coltin's calf, but the man made no motion to remove it. "We need to try." He backed towards Kin, at least a dozen Corrupted prowling around them, waiting to lunge. "There's too many." Blood dripped from his brow as he peered up, a bright spot of red among all the black ooze.

The wyverns battled from above, swooping down to crash into the Corrupted before launching again, misshapen bodies falling from their claws to the jagged rocks below.

Sephysis kept a pattern between them and the fissure, almost playfully dancing back and forth over a group of cat-creatures who batted up at the dagger with little success. Extending his will to the dagger, its blade nearly black with the Corrupted blood it had absorbed, he pulled Sephysis back to them.

"I say we make a break through the trees to the next clearing." Kin glanced behind them at the tree line. "You able to make it with that thing?" He gestured at the claw still protruding from the faction man's leg.

"It's shallow. Go," Coltin ordered, creating a barrier between Kin and the Corrupted. "I'll cover you. I'll be right behind."

"Seph will cover us. You first." Kin grabbed his shoulder roughly, encouraging him forward, but he didn't budge.

The fire in Coltin's eyes told him it'd be easier to move a mountain.

"Fine," Kin growled, hurrying towards the trees. He looked back, cringing at how many Corrupted faced off against Coltin, but forced his feet to keep moving.

The next clearing. Then Xykos could land, he could mount. They could get out of there. Thirty yards. Twenty five.

Huffing sounded behind him, and he dared glanced back at Coltin charging through the trees. The tooth had dislodged from his leg, leaving a trail of blood behind.

Black shapes darted through the trees, chased by the red streak of Sephysis weaving in and out of the dense foliage.

Ten yards.

Coltin barked a shout as Kin looked at him, the man's eyes wide on their would-be escape. Kin faced forward and stumbled at the sight of the giant Corrupted landing in the clearing.

Oh, gods.

He recognized the leather bat-like wings and jungle cat patterned body. Had seen it countless times. Had even ridden it. For the beast that towered over them was once Alana's mount.

Baellgaith.

"The *fuck* is that?" Coltin skidded to a halt next to Kin, panting.

The head, like that of a leopard and a bat made into one, opened its maw of razor sharp teeth and let out a high-pitched scream. It made Kin's ears ring, and he tried to pull Sephysis closer, but the dagger held off a horde of Corrupted coming from behind.

The horse-like body quivered, but stood fast where it was fifteen feet away. A clicking purr rumbled from its chest as its dark eyes focused on Kin. He could see himself in the reflection of its crimson irises, a strange knowing in the depths.

A wave of confusion broke into Kin's awareness, Sephysis stilling behind him for a moment rather than continuing to lash at more adversaries.

"Why isn't it attacking?" Coltin breathed, eyes darting between the largest Corrupted and the strange quiet that had settled in the forest behind them. "Where are the Corrupted?"

Baellgaith chortled, stepping closer to them and tilting its head.

Sephysis lunged again in Kin's senses, chasing now, rather than defending. Kin could hardly focus on the dagger as Baellgaith neared him, his heart pounding. He recognized the friendly chitter the creature used to give Alana.

It recognizes me.

"These Corrupted don't belong to a summoner." Kin cast a daring glance to Coltin. He could barely believe how many there had been. How many Corrupted had been free of a leash. "This isn't Uriel. This is one of Alana's."

Baellgaith's nostrils flared with each huff, scenting Kin the closer he got.

"And you trust it?" Coltin didn't sound convinced, strafing around the creature while its attention remained on Kin.

"Not really," Kin confessed, looking down at the cat-like paws, claws hidden somewhere within. "Pretty sure *wild* Corrupted are still just as dangerous. But Baellgaith seems to remember me." When he received no reply from Coltin, he looked sideways, but the man wasn't there anymore.

As if in answer to his comment, the Corrupted gave another deep purr, like stones tumbling against each other.

Exposed, Kin's chest tightened. He sought Sephysis through their bond, finding the dagger had made its way back to the fissure, still focused on picking off more Corrupted. Too far away.

Baellgaith took another step, close enough now that its reeking breath reached Kin's nose. It chortled again, lips curling to reveal long, serrated teeth.

"You remember me..." Kin spoke cautiously, trying to keep his heartbeat steady. The creature could likely sense his growing panic, no longer subdued by Sephysis's power. "Alana wouldn't want you to hurt me."

The beast seemed to smile, showing the entire row of teeth as grey saliva dripped from its jowls. It took another step, forcing Kin to back up. The purr altered to a growl, claws extending into the forest floor.

Kin pulled hard on the bond to the bloodstone blade, and Sephysis reluctantly drew back from its massacre. He sensed it weaving through the trees behind him, but far too slow.

Baellgaith lunged without warning, and Kin threw himself away from the claws. His wet boot slipped on the meadow grass, and he fell mere inches from where Baellgaith's claws tore at the dirt.

It turned, roaring wide at Kin, before the sound cut off. Baellgaith's head dropped from its body, mouth frozen agape, and rolled sideways as its body collapsed, Coltin sitting on its back. Sword in hand, the spy leapt from the beast's back before it could pin him under it. "We need to get out of here."

Sephysis whirled into the clearing in a flash of red, circling the headless corpse as if disappointed.

Kin only nodded, trying to soak in Sephysis's indifference as he pulled the blade back to him. Comfort washed over him as the hilt came to rest in his palm, and he held it tightly as he rose to his feet.

Coltin lifted two fingers to his mouth and let out a sharp whistle, calling the wyverns.

Howls broke from the clearing they'd first fought in, whatever time Baellgaith's roar had bought them now dwindling. The roar Kin had thought was the monster defending him. But no, not defending.

Claiming.

Xykos landed first, streaks of maroon and black blood coating his scales. The second wyvern landed a breath later.

"We need to get into the sky." Coltin glanced back in the direction of the cavern.

Sephysis buzzed in Kin's hands, but not as urgently as before. It'd been satiated by the bloodshed, making it far less eager. Kin took the opportunity to secure the dagger back to his thigh as he hurried to Xykos. "Dak." He hardly had to state the word for Xykos to crouch low, allowing Kin to throw himself up into the saddle. He only just latched his harness before he gave the command for Xykos to launch into the sky, Coltin close behind.

Chapter 14

THEIR BED FLEXED BENEATH HER, waking Ahria. She blinked, nausea rolling her stomach at the distinct lack of sleep as she tried to gain her bearings. The curtains were still drawn, and no sunlight seeped in the cracks.

The bed shifted again, and she rolled over, facing Conrad, whose body twitched in sleep.

Sweat beaded on his brow, his breath coming in sharp pants.

"Shit," she whispered, propping herself up onto an elbow as she touched his cheek, his shoulder. "Hey, wake up." She repeated it several times, keeping her tone gentle as she stroked his dark skin.

His eyelids fluttered, lips parting to suck in a deep breath as they finally opened. His body tensed instantly, tremors still shaking his muscles.

"It's all right," she murmured, trailing her fingertips over his forehead. "You're safe." She pulled her body closer, entwining her leg around his.

He shuddered as he wrapped his arms around her, pulling her hard against his chest. He kissed her head, his heart pounding in her ear. "I'm sorry," he whispered, nuzzling into her hair with another kiss.

"Shh…" Ahria smoothed a hand over his head, lowering herself into him and kissing his neck. "I'm right here. No need to apologize."

"There's always need." He ran his fingers along her bare side to her hip, soothing her unsettled stomach. "You need sleep, too."

She trailed the tip of her nose up his neck to his jaw, where she kissed again. "I get plenty of sleep."

It's almost true.

She'd been feeling a bit better since seeing the healer, but the bedrest only helped so much. And right then, with Conrad's hard body pressed against hers, thoughts of sleep quickly slipped away.

He breathed deep, a sigh rustling the hair on top of her head. "Aren't you going to ask me if I want to talk about it?" A smile tinted his tone.

Ahria huffed a breath over his cheek, resting her head against his chest. "*Do* you want to talk about it?" Her hand eased down his chest, dancing lightly over his stomach in slow, circular patterns. She looked up at him, hesitant hope blossoming within her.

His fingers touched her chin, lifting her face to his. He kissed her, soft and long as his fingers brushed her own, entwining and taking her hand from his skin. He brought it up, pressing her knuckles to his mouth before nuzzling his cheek into her hand. "I would like to try."

Ahria blinked, and she studied his face, furrowing her brow. "Talking?"

Anticipation steeled her insides. As much as she'd longed for the day he'd open up to her, she dreaded saying the wrong thing. Doing the wrong thing that would have him take it all back and never try again.

He remained close, his legs still tangled with hers as he stroked her arm and shoulder. "It's always the same. It's always him. Always Uriel. And it's back in that damn bunker beneath the ocean." He closed his eyes, squeezing her slightly. "You always die."

Falling silent, Ahria nuzzled her face into his chest, drawing more circles over his skin as he held her. She waited, not daring to push for more, even as her heart constricted.

"He's always laughing at me. And that's exactly what he did when I tried to help Damien. He *laughed* at me and threw me aside like a doll." His body trembled, and she held him tighter. "I'm nothing. In the dreams and in life. I don't have the Art like you, or everyone else. Even Kin has Sephysis now. I have no business being part of Taeg'nok. I'm useless."

Ahria jerked back, looking at him. She'd known he had insecurities, but... "Conrad," she whispered, touching his face. "You're not useless. Uriel may have laughed, but that's *his* mistake. You may not have the Art, or some strange ancient dagger, but you've saved *me* more than once. I may need the Art to play my role, but I need you even more. You could never be useless."

He met her eyes, doubt still hovering in his face. "I just don't see how. All of this is so far outside of what I ever expected my life to be." He caressed his fingers over her jaw. "I don't regret us. You're the one thing that has ever made sense in this life. The only thing that matters to me. I just wish I could *really* be there for you in all of this, but I don't know how. I'm not afraid of what Uriel can do to *me*. But these dreams... Every time I lose you, I'm not enough. I wish you knew how out of place I felt at all those meetings. I don't belong with that group of people planning how they'll save the world. I'm just a ship's captain."

"That's not true." Ahria shook her head. "Not everyone in that group has some amazing skill. Liam's just a man, and from what I understand, Katrin's connection to the Art is average."

"You just tried to use the man who works directly with the dragons and was instrumental in bringing them back into the world, and the queen of Isalica as examples." A thin smile crossed his lips. "She still has the Art, and that neat ability to portal people just about anywhere."

Scowling, Ahria still shook her head as her heart picked up speed. "You're the prince of Ziona, and half your blood is alcan," she whispered. They rarely spoke of it, since he hardly recognized it within himself, but it was true. "You don't know what that could aid us in. It saved you during the bunker attack, didn't it? Or you would have drowned. You helped Rae while she was a wreck over Damien. Helped my uncle with repairs. And you help me all the time. If there's anything I'm learning from this, it's that every piece of the puzzle is equally important, even if you feel insignificant. Because to me, you aren't. I wouldn't be able to do any of this without you."

"Yes, you could. You're the strongest—"

"No," Ahria choked out, and the half-strangled word silenced him. Emotions rushed through her veins as she stared at him, eyes burning. "I've lost... *so* many people that I love. I don't care if you have the Art. You keep me together when the world tries to rip me apart." Tears slipped sideways down her skin. "It doesn't matter how *useless* you think you are, because I *know* different. I need you just as much as I need air, and I'll be damned if I let you think otherwise." Her throat constricted, her hiding aura a feeble attempt to keep her power hidden. But who would be here to feel it and care? She let it slip, but it didn't let her breathe any deeper as she imagined Conrad truly believing the words he'd told her.

Useless.

It broke her heart.

Cupping his face, she sucked in a shaky inhale and willed the flicker of blue flames on her fingertips away. "You have a purpose with me. With all of us. A role to play in taking out the piece of shit who took everything else from me. We may not know what it is, yet, but you have one. I promise. And it will *not* be useless."

His eyes had grown glassy in the dim light, shining in the sparks of blue she couldn't fully control. Taking her hand, he kissed her knuckles and the flames, unafraid. The sun fought to seep through the bottom of the curtains as it rose beyond, and Ahria swallowed as the azure fire finally subsided.

"I hope you're right." Conrad stroked her cheek. "Even if I don't see it, yet. I just don't want to be the one who gets in the way of defeating Uriel." He sucked in a breath through his nose, shifting up onto his arm beside her. "But no matter what, I will always endeavor to be here for you. However you need me. And if that's in the room—whether it's a meeting or with the prison at Taeg'nok—then I will be."

"You won't *get in the way*." She scrunched her face at the absurd notion. "We have no idea what exactly we'll face, and you never know what will end up making the difference between victory and defeat." She swiped a hand over her face as something warm settled in her chest, threatening to renew the tears. "Thank you."

He made a face, running his thumb beneath her eye where it was still wet. "You have nothing to thank me for. I should have told you a long time ago. I'm the one who should thank you. For how patient you've been with me."

Ahria swallowed, briefly smiling. "I don't want to lose you."

"I know." He stroked the hair from her forehead before placing a gentle kiss there. "And I don't want to lose you. That's why this whole thing is so insane. Less than a year ago our biggest worry was how to steal that ugly ass hat from Warrin."

Memories of that tavern, the fire wine, the smoky scent of the city came flooding back to her. The rich scent of him as they'd gotten close. And the lush taste of him when they'd kissed on the beach under the docks.

Her stomach flopped over. "Getting caught on your ship was the best thing that could have happened to me," she whispered, muscles finally relaxing within his warmth. "I fell so hard for you, and I'm so glad I did."

"The feeling's pretty mutual." His arms tightened around her, pulling her against his chest as he kissed her forehead again, each little kiss sending a wave of shivers down her spine. "Can't just call you a stowaway anymore, though, Mouse."

Ahria chuckled, hovering her mouth over his. "I mean... could you ever have called me *just* a stowaway?"

He smiled, his breath tickling her lips. "Not after you put Merril on his knees in less than a breath. Took a bit longer for you to get me into that position, and now I quite happily will take it before you... any time." His fingertips danced down her side.

Heat bloomed over her cheeks, the discomfort in her body finally easing for the first time in weeks. Lifting her chin, she grazed his mouth. "On your knees, huh?" Images of him kneeling before her made her core tighten.

"Mhmmm." Conrad ran a line of kisses along her jaw, breath hot against her neck. "Would you like me there, now?" His tongue left a trail of goosebumps as he moved towards her breasts.

Ahria smiled as he eased her onto her back, breath quickening. "Only if I can return the favor after," she murmured. A rush of satisfaction tore through her when his gaze snapped to hers.

Conrad's lips slowly spread into a grin as he shifted on top of her, placing a teasing kiss on her abdomen. "I can agree to those terms." He moved between her legs, his hands running down her hips and thighs as anticipation built within her.

And when his mouth closed over her, the morning became a blur. The times before, to rid their minds of the Corrupted that lurked within, could hardly compare. Instead of the lazy pleasure they usually enjoyed, this became faster, more demanding. The ecstasy he evoked, over and over, left them both slick with sweat and heaving for breath.

They didn't speak as they held each other, and Conrad slipped back into sleep despite the breakfast bell ringing distantly down the hall.

Ahria let herself enjoy the comfort of his arms, her body a blissful puddle of pleasure beside him. But her mind wouldn't quiet enough for her to join him in sleep.

His words haunted her, and not just because they made him feel insecure.

A truth lingered beneath them that sent a jolt of fear through her.

He could be killed.

Easing out of his embrace, Ahria crossed the room to where his belongings rested against the wall while pulling her silk slip over her head. They'd yet to unpack fully, with all the meetings and stress, but she stared at his pack. Her gaze wandered to his sheathed swords before narrowing.

Rae said Damien made her a bow.

Curiosity had her picking up his steel sword, glancing back at him to ensure he still slept.

She brought the weapon back to the bed, leaving the copper faction sword with his things.

Ahria had no idea if she could forge a weapon made out of her power, but a voice in the back of her mind suggested it wasn't something only a Rahn'ka could do. A memory darted through her of Talon summoning a wicked, bruise-colored blade from his power, and she focused on that.

But she had no clue how to accomplish it. And Amarie had warned her not to take too much at once...

Steeling herself, Ahria silently slid the sword out of the sheath, admiring the intricate etchings on the steel near the hilt. The guard curled like leaves, the pommel boasting the carving of a thistle head. She wondered what queens of Ziona might have wielded the blade before it fell into Conrad's care.

Resting it on her lap, she glanced at Conrad once more.

His eyes remained closed, chest moving peacefully in sleep.

Returning her attention to her task, she nodded to herself.

I can do this for him.

Shutting her eyes, Ahria dove into her power.

Ice drenched her, yet flames licked at her feet.

Ahria's body shook so violently, it couldn't have been her own doing.

Sleep clung to her senses, blurring her surroundings and dulling her awareness. But her body kept shaking, rocking back and forth until she became aware of a voice.

"Ahria, wake up. Ahria!"

Conrad.

It was him, but... Gods, he sounded terrified.

Has Uriel found us?

Ahria forced her eyes to open, a deep nausea rolling her stomach. Her hand flexed, vaguely aware of the damp sheet under her.

The shaking stopped, and someone stroked sticky hair away from her forehead with a cool cloth.

Conrad's voice came again, but she couldn't make out the words. Another voice, somewhat familiar, responded, then a loud bang.

Shivers broke over her body, and she blinked, trying to focus. Trying to speak. But her throat, parched like she'd spent a week in Xaxos, couldn't make a sound. She choked, coughed, and pain scorched over her skin.

Ahria gasped, crying out in a moan at the unexpected agony. It lurched through her until she lifted her head enough to vomit what little remained in her stomach over the side of the bed. "What's... What's happening...?" Her voice was hoarse, shaky, and she hardly recognized it as her own.

Conrad's warm hands ran over her body. "I don't know. You were shaking the bed with how hard you were shivering. It woke me, thank the gods." He pulled her hair back from her face with a gentle stroke, passing a fresh cloth over her mouth. "A healer is on the way."

Another tremor shook its way through her, and she grimaced as her skin burned. Burned, like heat roasted her from the inside out.

"Everything hurts," she managed between clenched teeth. She'd dreaded the symptoms the day before, worrying about carrying a child... But now she wished it was as simple as an unexpected pregnancy. Whatever was wrong with her wasn't going to just go away like the healer had said. Something in her gut told her it might never go away at all.

Rolling onto her back, she stared at the ceiling, willing it to stop spinning. Tears slid down her temples when she blinked. The pain in her muscles peaked again, and she rolled onto her side, facing Conrad this time.

The door to the room opened in a rush, hurried footsteps crossing the rug towards them. Another set of hot hands grazed her shoulder, and she recognized the gentle touch of the healer from the day before.

Conrad rattled off words that she tried to keep up with, but a distant ringing had joined the spinning, even when her eyes were closed.

The healer spoke while softly examining her, then paused. "Did something happen with that?" the healer whispered, something in her tone suggesting she gestured, but Ahria didn't look.

Conrad leaned over her, looking down at the floor beside their bed. He remained beneath the sheets, still naked, and her in nothing more than a sheer slip.

She couldn't summon the energy to care.

"I don't know." Conrad sounded strange, a tone she hadn't heard before. "She's not cut."

Cut.

The word floated through her, making no sense.

"I can't find anything unusual." The healer's tone had taken a similar shift as Conrad's. Panic, she realized. Fear. "In those cases, it's always just a regular chill. It'll pass."

"This isn't passing. It's getting worse." Conrad moved, taking the top blanket from the bed with him as he stood, wrapping it around his waist.

"What were you doing when this happened?" The healer directed the question at Ahria, stroking her hair back from her ear and speaking quieter. "Were you sleeping? Did you feel fine before falling asleep?"

The questions echoed through her, and she tried to remember. Conrad had opened up to her, and they'd made love. He'd fallen asleep, and she'd drifted off next to him.

Right?

Ahria furrowed her brow.

No. She hadn't fallen asleep. She'd tried to...

"I was using the Art," Ahria whispered. "I don't remember anything after that."

Silence hovered in the room for several minutes before the healer finally spoke again. This time, to Conrad. "If this illness is related to the Art, then I can't help you. It is out of my realm of knowledge."

"It only solidifies what we need to do, then." Conrad looked to the open door, where the two guards nervously peeked inside. "Go to the dock. See that a ship is outfitted for travel to Isalica right away."

"Yes, your highness."

"What's happening?" Another familiar voice came from the doorway, and the guards hurried to move out of her way. Talia's wide eyes landed on her son and then Ahria.

A golden shape shoved past her through the doorway, and Andi launched into the room. The dog raced for Conrad before stopping part way, tail stiff as she eyed Ahria.

Ahria suddenly craved the comfort the dog's warm furry body could offer. "Come here, girl," she murmured, patting the bed, but the dog didn't move. And then her stomach sank when Andi *growled*.

"Hey!" Conrad's sharp command silenced the dog, who whimpered as she slunk closer to him. "What's that about?" Andi leaned hard against his leg, her weary chocolate eyes moving back to Ahria.

A soft conversation unfolded between Conrad and his mother, but Ahria closed her eyes and thought of happy memories. Anything but the pain.

Isalica.

But it wasn't the destination that had made Conrad decide on such action. Katrin. Damien. Probably the only two healers who would know where to start.

If I make it there at all.

Chapter 15

THE THUNDER OF APPROACHING DRAGON wings roused Liam from his chair. The warm, damp air of Draxix hit him as he stepped out onto the front porch of the cabin, looking to the clearing as Zedren's wings made the distant trees tremble.

A faint vibration echoed through the ground as the dragon landed, his massive head swinging to face the human who leaned casually against the worn post holding up the roof of the porch. It felt like only yesterday he'd built this place, but now the paint peeled in spots and a few boards needed replacing.

"Let me guess. No luck." Although he directed the statement to Zedren, Liam focused on the movement against the cliffs to the left, to a massive cavern burrowed into the stone.

Zaniken's teal scales glimmered in a sun shaft as he extended his neck in curiosity, Jaxx stepping out beneath his bent head.

Looking at his son, it was like Liam looked in a mirror of his youth, though the boy had an interested expression that looked more like his mother.

Zedren huffed, but didn't answer right away, looking at the far smaller dragon as the pair approached.

"News?" Jaxx wore the loose undergarments of his elaborate riding gear, stripping both from him and his dragon.

Liam was envious of everything the dragons had provided to the young man, including the Art-infused armor. But pride swelled his chest for his son being the first and only true Draxnathar in thousands of years. He and Zaniken shared a unique bond, forged in the pit of Thrallenax as Zaniken hatched. It enabled them to fly together in ways anyone else could only dream of.

"The Primeval have demanded a trial before they will allow the king and Rahn'ka an audience with them." Zedren's voice, like all the dragons, was like two stones grinding together. "It is the best outcome possible, as no one sees the Primeval without first proving their worth."

Liam fought to control the sense of relief, knowing this was far from over. "What kind of trial?"

Zedren swung his head towards the northeast mountain range, where the mountain the dragons called Oias dominated the skyline. Not as tall as the Isalican mountains, but the steep sides made it a formidable structure.

"They will need to climb to Oias's summit." Zedren lowered his head again. "Without the aid of wings."

Liam winced. "That'll take some time after they arrive. I'm surprised they're not here yet." He looked at the horizon beyond the cabin, where the lake water below the portal entrance glowed like liquid crystal. "What about our request for more dragons to aid our cause?"

Zedren paused before shaking his head. "The Primeval have granted nothing." Before Liam could voice his annoyance, the dragon continued, "But I may have another willing to join our cause without the Primeval's orders. She is young, but an accomplished aerial fighter."

The corner of Liam's mouth kicked up. "Aren't all dragons young in your eyes?"

The emerald dragon huffed a breath of smoke at Liam. "I am not as old as you seem to believe. Dragons can live for millennia. The Primeval remember a time before the Sundering."

"Aren't you over a thousand years old already?" Liam drawled.

Zedren narrowed his eyes. "What's your point?"

Liam lifted his hands, smirking. "Only that you're older than a lot of dragons."

Zaniken chuffed. "He's got a point, Zedren. Not many from your clutch are still around."

Zedren's expression darkened, and Liam could sense the dragon's mind must have drifted to painful memories. He didn't know why so many of the older dragons were gone, but he'd been there when Zaelinstra fell. Zedren's mate and élanvital.

Guilt for bringing it up curled in his gut.

"It doesn't matter." Liam straightened, waving a hand. "What matters is that you were successful in getting Matthias an audience with the Primeval. Hopefully they'll be able to tell us something helpful about Uriel."

"Many dragons know well the evil that beast is capable of." Zedren's mood hadn't seemed to improve much. "But the Primeval will know more about how he came to be."

"It's more about figuring out what he's trying to do."

The dragon growled. "To know what he will do, you must first understand what he has already done." The last words came out as a snarl, and the dragon lifted into the sky with a mighty flap of his wings, not looking back.

Jaxx shook his head, peeling his loose white undershirt off. On his chest, he bore an intricate tattoo in the dragon's language in black ink. "You shouldn't have brought that up," he muttered to Zaniken, then eyed his father. "And you should know better than to tease an old man about his age, shouldn't you, *old man*?" But he smirked with the words, striding past and entering the cabin.

Liam frowned. "I was merely making an observation." He followed his son into the cabin's front room. "Breakfast is on the counter in the kitchen. Though it's probably cold by now."

Jaxx strode straight for the plate of fried eggs and bacon, a loaf of bread beside it. He jammed a strip of bacon into his mouth before cutting two thick pieces of bread. "Cold bacon is still bacon," he muttered while chewing, picking up two fried eggs with his fingers and putting them on the bread along with three more slices of the fried, cured pork belly.

"Well, enjoy, because it's the last of it until you and Zaniken do that run into a city that I asked for a few days ago." They hadn't anticipated being in Draxix so long, and supplies had run thin weeks ago. Liam had been too stubborn to leave, with Zedren preoccupied trying to get to the Primeval. And Jaxx, even at twenty-six, still managed to get distracted rather than do chores. Though with his duties to the dragons, he supposed he couldn't blame his son.

"We were planning on going this afternoon." Jaxx faced his father, taking a big bite of the sandwich he'd made. He swallowed before speaking this time, picking up the parchment list of supplies they kept by the front door. "Was there anything else to add to the list?"

"Check with the barracks to see if there's any messages from your mother or uncle. Matthias should have been here by now." It was unlikely Matthias would have been able to send any word, considering where he and Damien had been heading. Or that Dani would have sent an update. But being isolated in Draxix ate at Liam's nerves.

Hopefully someone has gotten word about where in the hells Uriel even is right now.

"You got it." Jaxx stuffed the paper into his pants pocket. "Can you survive without me if I stay in the capital tonight?" He took another bite, humming.

Liam lifted a knowing eyebrow. "Stay?"

Jaxx rolled his shoulders. "I was going to stay with a friend."

"I thought you and Freya ended things?" He tread carefully, grateful his son was so open about his relationships, but worried if he said the wrong thing, that would end.

"We did."

"Someone new then?" Liam studied Jaxx, seeing the spark in his son's eyes.

Jaxx shrugged, but a hint of color touched his cheeks. "Maybe. He's a royal guard, but we haven't made anything official."

"Royal guard, huh? At least he's not a crown elite under me and your mom. That could have been awkward." Liam gave his son a grin as he roughly patted him on the shoulder. "Just be smart."

His son chuckled, nodding. "I will." He paused. "So you're all right if I return tomorrow, then?"

"I'll survive the loneliness." He looked back to the empty front room, imagining how it had been with all the bedrooms full, him and Jaxx cooking together while Dani and Varin sat in the living room. A drawing of Ryen's likeness, of him laughing, hung in a simple matte black frame on the far wall.

"Thanks, Dad." Jaxx stuffed the rest of the sandwich in his mouth, heading for the bedrooms. "I'll just take a quick nap and head out."

"Make sure to spend some time with your cousins, too," Liam called after him. "You know how much Zael loves Zaniken."

Jaxx laughed, disappearing inside a room. "Always do!"

Thinking about Matthias and Katrin's children made Liam's heart swell at the family he believed for a long time that they'd never get to have. A family still at risk because of the threat that hung over all of them. It made the time away a little easier to bear when considering what they fought for. And hopefully the children would all understand as they continued to grow in a world without Shades.

As Jaxx shut the door, Liam let out a breath and picked up one of the remaining strips of bacon.

The memory of Ryen, stealing slices of bacon as soon as they came out of the pan at their home outside Thrallenax, jumped into his mind. A ghost in the kitchen that only hardened Liam's resolve. "We'll win this for you, Ry," he whispered to the empty air. "I promise."

Chapter 16

KIN'S EYELIDS SAGGED AT THE tedium. He hadn't gotten enough sleep the night before, which made the morning meetings drag even more than usual. And there were plenty more filling up his afternoon.

With the wyvern lessons now less frequent, he could no longer use them as an excuse to avoid meeting with various advisors and so-called experts. And now he swore his advisors purposely loaded him with enough obligations to keep him exasperated from dawn until dusk.

The guards stationed outside his chambers saluted as he pushed through the doors.

"No visitors for at least the next thirty minutes." Kin met the gaze of one of them. He'd seen the man before, but couldn't remember his name. He could hear his mother's voice in the back of his head, reprimanding him for not making an effort. "Please."

"Yes, your majesty." The guard gave a curt nod. "Not even Lord Delphi?"

Kin rubbed at his eyes. "Especially Lord Delphi." He didn't need him showing up, trying to squeeze in a fast refresher on Xykos. "Thirty minutes."

His mother's lessons in manners waned under his exhaustion as he shut the chamber doors tightly behind him. Crossing into his bedroom from the sitting room, he squinted at the unexpected brightness.

Damn it. They always open the curtains.

Despite the snow cresting the top of the black mountains behind Jaspa, the hearth's flames stifled the air in the room. He pulled at his formal collar as he walked to the windows, throwing one open to take in a cool breath of fresh air.

Leaving the window cracked, he drew the curtains and flung his tunic over the back of a chair. His fingers unlatched the sheath at his thigh without much thought. He barely glanced at Sephysis as he tossed the tangle of leather and bloodstone to the end of the bed. The dagger lay dormant as he kicked off his boots and unfastened his belt. Removing his breeches, he slid into bed with his shirt and undershorts still on, pulling the heavy blankets over himself.

As soon as his head hit the pillow, the noise of the city and crackle of flame blurred into a gentle haze.

Sleep stole him in a matter of breaths, and he wasn't sure how much time passed before he woke to an unnerving sound. He groaned, rolling over, as the noise became clearer.

Long, slow scratches.

Kin jolted upright, visions of beady-eyed Corrupted filling his mind, and lunged for Sephysis at the bottom of the bed. But the dagger wasn't there. His hand tangled with empty leather, and his stomach dropped.

Blinking, he paused, the scratching noise still cutting through the chamber. He hurtled out of bed, yanking the curtains open.

Whirling in the fresh light, he half expected to see a monstrous creature clinging to the ceiling above his doorway, but...

Only the familiar glimmer of Sephysis's red blade as he spotted the dagger on the opposite side of the room.

Kin narrowed his eyes at the bloodstone dagger, free of its sheath, hovering over his desk. The dark mahogany bore damage from the blade's tip. "It was you?" He let out a breath, trying to calm his racing heart as he strode over to see what Sephysis had done.

One vertical line crossed by two arched horizontal curves. Surrounded by a circle.

"What is this?" he mumbled.

The mark had been repeated several times on the wooden desk, in various sizes. But each perfectly replicated.

Kin watched as Sephysis continued the largest of the symbols it'd created, slowly scoring with precision. He waited until the symbol was complete, Sephysis about to begin another pass at the outer circle. Grabbing the hilt, Kin took the dagger away, tightening his grip against expected resistance.

But Sephysis didn't fight him. It merely pulsed against his palm, the heat of its energy merging again with his.

Kin tried to sort through the feeling of it, trying to understand what might have led to this. The dagger had tried to communicate, but nothing Deylan had mentioned suggested the blade would be capable of such a thing. Yet... this felt important. To Seph, at least.

A few raps jarred Kin's focus from the dagger, someone knocking on the sitting room door.

Pushing his will into Sephysis, Kin released the bloodstone blade, and it lazily glided back to the bed and its sheath. He picked his breeches up off the floor, slipping into them as he contemplated the dagger. It lay dormant, as if nothing had even happened as he picked it up. Not bothering to secure it to his leg, he carried it with him to the door.

How has it been thirty minutes already?

A messenger stood in the hall when Kin opened the door, bowing quickly before offering a rolled parchment. "Word from Ziona, your majesty."

"Thank you," Kin muttered absently, taking the parchment. As he stepped back, the guards closed the door for him. Setting Sephysis, sheath and all, onto the low slung table in front of the sitting room hearth, Kin broke the wax seal of the Zionan royal crest.

The first words made his heart pick up its pace.

> *Kin,*
>
> *Ahria is unwell. We've spoken to the best healers in New Kingston, and no one can figure out what is wrong. It is Art related, so we've departed for our rendezvous in the hopes that our friends there can help. We should arrive in the second week of Winter. Perhaps you could join us in this early arrival? Your company may help as well. I wish I could explain more. You're the only one with this information and I leave it to you whether or not to share it.*
>
> *Regards, Conrad*

He quickly reread the letter, trying to glean what all Conrad was trying to say. He obviously kept it brief and vague out of precaution, and had chosen to send a message to Kin directly rather than relay it through a faction communication device.

Conrad and Ahria would be arriving in Nema's Throne in two weeks, far sooner than he'd anticipated needing to leave Feyor.

If Ahria is sick...

That could mean any number of things. Art related? It was possible she'd injured herself practicing with her power. Or that someone else had done something to her.

The possibility heated Kin's blood, and the dagger hummed its agreement.

The planned rendezvous had no specific date, considering no one knew exactly what it would take to accomplish all they needed before trying to imprison Uriel. Kin wondered if Katrin or Damien would even be anywhere near Nema's Throne by the time Ahria and Conrad arrived. It was possible they'd be the first there, and be no better off than they'd been in New Kingston.

Kin read over the note one last time, making certain he hadn't missed anything before he crumbled the parchment and stood. Throwing it into the hearth, he watched the flames catch on the paper. He waited until its ash fell against the bricks before picking up Sephysis, securing the sheath to its usual place.

Arrangements needed to be made if he was to depart so soon. More meetings would need to be crammed in to ensure he'd done all he could. He could justify a week. One week before he needed to leave on a wyvern to get there in time to meet his daughter.

Good thing I already know how to...

Kin frowned at the thought. At how Coltin had pushed him to learn to fly faster, just in case.

He's going to rub that one in.

Worries about the symbols carved into his desk vanished as Kin retrieved his discarded tunic, still pulling it into place as he opened the doors to his chamber. The guards reacted with a salute as Kin walked quickly between them.

It was obvious who the only person he could trust in the palace was. Especially after their accidental encounter with a den of wild Corrupted.

Coltin would be in his office, so he headed straight there. The man would know how to help expedite his departure, and could contact Deylan to keep him in the loop. Even with the faction currently unable to assist, working together moving forward was still paramount.

Not to mention Deylan is my brother now, and would probably want to know what's going on with his niece if he doesn't already.

Kin frowned, lifting his fist to knock on Coltin's door.

Not that I know what's going on.

Chapter 17

Winter, 2632 R.T.

DAMIEN URGED THE ENERGIES HE'D absorbed from the sanctum to separate from his ká for the first time in weeks. The disconnect left him hollow for a moment, but gradually his own power settled back to its usual place.

Every muscle weighed heavily with exhaustion.

Mirimé's tail swished back and forth in front of the runes carved on one of the six pillars surrounding the prison. Damien hadn't allowed himself to fully appreciate the magnitude and odd beauty of the huge obsidian cube.

"It felt fitting that we finish here," Mirimé mused, their fox head tilting curiously towards the black shape. "Seeing as this is the purpose of your visit." Slight disdain still lingered, though he doubted it was directed at him. The guardian had warmed considerably since their initial arrival, surpassing all his expectations.

And, if Damien was being honest with himself, they'd been an incredible instructor.

He turned from the prison, focusing on the guardian. "It won't be nearly as long before our next visit, seeing as we plan to lure Uriel here in the coming months."

The fox's upper lip curled at the name, but they nodded, almost human-like. "Just assure me I will not end the same way Hedenmé did, back when the world shattered."

It took Damien a moment to realize who the guardian spoke of. He'd never heard the name. But the sanctum that had held the original prison in Lungaz had once housed a guardian, too. Though, with the area now devoid of all Art, one could only guess what might have happened to Hedenmé.

"We won't let that happen." Damien rubbed at his fatigued arms. He hoped the guardian would believe him, even if he wasn't entirely certain. History had an odd way of repeating itself. But the idea of all this work leading to Uriel one day escaping his prison again... He refused to let the idea consume him.

Mirimé sighed. "You're certain you must leave? I've grown... accustomed to the company."

Damien smiled. "Does that mean you accept me as the Rahn'ka?"

The fox's head quirked to the side. "Weeks ago, I made the acceptance. But you needed to finish your trial."

"Of course." Damien held back his chuckle. "Would have been nice to hear it aloud before now, though. I appreciate the training you provided me. It's been a while since I learned something new. And from someone willing to actually tell it to me straight instead of speaking in riddles or just telling me to go read a bunch of books." He bowed his head to Mirimé. "Thank you."

The fox smiled, mouth opening in a relaxed pant. "More lessons await upon your return. And I'm happy to offer them to your children, as well."

Damien grew more serious. "When the time comes. When Uriel is locked inside there." He pointed with his thumb at the gleaming obsidian.

Matthias's voice echoed through the hallways from above. "Zelbrali is here!"

The Rahn'ka wasn't sure if he'd ever get used to flying on the back of a dragon. Heights weren't his favorite thing, but it was better than trudging for weeks through the snow.

"That means it's time." Damien bowed again to the guardian. "Be well, until next time." He didn't wait for the guardian's response, accepting a vague nod as he climbed the stairs through the sanctum.

He couldn't call them ruins anymore, not after all he'd done. Even with his barrier back in place, his ká reverberated with each step. Each stone as he ran his fingertips along it. He'd lived in Sindré's sanctum for long periods of time, but he'd never felt as connected as he did to this one. Like there was a part of him in each assembled piece.

Matthias had packed their camp already, loading the supplies onto Zelbrali's back. The dragon's golden scales shone in the bright, partly-cloudy day, glittering with the illusion of warmth. The flight to Draxix, through Thrallenax, would be long and cold, with few energy sources for Damien to use to keep them warm.

A familiar voice tickled Damien's senses, piercing the barrier he kept in place. His heart leapt, a mix of happiness and anxiety swirling through him as he looked up to the sky.

Rin screeched, as if aware they were about to leave. Rae's hawk would never find them in Draxix, though they'd never tested the theory. The hawk, smaller and less of an asshole than Din had been, soared down from above, and Damien barely raised his arm in time to catch it.

"Hey, Feathers," the Rahn'ka murmured, stroking the hawk before pulling the rolled note from its leg.

Matthias kept quiet as he read.

Lieutenant,
Beansprout is doing great, no sign of
anything yet. Jarrod is home with her. I'm
leaving for Eralas with Maith. We've
received word things might be unraveling
there, as an Elder has reached out about our
treaty. Will update you when I learn more.
Love, Dice

The anxiety faded, overshadowed by relief that their daughter hadn't begun to show signs of being a Rahn'ka yet. The nickname he'd given her as a child brought a smile to his mouth as he folded the paper back up and put it in his pocket. He brushed his hand over the feathers of the hawk still perched on his arm, sending a pulse into its ká, which elicited a happy chitter.

Jarrod can help Sarra like he helped Corin, if need be.

"Good news?" Matthias waited, having already retrieved a parchment and charcoal from the packs for him to write a reply.

"Some. Sarra hasn't started to show signs yet, which is good. I'd rather be there when the voices start. It can be... overwhelming." He reached for the supplies as Matthias held them out to him. It felt odd to be so open with the possibility of his child becoming Rahn'ka, yet freeing to finally be able to speak plainly with Matthias. "Thanks.

Hold this for me." He bumped his arm, and Rin flapped once to hop to the king's extended limb.

Matthias stiffened, eyeing the aerial predator suddenly on his forearm. "You look more dangerous than our owls."

"Rin's about as dangerous as a potato."

The hawk clicked its beak, head tilting as it asked for scratches from an oblivious Matthias.

"He wants you to scratch his head." Damien looked around for something to write on for a moment before turning to Zelbrali. "You mind?" he asked as he put the parchment against the hard scales of the dragon's flank.

"I'm not a writing surface." Zelbrali rolled his eyes, but didn't pull away. "Just be quick. The wind is changing. We need to fly."

Damien nodded as he put the charcoal to the page, vaguely aware of Matthias's growing amusement as Rin inched up his arm, happily chittering at the king's scratches into his feathers.

> *Dice,*
>
> *Good news about Beansprout. Our first stop took longer than expected, but all is taken care of. Headed for our second, and hopefully Liam has been successful. Be safe in Eralas. And give Maith shit for me.*
>
> *Love, Your Lieutenant*

He stored the paper-wrapped end of the charcoal between his teeth as he tore the smaller strip of parchment off and folded it tightly. He turned back to Matthias, finding his friend grinning at the hawk and scratching under its neck. "Sorry, I need your new buddy." Damien handed the charcoal back to the king as he extended his arm in an unspoken command to the messenger.

Rin's beak clacked in disappointment as it hopped back over to Damien. Waiting patiently, the hawk looked at Matthias as Damien secured the paper under the cuff.

"Go to Rae." He gave the creature a final scritch under the chin before he lifted his arm. The hawk took to the sky with a call, and Damien wished he could fly south, too, to see his wife. "She'll probably be in Eralas already when Rin finds her."

"What's she off to Eralas for?"

"Seems an elder was reaching out regarding the treaty with Helgath. And if the auer are following up on that agreement, it could mean trouble." He sighed. "Not that we needed more."

But Rae will be fine.

Zelbrali shifted behind them, extending his wings briefly. "We should go."

The Isalican king climbed onto the massive beast, taking the highest seat on the dragon's neck. As Damien watched Rin gliding south, Matthias laughed. "Don't forget to put clothes on, Rahn'ka. Winter in Isalica doesn't bode well for the half-naked, Art or not."

Damien reached for one of the packs as Zelbrali crouched to allow him access. He pulled the first shirt he found over his head, wrapping and buttoning his cloak next. He'd worry about looking better when and if they gained an audience with the Primeval. "If I didn't have to bother with keeping you warm, too, I could have gone without." He ducked under Zelbrali's wing, running his hand along the dragon's rough scales to reunite himself with the electric current of his ká. Zelbrali was the only dragon he'd had close experience with, and if the rest were anything like him, dragons' ká were infinitely more complicated than humans'.

"And trust me, your Art is greatly appreciated." Matthias stroked the dragon's neck. "At least it's good weather for flying. If it holds, we could be there by tomorrow night."

"And now we'll hit a storm," Damien grumbled as he hoisted himself up to the saddle behind Matthias. "Did Liam send any word about his progress? Do we know what we're walking into?"

"Nope." Matthias looked back at him. "But I didn't expect him to, either, unless we needed forewarning. So I'll take it as a good sign. He should be waiting for us at our regular spot."

"You don't think the dragons will be angry with you for bringing someone new in?" A strange anxiety lingered in Damien's chest. The fact that dragons even existed was still relatively new to the world, let alone that they had their own civilization in a hidden country beyond portals. And now they had to worry about things like politics with the creatures, considering they may hold vital information about Uriel.

Because Uriel was once a dragon. In his original form before becoming the parasite he acted as now. Zaelinstra had been the one to tell Matthias so many years ago. Yet, they'd never learned more, or what they could do with the information.

It would make sense that the Primeval could have knowledge that could help them.

"They may be upset at first, but if I vouch for you, it will help ease their concerns about a newcomer. I don't think they will make meeting with their leaders easy, though," Matthias said over her shoulder. "But all the dragons I've met have genuinely wanted to help our world. Let's hope the Primeval are the same. Ready?"

Zelbrali shifted beneath them, his muscles primed to take them airborne.

"Almost." The tightness in his chest at the thought of lifting off the ground only grew worse. "What do you know about the Primeval? Is it a group of dragons like the auer Elder's Council?"

"I know very little. But Katrin read once that the Primeval were made up of the dragons' eight most powerful leaders and they have a unique connection to Pantracia. I've never met one, none of us have. So now you know as much as I do." Matthias reached behind him, grabbing the strap around Damien's left thigh and cinching it tight without asking if the Rahn'ka needed help with his blind side. "Not that we wouldn't catch you if you fell, anyway."

"Not really helping this whole fear of heights thing." Damien patted the buckle on his right thigh. Ever since the tumble from an upper window in the Veralian palace, looking down had sent butterflies through his stomach. Even harnesses didn't help. The only thing that did was knowing he had control, but being on a dragon was far from that.

"Isn't it more a fear of splattering on the ground below?" Matthias chuckled, his gaze discreetly tracking over each buckle securing Damien before the king faced forward, apparently satisfied with his friend's safety. "Let's go, Zel."

"I mean, I think splattering on the ground pretty much sums—" As the dragon lurched into the sky, Damien's stomach stayed on the ground, his eye squeezing shut.

He kept it that way most of the time they were in the air, focusing on his breathing to meditate. The landings and take-offs were the worst, but at least the weather held for the entire first day of their journey, through the night, and into the following day. Zelbrali kept their flight smooth, and he could almost forget they were thousands of feet above the ground even when he opened his eye to stare ahead at the horizon. He'd still close it from time to time, since meditation kept the cold surrounding them tolerable, though it still bit through all the layers of fur he wore.

That morning, they'd departed from New Linsbane where they'd indulged in rooms at an inn to recover from the chill of the mountains north of Orvalinon. Zelbrali had banked north, despite their destination, to catch a wind current off the coast.

Damien relaxed a little more at the prospect of having ocean beneath them, rather than unforgiving stone, and settled into a meditative state.

Hours or minutes passed, he wasn't sure, before Matthias smacked his knee a couple times. "I know it's asking a lot, but you should really see this view."

When they'd flown each previous time, the clouds had been both a blessing and a curse. It had shortened the durations they could fly, with the collection of frost on Zelbrali's wings, but they'd also acted as a visual barrier between him and the ground. Though, it'd made it impossible to enjoy any kind of view.

Today, only a few clouds dotted the sky, and he knew once he peeled his eye open that it'd be...

Breathtaking.

Damien momentarily forgot his fear as he gazed down the strait between the two northern continents. Cliffs dominated most of the shoreline on either side, shadowing the water within. Snow glittered in the northern stretches, drawing his sight over Matthias's shoulder.

The peaks of the Yandarin Mountains jutted up in the distance, but Thrallenax towered over them all. Its high stoney peak was too steep for snow to stick to all parts, but the white sections gleamed in the sun. The mountains sloped below Thrallenax and met the white-dusted tops of pine trees, where the lowlands had still been spared the harsher winter storms. Sheets of snow clung to life in the shadows, but much had melted, leaving the stone cliffs shining as water trailed towards the sea. Massive icicles from the previous night's freeze still hung on every sharp edge.

Damien drew his gaze back to the distant mountains, squinting at where Nema's Throne stood at Thrallenax's base. He couldn't make out the capital's white towers, still too far with the mountains between. Thrallenax dominated the horizon like a looming giant, and its mere presence whispered the secrets that it held. A halo of wispy clouds danced around the peak, and as he watched, the air churned darker towards the lowlands.

Encroaching from the west, grey storm clouds swelled around Thrallenax.

"Shit," Matthias muttered, gaze pointed in the same direction. "What do you think, Zel?"

"That is not a storm I wish to fly through," the dragon rumbled, vibrating the saddle beneath Damien with his words.

"We'll have to make camp." The king sounded disappointed, but stoic. "Arriving tomorrow won't change anything."

Damien considered asking if they'd be able to make it to Nema's Throne, since a bed in the palace would be far more comfortable than a camp.

I've grown too soft. I used to sleep in the wilderness all the time.

"You think the storm will pass by tomorrow?" Damien squinted at the clouds again, dark with brutal promise.

Matthias turned towards Damien. "Isalican storms usually hit hard and fast. It could be a rough night, but it will probably be clearer come morning."

"I can find us a cave after we land."

"The portal is *where?*" Panic scorched through Damien's gut.

Zelbrali's chuckle only spiked his irritation.

They flew towards Thrallenax the next day at a revived pace, cutting through the spent storm clouds instead of bothering to fly above them.

The night had been rough, as Matthias had warned, but it could have been worse. With Damien's power, they'd kept the snow at bay as the rest of the area received over two feet of white powder. Zelbrali hadn't stayed, but he'd given them a blazing fire as a parting gift.

"You knew it was inside the mountain." Matthias's voice hid most of his amusement. "They couldn't put it somewhere anyone could accidentally find."

"Didn't you all *accidentally* find it?" Damien countered, his palms sweaty against the saddle handles.

"True," Matthias admitted. "But we were plummeting to our deaths, about to burn alive in magma, so it was a welcome discovery."

Damien shuddered. "And you're sure it's still there? The exact spot?"

"Has been for centuries," Zelbrali huffed, and as if predicting Damien's next question, he went on, "It encompasses the entire pool. We won't miss it."

Rae won't believe any of this when I tell her.

He missed her and their kids sorely, damning fate each time it pulled them apart.

The entire time they soared up the mountain, Damien imagined the look on his wife's face and the brightness in his children's eyes as he told them stories. They weren't as young as they once were, hanging on every word that came out of his mouth during their bedtime tales, and he missed those days dearly. They'd passed by far too fast. And now he barely saw Bellamy as he went off to train with the guardians.

And Sarra might be doing that soon, too.

He suddenly yearned to be home. But the steady drumbeat of Zelbrali's wings and the icy wind against his face reminded him he was about to dive into magma instead. To face beings no human had seen in millennia. Assuming Liam had succeeded in gaining them an audience with the Primeval.

Zelbrali angled sharper towards the mountains, aiming for a stark wall of rock.

The Rahn'ka's heart leapt faster. "What is he..."

"Trust the process, my friend," Matthias said through a tight jaw.

I guess even he is affected by this.

But they flew at merciless stone, closer and closer. Then Zelbrali banked, hard enough that Damien momentarily lost his grip on the handles, the pressure against his thighs doubling as the harness did its job. But he spied the opening.

Too small. That jagged cave in the side of the mountain, hidden behind the sharp turn they'd just taken, would never fit Zelbrali's wingspan.

Matthias leaned forward, and he followed suit, barely able to hear even the wind over his thundering heart.

Closer and closer. To that too-small opening. But Damien forced his eye to remain open as Zelbrali promptly tucked in his wings, becoming a living arrow, and shot into the cave. The dragon didn't even touch the sides as they soared through, close enough that if Damien reached a hand above his head...

Hot air hit him, the tunnel finally ending, and the dragon's wings snapped open. The sudden slow pushed Damien hard into Matthias's back, the harness still straining to keep him in his seat despite his death grip on the saddle. Heat raged through the cavern, shimmering off Zelbrali's scales.

They plunged downward.

Nymaera's breath.

Molten stone simmered below them in a lake of orange and red. It glowed against the dark rock of the mountain's interior, a jagged cylinder leading up from the magma bed below. The cavern disappeared into darkness above them, keeping the secret of just how large it was.

A low rumble pressed against his ká, as if the mountain itself questioned his presence here. For a moment, he wanted to open up to it. Hear the voices of the stones and magma that he'd never encountered, but Zelbrali's dive towards the hells only made him harden his barrier.

The dragon didn't balk. Nor did the king as they flew straight for what looked like certain death.

The heat grew unbearable, rising too fast for him to shield from it. He held his breath as they approached the bottom, face burning.

He closed his eye, and a breath later, the heat winked out. A steady warmth replaced it, fresh air surrounding him as the dragon banked again, leveling out.

Daring a look, Damien gasped at the water racing right under them. They flew over a massive lake, framed on all sides by humid jungle.

I didn't even sense the portal.

Damien blew out a breath, his mind whirling as he tried to process all that had happened in only a few moments. His body shivered, still trying to figure out what temperature it was supposed to get accustomed to. Then the hum began. The plethora of voices echoing from across the water.

"That was intense," he murmured, only vaguely aware that he'd even spoken as he took in the terrain with awe. Land so few humans had ever seen.

Draxix.

Something akin to honor flowed through him, gratitude following in its wake. At what a privilege it was to see this place. To be here.

"Always is," Matthias breathed, the king's shoulders finally relaxing, too.

Zelbrali blew out a puff of flame, as if sharing the sentiment, before he rumbled, "Welcome to Draxix, Rahn'ka."

Chapter 18

SALTY AIR WHIPPED AGAINST RAE'S braids, cooling her scalp between the thin rows over her ears. She'd woven the hair on top into a braided mohawk, all tightly secured by a leather tie at the back of her head.

Maith strode beside her, his steps as quiet as hers as they approached the waiting gangplank, each with a pack slung over their shoulder.

The scent of wet wood mingled with the salt and fish of Rylorn's air, reminding her of the comfort of the Herald. Her mother's ship.

Weeks had passed since she'd received Jarrod's reluctant agreement for her to go to Eralas. Despite what he probably thought, she needed that assent. Ever since the underwater attack, the stakes had seemed steeper. She wouldn't have faulted him for opting to keep her in Helgath.

While she waited, preparing and fitting her outfit with as many blades as possible—along with an Art-nullifying earring, just in case—she'd spent every moment she could with Sarra. Monitoring her for any sign of the Art, of course, but also catching up on missed time. They were some of the best weeks, full of horseback journeys, Sarra trying to teach Rae how to cook, and experimenting with kohl around Sarra's eyes. In that moment, she'd looked so much like a young Rae, the Mira'wyld had nearly wept with pride.

"Whenever I get that hawk of yours nowadays, I worry it might be bad news. But I like this simple asking-for-a-ride situation much better." Andi leaned with her hip against the break in the banister at the top of the gangplank. Her traditional long braid laid over her shoulder, just touching the hilt of her rapier at her side.

Rae smiled, seeing through her mother's dry humor. "And, thankfully, no one is dying this time." Her own words sparked images of Damien lying in the faction's infirmary, clinging to life. And although he'd recovered, she wondered how many more times that would be the outcome. How long it would be until their luck ran out.

We might all be dead in a few months if this plan fails.

"Welcome news." Andi gave Maith a simple nod in greeting as he stepped onto the Herald's deck beside Rae. "Usual quarters for you, Chief Vizier Maithalik." She gestured towards the bow of the ship. "I've already got a bottle of whisky with mine and Rae's name on it waiting in my quarters."

The auer bowed before lifting three fingers to his forehead, lowering them in a traditional greeting. "You have our gratitude." His mouth quirked into a smirk as he gestured to Rae with his chin. "And our coin."

Rae held up a pouch, heavy with silver florins, and chuckled under her breath. "The crown always pays well."

"Which is one of the reasons I'm willing to take on such ventures." She took the pouch, deftly securing it to her belt with one hand before murmuring to Rae, "Not that anyone could stop me from helping my daughter."

Smiling, Rae's chest warmed at the title she still didn't take for granted. "Unless they outbid me," she teased, walking past her mother. "I'll go put my things in your cabin." She paused before Maith, angling her chin up to meet his gaze. "Try not to roll off the bed this time, hey?"

Maith smiled, following her for a step before turning to make his way to the cabin under the raised bow deck. "I shall create a blanket fortress to keep myself contained."

Years ago, they'd shared sleeping quarters so Maith could help Rae through her night terrors. But over time, and with Damien's help to heal her mind, they'd lessened enough that she no longer feared sleeping alone. Though she knew the offer stood, should she need it. And even her husband had encouraged her to take him up on it, rather than struggle through it alone.

She watched the auer close the door behind himself, content to get settled before they disembarked. Turning to Andi, she smiled again, though without the same humor. "Thank you," she murmured, knowing that Andi would sail the Herald to the ends of Pantracia for her, regardless of payment. But she kept the sentiment to herself while in earshot of the crew, and made her way to the captain's quarters.

Andi followed without further word, only needing to glance at her first mate, Keryn, to ensure the ship began the launch procedure. As the captain closed the doors to her quarters, Keryn's strong voice bellowed over the sounds of the Rylorn dock and ocean winds.

"So what danger am I sailing you into today?" Andi crossed to the familiar set of overstuffed chairs at the back of the cabin while Rae set her pack on the bed.

"Who said you're taking me somewhere dangerous?" Rae kept an air of innocence to her tone as she sat on the mattress.

"There's always something. And I know what you and your friends are up to." The coins in the gift pouch jangled as she put it on the small table between chairs before she picked up a bottle of amber liquid. "I've been keeping my eyes and ears open too, while continuing business as usual. I haven't heard anything unusual. Just quiet hope for real peace between the countries with a new king on the throne in Feyor. But that just means something's about to come to a head." She filled two glasses halfway.

Rae clenched her jaw at her mother's awareness. Ignorance would be safer for most, but Andi had never balked at dangerous knowledge, not if it meant being a stronger ally for her daughter. "That's good. We've received rather cryptic reports that there may be trouble in Eralas. Of what kind, we don't know, which is why I'm heading there under the pretense of Mira'wyld training to gain better access to the situation."

"I'd think you have enough on your plate without getting involved in the problems of the auer." Andi crossed the room to give her the glass of whisky, her own resting in her hand as she leaned against the poster of her bed. "Lanoret's back on his feet, but not with you. Which means he's somewhere else equally dangerous."

"Damien was in Isalica, but I suspect by now he's in the dragons' land." Rae didn't miss the sparkle of interest in her mother's eyes. "But the correspondence from Eralas came as an official test of our treaty. Our armies. Our armada. They're ready to move, if need be. The letter hinted at... shadows. So I must make caution a priority."

"I'd say that's for the best." She nodded before taking a long swig. With only a minute wince, she smiled down at her daughter. "How are my grand-babies?"

Rae's smile broadened. "Bellamy is doing well. He saved Damien's life, after I saw you last." She swallowed the rise of emotion. "He's come so far in his use of the Art and everything else. He's such a young man now. He's even shaving his face." She huffed. "Sarra is good, too. No sign of power, yet, thankfully, with all this going on. But she's happy, usual bouts of teenage angst aside. There's even a boy she likes, back at the palace, but she's shy. She's so much like her father that way."

Andi smiled, but Rae could see the regret in it. "I don't see them enough. Maybe when all this business is over I should make my way inland for a bit."

"They would love that." Rae sipped her whisky. "We all would. You know you're always welcome and your rooms are never used for anyone else." She tapped a finger against the side of her glass, thoughts of family swirling around in her mind. "Can I ask you something?"

"Of course. You always can." While their relationship had started on rocky ground, Andi had changed over the years. With Rae's acceptance of her, despite Andi having abandoned her as a baby, the captain had embraced her role and proven herself time and time again.

"What do you know of your parents?" Rae tilted her head, keeping her voice gentle. "Sometimes Sarra asks me about my grandparents, and I wish I could tell her something. My father's mother passed when I was quite young, and he never knew who his father was."

An unfamiliar look settled on Andi's face. Surprise, which she didn't openly show often. "My mother was a weaver in Capul. I broke her heart when I ran away to join a crew when I was only sixteen. She died a couple years later." Rae's heart sank as Andi settled down onto the bed beside her, resting her drink in her lap. "My father..." She blew out a breath. "I only got my mother to talk about him a few times when I was a child, and usually only after she'd had a few drinks. He was never there. I don't even know if he's aware I exist."

Rae lowered her gaze to her drink before downing the rest. "I'm sorry." She sucked in a deeper breath. "I don't know why I was hoping the question would have a happy answer."

Finding an alcan who didn't want to be found—or even just didn't know someone was looking—would be beyond impossible. Especially without any information about him.

Andi shook her head. "It's important to remember. We learn from our parent's mistakes, don't we?" She gently elbowed Rae in the side with a smirk. "I'd say you have."

Her mother's words struck a chord in her chest that instantly brought emotion to burn her eyes. "So have you." She smiled, nodding. "Some would even say that the changes you've made were more difficult. You're priceless to all of us."

Andi patted Rae's knee, her throat bobbing. "I was lucky you even gave me a chance." She coughed lightly, lifting her drink. She made a soft grunt as she pushed herself to her feet. Passing by her large map table, she slid her nearly empty glass on to it before opening the glass cabinet doors of her bookshelves. She retrieved a small wooden box that had been tucked at the bottom behind a stack of books.

Rae said nothing, studying the uncharacteristic hesitation in her mother's movements.

Andi stared at it in her hands for a moment, bumping the cabinet closed with her hip. "I chose to never give him the chance, though." She tapped the plain top of the box with her thumbs as she walked back to Rae. "But you can, if you want." She held out the box to her daughter.

Eyes widening, Rae stared at the box and then Andi. "What is this?" She took it carefully, the smooth base fitting in her palm.

"After my mother died, I was looking for answers. For... a family." She sat down again, tucking a leg beneath her on the bed. "It took a long time, and a lot of resources, to find any information on an alcan named Adamonicus. I never *found* him, per se, but I did get close. I know he lives in an alcan city in the northeast ocean."

"Near Isalica." Rae ran a hand over the top of the wooden box. "Why did you stop looking?"

A small smile crept onto Andi's face. "I stopped looking for a family because one found me instead." She placed her hand on Rae's knee. "One I'm incredibly grateful for. And the importance of finding him just wasn't there anymore."

Rae swallowed, understanding perfectly well what she felt. "Can I...?" She gestured to the box, and with Andi's nod, she opened it.

Inside, on a velvet-cushioned bottom, lay a marble-sized glass sphere with intricate carvings covering its surface.

Her brow furrowed as she picked it up, studying the tiny markings. Little waves broken up by etched stars. "This is..." A murmur of the Art dwelled within, dormant. "Is this a ward key?" She'd seen something similar in Eralas, though that one had been composed of oak.

Andi nodded. "One that will grant you access to that alcan city, if you can find it." She shrugged. "I never was able to find exact coordinates, and the place is shielded in a way that you can't see it until you're through the ward."

Rae blew out a slow breath, placing the trinket back into the box. "And you're fine with me pursuing him?"

"Adamonicus is your grandfather, and if you want to know your blood, I won't stop you. Just because I'm content not knowing, doesn't mean you can't go find those answers yourself." Andi lovingly brushed a loose strand of Rae's braid behind her ear. "But maybe after you've sorted through all this Uriel business?"

Chuckling, Rae snapped the box closed. "After. Most definitely after." She smiled. "Thank you. Do you know the name of the city?"

"Luminatrias," Andi whispered. "The City of Light."

Chapter 19

TENSION EASED FROM MATTHIAS'S SHOULDERS, the welcome warmth of Draxix seeping through his muscles.

Zelbrali's roar exploded through the air, rippling the surface of the lake, and the king smiled at the dragon's love for being home.

The crystalline water reflected the dragon's golden scales, clearer than any lake he'd witnessed in other parts of Pantracia.

Is Draxix technically part of Pantracia?

Matthias stumbled over the thought before dismissing it for irrelevance. He turned, looking at Damien, and his smile returned at the awe radiating from the Rahn'ka. "Nothing else like it, is there?"

"Even the air feels different. And I wish you could hear the ká here." Damien closed his eye, but no longer out of fear as he drank it all in. But his eye snapped open as Zelbrali shifted upward, beating his wings harder to carry them over the tops of the trees.

Birds squawked, their colorful wings shining in the sun as they flew from their roosts among the trees. They looked so different from anything else Matthias had seen, and it only furthered the thought of what a different world this was. He'd asked Zelbrali once, where this continent was situated in relation to the mainland, but he'd refused to provide the information. Uriel had attempted to find the geographical location once, through Dani and Liam's son, but Ryen's sketches of the stars had never fallen into the master of Shade's hands. And Zaelinstra had advised them to keep his failed task a secret from the rest of the dragons.

But Uriel would have other means of finding Draxix, especially if he hunted for the portal. The entrances to Thrallenax were guarded and warded at all times, but the ever-changing nature of mountains led to endless possibilities of finding an unknown tunnel within. They would never be able to guarantee the prevention of a Shade entering the sacred mountain.

Matthias, even with his years of experience as Uriel's

host, couldn't imagine a Shade leaping into magma just to see if a portal hovered above the surface.

Yet, if Uriel was desperate enough...

He pushed the dread away, rolling his shoulders as Zelbrali banked west, taking them closer to their usual meeting spot with Liam.

He'd helped Liam build the small cabin perched on the edge of a short rock cliff that jutted up from the forest. The natural clearing behind it allowed plenty of space for the dragons to land before more cliffs rose behind it.

A slight hollow had formed in the cliffside behind the cabin, where Zaniken had built himself the beginnings of a roost. The stone had melted in places, reforming into smooth, sloping curves.

The small copse of jungle trees at the back of the landing had been partially buried by displaced rock, still marred with claw marks from Zaniken's construction.

No paths led up the rock face in front or behind the cabin, only approachable from the sky.

Liam stood on the deck of the home, positioned on the backside near the cliff. The sun lit the grey in his hair near his temples, and with the mug in his hand, he looked like his father had on the porch of their farm house. All he was missing was the constant cloud of pipe smoke as he waved and strode to greet them.

Zelbrali slowed his descent, wings kicking up dirt and

leaves from the ground as he landed.

"And here I was worried I wouldn't hear back from the Primeval in time," Liam shouted from the porch, stepping down the three stairs to the grass. "What took you so long?" He eyed their heavy cloaks, snow still melting on their collars. "Rough weather?" He grinned, likely well aware of the snow that had hit Isalica the day before.

Matthias huffed, unbuckling his thighs. "The sanctum guardian had a long list of laundry for our Rahn'ka. The storm only slowed us down by a day."

Damien shifted behind him, no doubt eager to get his feet on the ground. "Gods, the wildlife and flora here are so..." His voice sparked with excitement as he unfastened himself in record time and scrambled to the ground. He kicked off his boots, not caring that the king and Liam watched with raised brows, and sighed as his toes sank into the grass. "Unique."

Matthias shared a look with Liam, smirking. "You think he'll be sad when we remind him he can't live here?"

Liam crossed his arms, resting his mug against his bicep. "I'm just hoping he pulls himself together before you two meet with the Primeval."

Zelbrali turned at the statement, eyeing the older soldier as Matthias joined Damien. "You were successful, then?" Even the dragon sounded surprised.

"They agreed to meet with me and Damien?" Matthias

echoed the sentiment, impressed with the results when it had felt like a long shot.

"They did," Liam confirmed, but he wasn't saying everything.

The king narrowed his eyes. "There's a catch."

Damien seemed to only half pay attention as he stripped off his cloak, dropping it onto the ground, and sat down right where he'd stood. Pushing his palms to the lush grass, he tilted his head back and took a deep breath.

Liam quirked an eyebrow before looking pointedly at Matthias for a moment. "There's a catch." He gestured to the door. "Did we want to go inside and discuss it, or..."

Damien minutely shook his head. "I'm listening. I can tell you don't seem terribly worried about the catch, so it can't be too bad."

Matthias blinked at the man sitting in the grass, finally removing his own cloak as his body warmed. "Liam has been a soldier since you were learning to dress yourself, so even if he *was* worried, you wouldn't be able to tell without cheating." He lifted his gaze to his brother. "But it isn't too bad, right?"

Liam shrugged. "I'm grateful I'm not the one who needs to do it. There's a bit of a trial you will need to complete."

The Isalican king frowned. "Is it at least both of us this time?"

He wasn't sure how much more sitting around, tending

to Damien's hunger, he could take.

Zelbrali meandered away from them before laying on his belly and stretching his wings over the grass. His eyes closed, breathing evening out as he enjoyed the sun.

"If you mean both you and Damien, yes. But not Zelbrali. Or Zedren, or any dragon. You have to get to the Primeval without them." He glanced at Damien again, talking over Matthias's shoulder with a smirk. "Hope you can climb rocks as well as you talk to them."

Unease curled in Matthias's gut. "*Where*, exactly, are the Primeval?"

"Judging by his tone," Damien started, still not opening his eye as he raised a hand and pointed towards the mountain range in the northeast. "I'm guessing over there."

The cliffs rose sharply from the rainforest below, eroded clay-colored stone with hundred foot rock faces softened by the wet climate. They were only broken up by small strips of foliage that'd found purchase in the narrow gaps of level ground.

Matthias glanced at Liam before focusing on the mountain range. The highest peak stood hundreds of feet tall in the distance, though no snow frosted the top. The tropical terrain boasted waterfalls at each tier, winged creatures screeching and circling above the palms far below it.

Those are rather large for birds.

Liam grinned. "At the very top."

The king lifted his gaze, but the summit of the highest rise wasn't visible from where he stood, the angle preventing him from being able to see whatever rested on top. *If* anything rested on top.

Damien let out a slow sigh. "I don't know about you, but I'm pretty tired of trials."

"I don't know," Matthias scoffed, pushing his sleeves up over his forearms. "I think I'm ready to get started. Been sitting on my ass for too long."

"You can leave tomorrow morning, if you'd like a good night's rest on a bed tonight. Jaxx won't be back, anyway." Liam approached, helping Matthias unlatch their packs from Zelbrali's saddle.

The dragon still laid in the grass, sunning his spread wings. "Where is Zedren?" he asked lazily, though the dragon likely missed the company of his own kind.

"He's gone to Nema's Throne with a new ally to show her around." When Matthias quirked a brow, Liam continued, "Her name is Zanmea. She's a young dragon, but wishes to aid our cause. If you see them without me, she'll be the dark grey one."

"Can't argue with more help." Damien stood, rolling his shoulders as he approached. "Though, probably best to keep the dragons away from the sanctum for now, so

Mirimé doesn't get too riled up again. That part of Zanmea's tour will have to wait."

Zelbrali snorted, his wings shuffling. "The little spirit creature is intolerant."

"Noted." Liam smirked, hauling two packs towards the cabin.

Other than refilling their food stores, the packs would have to remain as they were—full and ready to go. The journey up that mountain would take at least a week, but a bed for the night sounded wonderful.

"Anything we should know about meeting with them? The Primeval?" Matthias glanced at Damien, though the question was directed at Liam.

The crown elite shrugged. "The instructions were communicated through Zedren, and that was all he shared. I wish I had more to tell you." He paused at the doorway, waiting for the other two. "You need to climb to the summit after we drop you off at the base, and you have to do it without wings."

"Any rules against the Art?" Damien looked at Matthias. "My climbing skills are a little rough, and I might need that handy trick of yours."

Matthias chuckled, but Liam replied, "Unless you use it to grow wings, the Art is fair game."

Chapter 20

"AND HOW IS THIS PERSON connected to you?" Maith's distrust lingered within his murmured tone from where he sat opposite her in the carriage.

"I told you," Rae sighed. "She's Talon's sister. Kalstacia was there when Amarie went into Slumber and facilitated her healing and training after they woke her."

"And this makes you trust her?"

Rae rolled her lips together, neck still sore from sleeping on the carriage bench. "Mostly, yes."

"A stunning advocation." Maith's lips flattened into a line.

Summoning all the patience she could muster, Rae shrugged. "It gives me an excuse to be in the city, which is what we were hoping for, anyway. Whether she can be trusted is hardly relevant, since I don't plan on sharing any pertinent information with her."

Andi had made port outside Maelei, close to the Mira'wyld compound. It was the expected arrival location for her training, but Kalstacia's request to meet in the city had been fortuitous.

"The banishment of the Di'Terian siblings was a rather public affair. You may draw attention to yourself by meeting with her. And in such a public place?" Maith pulled aside the curtain of the carriage window, peering out at the Quel'Nian street. They grew closer to the center of the city, the streets narrowing and the architecture more elaborately shaped from the trees.

Rae agreed with him there, at least. "She chose the spot because she's a member of the Menders' Guild. But the good news is that there are plenty of elements in the garden, and the elements are mine."

"To what end? Will you destroy the entire courtyard?" Maithalik made no effort to hide the dryness of his words.

She couldn't help the roll of her eyes. "No, of course not. But you're worried about me, and I'm telling you not to be. She's on our side, even if she's hardly aware of it."

"I'll take your word for it."

Rae looked at him from the corner of her eyes, frowning at his sarcasm. The auer would be on guard the whole time, but she supposed that was why Jarrod had insisted he accompany her. He bore two thin swords across his back, his light-grey hair secured at the back of his head in a short ponytail.

Gazing out the window again, she watched the sky. Rin had yet to return, and worry knotted her insides. Damien had promised to be prompt with his replies, but if he'd already reached Draxix by the time she sent her hawk...

Rin could have been delayed by a storm, too.

They passed beneath the woven branches of the archway to the heart of the city, and Rae exhaled her concern for her husband. The Sanctum of Law dominated the area, towering over the other lower slung buildings. The lofty structure, crafted from what had once been a monstrous oak tree, boasted a crystal ceiling with a skeletal metal frame. Glass spires stretched towards the sky, glittering in the sunlight like geodes.

The carriage followed the road that wound in front of the Sanctum, but came to a stop at a delicate archway of cherry blossoms, eternally in bloom despite the season. The gardens in front of the Sanctum serviced the three uppermost guilds. The Menders' Guild, the Architects' Guild, and the Guild of Swords.

On the other side were the dormitories. The first place she'd ever crossed paths with Amarie so many years ago.

"Gods, I hate being here," Rae muttered.

Maith kept watch out the window. "Too many bad memories?"

"It's not that." Her stomach twisted as she imagined the sky falling into blackness under Uriel's attack. "Just... every time I come to this city, something awful happens."

"You are rarely superstitious." Maith finally looked at her. "You've returned several times already for training. Did something terrible happen each of those times?"

"I never came to Quel'Nian for those training sessions," Rae breathed. "It's just *this* city."

Maith hummed. "Then let's not be here longer than necessary, if only to keep your stress manageable."

Rae groaned and knocked her fist on the carriage ceiling. The door swung open a moment later, and Maith exited first. He paid the driver as Rae stepped out, every sense on high alert.

But nothing seemed amiss.

People bustled around the courtyard, in and out of the gardens and dormitories. Two guards stood sentinel at the steps leading into the Sanctum of Law, as was standard practice. Whatever concerned Qualtavik clearly hadn't affected security measures.

Just another day.

Rae let out her held breath, vaguely aware of the carriage departing. They hadn't bothered to bring their packs, leaving them behind at the residence in the compound. She debated removing her cloak, but carrying it would be a greater burden than dealing with being a little too warm. "Are you sure you don't want to find Qualtavik while I meet with Kalstacia?"

Maith shook his head. "I will find the elder after. It is best if we stick together." He, too, seemed unnerved at the lack of chaos in the capital. "Though I'm now wondering if he wrote the letter in a drunken haze and Jarrod readied the armies for nothing."

"One way or another, we need to find out." Rae started for the gardens, distinctly aware of each blade hidden on her body and how it moved with her leathers. The weight of each one. And the compass-size communication device tucked into the inner pocket of her cloak. Though the tiny Art-repressing earring hidden in the breast pocket of her tunic felt the heaviest.

They entered the gardens, and the noise of the city dimmed. Even while able to see multiple groups milling along the various pathways, the dense foliage and size of the gardens made her suddenly feel isolated.

"Do you know where to meet her? The gardens are expansive," Maith murmured.

"Most people who learn Common as a second language don't use words like *expansive*. Or *advocation*, for that matter." Rae smirked at him, but he only quirked an eyebrow back at her. She sighed. "No. I'm hoping she finds me."

"I like to ensure my vocabulary is *comprehensive* so that I may express myself with accuracy and precision." Maith narrowed his eyes, but a glimmer of mirth danced within.

This is why I told Sarra not to give him a thesaurus.

He led the way as they wandered deeper into the garden, keeping them on paths that were more exposed to view, despite his earlier concerns.

They walked slowly, Rae keeping her eyes on the distant building belonging to the Menders' Guild. It'd been so long since the last time she'd seen Kalstacia, she wondered if she even truly remembered what she looked like. But when the auer came into view, carefully crossing a patch of clover-dabbled grass, Rae could have easily picked her out from a crowd.

Her dark hair was cut just below her jaw, as it'd been when they first met. The bottom curled gently against her jawline, framing her dark features. Her pale lilac dress fit perfectly to her form, obscuring her feet as they stepped with auer grace.

She smiled as she drew closer, lifting three fingers to her forehead before arching them down in greeting, which Rae returned. "Thank you for agreeing to meet with me. When I didn't hear, I'd feared perhaps you'd forgotten me." She gave the same greeting to Maith, offering him a welcoming smile. "Maithalik, I know by reputation already. It is a pleasure to meet you formally. I'm Kalstacia Di'Terian."

Maith returned the greeting, but Rae spoke.

"I apologize for not writing back. I tend not to put much in writing, these days."

Kalstacia nodded her understanding.

"It is a pleasure to meet you. How may we be of assistance?" Maith tilted his head, the picture of diplomatic elegance.

Kalstacia's smile tightened. "I need to ask for a favor. Which I understand you don't necessarily owe me." She met Rae's gaze. "It pertains to my late brother, Talon. And Amarie."

Rae's shoulders drooped. "I am sorry for the loss of your brother. And if I can grant your favor, I'm happy to."

The auer's embarrassment turned to surprise. "Thank you. But your knowledge of my brother's passing gives me hope that you may be able to assist me. However, I need to ask first... how do you know? I didn't think his death would be news enough to reach the Helgathian royal council's ears."

Motioning to a nearby table, grown of roots and branches, Rae sat. Once the other two had joined her, she shook her head. "It was not news that came to Helgath, but it was news that came from a friend. Amarie told me of Talon's death."

Delicately folding her hands together, Kalstacia blinked. "I only learned the mysterious news of Amarie waking from Slumber a month ago. And her subsequent disappearance from our shores. I assumed she was out in the world wandering without memories... which was the purpose of my request to meet with you. With news of Talon's death, I knew I needed to find Amarie. For her daughter. But if what you say is true..." Her jade eyes swirled with a plethora of thoughts Rae could only guess at.

Rae stiffened, sitting straighter. "You know Amarie had a child?" She scoured her memories for the time she'd visited Talon and Kalstacia, but they'd failed to mention a baby. "Did you know this when I first met you?"

That knowledge would have changed everything. The entire plan she and Damien had come up with revolved around Amarie's power and keeping it hidden. And although learning of Ahria had put all Amarie's volatile emotions during their travels together into perspective, the more important aspect had been their plan to kill Amarie and force her power into the obsidian dagger. They never would have attempted such a feat had they known she'd birthed a female descendant for the power to pass to.

"I knew about Amarie's pregnancy. I confirmed it for her when she first suspected it. But the child wasn't Talon's, so things were... complicated."

Maith caught her gaze, and she read the message in his expression.

Don't get caught up in the past. You can't change it now.

Rae swallowed, urging her shoulders to relax. "Amarie has regained her memories. She has also reunited with her daughter and is married to the new king of Feyor."

The relaxation that started in Kalstacia's shoulders at the beginning of Rae's news promptly changed with the mention of her marriage. She opened her mouth, but then closed it again before she shook her head with a short chuckle. "I am clearly well out of the loop of events. Ahria sends me letters from time to time, but I suppose she has been rather distracted after her father's death." She rubbed her thumb along the skin of her other hand. "So you know Ahria?"

Nodding, Rae sucked in a deeper breath. "I do. Ahria is doing well, all things considered. She was in Ziona, last I knew, being courted by their crown prince. From what I understand, Talon's death was very difficult for her. Alana's, too, took a toll."

Kalstacia's expression abruptly hardened, a slight twitch giving away that this, too, was news to her. "Alana?" Her voice held an unfamiliar tone. Anger, oddly twinged with sadness.

Rae glanced at Maith, realizing her mistake. "I'm sorry, I shouldn't have said anything. I thought you'd have heard, somehow."

Kalstacia swallowed, gently shaking her head. "I had no love for my younger sister anymore, but this news is still surprising. You don't need to apologize. I appreciate knowing." She straightened, clearing her throat. "Do you know how it happened?"

"I do, but I'm not sure you'd believe me." Rae blinked at Kalstacia.

The mender quirked an eyebrow. "You've already implied Ahria mourns her, which is curious enough. I know the shadows my sister lived within. Talon may not have gone into great detail, but I was here when the shadow beast consumed Eralas's sky. I can guess who she chose to associate with after her banishment."

"Fair," Rae murmured. "Those shadows killed your sister. But not before she saved Amarie, Ahria, *and* Ahria's prince from death at her master's hands. They lived because of her. It may not atone for all her wrongdoings, but you should know that in the end, she chose the right side. She chose her family."

Kalstacia's firm expression softened, but only for a moment. "Thank you." She lightly bit the corner of her mouth. "With all the information you've shared, I'm not entirely sure I have a favor to ask anymore. I now know

Amarie is safe, has her memories, and has found her daughter. I had hoped to ask you to use your political power in Helgath to help find that information, rather than offer it so readily."

Rae smirked. "So you're saying I should have held out for a better offer?" She shook her head. "Would you like me to pass along a message to Amarie for you? I intend to see her in a few months' time. As an alternative, though, you can always write to her. If you send correspondence to the royal palace in either Feyor or Isalica, she would eventually receive it."

Kalstacia smiled. "It seems Amarie has found her way in this world if there are *two* kingdoms I can contact to reach her. I will write, but should you see her before my message reaches her, please only remind her she has a sister in Eralas who still cares deeply for her."

Warmth blossomed in Rae's chest. "I will tell her. And..." She paused, her smile growing. "Ziona's royal palace is also an option, given Ahria's relationship. And, well, Helgath..."

"Four kingdoms, then," she laughed. "I feel there is far more to this story than I can possibly know in this short meeting. Though, I'd hate to take any more of your time in asking you to share the details."

Rae ignored Maith's look of warning. "You will have to visit Helgath when this is over, and we can fill you in on everything that's happened."

Kalstacia's eyes sparkled at the implication Rae had let slip. "A grander scheme is in the works, then. Please, if I can be of assistance, I hope you will ask."

"Of course." Rae let the lie slip off her tongue, even though she had no intention of endangering any more lives than necessary. "Hopefully, things will—"

Maith gripped her arm suddenly, so tightly it caused pain.

"What..." Rae flinched at a deafening screech that echoed from above. Her heart leapt into her throat, thundering at the sound that so closely resembled one from her nightmares.

Impossible.

She stared at the sky, rising slowly to her feet as Maith released her. The blue of the sky had shifted, taking on a strange green sheen. But even as she watched, cracks appeared in the ward surrounding Eralas. Lightning crackling along the tearing edges.

Cries of terror and astonishment rose around them from those gathered in the garden. Somewhere, a chime rang, turning into a single high-pitched warning.

"You should get inside," Rae told Kalstacia. "Better yet, get out of the city."

Before the mender could reply, a black monstrosity appeared from the north, wide wings coasting slowly over the city. Black flecks flaked off its scales like ashen snow, and it bellowed again.

A dragon, yet... not.

Maith drew his swords. "What in Nymaera's name is that?"

"Corrupted." Kalstacia breathed. Her demeanor shifted to a battle-ready calm. Her hands glimmered, and the familiar pressure of the Art entered Rae's senses as Kalstacia wove the fabric around them.

"I've fought Corrupted plenty of times," Rae growled. "But now he's got Corrupted dragons? You've got to be *fucking kidding me.*" She gave Maith a pointed look. "See? Awful things. Always awful things."

"You win that argument." Maith backed up. "We need to get out of the gardens. We're in plain sight here."

Waves of screams coincided with bursts of fire as dark shapes dropped below the dense canopy above the capital city. They drew long lines of devastation towards the south, branching away from the Sanctum of Law.

Wouldn't they go for the elders first?

Moving towards one of the garden hedges so they weren't as exposed, Rae looked up rather than follow Maith. He jerked to a stop mid-stride towards the gate they'd entered, concerned annoyance in his expression.

"How many do you count?" She still stared at the sky, though the canopy of trees beyond the sanctum and its courtyard made counting the Corrupted difficult.

"I've seen maybe three, but I hear four." Maith looked at the mender. "You should go. Do you know a safe route out of the city?"

"There are several, but I cannot leave." Kalstacia looked back towards the Menders' Guild. "I'll be needed here."

"You'll be dead here," Maith hissed, looking at Rae. "We need to leave. Now."

"This is the master you spoke of, isn't it? The one Alana served." Kalstacia hissed. "Is he part of whatever it is you're involved in?"

Rae's promise to Jarrod scorched through her mind as she nodded to Kalstacia's questions. She'd sworn to flee. To run from Eralas at the first sign of trouble.

Suddenly remembering the faction device in her pocket, she yanked it out and flipped it open. Before she could spin the dial to any of the letters, the thing whirred and clicked on its own. She waited for the dial to stop, to spell a message, but... nothing. It spelled nothing, endlessly spinning.

Shit. Something must be blocking it.

"We can't continue to stand here." Maith's tone had an undercurrent of panic Rae had only heard a handful of times in their years together.

Kalstacia pulled up her skirt, tucking it into her belt in preparation to run. "If you're working against the creature to blame for my family's death, then I'm with you."

Rae considered arguing, but the roar of a Corrupted spurred her feet to move. They ran, Maith leading the way with graceful movements, back to the courtyard in front of the Sanctum of Law. Their carriage was long gone, and they skidded to a halt on the cobblestone.

The open space in front of them sat eerily empty. No civilians. No soldiers. "Why is it so quiet here?" The guards typically stationed at the front entrance were gone, too. "The elders are here. Where is their protection?"

"Maybe they aren't here," Maith offered, uninterested in her observation. "Wherever they are, they'll have a thousand guards around them."

"They were scheduled to be in session today. They're here." Kalstacia narrowed her eyes at the barren front steps.

Rae looked down at the faction device in her hand, where it still whirled and buzzed without meaning. Slipping it back into her pocket, she turned to the mender. "You're not safe with us."

"Why isn't she?" Maith ground out. "We're leaving."

"No. Something is happening here. The Corrupted attacked and then all flew south. They're drawing everyone away from the sanctum. And if the elders are inside..." Rae glanced around. For what, she wasn't sure. Something.

Anything to give her a hint of what could be the objective. Because burning civilians and creating chaos would be a secondary goal for Uriel.

Kalstacia gestured with her chin towards the north side of the Sanctum. "There's a back entrance, where the elders' private meeting chambers are. We need to get inside and help if something is wrong."

"Raeynna..." Maith warned, but he didn't touch her. Didn't dare try to force her hand.

Rae's gaze landed on the crystal ceiling. The vantage point. "Go that way with Maith," she instructed, not taking her eyes off the clear dome supported by a metal skeleton. "Erdeaseq and Qualtavik are our closest allies. They tried to warn us. Help them." She locked eyes with Maithalik as he opened his mouth "I know, all right? Just please do it."

Before he could question her again, Rae sprinted for the sanctum. She gathered her power in her veins and used it to funnel the wind beneath her feet. The smell of smoke burned her nostrils as she leapt, carrying herself on the Art-laden wind to land at the base of the crystal roof. Panting, she didn't look back as she climbed higher over the panels, keeping her weight on the metal portions of the structure. She needed to get high enough to see over the galleries within the sanctum, to see the central chamber where the elders...

Rae froze, heart skipping a beat as she beheld the elders standing below. She retreated a few inches, ducking out of sight as she processed what she saw.

At least two bodies sprawled on the upper platform of the chamber, near the elders' throne-like chairs. But several of those appeared to be knocked over. Another pair of bodies lay near the gold inlaid circle at the center of the room, where those under trial would wait. Guards, probably. But there were more alive than there'd been dead, standing along the crescent-shaped stairs formed of roots.

From the distance and through the crystal, she couldn't make out their faces clearly with such a short glimpse. But dark shadows lurked at the feet of one figure, who stood at the center of the crescent. It was enough to know the precipice of danger she hovered at. Her Art thrummed through her, static sparking at her fingertips as her internal storm brewed. She needed to shut that down, lock it away tight, but her skill with a hiding aura might not be enough.

Rolling onto her back on the roof, Rae looked at the sky, at the smoke billowing from the west. Whatever was happening out there, it had to be a distraction from what was inside. *Who* was inside. And she didn't dare think his name, as if it might summon his awareness of her.

Laying her palm over the breast pocket of her leathers, she took a deep breath. It had been brought with her *just in case*.

Just in case something required her to hide in plain sight.

With steady hands, she withdrew the thick silver earring, opening the tiny hinge and inserting it through the upper cartilage of her left ear. A cold jolt shot through her, chilling her veins and halting the flow of her Art. Her muscles trembled at the loss of energy, her stomach clenching.

Rae swallowed, taking a few calming inhales before rolling onto her front again. Climbing those few inches that allowed her to peer down into the Sanctum of Law, she all but held her breath.

Voices couldn't penetrate the ceiling crystal, but she focused on their mouths, their expressions.

An auer she didn't recognize—definitely not one of the elders—stood with Lo'thec while Olsaeth and Ekatrina strode along the top of the stair, pushing the other elders down to the lower level. His body was gaunt, signs of age evident even from this distance. Pale grey hair cropped short to his scalp, unable to hide the dark blemishes on his skin.

And the two bodies near the feet of the unfamiliar auer...

Paivesh, one of the kindest of them, and Ietylon, the eldest. Her eyes stung as she failed to pry them off the elder who'd single-handedly changed Amarie's fate. The one who'd listened when the others hadn't taken her seriously. Her friend had told her all about it, and the life it had saved.

Dragging her attention to the others, Rae watched as Lo'thec nudged Paivesh's body with his foot, pushing her lifeless form from the path of the unknown auer who crossed to the arch judgment's seat. His lips curled into a smile as he spoke, gracefully sitting in the spot meant for the auer now on his knees before Olsaeth.

Ekatrina used Ietylon's fallen cane to hit Kreshiida in the back of her knees, sending her into a matching pose next to the leader of the elders. Beside her, Qualtavik lowered himself without waiting for Ekatrina to use force. The last elder, Tyranius, followed suit, his white hair falling in front of his shoulders.

Rae glanced at the back entrance, where Maith and Kalstacia had been headed, but there was no sign of them.

A voice boomed through the space, but the words were muffled. The auer on Erdeaseq's chair tapped his fingers on the armrest, addressing them all. Shadows swirled under those fingers, and Rae's stomach turned.

Qualtavik's back suddenly went rigid as he was yanked to his feet. A tendril of shadow emerged from the layers of his cloak. It slithered around his neck, breaking into small thorns that sank into his dark skin. He grimaced, but defiance hardened his eyes even as his scream shook against the glass at her fingertips.

Fear, sharp and undiluted, stabbed through her chest. Qualtavik had always been fair to her, and had been their main point of contact with their treaty. He'd tried to warn them...

Uriel's expression darkened, his hand twitching as he wove more shadows up Qualtavik's body.

Movement from Kreshiida came in a jolt as motes of green, which usually flowed along the walls of the sanctum, whirled in a cyclone around her. Everything shook as the ground beneath Uriel ruptured. A geyser of woven vines and branches erupted, devouring half the upper platform, including the throne Uriel sat upon. It vanished, wood crunching as the branches wrapped tighter to form the trunk of a massive tree shooting towards the sky.

The tree shattered through the crystal dome thirty feet away from Rae and she threw up her arm to shield her face. Shards flew at her, scraping along her leathers. She held in a cry as a slash appeared across the back of her hand, shuffling sideways to avoid the cracks spreading towards her. More glass rained down below in a cascade of prismatic light, leaving a layer of sparkling debris on the sanctum floor.

She stared at the tree, borne within seconds from the female elder who'd lashed out to protect Qualtavik. The shadows had faded from him, and he collapsed to the floor, his gasps for air now audible.

Kreshiida had never liked her. Or Amarie. And had made that opinion well known. A part of Rae had almost believed that if there was betrayal within the Elder Council, it may have been Kreshiida. But she'd lashed out in defiance, and Rae dared to hope the elder's Art had conquered another of Uriel's hosts.

But Lo'thec, Ekatrina, and Olsaeth only blinked at the tree, utterly unconcerned before looking at Kreshiida, locks of her white hair sticking to the perspiration on her neck from the strain of her power.

"Perhaps she wants the offer for herself," Lo'thec mused in a rough voice to Ekatrina, speaking Aueric.

Black oozed from the gaps between woven branches, and the darkness curled over the fallen crystal as the tree quivered. The wood turned sickly grey, the array of green vanishing as quickly as it had appeared as leaves turned to autumn colors and then brown and finally flaking into ash. The vines and branches withered, curling in on themselves as the master of Shades took hold. Blackness surged through its roots, and in a blink, Uriel was there. Shadow molted away from his body, just in front of Kreshiida. His hand shot out, grabbing her by the throat.

Rae quivered as she watched the female elder's eyes widen.

"I will never let you in," Kreshiida rasped, upper lip curling. "Never."

"I know." Uriel's grip tightened on her throat, lips contorting in pleasure as the elder lost her stoicism as pain ravaged her. It passed over her in a wave, and she let out a stifled scream, her face hollowing as she rapidly aged before Rae's eyes. Her arms thinned, bones becoming more defined beneath her skin as her dark complexion paled. Her body shriveled, like the tree she'd sprouted from nothing, every ounce of living energy taken. As Uriel finally released her, Kreshiida's broken body disintegrated into the elegant red dress she'd been wearing, now just a pile on the floor with bits of dust.

Qualtavik had recovered only just enough to back away, but Lo'thec held him in place as Uriel turned his attention towards Tyranius and Erdeaseq.

"Your people have already fallen." Uriel held out his hands, as if to gesture to the city beyond. Now with the ceiling shattered, the elders would be able to hear and smell the chaos of outside as well as Rae could. "Your little council is destroyed. Eralas is mine, and you'd be better to accept me and remain alive, or..." He glanced at Kreshiida's crumbled body. "I can use you either way, really."

"You're an abomination." Erdeaseq hissed in a tone Rae had never heard before. His attention turned towards the auer behind Uriel. "And you are traitors to your people."

"Our people?" Olsaeth scoffed, spitting on the floor. "Our people are weak. A fragment of what we used to be. Of what we could be. We're going to fix that."

"By killing what's left of our population?" The arch judgment looked between her and Lo'thec. "By betraying what we have fought to uphold?"

Lo'thec smiled as Olsaeth forced Qualtavik back to his knees beside Erdeaseq. Blood ran from Qualtavik's neck, splotching the collar of his robes.

Uriel centered his gaze on the bleeding elder. "By helping with a regime change." He touched the man's face with one finger, trailing it down his cheek in a mocking tear. "Answer my question. I doubt I must repeat it."

Rae braced herself to witness Qualtavik's death. She knew the question without needing to hear it. The only question Uriel ever asked of those powerful with the Art. And he wasn't hoping the elders would become his Shades.

No, he wanted a new host. Needed one based on the condition of his current body he'd already burned through.

A small sound came from the huddled, quivering figure of Tyranius rather than Qualtavik. A muttered word, lost in the distance between them and Rae.

Erdeaseq's head whipped towards the elder beside him, horror in his gaze.

Rae's heart leapt into her throat as Uriel's attention turned, too.

"Say it again." Uriel stepped towards Tyranius as the elder lowered his head further towards the floor.

"Take me. No one else needs to die." Though muffled, the terror within the words was clear. "I accept you."

With a twitch of a finger, Uriel's shadows snapped Qualtavik's neck. The elder fell, limp, in a heap at the master of Shade's feet.

Tyranius balked, staring at the dead elder. "I said no one else dies. I accepted you. I said—"

The back of Uriel's hand knocked the elder off his knees, sending him sprawling across the sanctum floor. "You have granted him the mercy of a swift death and nothing more. And now, you are mine."

"No!" Erdeaseq shot to his feet, the Art swelling in a pale green glow around his hands. Power lanced through the air, exploding through the structure. Sheets of pure crystal fell from the roof as the sanctum shook, crumbling against the tremors rocking the capital city. The vines along the inner walls retracted, sinking towards the bottom of the structure. The stones they held in place broke, their support falling away.

A well of shadow bubbled up beneath her, engulfing not only Uriel, but those who'd betrayed their people. Rubble rolled off of the roiling surface as it struck the shadow, falling faster with each breath.

The crystal beneath Rae shattered.

She grasped the metal frame in desperation to keep from falling. But walls kept failing and wood kept cracking. She strained to reach another bent metal frame. As her fingers closed on it, the metal let out a protesting screech. It bent, collapsing, and Rae's grip slipped.

She fell with the ceiling, with the walls, as everything crashed down under Erdeaseq's power. All the air left her lungs as she landed in the rubble, plumes of dust enveloping her.

"Fool!" Uriel barked as his sphere fell to the ground. A black serpentine tendril rose from the debris near where Erdeaseq landed on his knees. The shadow slashed across the arch judgment's middle before it flung the auer into a pile of destruction not far from Rae.

She didn't dare move or speak, still reeling from the pain arcing through her body. She didn't know if anything was broken, but laid perfectly still, praying the rubble hid her as Uriel's attention returned to the one who'd accepted him. The last remaining elder loyal to Eralas.

Tyranius crawled backward, away from Uriel, shaking his head. "You broke your word."

"I am not bound to such words until I've taken you." The gold in Uriel's eyes glittered. "Or are you retracting your offer and choosing to die?"

Tyranius recoiled as shadow inched across the cracked floor from Uriel's feet. She wished she could yell at the sole remaining elder. Tell him not to accept because then perhaps Uriel would never find a suitable host. But she was alone. Maith and Kalstacia were nowhere to be seen, possibly dead in the collapsed hallways of the sanctum. And beside Uriel stood three immensely powerful auer.

She had nothing and no one to help her, and if Uriel saw her, she'd be as dead as the rest of the elders. The knowledge sat heavy in her gut, and she prayed Maith and Kalstacia were still alive.

Ten feet from where she hid, Erdeaseq's hand moved. She sucked in a shallow breath and looked at him.

His arm lay over his midsection, where blood seeped through his robes. But his eyes met hers.

Tears flooded her lower lids, and she shook her head, lifting a finger to her lips. He nodded, so slight she wasn't entirely sure he'd meant to, and then his eyes slid shut.

Her heart hammered in her chest, tears wetting her cheeks as she looked at Uriel.

Tyranius's throat bobbed. "If you agree to leave Eralas immediately... I accept you." He breathed the last words, face wan with fear.

"Catching on quickly with how this works." Uriel sneered but shrugged. "I was planning on it, anyway."

It was so fast it stole Rae's breath.

Shadows lurched from Uriel's body, fanning out in a mist of darkness, causing the host to collapse. It curled upon itself midair, stretching through space like a swirling cloud of serpents. And before the elder could react, it lunged for him. Tyranius screamed, but no sound came out as Uriel's essence plummeted into his open mouth. It leaked out of his eyes, his ears, as it shifted and settled. The abandoned body collapsed, and Rae swore a shuddering breath vibrated his chest before he, too, died on the broken sanctum floor.

Rae swallowed the nausea rising in her throat, unable to tear her gaze away from the eyes that were quickly consumed by inky blackness.

No one and nothing moved as Tyranius rose to his feet, calm and steady. He rotated his neck, stretching his jaw before humming. "This will do just fine." He looked at Lo'thec and snarled, "It's time to go. I need to make a stop in Aidensar, but I will rejoin you after you take care of the prison."

The...

She couldn't get a breath down.

Aidensar.

Corin was in Aidensar. With Amarie, Dani, and Katrin.

Gods. Fuck.

And the prison? Uriel knew where it was? Her mind raced, but she lay powerless as Uriel, in his new host, vanished into shadow.

Lo'thec looked at Olsaeth and Ekatrina, their master

now gone. "You heard him. I'm taking the Corrupted north but you'll remain here. Continue as we discussed." The two female auer nodded, lifting three fingers to their forehead and sweeping the gesture down.

Rae looked at Erdeaseq, but he was either dead or very good at pretending to be.

Wing beats filled the sky above them, drawing her gaze to the horrific, Corrupted dragon now descending on the destroyed sanctum. The dark scales were dull, like old lava stone rather than shimmering with undertones of color like Zelbrali's. Its shorter neck supported the slightly larger, more wolf-like head, and tufts of matted fur ran along the spine and underside.

It landed amid the rubble, clawed feet scraping the ground as a purr like a rockslide rumbled in its chest.

On the rump, a brand burned through the scales, the mark of its summoner that bound it to their maker's will. A vertical line with two arched curves running through it, all surrounded by a circle. She'd seen the emblem on a pendant Lo'thec wore, though she didn't dare look now to confirm.

But it means he's the summoner.

Rae breathed faster, realization dawning that she had a choice. A choice to stay, find Maith, and report all of this back to Jarrod as quickly as she could.

Or...

Her eyes locked on the harness crossing the dragon's belly. It was elaborate and loose in some sections. Her mind quickly determined the best ways to abuse the design.

Lo'thec was heading to the prison with Corrupted. To destroy it, most likely. The futility of what little she could do burned through her, but she couldn't. She couldn't just sit back. Not when Damien could still be at the sanctum, the prison, unaware of the danger flying his way.

As Lo'thec rounded to the other side of the dragon to mount, Rae summoned all of her strength and burst from the rubble. She ran for the Corrupted dragon, sliding on her hip to avoid its wing as she maneuvered beneath it. Reaching the lower harnessing, she made quick work of the buckles to secure herself to the beast's belly.

It shifted, as if noticing her movement, but Lo'thec's sharp tone and a yank on the reins drew its attention back to him. The rumble of its reply vibrated deep into Rae as she pressed herself against its underside, hoping it would mistake her for the pressure of its harness.

Glass and stone crunched as the Corrupted dragon turned. The sound of leathery wings spreading kept Rae perfectly still as the ground beneath her disappeared.

Chapter 21

NOTHING ABOUT THE BIG WHITE panther stalking ahead of them blended into the jungle. Amarie could see Dani weaving through the trees from thirty yards away. The Dtrüa's pure white fur found no camouflage in the murky Aidensar forest, but her cat senses were invaluable, negating the risk of possibly drawing attention. She'd identify any danger well before it came close to their group, which helped ease the anxiety constantly coiled in Amarie's gut. She knew the dangers of the Sarian forests all too well, and had encountered enough grygurr in her lifetime already.

It'd be easier if they passed through undetected, but Corin's deafening footsteps were just as likely to draw attention as Dani's ghostly color. So Amarie kept her hand near the hilt of her sword, knowing it was only a matter of time before she got to see just what kind of fighter the Helgathian royal was.

They'd been lucky their first two visits to the forest floor, and Amarie felt the mounting anxiety in herself that their luck was bound to run out.

This time, Katrin had stayed in the city to do more research in Kiek's royal library. They hadn't been successful in finding an appropriate relic for Melyza, yet, and they'd agreed the queen's time could be better served searching for more answers to all their problems in previously inaccessible texts.

As they traversed the deadly forest floor, Amarie almost wished she had stayed, too. It'd been years since her last grygurr encounter when she'd traveled with Talon, but it wasn't that memory that caused the persistent tension in her shoulders.

Trist is long dead.

Walking around one of Aidensar's giant trees, Amarie kept her feet as silent as possible. Peering into the foliage ahead, she looked for white fur but didn't see Dani.

"Always feels like we're being followed," Corin muttered under his breath. "This forest is creepy."

"Won't disagree there," Amarie whispered, scanning again for the Dtrüa.

Dani's tail flicked behind her as she emerged from the

underbrush, closer than she was a moment before. Her cloudy eyes met Amarie's before she nodded and pranced off ahead of them.

How a cat as large as her could *prance* was beyond her.

"We sure we're going in the right direction?" Corin had played the skeptic since they'd taken the lift down from Kiek. The operator had barely waited for them all to step off before reversing the Art-crafted pulley to ascend once more.

Amarie scowled at the glimpse of distant crags that sheltered the foreboding Aidensar ruins. "Unfortunately." She kept a hand on the hilt of her sword, her power locked down tight. "We're almost there."

"That doesn't sound unfortunate to me."

You weren't murdered inside them.

Corin swung the sword at his side to remove the dense brush ahead of them, which Dani had easily slipped through. "Sooner we get something for Melyza and return to Lramandoo's, the happier I'll be."

"You just want more garlic flatbread." Amarie's voice lacked the mirth she intended. "But I agree with you. This is not my favorite place."

Corin slashed at another unfortunate bush. "Does make me miss the desert." He slapped his hand at the back of his neck, destroying some small insect trying to make a meal of him. "It's almost winter, but this place is making me want to strip off layers." He paused. "But I guess that's true in Mirage, too."

"And expose more skin for the bugs? No, thank you." Amarie drew her sword under the pretense of helping cut a path through the thickening brush. But it felt slightly better to have the weight in her hand. A crow cawed somewhere beyond her vision, and bile rose in her throat.

"You doing all right?" Corin eyed her, lips pursed in concern, even as he smacked the side of his clean-shaven jaw.

Amarie glanced at him, every instinct telling her to shove off his concern. But they were a team, and teammates were honest. At least, most of the time. "I've been better," she admitted, continuing their pace.

But then the smell touched her nose. *That* smell. Mold, decaying flora, damp rock, and the musty, old scent only achievable by truly ancient places. It turned her stomach, and a tremor shook her hands.

As Corin cut away more brush, their eyes fell on where the forest gave way to stone. Vertical rock took the place of trees, as wide and tall as a stout mountain, but Amarie suspected the formations were less natural than commonly believed. She'd been inside, once, and seeing the outside again, with its strangely clean-cut edges and flat sides, only reinforced the notion.

Dani padded towards them from the north, and her body morphed.

Amarie didn't think she'd ever get used to seeing how her fur smoothed into skin, her face reshaping, flattening, and her body bending to become human.

"There is an entrance just north of here." Her breathy voice somehow matched her stark-white hair. "We should be able to fit inside."

Inside.

Amarie clenched her jaw and nodded as they continued on, tightening her grip on the hilt.

"Hopefully this one hasn't already been pillaged." Apprehension lingered in Corin, his blade remaining in his hand despite the more open ground. He glanced behind them, looking back to the dark trees.

"I saw no tracks, smelled no others," Dani confirmed. "But until we look within, we will know not." The Dtrüa kept to her human form as they all strode north. "Someone should stand watch outside."

Amarie hardly heard her, unable to force her gaze away from the narrow crevice ahead. The sliver of shadow that led inside.

Inside.

Her stomach lurched, threatening to eject her breakfast.

As they grew closer, Amarie's heart thundered in her ears. Whips of shadow lashed at her memories, her legs mangled, her blood a pool surrounding her.

Something closed on her right shoulder, and Amarie spun, raising her sword at her attacker, and steel met steel. The clang reverberated through her muscles, and her eyes focused on Corin.

"Whoa!" He lifted his free hand towards her, holding the block as her body began to shake. "It's just me, Amarie."

She stepped away from him, acutely aware of Dani's attention. Swallowing, she bowed her head, inhaling as slowly as she could. Counting. Releasing the breath. "I'm sorry."

"No harm done." Corin lowered his sword to his side. "But you're jumpier than a field mouse."

Dani approached and kept her voice low. "You have been here before, and you're afraid."

Not a question, but Amarie replied anyway. "I... I was somewhere near here."

"What happened?"

Amarie looked down at her feet, seeing deep carvings in her flesh. The bindings that bit into her wrists. Her chest rose faster, the truth stuck in her throat as she whispered hoarsely, "I died."

"Nymaera's breath." Corin pursed his lips. "I thought that was near Hoult. Didn't think Damien came—"

"No." Amarie choked on a dry, humorless laugh. "This

is where I died the *first* time." She met Corin's now deadpan stare. "A Shade tortured and murdered me in ruins like these. I... I thought..." She swallowed. "I can't. I can't go in there."

Dani put a hand on Amarie's arm before angling her head towards Corin, silent.

"Think you can do this one alone, Dani? Hopefully whatever you come across and pick up first will be enough." Corin glanced towards the dark crevice. "I think I better stay out here, too."

Amarie let out a breath. A small part of her had worried they'd be angry for her not saying something sooner. For not warning them that she might be useless in this quest. But Corin's acceptance washed over her like warm water, calming her insides just enough.

"I can." Dani squeezed Amarie's arm before letting go and stepping towards the crevice entrance. Her leather-slippered feet made no sound as she moved, crouching. "I will be as quick as I can." Her mantle of fur spread as her body shifted, four paws hitting the cold ground before she disappeared inside.

Amarie backed up, keeping the forest and the crevice in her field of view. "I know I should have said something sooner." Shame spiked through her chest. "I thought I could handle it."

Corin gave her a soft smile as he angled towards the

forest. "I understand. I still have issues going down into the palace dungeons, even though I tell myself I can do it every time. And my trauma is over twenty years old." He watched her for a moment. "Yours isn't nearly that far away. How old were you?"

"Twenty-two." Amarie rolled her lips together. "Two years ago, if you don't count those I slumbered or trained."

He let out a breath. "They don't count if you can't remember them. You were too young. That's all that matters." Chewing his lip, another question formed on his face before he spoke it. "Did your revival have something to do with the Berylian Key power? Since Damien wasn't involved?"

"It did." Amarie exhaled, her nerves raw as she recalled her first time in the Inbetween. "I was dead for a couple hours, but for me it felt like a whole day. I talked with my mother, who passed when I was a child, and she explained that the Key's power would continue to bring me back to life until it had a female descendant to pass to."

Corin's jaw twitched. "So, you hadn't had Ahria yet. But when you died and Damien brought you back... that's how she got the power, too?" He shook his head. "I bet that whole situation is strange. I don't know how I'd feel if I'd missed so many years of my daughter's life."

Guilt punched her in the gut. "It feels awful," she whispered, meeting his gaze. "Even though I'm proud of her. I've only got like ten years on her, so I hardly feel qualified to give her advice."

"Trust me, that doesn't change." Corin gave her another light smile. "I sure as hell hardly know what to tell Brynn."

Amarie huffed, her shoulders finally easing. "But the thing is, I don't know if I would change it if I could go back. She had a good childhood, a great family. And who knows what danger my presence would have brought."

"Isn't that what we always strive for, for our children? A better life than we had?" He turned more towards her. "That's why we're doing this."

Nodding, she sighed. "I just didn't realize she'd get caught up in it." She shook her head. "Hells, I didn't even know *I'd* get caught up in it."

"Another inevitability of life, I've found. It always surprises you. You think I thought I'd get caught up in a civil war and overthrow a king?" He chuckled. "I honestly used to think I'd be the one to run the horse ranch when I was a kid. That'd have been a boring life."

"Compared to ruling Helgath with your husband, the king?" Amarie scoffed. "I don't know, horses can be... the best."

He lifted an eyebrow. "I feel like there's a story there."

"I was very alone in life before all this." She gave him a pained smile. "And although it is *truly* amazing to have all of you as allies and friends, I only had one companion back then, and I miss him."

He nodded solemnly. "I can only try to imagine what you've gone through, despite being so young. I hope, for you and all our children, this is over soon."

Amarie's mouth pulled into a smile, the comment about her youth sending a warm memory of Talon saying something similar through her. "Me, too. But I—"

The faint crack of a twig stiffened her spine, silencing her tongue.

Damn it.

They'd been careless. Too loud. Too relaxed. Forgetting what surrounded them.

Corin tensed at her side, facing the shadows of the forest. His sword arm remained relaxed at his side, but his knuckles whitened.

Amarie angled her body away from Corin, scanning the trees. "You may have been right before," she whispered. "I don't think we're alone."

He grunted. "I don't see anything. Damn bushes are too thick."

Amarie sucked in the tiniest bit of her Art, expanding her pupils and brightening her vision. And there, between the branches...

A pair of large orange eyes.

Chapter 22

"I'M OFFICIALLY READY TO GO back to sitting on my ass," Matthias muttered, hands scraped and dirty from climbing the giant boulders that blocked their path.

"What does that feel like?" Damien glanced back at him with a teasing grin. "Sitting on your ass, I mean."

The first three days had been difficult, but the path only got steeper, sharper, with less opportunities to hike and more necessity to climb. Now, on their sixth day of climbing, things had only gotten harder. He'd healed Matthias's hands several times, since gloves only hindered his grip. But Damien had opted for the leather barrier, since he couldn't heal his own injuries without a nearby sanctum.

They were getting closer to a point where they'd need to climb again, since the boulders ended in the sharp rise of a cliff.

Fantastic.

"Better than this," Matthias grunted, a smile tugging at his lips. "But you don't get to complain. I've saved your life three times already."

"Only because I'm the idiot going first," Damien mumbled.

Matthias countered, "Can't jump if *I'm* dead."

"But you could if you were still mid-air." He didn't actually mind going first. In a way, it allowed him to focus on where the next hand was going rather than being tempted to look down.

Pushing aside the vines and branches of a jungle tree that'd somehow found root in the soft stones, Damien faced the coming rock face. As he leaned his head back, it pressed against the bedroll tied to the top of his pack. He hadn't really noticed the extra weight on his shoulders, but had to admit it was only because he could bolster his ká against it. All things considered, he actually felt physically well, certain that the time with Mirimé played a part in how in shape he was. The physical recovery had been needed after the month he spent in a coma.

"True. You want to take a turn eating my gravel?" Matthias chuckled, dodging a rock Damien purposely rolled his direction.

"After you." Damien stepped aside, gesturing to the cliff face. "Looks like this is one of the big ones, which means we're getting close." He recalled looking up at the mountains from where Zelbrali and Liam had dropped them off. The most exposed cliff faces were those near the top, which meant they'd be adequately exhausted from the days of rough terrain and hiking before the serious climbing even began.

Matthias frowned, climbing onto the boulder Damien stood on. Behind, and to their left, a sheer drop. The only way forward was up. The king sighed. "This better be worth it."

Damien looked out over the valley of Draxix, avoiding glancing down at the drop off the edge of the boulder. "I was going to say the same thing." He looked up at the cliff again, then met Matthias's stormy eyes. "Are we certain it is? Should we be focusing our attention somewhere else, with how close we are to imprisoning him?"

"We're so close now. It's too late for reconsidering. Let's go. We can take a break at the next landing." Matthias touched the rock wall, finding purchase, and started the climb. He tested each hold before putting his full weight on it, the same as Damien had.

Thirty minutes of grueling climbing left the king panting by the time he reached the top, looking down at Damien. "Almost there!"

"You're sure I can't just use my Art to create some platforms or something?" Damien's muscles ached, regardless of how much of his ká he pushed them. He leaned against the rock, feeling the cool stone against his cheek as he reminded himself not to look down. He kept remembering how he'd used his Art to move stones from the palace tower as he climbed after his near death.

This would be so much easier...

"Do you want to get to the summit only to have the Primeval angry that we cheated?" Matthias started, suddenly, his boots scuffling. "No!" he shouted, moments before Damien touched his next hold. A hold that Matthias himself had used. "Not that one."

Damien's gut lurched, knowing exactly how Matthias had come by the knowledge. "Great," he muttered, reaching for a much higher stone. He huffed as he heaved himself up, listening to the surrounding energies about where to put his foot rather than looking to confirm. "How many times are we up to at this point?" He considered blindly reaching for the next handhold without testing, knowing Matthias would correct him if he was wrong.

"Three."

"You said three earlier," Damien growled. "Lying bastard." He yearned for the top of the cliff, his heart thundering as he scrambled another body length up.

"All right," Matthias breathed as he reached down and clasped Damien's forearm, hauling him up the rest of the way onto the landing. "It might be closer to seven or eight, but I didn't want to freak you out. There was one place two days ago that used a few jumps all on its own."

Damien breathed a sigh of relief as he crawled onto the ground, savoring the feeling of being horizontal instead of vertical. The grass of the landing tickled his nose, and he eagerly accepted the latent energy the foliage around him offered to his ká. "What were we thinking doing this without ropes? Or actual experience?"

"You mean like how we do everything?" Matthias smirked. "Liam's ropes weren't long enough for this climb and returning to the city for supplies would have wasted time. We're here, aren't we? Alive. We'll make it."

"From what you say, there's a few dead Damiens in alternative timelines that would disagree." He rolled awkwardly onto his back, forced at an angle because of the pack.

"I don't think it works that way. And to be fair, sometimes you're still alive when I jump." Matthias offered him one of those stupid, shit-eating grins before adding,

"We should take a break, though. My hands won't stop shaking from that stretch."

Sure enough, Damien peered over, and the king's hands not only shook, but bled, staining the sparse grass.

The Rahn'ka didn't bother asking as he stripped off his worn gloves and grabbed Matthias's wrist. He'd done it enough in the past few days, that connecting to his ká came in an instant. It only took a slight suggestion from his Art for the king's flesh to respond. It rapidly progressed through the stages of healing, the cuts closed and scabbed, then turned to pink scars that faded to his smooth palm.

Finishing, he pulled back and examined his own hands. No new cuts, just the one still healing where a rock had sliced through the leather of his first pair of gloves the day before. Setting them down, he crossed his legs beneath him and loosened the straps of his pack from his shoulders.

Matthias let out a breath, closing his eyes and leaning against stone.

Damien wouldn't argue with the break, exhausted from the weeks of intense work. He gazed over Draxix, smiling faintly at the group of wyvern hatchlings swooping around each other in a game of chase over the lower jungle.

The wildlife here differed from the continents of Pantracia. Monkeys howled through trees, staring at them from vines, while brightly colored birds had dappled the sky. This far up the mountain, though, they only saw the occasional snake or falcon. And draconi.

A wyvern rose from the lower jungle in the distance, and Damien watched as it came closer. Perhaps the mother of the hatchlings. But as it soared nearer, his chest tightened.

Dragon, not wyvern. Gold scales glittered in the sunlight.

Matthias noticed, too, and glanced at him but said nothing.

Zelbrali barreled closer, barely slowing, and Damien's heart picked up its pace. The dragon spread his wings wide, blasting them with wind as he came to a fast stop before he latched onto the mountain. One foot on the landing edge, the other halfway up the next rise, he swung his massive head down to the two men. "I bear grave news," he growled.

"What's happened?" Damien jumped to his feet, followed by Matthias. He tried to control all the places his mind leapt, considering how widespread everyone was.

The dragon's eyes shuttered, his tone softening to an impossible level. "The auer have suffered an attack. Eralas has fallen."

Matthias's gaze shot to the Rahn'ka's.

Terror punched him hard in the gut. "Who attacked?" It was all he could manage as his mind rushed to fill him with horrific images of what happened to the beautiful island.

"Corrupted," Zelbrali hissed, anger spiking in his tone.

"That's impossible, Corrupted would never make it past Eralas's wards." Damien tried to control his voice, but panic clawed at him.

"The wards were down." The dragon bowed his head, empathy flowing off him in waves at the knowledge that Damien's wife had been there. Empathy that Damien didn't want. "The wards are *still* down."

Damien's mind whirled. He debated sitting down to meditate, to see if he could reach out to Rae and ensure that she was safe. But there was no way it would work. He had a hard enough time accomplishing that when he was in the same country as Rae, let alone a different continent. He laced his hands behind his neck, trying to control his unraveling emotions.

Why the hells would Uriel attack Eralas? They're not part of this.

Matthias studied him, then carefully asked, "What do you want to do?"

Damien was silent as he tried to consider every angle. Every option before them. "What I *want* is to know my wife is all right." He gritted his teeth, looking up at the cliffs that still hung between them and the Primeval. "What in Nymaera's name would Uriel want with Eralas? Did he ever think about doing something like this while he was in you?" He looked desperately at Matthias. He wanted him to say yes. That this had been a plan of Uriel's all along. Because then it would stop the wild thought that Uriel had gone there for Rae. As a completely isolated member of their six required to imprison him.

The king shook his head. "He only obsessed over it for a short time after Amarie fled there. I never knew of any plans to destroy it. Last I knew, he even had a couple auer allies, but I don't know their names or faces. Correspondence was only ever written, and in code he obviously never explained to me."

"You must continue your journey." Zelbrali seemed to read Damien's mind. "If you abandon this trial, you will not receive another opportunity. We have a dragon and rider standing by in Nema's Throne in case the threat nears the capital."

Matthias's brow twitched. "Who?"

"Jaxx and Zaniken."

The king nodded and met Damien's one-eyed gaze again. "Rae is smart. Adaptable. She survived it, I'm sure."

If she wasn't the intended target.

Damien's dark thoughts left every inch of him tense. Even Matthias's assurance did little to ease his fear. But they had little choice. Little power, even if Rae was hurt or worse. He sucked in a breath as he closed his eye. "Why would Uriel attack Eralas?" he repeated the question quietly to himself. But it didn't matter. Not in this moment with the cliffs of Draxix and the Primeval somewhere above them.

Maybe the Primeval will know something. Be able to explain why Uriel does what he does.

No one answered his rhetorical question, but Matthias murmured, "It's your call."

Damien breathed one final time with his eye closed before he rolled his shoulders. He looked down to his pack before scooping it off the ground and pulling it back on. "We should get moving again." He gestured to the thin copse of trees they'd need to make their way through before the next cliff. "We need to keep going."

Chapter 23

I'M SURE THEY'RE FINE.

Katrin busied herself pouring through the stack of books she'd gathered on a modest desk nestled at the back of the royal library. She hadn't known entirely what she was looking for, but over the past weeks, her pile had continued to grow with any and every mention she could find about the ruins outside of Kiek.

Her other topic of interest had been harder to find text on. Uriel was never mentioned by name, a feat she wasn't sure how he'd managed. She primarily found information related to his Shades, with hypotheses about a potential puppet master.

Maybe I should write a book about him after this is all done.

She was likely the most familiar with what he really was, other than her husband, of course. But she doubted Matthias would want to dedicate the time to write such a tome. But the thoughts of it were premature. They had to rid the world of him first.

Movement out of the corner of her eye made her heart jump, body following suit before she focused on the familiar assistant.

"Evannika, you startled me." Katrin placed her hand against her chest, willing it to still.

The woman gave an apologetic smile, a pair of books clutched to her chest. "Apologies, your highness. I have very quiet feet." She set the books down next to the one Katrin was reading, her long sleeves ending in a point over the back of her hand. The fabric extended into a woven ring around her middle finger, holding them in place. "Have your friends successfully retrieved a relic, yet? Did they find the ruins?"

"They're out making an attempt as we speak." Katrin rubbed at her eyes, urging them to focus. The pot of tea to her right had already gone cold. "And, please, formalities are not necessary. My name will do."

"I'm sorry, your—uh, Katrin. Habit." A bit of color touched her cheeks as she smiled wider and sat. "Which would you like help with?"

"I'm not entirely sure." She shook her head at the stack,

searching the titles on the leather bindings. "I've been rather curious about the formation of the mountains here in Aidensar. They all seem ripe with ruins. But that's more of a personal curiosity than something completely relevant. I'm hopeful I pointed my friends in the right direction today."

"I believe you did, if you used the information we found yesterday." Evannika blinked at her, a glint of something beneath the look. "They aren't truly mountains, you know." She'd lowered her voice, like it was a secret, but the woman often made outlandish statements as if they were indisputable fact.

Like how she'd said some of the ruins in the mountain were literally sideways, and therefore, extremely dangerous. If someone turned the wrong way and fell *down* a hallway, it would be certain death.

Katrin wasn't sure whether to believe her, but she'd passed along the warning half-heartedly, regardless. She had no idea what could possess an ancient civilization to build something sideways.

She'd seen the massive stone cliffs herself on the first two excursions into the Aidensar forest with Amarie, Corin, and Dani. The way the grey rocks looked perfectly measured and cut beneath the overgrowth that grew over them. She knew mountains, being from Isalica, and even if Aidensar was an entirely different climate and region, the structures still seemed man-made rather than natural. So perhaps there was something to Evannika's claim.

"Has there been research into what formed them, then?" Katrin met the library assistant's gaze. "If they're not mountains? Someone must have looked into it..."

Evannika tapped the cover of one of the books she had just put down. "They're cities. Ancient, forgotten, destroyed cities."

Katrin lifted her brow, slipping the book Evannika pointed at into her hands. The leather binding cracked as she gingerly flipped open the pages. The text was Aueric, the intricate lines drawing together in a language Katrin had always struggled to read. Flipping through, she found a drawing easier to understand than the words, and it reinforced what Evannika suggested.

The towers and structures depicted on the page reminded Katrin of Eralas. She'd never visited the island, but seen enough from the decks of ships from a distance. But her eyes didn't linger on the drawing, which, based on the various structures, appeared to be a massive city. Instead, they wandered to what was drawn below... the tops of trees as if the city itself hovered above them. Clouds etched along the outer walls of Aueric architecture.

"It was known as the City in the Sky." Evannika's tone held a note of awe, that Katrin couldn't fault her for. "Crynetheus."

"By the gods." Katrin ran her finger gently over the etching, scanning to the page beside it, trying to pick apart some of the Aneric words. "I didn't know the auer were ever this far inland. This must have been magnificent to see."

The library assistant leaned forward, placing her elbows on the desk. "The auer ruled all of Pantracia before the Sundering. Aidensar was the hub, connecting all the ley lines, and when the City in the Sky fell, so did their reign."

Katrin tried to wrap her mind around the idea, but it sounded so bizarre. "I thought the Sundering was merely a restructuring of the ley lines. I know there used to be hubs, but I was taught in the Isalican temples that when the current recorded timeline began, there'd been a natural shift. That the gods and Pantracia herself had decided the Art needed to be shared. But you think that's what made Crynetheus fall from the sky?"

Evannika nodded, her fingers twitching excitedly. "The Sundering did a whole lot more than restructure ley lines. It ended the auer rule of Pantracia. With so many killed when the continents broke apart, and the Art readily available to many humans, they couldn't regain control. Then the humans banded together to make their kingdoms. *That's* when recorded time began."

"How do you know this?" Katrin felt a heat rising in her.

"It is my job to know. I helped our previous head librarian write a book on the Sundering last year, and we compiled more information on it than I've ever seen in one place."

Katrin rapidly sorted through everything she knew about the Sundering. Which wasn't much. "Did you cover the formation of Lungaz in this book as well? From what I understand, that may have been related to the Sundering too?" She didn't say his name. It was better not to burden Evannika with the knowledge of him.

Evannika shook her head. "No, we didn't research Lungaz, as we believed it wasn't related."

Katrin already knew in a way it was, considering whatever had happened during the Sundering had also released Uriel from his former prison. It'd been naive to think it was a mere restructuring of the fabric of Art surrounding the world. Of course there had been more destruction. Evidence of it lay everywhere across the land in ancient ruins no one ever had an answer for. Recorded time had marked the beginning of *human* history, and suddenly, Katrin found herself curious to what the world was like before that.

An auer empire?

It seemed a crazy thing to consider with how few auer there were in the world now, mostly hidden away on their island. And awfully protective of their knowledge. She'd requested access to their libraries multiple times over the years, always to be denied.

It's because they have plenty to hide.

She shook her head, carefully closing the book before adding it to a pile on the edge of the desk. A pile she'd be requesting to borrow from the royal council to take back to Isalica. "Do you have a copy of this book you assisted in writing? I'd be very interested..."

"No." Evannika shook her head again. "The only copy was destroyed shortly after its completion."

She hid the disappointment. "What about the librarian who wrote it? Where are they now?"

Evannika frowned, pain etched over her face in a subtle cringe. "She... She is the one who destroyed it. She burned it, burned her whole study and all of our reference material, and she died in the blaze."

Katrin's gut twisted at the graphic end. Destruction of the text only furthered the idea that it might have contained extremely sensitive information. Something the author clearly didn't want shared with the world. Enough so to let herself die, whether by design or accident. But now, Katrin had Evannika. She was likely the closest the queen would ever come to knowing what was actually on the pages.

But is this the wisest thing to focus on? There are more important things...

"I'm very curious and would love to speak with you further on this." Katrin looked away from the book on Crynetheus and focused again on her pile of more pressing interests. She stared at the one she'd picked up on a hopeful whim.

Ancient Weapons and their Origin, Volume 4.

She hoped Volume 4 was far enough into the series to reach the S's. Since this particular author had decided to organize his research alphabetically.

"Have you narrowed down the location of the woman you seek? Melyza?" Evannika tilted her head, picking up a book at random and flipping through the pages.

Her question seemed oddly timed with Katrin's errant thought about Sephysis. "Oh, yes. We did have a bit of luck on that front as well. Which is why I'm extremely hopeful that my friends are able to find something helpful today." She plucked the ancient weapon book from the pile, flipping to the index at the front.

Evannika smiled. "If you do find a relic to offer her, where will you take it?"

The question was... strangely specific. "The royal council gave us a general direction. With Melyza being auer, my friends should be able to sense her Art to help with the exact location once they're in the area." Her fingers paused on the page as she considered a random thought. "I wonder if Melyza will know more about the

Sundering... or if that's why she chose Aidensar after her banishment."

Evannika hummed, sitting up straighter. "She probably chose Aidensar because it reminds her of Mentithe."

"Mentithe?" The word felt distantly familiar, like she'd heard it before.

The library assistant paused, a ripple of hesitation passing through her like she hadn't meant to say the word. She glanced behind her, then focused on the Isalican queen with intense eyes. "Pantracia was birthed in the Sundering," she whispered. "Because prior to that, it was called Mentithe."

Katrin narrowed her eyes, focused only vaguely at the book in her hands. Evannika spoke things that she should hardly put real stock in. It sounded insane. But Katrin had lived through insanity with all Uriel had inflicted. And knowing the dragons as well... Ideas like Mentithe and an Aueric empire didn't seem so crazy.

The dragons might know more.

It shifted her thoughts to her brother, who was likely in Draxix now, seeking exactly that kind of information. And hopefully he'd have luck with securing a meeting with the Primeval. Their closest dragon friends hadn't been alive long enough to know about the Sundering, so she doubted asking Zelbrali or Zedren would provide much insight.

Katrin repeated the old name for the world in her mind again, wondering where she'd heard it before. She needed to focus on more pressing matters... Sephysis, Melyza... Uriel. But something kept drawing her back to Evannika, who still watched her intently as if expecting some reaction.

"What was the late librarian's conclusion?" Katrin would need to forgive herself for the distraction. "What did they believe caused the Sundering?" As much as she wished she could believe it was the will of the gods, like the temples had taught, experience suggested otherwise.

Evannika blinked again, expression impossible to read. "She kept that information close to her chest, sadly. But I saw a reference that it involved an ancient, bloodstone blade."

Oh, gods.

The pieces clicked together, slowly parting Katrin's lips. Her eyes trailed down the page, to where the S's began. And there it was, dropping her heart right out of her chest.

Sephysis, the bloodstone blade of Fylinth, destroyer of Mentithe, and protector of the light.

Katrin read it again, mouth dry.

Destroyer of Mentithe.

Chapter 24

THE GLOOMY FOREST LOOKED THE same, but something hid within, watching them. The hairs on the back of Corin's neck prickled as he scanned again, urging his muscles to be ready.

"There's at least four grygurr," Amarie whispered to him, but he couldn't see a damn thing in those trees. "If there's a shaman, don't approach it."

"How do I know if it's a shaman?" Adrenaline spiked, tightening his voice as he kept his back angled towards hers.

"It won't look like a warrior. It will have a staff, beads, and no blades." Amarie drew her dagger with her other hand.

"Could they just go away? Or..." He only had stories of grygurr to go off of. And if the stories held true, he already knew the answer. Despite the creatures usually acting as scavengers, they'd been warned the grygurr were protective of the ruins. This was why they'd needed another person to go to Aidensar with Amarie, to be prepared for unexpected complications like this one. Yet, he suddenly felt unqualified for facing the cat-like beasts.

"We don't have an auer with us, so that's unlikely. We're in their territory." She never once looked at him, remaining focused on the trees, eyes unnaturally bright. Lifting her chin, she spoke to the forest with a raised voice. "We don't want to fight you. But if you attack us, we *will* kill you."

The trees remained still and quiet.

"Why do I doubt that worked?"

"Because it didn't," Amarie hissed, spreading her stance.

A familiar tension rose through his limbs. The dance that hovered before a battle, when both sides were watching the other. Waiting.

Would help if I could at least see where they are.

"If you get in serious trouble, shout," Amarie warned. "My Art is a last resort."

He frowned, but knew that dance, too. Damien had always been secretive with his power, but keeping Amarie's contained was even more important. Though, he doubted the grygurr were reporting to Uriel.

Amarie breathed. "Incoming."

Brush crunched as massive beings charged from the forest.

By the gods.

They were huge. Seven, eight feet tall, with shoulders twice as broad as his. Corded muscle ran the length of their bodies, interrupted by basic clothing and belts boasting a few secondary weapons. Exposed from the undergrowth, their skin shimmered under the dim light, dappled with leopard-like spots and streaks of mud.

Corin's back left Amarie's, her actions lost to him as an axe descended at his neck. Instinct took over, and he parried with his broadsword, clawed fingers holding the axe mere inches from his face.

The creature growled, and moist, rank breath hit Corin like a blow. Steel clanged behind him, but he didn't dare shift his attention.

But the monster before him moved too fast, grabbing Corin's tunic with a clawed hand and lifting him clean off the ground.

With a startled shout, he managed to block a swing at his stomach while his feet hung.

Amarie yelled, rolling away from the two grygurr who advanced on her.

"Trespasser," the grygurr holding Corin hissed, slamming his pommel into Corin's sword arm. His grip failed with the blow, and his blade hit the ground. Grappling the tufts of hair around the grygurr's wrist, he kicked at the concave abdomen. But the thing held him away from its body, lip curling to reveal sharp, yellowed teeth.

A new snarl tore through the air and a streak of white fur launched at the grygurr holding him. Dani tackled them both, claws and teeth tearing grygurr skin. The beast howled, kicking her off with a clawed foot. She tumbled through fallen leaves before finding her feet and charging again, blood staining her maw.

He scrambled across the ground to his sword, rolling to his feet. The grygurr who'd held him had shifted his focus to Dani, two more squared off with Amarie.

There was a fourth.

There wasn't time to consider exactly where it'd gone as he rushed towards Amarie and her opponents.

Amarie dodged a cutlass, while the Dtrüa circled with the third. The Berylian Key withheld her power, using her blades to fend off the attacks. But she couldn't get any of her own in between her two adversaries, constantly on the defensive and losing ground as they backed her towards the rock face.

Dani tried to break away from her grygurr, but he leapt at her and forced her into a tackle, claws flying as they locked together.

Corin roared, pulling at the adrenaline rushing through him as he charged the side of one of Amarie's opponents, his sword swinging low to avoid the long arms of the grygurr.

The creature spun to meet him, catching Corin's blade with a bare hand. Blood bubbled around the steel, running down the sword as the grygurr snarled at him.

Well, fuck.

A low, ominous chuff came from the forest. And to his shock, all three grygurr stilled. The one holding his blade didn't move, fingers tight around the steel and eyes locked on Corin, but the blow he expected didn't come.

Amarie panted, sword raised, and dared a glance at Corin. Then Dani. The white panther stood facing the third grygurr, blood splotches over her face and fur.

A gentle thump accompanied tiny clacking sounds as the fourth grygurr finally emerged from the forest. A thick curtain of beads adorned its neck, covering its broad chest. More clattered against the staff, a curved bough riddled with carvings of fine familiar-looking runes.

The shaman chuffed again, and the three warriors receded a step.

What is happening?

Amarie looked just as surprised, her empty hand flexing at her side.

"You." The shaman focused on Corin. Not the Berylian Key. Not the Dtrüa. Just him. "Why carry de power... when it runs not in your veins?" Each 'R' sound came out of him like a growl.

Corin blinked, confused to be hearing things he understood from the fanged mouth. He refused to let go of his sword, blood still running down the steel as the grygurr held on. He eyed the shaman's staff again, the origin of the carvings sinking into his battle-focused brain. "Rahn'ka." He spoke carefully, not wanting to break the tenuous pause between them all. "You mean Rahn'ka power?"

Damien and Rae had told him the stories of their encounters with the grygurr. Rae had thought her husband was crazy when he actually talked to a pack of grygurr near the Olsa border, and they had acknowledged Damien's power and left them alone. Damien had plenty of theories about the origins of the grygurr, but the one thing he knew for certain was some shared past with the Rahn'ka. Thousands of years old, but still something that connected him to the infamous creatures. They weren't the beasts the human cultures had painted them as, but civilized and their own society.

Yet, all that knowledge didn't make the teeth still snarling near his face any less imposing.

"You... are no Rahn'ka." The shaman took a step closer, thumping his staff on the ground once more.

"But I do carry some of his power," Corin acknowledged, lifting his free hand in a placating gesture. His heart pounded in his ears. "Think your friend here could let go of my sword and maybe stop smiling at me so threateningly? Then I can explain."

The shaman paused before giving another chuff, and the grygurr holding his sword finally let go. Blood dripped from his hand, but he seemed utterly unfazed. The other two grygurr also stepped back again, giving Amarie and Dani more space to breathe.

His sword finally free, Corin let out a sigh of relief as he lowered it to his side.

"Please tell your friends not to overreact." He looked at the other grygurr before facing the shaman, who gave a subtle nod. Dropping his sword to the ground, Corin rolled the sleeve of his left arm away from his wrist, exposing the metal band etched with runes similar to the shaman's staff. Running along his skin beyond the band were dark blue etchings, shaped like a blade.

Damien had given him the tattoo years ago, along with the power that went with it, but he often thought nothing of the silver bracelet he never took off. A gift for his thirtieth birthday that he'd rarely needed to use.

But in that moment, he dove into himself to find the familiar tangles within his soul. Old threads, still oddly fresh.

"You know, you're lucky." Damien had patted Corin's shoulder as they stared down at the pale blue shape held in Corin's left hand. The azure dagger, serrated near the hilt with an elegantly carved guard that reminded Corin of Sindré's antlers, felt like nothing as he turned it over. "I wasn't sure you'd be able to summon it."

"Why?" Corin frowned, looking at his brother, who smirked.

"Because you don't have the Art. Makes it almost impossible to find the right strings to pull. But I guess you still remember some of my old lessons." Damien moved his hand over the silver bracelet and the blade vanished in a wink back into his skin. "Guess something else good can come out of that test the guardians put us through."

Corin looked down at the tattoo, the skin not needing to go through any of the healing phases like normal ink. Damien's power had not only created it, but healed it, too. The tingle of the power still hummed there beneath the skin, and it felt comforting, even if Corin had loathed every moment of being the Rahn'ka so many years ago. But evidently, something still held on within him, some distant part of him still understood how to access his ká even if the guardians had returned the gift to his brother.

Corin reached for the power again, bringing the dagger to life.

The pressure in the air shifted, and despite the sudden appearance of a glowing blue blade in Corin's hand, the grygurr didn't even flinch.

Amarie scoffed. "You never mentioned having a *Rahn'ka* weapon."

Corin shrugged. "It didn't seem important." He marveled at the thing in his hand for a moment, having forgotten what it looked like. A power he took for granted. "Perk of being the Rahn'ka's brother."

On his other side, Dani returned to her human form, drawing the attention of each of the grygurr. They stared at her, chuffing quietly to each other.

"You travel wid interesting company." The shaman peeled his eyes off Dani, studying the blade Corin held once more. "Bruder of de Rahn'ka." He paused, and no one moved or spoke as he considered. "Why are you here?"

Dani took the cue and walked back to the crevice she'd emerged from, picking up a tarnished metal item and returning to the others. She clicked her tongue as she approached the shaman without hesitation. Holding out the object, she gave no reaction as the grygurr took the item. "We came to retrieve an offering for the one named Melyza who resides in the mire beneath the human city."

The grygurr turned to each other, chuffing again in some guttural language he had no chance of understanding.

"No," Dani interrupted them, blood still marring the skin around her mouth. "We do not aim to hurt her. Just talk."

Corin furrowed his brow. "You understood them?" Even as he asked, he realized it made sense. She could transform into a panther, so it stood to reason she knew how big cats communicated. And if what Damien theorized was correct, the grygurr were ancestors of partially transformed beings, and Feyor had used their blood to help create the Dtrüa.

"I know the basics," Dani murmured.

More chuffing followed, before the warriors put their blades away and returned to their shaman.

"We will take you." The shaman placed the relic back in Dani's hand. It was an urn-like vessel, without a lid, covered in carvings Corin couldn't make out from where he was. "To de swamp. Come."

Dani didn't move as the grygurr all turned, heading southwest into the forest.

Amarie stepped towards Corin. "I guess we follow them?" She looked at Dani, who passed her the relic.

Corin stared after where the grygurr had effectively disappeared back into the trees. "I guess so. Hopefully they stay as friendly as they seem." He looked over at Dani, taking in her grisly face. "You... uh... got a little something..." He touched the skin around his own mouth.

Dani tilted her head at him, cloudy eyes amused. "What is it? You know I cannot see you clearly." She chuckled, though, and his sudden worry at offending her melted as she shifted back into her panther form.

"I don't think she cares," Amarie whispered to him in a playful, conspiratorial tone. As Dani loped after the grygurr, she moved to follow. "I think your brother's little gift is earning us an escort through their territory. Maybe lead with that next time."

Corin looked back down at the glowing blue blade, admiring it one more time before he tensed the muscles in his arm and it winked out. He stooped to pick up his steel sword, wiping it against his leg before he finally sheathed it. "Self-righteous bastard still gets to save the day, and he's not even here."

Chapter 25

"OH, THAT FEELS GOOD," AHRIA sighed as she stepped into the sun.

Conrad kept an arm under hers, hyper aware of every wobble of her knees. "I'm sure it does."

They'd sailed through a storm, and during those days, Ahria hadn't left their cabin. With the violent sways and chilled air, even she had agreed it would be best to stay within the dry, warm bedroom with a bucket nearby.

A thick pelt lay over her shoulders, pinned to her woolen cloak. Her face was paler than usual, her frame leaner than he'd like. But she'd been eating more in recent days, claiming she felt better as long as she didn't use her Art.

Though, she never felt truly fine. Even with her

attempts to hide it—not out of secrecy, but a desire to ease his worry—he could tell. Her appetite, which had been a force of nature before, hardly sustained her.

Their boots thudded quietly over the wooden planks as they crossed to the gangplank. The large royal ship bore soldiers along the exit, heads dipped in respect.

A carriage waited at the end of the dock, understated but well-equipped judging by the wagon traveling behind it with supplies. Four mounted guards waited in front, a fifth leading them, with four more behind the carriage, all on Isalica's trademark grey horses.

A light dusting of snow coated the cobblestone, defying the morning sun. Beyond, there wasn't much of a town like Conrad expected. Only large structures that were probably storage facilities lined the road that led away from the harbor. He caught glimpses of a few workers in fur-lined coats moving between the buildings and under large stone archways, the crest of Isalica carved on each keystone. They framed the roadway that led from the port, a small decorative detail for visitors who arrived to landlocked Nema's Throne by ship.

As they neared their escort, a pair of footmen gracefully opened the double doors of the large carriage.

Ahria leaned on Conrad's shoulder. "Who arranged all this?"

"He did." Conrad gestured with his chin to the rider in

front. "I've been exchanging letters by owl with Micah since we left New Kingston."

The man dismounted at their approach and strode to them. "Welcome to Isalica." Micah shook Conrad's hand before giving Ahria a once-over. "How are you feeling?"

"Tired, honestly." Ahria's throat bobbed. "It's been a long journey, and I'm ready for it to be over."

"Almost there," he murmured, taking her hand and squeezing it before letting go. Looking at Conrad, he nodded. "I've sent word to your mother of your arrival this morning. I will keep her updated once we arrive back at Nema's Throne, if that is acceptable to you both."

"I could have done that." Conrad eyed Micah, sensing the man would have been sending letters to his mother even if there was nothing to report on. "But that's fine. As long as it's not a hassle for you, but I suspect it's not."

Micah smirked. "Not really." A breath passed before he stepped back and motioned to the waiting carriage. "There's tea inside, along with food and a bed, should you need it."

"Thank you," Ahria stepped ahead, accepting Micah's offered hand as she climbed into the carriage.

Conrad lingered behind, watching Ahria as she moved towards the back of the carriage where all the things Micah described waited. He looked again to the right hand of the Isalican king, studying his features and seeking the kindness his mother had spoken so highly of. Of course, he'd already seen it. In the gentle way he'd helped Ahria, and the softness in his eyes when he spoke to Talia.

Micah met his expression without balking. "Is there anything else I can do to aid the rest of your journey?" he asked quietly, tension lingering in his jaw.

"Journey, no. I think you've attended quite well to that, thank you." He'd been exchanging letters with Micah, but they'd pertained only to business. Now, standing in front of the man, memories of his conversation with his mother re-emerged. He looked into the carriage at Ahria, where she eased herself onto the bed built into the front. "I have questions, but I'm not certain now is the time to get into it."

Micah glanced into the carriage then back at Conrad. "If Ahria wants to sleep awhile, you're welcome to join me up front. I can always free up a horse for you." Now that Ahria settled, the tension ebbed from Micah's face until he radiated only calm.

Conrad debated the warm interior of the carriage, perplexed by his desire to remain in the chill open air. He'd only be smothering Ahria if he remained with her, he decided. She'd made it clear she didn't want to be constantly fussed over, sick or not.

"I'd like that." Conrad nodded. "Let me just make sure Ahria doesn't need anything."

With a single nod, Micah stepped away. "Of course." He strode back towards his horse, addressing one of the other riders. "Jecklyn, ride with Werden for now. The prince needs your horse."

The rider gave a stoic salute before following orders and heading to sit with the carriage driver.

Conrad climbed into the carriage, ducking his head as he moved to the bed where Ahria had already snuggled under the blankets, her boots abandoned on the floorboards. He examined the tea setting on a small, rimmed shelf built into the wooden wall, catching the scent of peppermint tea popular in Isalica.

He touched her lower leg through the blankets. "You all right if I ride outside for a little while?"

Face half-smushed into a pillow, Ahria peeked at him, the shadows under her eyes tightening his throat. "Of course. I was just going to sleep a little, anyway."

Conrad tried to give her a reassuring smile as he crawled slightly onto the bed to place a gentle kiss on her forehead. "Don't hesitate to stop us if you need anything."

"Maybe you can pass me a cookie?" Ahria blinked at him, a soft smile on her lips. Her optimism hadn't faded, hope still prevalent that Katrin or Damien would be able to help her. "I can't reach." She extended her arm, reaching for a plate that was halfway across the carriage on a side table. It bore fruit, cheese, and thin, wafer-like cookies.

He chuckled, kissing her forehead again. "I'll get you the whole plate." He did as he promised after he stood from the bed, transferring a few pieces of fruit onto the cookie tray as well before nestling it among the blankets at the edge of the bed. "The tea smells good, too. I wouldn't be surprised if Micah brought one of Katrin's blends that might help you feel better."

"I will try it," she promised. "Go enjoy some fresh air. I'll be fine."

He nodded, ducking towards the carriage doors. He paused as he started to climb out, looking back at her. "I love you, Mouse."

"Love you too," she murmured.

Gently closing the door behind himself, Conrad made his way to where Micah held the reins of a riderless horse. Touching the faction blade on his belt to keep it from getting in the way, Conrad mounted with practiced ease and adjusted to the saddle. He looked at Micah, giving him a brief nod in response to his inquiring gaze.

Micah nodded back, looking to ensure the Zionan guard from the ship had concluded loading Conrad and Ahria's belongings onto the back of the carriage. But they'd already returned to the ship, just as Conrad had instructed. There was no need for his own guard while in Isalica, trusting Micah would keep them safe. Though, it had taken some convincing to sway the captain of his small personal guard.

He swore he could still see the scowl on her face from where she stood on the ship.

If Micah thought anything of his choice to leave his guard, it wasn't apparent in his expression as he let out a sharp whistle. With the command, the four guards at the front moved forward, the carriage lurching into motion behind them.

After they rounded the port bend, Micah picked up the pace to a steady trot before looking at Conrad with a knowing grin. "Missing the sea under your feet yet?"

"Always. But being on a ship as a prince is remarkably different from how I wish it still was." He, of course, hadn't been allowed to assist with any of the ship's operation, despite his protests. His captain of the guard had pointed out it would be a distraction to the crew, rather than helpful, and he'd accepted it wasn't worth arguing.

"Perhaps you need a body double to fool the crew next time, while you secretly work the ropes like you want to." Micah chuckled. "Matthias used to take full advantage of me being 'prince' while he did very *un*-princely things."

"Not a bad idea. Maybe when all of this is over..." Conrad looked to the road ahead, the few workers he saw before pausing to politely salute in their direction as the escort made their way to the open road beyond. "It is rather tedious being royal, sometimes. But, I suppose you know that just as well, having played one."

"For many years. So, yes, I'm rather familiar with your position. But I usually had the pleasure of removing the mantle at the end of the day... or week." He looked sideways at the Zionan prince. "But I was raised within that life, for better or worse. It also means you can't trust all the stories and gossip you hear about my king, for not all of it was him." His expression darkened. "And I'm not referring to the twenty years of shadows."

"I can't say I paid much attention to politics before I was forced to."

Micah chuckled, rolling his shoulders. "I don't mean it like that. I hardly expect you'd have heard anything about Matthias. I meant it as a downside to having the stand in. Sometimes you get a reputation you may not have earned. Or wanted."

Conrad arched a curious eyebrow. "What kind of reputation did King Matthias have, then? That... may or may not have been you."

"Well, obviously that he was handsome, hilarious, and well spoken." Micah smirked, but shook his head. "Though people often thought he spent a lot of time with women, though not with any one woman in particular. We were far more prolific back then, but everyone always had a good time."

"And is that what you're doing now, having a good

time?" Conrad studied the man's face as it sobered.

"Are you referring to your mother?"

"She is a woman you seem to be spending time with." The desire to protect his mother rose in him like a wave, with an uncertainty about Micah. He hadn't had reason to doubt his intentions, not really. But there were still questions. And if Talia was genuinely finally allowing herself to heal from the void his father left behind, Conrad wanted the recipient of her affection to be worthy.

Micah nodded, humming. "That she is." He faced forward but remained relaxed. "And we *are* having a good time, but things are much different than they were thirty-five years ago. Are you concerned about my intentions?" As the man looked at him again, Conrad found nothing teasing or condescending about the question.

"Can you blame me?" Conrad kept his face serious as he held Micah's gaze.

The Isalican shrugged. "Not in the slightest. And I will answer any questions you have." There was the openness his mother had mentioned, and Conrad couldn't deny how it eased his mind already.

They'd emerged from the rows of storage facilities, the road ahead curving up the snow-patched hillside into a copse of pine trees. The fresh chill breeze bit at his skin as he considered what it would be like to have Micah for a stepfather. Though the thoughts still felt so premature considering how much was unknown. They didn't even know what the world would be like in a month if the others succeeded against Uriel. Or failed.

"How serious is it? This relationship? I already know you've slept together, but I'd like to hear it in your own words." Conrad took his gaze from the scenery to focus on Micah again, to gauge his reaction.

Micah coughed, clearing his throat with a short laugh. "Well, it's serious enough that Tal clearly felt the need to mention that to you."

The nickname caught Conrad more off guard than he expected, but he didn't let it deter him. "She didn't. I inferred it when she mentioned you have trouble sleeping sometimes. Like me."

"Ah," Micah breathed, pausing before meeting his gaze again. "It is the burden of living as we do. Nightmares, difficulty relaxing. I've died more times than I can count, but I can't remember even once. Messes with your mind more than you know at the time."

Conrad hadn't thought of that before. He knew of Matthias's Art, his ability to wind back time to make it so events never occurred. Of course there had been times that people around him would have died, considering the danger they all lived in. Danger he was now a part of, too.

I hope this really can be over, someday.

"But to answer your question," Micah continued. "It's

serious enough that neither of us are open to seeing other people. Our countries come first, but I'd be lying if I said being apart from her is something I enjoy."

Conrad considered. "What is your official title in Isalica? I know you and Matthias are close, and you always seem to be around in political situations."

Micah shrugged. "On paper, I'm the King's Regent. I act as king when he is away, so I must always be caught up with anything that's happening. But I'm also Uncle Micah, which is an equally important title to me."

"And you'd be willing to give that up? Not the uncle part, but the other... To be with my mother?" Conrad focused his full attention, trying to read even the slightest twitch of Micah's jaw.

"Honestly, we haven't talked about it much, but both of us have expressed a desire to alter our lives so they may be better entwined. My first priority has always been and will always be to my king and country, but I also haven't spoken to Matthias in depth about this, either. I have a feeling I know what he'd say, but you must understand that even while he was a prisoner of Uriel, my entire life revolved around finding a way to free him. I am on the outside of those needed to trap Uriel, I know that, but it doesn't mean he needs me any less."

A flurry of different emotions twisted in Conrad with each new statement. He understood, yet didn't. He remained silent, unsure how to respond as he looked ahead to the approaching tree line.

"That all said, your mother means a lot to me. More than I expected, as I've never had much desire to marry or have a family beyond what I already have. But when all this is past us, and Isalica is at peace, I would consider retiring and joining Tal in Ziona if that is something she'd want, too."

Conrad nodded thoughtfully.

When this is past us.

"Has there been word from the others?"

"Kin is on his way from Feyor. Matthias and Damien are probably in Draxix by now, as is Liam. The rest of them are a mystery, but I'm used to that." Micah smiled softly.

Conrad considered Micah's evident comfort of being in the dark, wondering if he could feel the same way. Of course, there was nothing he could do to aid the group in Aidensar. Or possibly find a way to identify Uriel's new host.

But I can take care of Ahria.

"Hopefully either Damien or Katrin return soon, then." He glanced back at the carriage where his love likely slept. "I just wish I could do more."

"You're doing exactly what you're supposed to," Micah assured. "Just as I am. Our roles may be smaller, by comparison, but just as necessary. And, arguably, a little less dangerous. Don't forget how those six came to be one of the pieces needed for Taeg'nok."

Conrad opened his mouth to ask, but then realization dawned. Matthias had spent twenty years as a body-slave to Uriel. Amarie and Kin had been in Slumber for just as long, and had suffered immensely to get to where they were. Damien and Rae had worked with Jarrod and Corin to overthrow a corrupt monarchy, while balancing their responsibilities to immense forces of Art. And Ahria... Ahria hadn't asked for this, and suffered all the same under the weight she bore.

What little he had endured suddenly paled in comparison to all of them. "I suppose that's a way to look at it." He'd wanted so badly to be a greater part, but now... It felt foolish to have ever daydreamed it. "I had always hoped I could contribute more, though. Just to at least feel like I'm not the deadweight being carried along because I happen to be in love with Ahria."

Micah looked at Conrad, expression serious. "No one thinks of you as deadweight. Without you, who knows what would have happened to Ahria when she inherited the Key's power. Who knows how we'd be working with Ziona in this. And be careful what you wish for, because it's not over, yet. It's possible your trials have simply not yet happened."

Chapter 26

THE GRYGURR SHAMAN LED THEM to the edge of the Bergin Mire, pointing a bony, clawed finger in the direction they needed to continue traveling. They wouldn't get closer. Out of fear or respect, Amarie wasn't sure.

The journey through the Aidensar forest had been surprisingly fast, considering the shaman continued to lean on his staff. The warriors had remained in the underbrush, invisible to the three of them for the majority of the walk. It'd left a tension in the air, even if Corin and Dani trusted that the grygurr wouldn't become aggressive.

All Amarie could envision was the shaman sending lightning towards her, and her ending his life.

Had there been another way back then, too?

The inkling of regret, of past foolishness, nagged at her. Yet, those grygurr had killed innocent caravaners, and she'd acted in their defense. There'd been no choice, and despite the current peaceful escort, she'd not felt safe for a second during the journey.

Her power hovered just beneath the surface, ready to destroy them at a moment's notice.

Clutching the relic, Amarie strode through the swamp, Corin on her left and Dani in her panther form on her right. She hoped the item Dani had retrieved from the ruins was adequate, dread weighing on her shoulders.

They walked for what felt like hours, her legs tiring of the difficult travel through sticky, wet ground. The mud suctioned to her boots at every step, but they had to be getting close.

Far above them, the dark shapes of Kiek's city districts clung to the trees like frightened animals, barely visible through the dense foliage of the ancient trees. She tried to gauge what direction they faced, what part of the city loomed hundreds of yards above them, but the dim gloom of the swamps left her disoriented.

"I swear I've walked over this obscene lump of mud before," Corin muttered, kicking a mound of sticky brown.

"That's because you have." Dani's voice came from behind them, and Amarie turned, surprised to see the

Dtrüa again on two legs. "We've been by here already. I can smell our scents."

Amarie furrowed her brow, looking at Corin. "Melyza must have wards." She cursed inwardly at herself. Of course there were wards.

"She's auer. That tracks with everything I know about them." Corin glanced around, as if the massive tree trunks might give something away.

"Take this." Amarie passed the relic to Corin, breathing deeper until her power came to the surface. She kept her hiding aura intact, reaching out with her hand and energy to feel for the presence of another's power.

And, sure enough, Aueric Art lingered in the air. She huffed, shaking her head, and pulsed just enough of her ability into what hovered before them. It crackled against the energies that formed the invisible ward, spilling too much power into it, and it winked out, like a fire that burned too fast. The air in front of them shimmered like a rainstorm, parting to reveal a log cabin nestled in the trees not fifty yards from where they stood. They'd walked in a circle around the perimeter without noticing.

"She'll know we've found her," Amarie whispered, and Dani nodded.

"Guess we better go introduce ourselves, then." Corin trudged forward first, a hand moving to the hilt of his sword. But he hardly needed the steel with the Rahn'ka weapon he had hidden. He'd pulled the shirt sleeve back down to protect against the more aggressive bugs of the swamp, but she could just see the edge of the silver band.

"Feet or paws, you think?" Dani asked under her breath as the two women started their approach, following Corin.

"Feet." Amarie swallowed. "But if things go sideways…"

"Teeth and claws. I got it."

Nothing stirred in the cabin as they grew closer. Gentle puffs of smoke rose from the chimney, the only sign of life inside. A lean-to had been built outside with a hitch post, but no horse occupied the space.

Anxiety rose in Amarie's throat as they drew within fifteen feet of the doorway, the ground growing more solid beneath their boots.

Corin jerked, an 'oof' echoing out of his mouth as his feet stilled on the edge of a flagstone walkway. He took a sudden step back, rubbing his nose. Something in front of him in the air rippled, like a spiderweb swinging in the breeze. He extended a hand, pressing his palm to something invisible as he sighed. "I hate the Art."

A chuckle lodged in Amarie's throat, unable to escape past her nerves. She stopped beside Corin and touched the nearly invisible barrier. Sending her power through the fabric, she traced it back to the source but didn't disable it.

"I'm going to disengage this ward." She raised her voice, unsure if the auer would hear. "Or you can let us pass."

They waited only a breath before the cabin door creaked open.

Amarie lowered her hand, watching the woman descend the few steps to the stony path that led to where they stood. Bright green eyes met hers, reminding her of Talon with a painful squeeze of her chest. But Melyza's hue was lighter and clouded by a mass of black—the only indication of her age. By human standards, she appeared in her mid-thirties with smooth dark-olive skin. Long, curly, slate-grey hair reached to her lower back, her clothing simple but clean.

"It will take me long enough to replace the first ward you disarmed," she gritted out through a scowl. "Why are you bothering me?"

"We brought this for you," Dani offered, holding up the relic.

"I don't want it. Leave." Melyza turned to go inside.

"Please. We mean no harm. We just really need to speak with you."

Melyza waved her hand over her head, walking up her steps. "I have nothing to say. Not to a Dtrüa, not to Helgath's king consort, and certainly not to the Berylian Key."

Amarie's gut did a flip-flop.

Gods, she knows all about us.

But Dani had shifted after they'd circled the cabin, and it was possible she'd felt Amarie's power through her use to nullify the first ward. And Corin, well, his and Jarrod's faces had been plastered all around Helgath and the surrounding countries during the rebellion.

Melyza opened the door to her cabin.

"We found Sephysis!" Amarie blurted, and everyone hung silent as the auer froze.

Melyza stood like a stone, one hand on her door as if she still contemplated opening it. Suddenly, she released it and turned. "Did you bring it?" Her eyes searched over Amarie, but something in them already knew they hadn't. They stood in silence again, as Melyza's eyes darkened. With a sigh, her shoulders relaxed, and she lifted a hand. With a twisting motion in the air, the pressure of the ward vanished from Amarie's senses. "I suppose I'll put some tea on." She turned back to her door and stepped inside, leaving it open. An unspoken invitation for them.

Corin tested the air in front of him with his hand before taking a tentative step forward. He looked at Amarie, his eyes full of silent questions she couldn't quite make out. Except for the one asking if she really thought it was safe to go inside.

"I don't think we have a lot of choice," Amarie muttered, and the three continued forward.

Corin entered the cabin first, hand still on the hilt of his sword, followed by Amarie and then Dani.

Amarie looked around the space, which was small, but more than enough for one person. Plants grew everywhere, vines snaking around the ceiling and shelves, with smaller greenery tucked in between. Some grew small, bright peppers, while others looked like rosemary and thyme.

Melyza emerged in the main room from another doorway, the kitchen behind her. She moved silently across her own floor directly to Dani, plucking the urn from her hands before any of them could protest. She turned the thing over, inspecting it before giving a quiet hum.

Amarie and Corin exchanged a glance.

The auer took the ancient urn back into the other room, and when she came out a breath later, it boasted a young plant that looked like...

"Is that mint?" Amarie watched Melyza place it on a crowded shelf, disbelief echoing through her at the vessel's purpose.

Plant pots?

"Frost Mint," Melyza clarified. "And it needed a home, so the urn will do."

Dani clicked her tongue, nostrils twitching, but she said nothing.

They stood awkwardly in the cabin's front room, Corin never moving his hand from his sword, but the auer maneuvered around them as if they weren't even there. She approached the fireplace on one wall, dim embers burning within it. She swung a metal bar with a kettle dangling from it into the fire that began to grow for no apparent reason.

A small dining table occupied one side of the room, adorned with one chair, grown from the planks composing the floor. A comfier looking chair sat in the corner, under the abundant shelves for the plants.

"Have a seat." Melyza withdrew mugs of different shapes and sizes from an overhead cupboard, picking leaves off various plants to make tea. "And tell me. Where is my dear old friend now?"

Is she talking about the dagger?

No one sat.

"Feyor." Amarie glanced at Corin again, her power hovering just beneath her skin. Just because the auer hadn't yet tried to kill them didn't mean she was their ally. Perhaps she wanted the information first.

"Feyor is a long ways from where it was last." Melyza set the empty mugs on the table. She smiled apologetically as she looked at the single chair. "I don't get guests often." With a subtle gesture, Amarie could feel her Art swelling. The floorboards beneath the table cracked lightly as roots sprung up from beneath them, weaving together lazily in a distinct new shape.

"Where it was last... Isalica, you mean." Amarie finally eased herself onto the chair at the table, letting Dani lounge in the cushioned one in the corner next to a packed bookshelf. The Dtrüa flopped into it, putting on a perfect show of relaxation.

Corin stood by the door, and she doubted anything could convince him to move.

"Yes and no." Melyza barely focused as she grew the additional chair, forming the seat before raising roots to create the back. "For a long time, Sephysis was kept by my son."

Amarie kept the surprise from her face.

I guess she is willing to share information, too.

"I thought it hadn't chosen a wielder in a long time." Amarie narrowed her eyes.

Melyza shot her a suspicious sidelong look. "It never chose him. He inherited it from his father, who also kept it against its will."

"If you're worried about that, it is not being kept against its will now." Amarie wondered how one would keep the blade in such a state. The thing was volatile and powerful, and even the faction had to pull out all the stops just to contain it.

The auer stared at her, the intensity almost enough for Amarie to look away. "Are you saying it chose someone?" She asked the question slowly, carefully, before retrieving the kettle from the fire and filling the mugs.

The scent of bergamot and lavender, with the lighter notes of mint, filled the home, and Amarie could have sworn she heard Dani purr.

"It did." Amarie dared not share who, just in case this woman worked with Uriel. If the master of Shades had intended to bring her the blade, then she had to know more about it than him.

"The wielder will have their work cut out for them. If Sephysis is back in the world, it will be seeking vengeance for all its suffering. I had hoped it would be brought to me before anything irreversible happened." An undercurrent of emotion lingered in Melyza's tone, and her gaze turned to study the fire.

"Why?" Amarie tilted her head, holding her mug and enjoying the warmth. "Alana told us—"

"Alana?" Melyza's head snapped back to her. A dark wariness lurked within her gaze. "Her loyalties lie with Uriel. Do yours as well?"

"No," Amarie whispered, forming a fist with her free hand beneath the table, where her power gathered. "Alana betrayed him, in the end, and helped us. What of your loyalties?"

Melyza quirked a single thin eyebrow as she lifted her own mug to her lips. "I find that idea an interesting one. Though, I suppose Alana tended to shift her loyalties wherever best suited her."

The picture of comfort, Dani pulled her mug off the table and cradled it in her lap, snuggled into the chair like she could sleep there.

Nothing ever gets under her skin.

"You didn't answer my question," Amarie said softly.

Melyza smiled against the rim of her mug. "I suppose I'm similar to Alana in that way. I place them where it best suits me. And if you have Sephysis, and Uriel does not... that means I am *your* ally."

Amarie hesitated, letting silence fall for a few breaths before she released her hold on her Art. "Why does Uriel want Seph?"

A chuckle vibrated from the auer's chest. "A nickname. That's cute." She sipped her tea. "The information about that dagger is incredibly sensitive and even more dangerous. You mustn't share it with anyone you wouldn't trust with the lives of all your loved ones."

Amarie looked at Corin, who gave her a subtle nod. "We understand."

"That doesn't mean I trust *you*."

Opening her mouth to argue, Amarie paused and closed it.

She has no reason to trust us. It's fair.

Amarie sighed. "All right. Then what do you want to know?"

"I want to know everything you do about Uriel." Melyza lifted her chin. "All of it."

When Amarie looked at Corin again, he pursed his lips, but gave the same nod as before.

Dani hummed. "I hope you enjoy long stories."

The corner of Amarie's mouth twitched. "Long story indeed. You already know I'm the Berylian Key, but let me tell you about the first time I met Uriel."

And every time after that.

This wasn't the time to hold back—to be secretive—so she told the auer all of it. They sat for a long while, everyone listening to her talk. She shared each encounter with Uriel, her relationship with one of his Shades, and how Kin broke away from his master. When she spoke of Matthias, Melyza seemed heavily invested, even letting out a sigh of relief when Amarie reached the part of the story where Matthias was freed by the Rahn'ka and his friends.

Amarie kept sensitive, irrelevant details out of her story. Like her daughter. And as many names as she could.

"And now all of you, all affected by Uriel in your own ways, have gathered together." She eyed Corin and Dani. Both pieces of different stories about the master of Shades. "To what end? Why come together?"

Amarie glanced down at her empty cup of tea.

Is it safe to tell her?

Doubt, even if just a shadow, made her want to keep her mouth closed. "Haven't I given you enough to at least tell us why Uriel wants Sephysis?"

Melyza considered. "I told him to bring it to me in exchange for information. I intended to destroy it, which I suspect would have upset him after he learned the bloodstone blade is also part of what he hopes to accomplish."

"Which is?"

"Tell me, first. I will tell you his goals, if you tell me yours."

Amarie took a deep breath, weighing her options. They hadn't learned enough, yet. "We built a prison. Our plan is to use it."

Melyza frowned. "Impossible. You'd need Uriel's blood to perform Taeg'nok, and his original body was lost long ago."

"It was," Dani whispered, sitting sideways now with her legs hanging off the chair's armrest. "Until we retrieved the original lock from within the maelstrom."

The auer's attention slowly shifted to the Dtrüa. She parted her lips to speak, but nothing came out until she looked at Amarie again. "You actually built it?"

Amarie nodded. "With the help of our winged friends. It waits for him."

Melyza exhaled long and slow through her nose. "You have limited time to accomplish that. Uriel is more determined than he has been in centuries and seeks to cause a second Sundering."

Her heart stuttered, all the mentions in the ancient tomes she'd read years ago about the Sundering surfaced in her mind. "How? How would he do that?"

The auer shifted in her seat, leaning on the table. "With Sephysis," she whispered, despite the solitude and wards. "And *you*."

Amarie swallowed hard. "What does that mean?"

"It means that if Sephysis collides with the Key, Uriel will end this world as we know it." Melyza's tone left no room to doubt. "This time, the Art could be stripped from the lands, and all who wield it with it. You must never go near Sephysis. Never again."

Dread chilled Amarie's insides, knowing what the auer suggested was impossible. Not when she and Kin were both needed to imprison Uriel. "Are you sure?"

Melyza gave a grim smile. "Its name is Sephysis, the bloodstone blade of Fylinth, destroyer of Mentithe, and protector of the Key."

Dani frowned. "Protector of the light," she corrected, echoing Amarie's very thought.

"Light and Key in Aueric are the same word, but context determines the meaning. Someone did a shit translation. Though, that part of the title was only true the last time Sephysis was used to cause a Sundering. This time, things would be different because of the way the Art is spread. When it caused the first Sundering, the world was called Mentithe, and it was a great Aueric empire. Everyone has forgotten, and the auer, now a shadow of what they once were, are grateful that the now-powerful humans don't remember their history as slaves."

Amarie sat silent as Melyza continued, "Sephysis destroyed the Berylian Keystone to cause the first Sundering, but the blade preserved the power by channeling it into a bloodline. Which is where it got its name."

"How do you know all this?" Corin spoke for the first time. His hand had finally left his sword, and now his arms crossed against his chest.

"Because my husband was the one who imprisoned Sephysis, and we were both there when the Keystone shattered." Melyza's throat bobbed. "I was powerless, then, to stop it, but when the Key's power leapt to a nearby human woman, it nearly destroyed her, too. I helped her manage it, and when my husband tried to stop me, I killed him. Not to save the human, but because of all those years he kept me complicit with his crimes against our own people and the world. He used the dagger as a threat, but it no longer mattered. I finally had the power to stop him, and I took my opportunity."

Water welled in Melyza's eyes, a tangle of anger and sadness in her dark irises. "Unfortunately, my son continued Sephysis's enslavement for many decades after that, and when he grew tired of my attempts to make him see reason, he banished me from Eralas."

"Banished you?" Amarie's brow furrowed. "But only the council can do that. Who is your son?"

"If you have met the council, you have met him. Sephysis will be seeking revenge, seeking to end his life."

Amarie's blood ran cold.

Melyza bowed her head. "My son is Lo'thec."

Chapter 27

THE SWAMP'S SCENTS SWIRLED AROUND Dani in a haze of muddy green and brown, but sparks of pink and orange suggested they were nearly free of it. Back into the forest and that much closer to a lift back to Kiek.

With all they'd learned from Melyza, her head spun. They walked in silence, the others presumably just as distracted with their heavier-than-usual steps. The journey back would take another half-hour, perhaps more, at this speed, but fatigue eked through her muscles.

Her descent into the ruins had been... interesting, to say the least. The entire interior had been nearly perfectly sideways, creating dangerous drops and steep sloping hallways she'd not enjoyed traversing.

And all that trouble for a plant pot.

Following that up with a grygurr encounter that could have ended much worse, she supposed she should be grateful.

Twenty years ago, these escapades would have had a lesser effect, but at nearly fifty-four, she required more rest in between adventures.

Dani, can you hear me? Katrin's voice echoed clearly through her mind.

Dani paused her lope only briefly before replying. *Yes. Is something wrong?*

No. Not wrong, but I found something interesting. Maybe you could double check it for me?

Dani's step slowed as her vision shifted. She'd grown used to the abrupt change over the years she and Katrin shared their élanvital connection, but sharp sight still drew a soft gasp from her.

Distantly, Amarie spoke to Corin. "I think she's connected with Katrin."

Aidensar's royal library shelves expanded before her. The space was massive, larger than the one in Nema's Throne. She stood—Katrin stood—at the center, where the space opened in an oval, shelves pushed against the walls. A long hallway ran ahead of her, illuminated by large iron chandeliers, with yet more shelves.

Katrin looked down, leading Dani's vision to the book in her friend's hands. The handwriting looped in graceful curls, a stark contrast to the jagged scribbled image on the right page. She hadn't ever directly seen a Corrupted before, beyond her cloudy vision, but she recognized the wicked claws of a wolf-like creature, a serpent's tail curved above a spiked spine.

When Dani had first shared sight with Katrin, she'd been unable to read. The skill was useless to her, but in the time since waking the queen from Slumber, she'd taught Dani to read Common and a few Aueric words.

Is that a Corrupted? Dani sent the question through their bond, vaguely aware of Amarie's gentle touch on her shoulder to keep her walking in the right direction.

Yes, and Melyza knows something more about them. Katrin briefly flipped the cover of the book closed, showing Melyza's scrawled signature on the front. *This is an old journal of hers she gifted to the Aidensar royal family hundreds of years ago.*

Dani halted and heard the others do the same without question. She shifted to her human form and murmured a low, "Katrin needs something. Wait."

Katrin flipped back to the page with the image of the Corrupted, but her finger went to the text on the other side. *My Aueric is still pretty rough, but I'm fairly certain this page describes how the first Corrupted were summoned.* Her delicate fingernail traced to several lines at the bottom.

It says something here about closing. Closing... something. The gate, maybe? But you should ask her about this.

Dani nodded, even though Katrin couldn't see her. *We'll go back. Anything else?*

Katrin snapped the journal shut, pushing it onto the desk as footsteps sounded behind her. She turned, and Dani took in the figure of a middle-aged man, leaning lightly on a cane with spectacles high on his nose.

"Have you been able to find what you're looking for, your highness?" The man folded his hands over the top of his cane, smiling pleasantly.

In a brief conversation at the start of their research here, Katrin had mentioned the librarian had served in Aidensar's military, but an injury during training had landed him as a permanent fixture in the palace library.

"Yes, and Evannika has been quite helpful as well. Though, I'm wondering if you have any more of these journals of Melyza's?" She tapped the cover she'd just closed.

The man's brow furrowed. "Forgive me, but I'm not sure I know who you speak of who's helped you. And unfortunately, that is the only work by that author in this library."

Katrin stiffened, something Dani felt too. "Evannika. Your assistant. She's been helping me for weeks."

Gesturing with his cane, the librarian shook his head. "I'm sorry, but you must be mistaken. I have three assistants, but none with such a name. Valnys is the only female, and there's no way that miserable old hag has been helpful with anything." His grin grew at the joke about his mother, who Katrin had also mentioned, and the Isalican queen gave a half-hearted chuckle.

But a chill crept through Dani's veins on Katrin's behalf. Her own pulse picked up its pace.

"I must be, though your mother truly isn't so bad." Katrin's tone had shifted. "Thank you, Mister Adanac. I hate to be a bother, but could you send for another pot of tea?" She looked towards the pot, but Dani could tell Katrin focused more on the stack of books she and Evannika had assembled together.

What does that mean? Dani's voice darkened. *Where did Evannika come from then? Why help us?*

The librarian nodded, crossing for the door. "Of course, your highness. Just give a shout if you need anything else."

Katrin watched the librarian depart around a shelf before whirling back to the books.

Amarie's touch on Dani's shoulder seemed worlds away.

I don't understand. Katrin started sorting through the books, placing them in different piles as if following some order Dani didn't see. *Evannika was instrumental in a lot of my findings about the Sundering and the ruins. She even told me that the world used to be called Mentithe, and about the old auer empire. Why would she give me that kind of knowledge?*

What did Evannika ask you *about? Anything?* Dread pooled in Dani's gut. *Maybe she needed your trust.* Something jolted through the Dtrüa. *Katrin. The ruins I went in today, where I found the relic... They were sideways, just like she warned.*

Katrin's hands paused as she shook her head, blurring Dani's sight. She hurriedly finished the two piles, one far taller than the other. *It didn't seem like she asked about much of anything. Only told me things, except...*

Her hand went to the smallest of the books, still sitting where she'd put it a moment ago. The olive green cover with Melyza's name signed at the bottom of it.

Except what, Kat? Dani's skin itched, like she wanted to run, but she waited. There was more to this.

She kept asking me about Melyza's location.

Dani swallowed. *Did you ever see her bare arms?* The accusation stung, even to make it. Her own son had been a Shade without her knowledge, and later Liam had confessed that Ryen had only been wearing long-sleeved clothing for months.

Katrin's gaze shifted to a book in the smaller pile, and she grabbed it from the bottom. The queen evidently came to the same conclusion as Dani as she tore the book open to a page with another drawing. A series of geometric symbols along a single vertical line. *No.* Even in her mind, the word sounded hollow. *Dani, you need to get back to Melyza.*

What about you? If Evannika is a Shade, and she knows who you are... You could be in danger, too. Dani hesitated against her previous words to return to Melyza. *We should come get you first.*

Katrin snapped the book shut, standing quickly. Her skirt rustled around her ankles. *Probably a good idea.* She reached to the table in front of her, fingers closing on Melyza's journal. She glanced around before slipping it into her pocket, then grabbed her cloak to bundle it at her hip on top of it. *I'll meet you at the southwest lift.*

Hurry. Dani let the connection weaken then drop.

As her vision returned to herself, clouding over, she breathed harder. "Evannika doesn't work for the library. She asked about Melyza's location, and Katrin never saw her forearms."

Neither Amarie nor Corin needed clarification on what that meant.

The Berylian Key said, "What's the plan?"

"We need to meet Katrin at the southwest lift, then get back to Melyza as fast as we can to warn her." Dani shifted, paws hitting the solid forest floor. She lunged ahead, with the other two running behind her.

They'd disabled the auer's cloaking ward. They'd left her vulnerable.

If Evannika is a Shade...

Sure enough, Katrin waited for them at the south lift, the operator's anxiety thick in the air. But he hadn't left her, and for that, Dani admired his bravery.

With barely a word, they turned around, heading back the way they'd come.

When they reached the sticky swamp ground, Katrin spoke. "Go, Dani, we're right behind you."

Without waiting for further encouragement, Dani picked up her pace. Her paws flew over the soft ground as she hurtled towards the cabin. She didn't look back, scenting the others not too far behind her, though they couldn't keep up. They didn't need to. She just needed to get back... Get back and warn the auer.

What took them half an hour to walk through before, dissolved into a ten minute run.

Dani passed over the spot where the first ward had disguised the cabin, and the scent hit her. Trails of grey and black wafted over her vision, roiling her stomach.

Rot. Decay.

Death.

Dani barreled across the flagstone path, through where the second ward had stopped Corin in his tracks, the odor getting stronger.

Amarie, Katrin, and Corin's footfalls landed soggily on the stones behind her.

"Dani, hold up!"

The Dtrüa couldn't. Not if they'd led a Shade right to...

As she approached the cabin, she hesitated as Amarie shouted the warning again. The grey overpowered her vision, reeking through her nostrils. Unable to bear the smell any longer, she shifted. Clicking her tongue, she called out, "Melyza?"

The others came to a stop beside her, quieting their panting breaths.

"Something ripped the door off," the Key whispered, and her sword sang as she drew it.

Corin did the same, his breath interrupted by a slight gag. "Nymaera's breath."

Katrin stood silent, her scent almost completely hidden among the rot even though she nearly touched the Dtrüa.

No answer came from within, and Dani dared step inside, lowering her voice. "Melyza?"

"Oh, gods," Amarie muttered, voice muffled by fabric as she halted beside Dani. "Oh gods," she repeated, voice shaking. "We need to get out of here. *Right now.*"

Dani couldn't move, dark, blurry vision focused on the shadowed part of the room. Rot drifted from each and every plant in the space, but it flowed the strongest from

Melyza's cushioned chair. Where Dani had sat just over an hour ago.

"She's dead, Dani. We need to go." Amarie tugged on her, hissing under her breath. "Uriel was here. We *need* to go."

"Who's that?" Corin's voice was muffled behind his hand, but Dani followed the direction he spoke, where another cloud of black hovered on the ground in the kitchen.

Katrin's warm scent whispered past Dani, moving towards the rot without hesitation. Her skirt dragged through the dead leaves of Melyza's plants. "It's Evannika." Her voice sounded hollow. "Or what's left of her."

"We should go." Corin's voice, muffled by his hand.

The queen's voice took on a quiet, uneasy tone. "I have one of Melyza's journals, but were there books on that shelf before?"

A short pause came from the others before Amarie replied, just as quietly, "Yes, but they're all gone."

Chapter 28

KATRIN FACED DANI ONCE THEY were all outside, fighting against the instinct to gag at the lingering scent. "We need to portal to Isalica. We can send Corin back to Helgath from there."

"Matthias's study?" Dani asked.

"Yes." Katrin entwined her fingers with Dani's, urging her heart to calm. They'd already stayed too long. But the anxiety made it easier to grasp her Art, the adrenaline helping to fuel the portal that bubbled between them with little thought. Familiar places were always the easiest. Picturing Matthias's study, the scents, the sounds... the feeling of it all flowed between her fingers as she tangled her Art with Dani's.

A dark place in her mind caused the sheen in the air to ripple as she imagined Uriel walking from behind the cabin, but Dani's energy kept it in place. They stepped apart only a few paces, just enough for Corin's broad frame to fit through. Katrin nodded to Amarie first, urging her through the portal.

Corin followed without a second thought, Dani and Katrin slipping through immediately after.

Katrin's vision sparked with color as she crossed through the gap between places, a chilled breeze drifting over her skin before the warmth of Matthias's study greeted her. The familiar scent of him hovering in the air brought instant calm to her turbulent mind.

Even in his absence, the staff still heated the hallway outside the study, and it permeated into the chamber.

Amarie shut the open door, locking it as Katrin and Dani dissolved the portal.

The energy slipped through Katrin's fingers like water, a sensation she always enjoyed, but in the moment it felt even more of a relief. Uriel wouldn't be able to follow them here, and now he was half a world away.

Uriel.

He'd been there, not just a Shade. A Shade couldn't drain the life of a person, but Melyza's remains had been a husk. A dried shell of a body. And only one being in Pantracia could do that.

And Evannika... A plethora of questions came to her mind with her death, too. For a moment, she'd questioned what she'd jumped to conclude. She perhaps wasn't a Shade after all, just in the wrong place at the wrong time looking for Melyza, too.

But Katrin had turned her corpse's arm over and seen the dark shapes etched into her skin, still visible despite her body being drained of life.

The book in Katrin's cloak pocket weighed heavily, both due to the knowledge it contained, but also at her own theft. But leaving behind Melyza's journal, after all they had learned and still needed to, felt like the larger crime.

Hopefully Mister Adanac doesn't notice for a while.

More disturbingly, Uriel had taken all the books from Melyza's cabin, and they had no way of knowing what dire secrets they may have contained.

Everyone seemed to take a collective breath, enjoying the silence and peace of escape.

"Uriel could have known we were there," Amarie breathed, hands on the door as she leaned her back on it.

"We already knew he was seeking Melyza. It's within reason he was there for that purpose and our presence was merely coincidence." Katrin met her gaze. "I wasn't exactly quiet about who I was, and Uriel *does* know me. And Evannika..."

"Why was she there? Wasn't she the one helping you in

the library?" Amarie met Katrin's gaze. "Did I see what I think I saw on her arm?"

Katrin grimaced. "That was the conclusion Dani and I came to that led to the rush back. I'm sorry we didn't have time to explain."

"Why the hells would he kill his own Shade?" Corin's eyes darted to the back of the room as if he was searching the shadows as much as Katrin was.

Amarie let out a breath. "Uriel probably doesn't have enough power to maintain Shades. Looks like he drained her along with everything else here. Or maybe she said something she wasn't supposed to to Katrin?"

"She was rather excited about history." Katrin shook her head. "I should have known something was wrong with her when she kept asking about Melyza."

"So we led him straight to her." Amarie's throat bobbed. "We *killed* her." Color still hadn't returned to her face, and her hands shook until she formed fists.

Corin put a hand on Amarie's shoulder. "It's not our fault."

She turned wide eyes on him. "Then whose is it, if not ours?"

"His. He would have found her another way, and you know it. Melyza was never safe from him with the knowledge she had." Corin crossed his arms.

Amarie's head tilted, her jaw flexing. "I disabled that first ward. I didn't even..."

"Don't dwell on it. Knowing Uriel, he would have found a way to her whether or not we had been part of it." Katrin shifted, the bound journal in her pocket bumping her hip. "What matters is what we've learned. And that we use it to stop him from doing anything like this again."

The Key cast her gaze downward but said nothing more.

Katrin took a deep breath in the silence. "We need to stick to the plan. The others will be reuniting with us here in a couple weeks. Until then, we try to digest all we've learned so we can share it."

"I should return to Helgath and fill Jarrod in." Corin let his hand drop from Amarie, though his gaze lingered on her until she nodded at him.

Dani only nodded, lifting her hands back towards Katrin.

"Probably best to warn him and Rae that Uriel is in Aidensar, too." Katrin met Dani's hands, already pouring her energy in. "Jarrod's study?" She waited for the Dtrüa's acceptance before their power surged together.

The portal stretched as Dani worked with Katrin, sparking and brightening as it took shape once more. Sweat beaded on Dani's brow, her hands shaking as she drew long, deep breaths through her nose.

Snapping into position, the portal gleamed with undulating color.

But before Corin could walk through, the surface shimmered and Katrin's heart leapt into her throat. "Someone's coming through."

"Should we close it?" Dani's cloudy gaze darted to her.

Leaving no time for anyone to answer, a form emerged from the portal, and Jarrod's gaze met Corin's.

Relief sagged across the Helgathian king's face. "Gods, it's good to see you're all all right."

"What—" Amarie glanced at Corin, who looked just as confused by his husband's presence. "Were you waiting for us?"

"Aye." Jarrod nodded, shadows lingering behind his gaze. "Something has happened." His throat bobbed, but no one dared interrupt. "Smoke rises from Eralas. Dragons have been spotted."

"Why in Nymaera's name would dragons be attacking Eralas?" Corin turned his attention towards Dani and Katrin.

Dani shook her head. "I know not."

"Rae is there with Maith," Jarrod added tightly.

Katrin's heart thundered. "There has to be an explanation. The dragons may not like the auer very much, but they've never shown signs of thinking of attacking anyone." She met Dani's cloudy gaze. "Liam's in Draxix. Maybe he'll know what's going on?"

Dani nodded, her breathing shallow and fast.

"I have reason to believe that some or all of the auer elders had foreknowledge of the attack." Jarrod looked at Amarie, then Katrin. "You need to warn those in Isalica. We lost sight of the dragons during the night."

"Isalica will also send aid to Helgath. I suspect you'll be receiving quite a few refugees in the coming days." Katrin's mind already whirled with the implications. They couldn't be certain it was the dragons they knew who'd orchestrated an attack, but Liam would be the one with answers to that.

The Helgathian king gave her a single nod. "Appreciated."

"Uriel was in Aidensar," Amarie added. "But it was possible he was only there for a short duration. He could be behind this. Let us know if you hear from Rae."

"Aye," Jarrod whispered, then looked at Katrin. "I'll have General Auster communicate with your Sixth Eye liaison if we learn anything. And keep us updated on what's happening with the dragons."

Once Katrin nodded her agreement, Jarrod reached for Corin, and they passed through the portal to Helgath together.

Katrin met Amarie's eyes and read the emotions there. No one voiced the question.

What if Rae is dead?

Dani worked on closing the portal.

Katrin wished she could help, but her hands shook every time she started to raise them. "Amarie is right. It's more plausible that Uriel is behind the attack on Eralas than the dragons, but we shouldn't take any chances. Until we know more, let's stick to our plans. I've seen Rae survive a dragon attack before..." She said the words to try to calm the roiling of her own stomach. "I'm sure she's fine. We need to worry about where that flight of dragons is going next."

Chapter 29

IT WAS GONE.

All of it.

Rock... melted. Trees scorched.

Nothing remained after the blackened beasts unleashed their fire.

Ancient stone failed. Cliffs toppled down, swallowed by the ocean in seconds.

Rae shivered, chin quivering. A fire raged on the other side of the beach, its orange glow rippling over the sand in a cruel beacon of warmth.

But she didn't dare get closer.

Lo'thec sat by that fire, surrounded by his Corrupted draconi. The dragons all bore riders, but other than the

Aueric elder, none of those riders bore souls. It'd taken all of her focus to sneak away, out from the belly of the dragon before it crushed her, and seek shelter in a small crevice in the cliff base.

The prison was gone.

All their decades of work, washed away in a single night. Hopelessness loomed in the back of her mind, only overshadowed by the lingering fear that Damien had been within the sanctum.

He should be in Draxix by now.

Rae clung to the thought. To the hope. Moving forward without the prison was devastating enough not to add losing her husband.

In a move of stupid, drastic desperation, she'd attempted to send a message through the faction's device from the belly of the dragon. It had been in working order once more, but after sending the first three letters of her message, the flying Corrupted had jerked sideways and she'd lost her grip.

It'd fallen, disappearing into the fathomless ocean far below.

Idiot.

Wrapping her arms around her knees, she pulled them closer to her chest, the small box Andi had given her digging into her sternum from within her cloak pocket. She'd relieved herself further down the beach, but had eaten nothing save for a few pieces of dried venison stretched sparingly over the day. She removed her earring for a moment—just long enough to pull water from the ocean and filter it—and drank what she could.

Closing her eyes, Rae tried to block out the cold. Her mixed blood prevented her from falling into hypothermia, but it would only hold out for so long.

Visions interrupted behind her eyelids.

There'd been no build up, no warning, as they approached the prison with terrifying accuracy. The Corrupted dragons had blasted it, over and over, with flames hotter than the deepest hell. The cliffside itself had melted, cooling and reforming into a smooth patch of rock.

As the prison—and the sanctum housing it—had fallen, flashes of the guardian's power had rippled through the water. Vibrant waves of bioluminescent blue pulsing outward through the waves, growing more frantic as the structure collapsed in on itself. The Corrupted slammed into the cliffs above, causing rock to rain down. The waves had surged between the twin cliffs, breaking the island in two.

Rae wasn't sure if the waves of Rahn'ka power gave her hope, or only confirmed the demise of the guardian.

Perhaps it wasn't the guardian at all.

The dire thought burned her eyes. It couldn't have been Damien. He would have gotten out. He would have lived.

Survived. Better yet, he wouldn't have still been there at all.

Dark shapes had clouded the water as the prison sank, and Rae imagined more of those wicked sea Corrupted destroying the remnants of the structure.

She dug into her pockets, finding no more of the dried venison. Rising, she stepped silently over the rocky beach, away from Lo'thec's camp. In half an hour, she scavenged a handful of winterberries and edible roots, but it did little to stifle her hunger. By the time she returned to her hiding spot, quiet had settled over the traitorous elder's camp, and she dared a peek.

The Corrupted dragons lay with their heads on the rocks, eyes open. They wouldn't sleep, nor would the Hollow Ones she remembered fighting all too well years ago. But Lo'thec slept.

Rae shifted behind the rock, leaning her head back. She had no idea where they'd go next, but if Uriel kept to his word, he'd rejoin them soon. The thought sent a shudder through her, followed immediately by another shiver. Closing her eyes, she let herself rest, but kept her muscles tense and ready to move at a moment's notice.

She could stay here, instead of enduring more of the freezing air while strapped to the dragon's belly. Someone would come to the prison and find her eventually. But wherever the Corrupted were going... It wasn't good.

Little late to change my mind now.

Movement from the Corrupted, like a uniformed shudder passing through them all, drew her attention back to Lo'thec. The sun had only just begun to crest the eastern horizon, vibrant orange and yellow piercing through the purple dawn. The backdrop seemed wholly out of place as the Corrupted lifted their heads, turning to look towards the opposite side of the beach from where she'd hidden all night. A swell of black ignored the rays of the sun, rising from the sand and stone.

Fear trembled through her again, and she touched her earring to ensure it was locked tight. The tiny key lay tucked in her chest pocket, where the earring had been stored, but using it herself took time and focus and, in more usual circumstances, a mirror. Providing herself drinkable water had been important enough for her to risk relying on her hiding aura with Lo'thec nearby, but she wouldn't risk it again. Not with Uriel here.

The master of Shades corporealized from the blackness as if merely stepping from behind a curtain. Tyranius's familiar face looked contorted now by his possession, eyes turned to dark onyx with flecks of gold. His attire had changed, forgoing the auer's usual flowing tunics for a more Isalican style laced vest and leather breeches.

Strange that he still dresses like Matthias.

Rae's hands shook as she double checked all her blades. As if they'd be of any use against him.

Uriel's gaze turned north towards the sunken 'v' between the cliffs of the island, a satisfied smirk curled on his lips. "I see you were successful." He lifted his hand, a chain twisted between his fingers.

Lo'thec's spine went rigid, his blankets falling from him as he stood. "Does this mean you were as well?" Excitement lingered in his voice.

"Very." Uriel sounded so pleased it made her stomach flop. "Our original suspicions were correct. The journals held the answers I needed. Did you have any problems here?"

"No. Though our water-dwelling *friends* were rather annoying for my Corrupted." Lo'thec glanced towards the sea with a frown. "Plenty of the pests died, but I'm glad we won't be needing my water forces for our next stop."

Rae furrowed her brow.

Alcans?

She had assumed all those dark shapes under the water were Corrupted, but if Lo'thec meant the alcans had been killing his Corrupted...

Rae tucked that piece of information away to dwell on later.

"How much longer can you hold them here?" Uriel stalked around the campfire Lo'thec had maintained through the night.

One of the Corrupted dragons smacked another with its tail, earning a snarl and snap of jaws. It retaliated, but Lo'thec shouted at them, "Enough!"

The auer refocused on Uriel. "Three more days, maybe."

Uriel's upper lip curled. "You said you'd have a week."

"I guessed. Can't say I've ever controlled Corrupted *dragons* before. I can hardly even sleep without the tether thinning." Lo'thec twisted as one of the dragons growled, glaring at it. "Shut. Up."

The creatures had bickered like this throughout the night, but Rae hadn't thought much of it. She knew little about how the bond between a summoner and Corrupted worked, considering the stance Jarrod had taken against them after he ascended the Helgath throne, but now she wished she'd done more research.

Looking unimpressed, Uriel sighed. "Then we better get moving. It will take us another two days to reach Draxix."

Rae's stomach dropped out, time slowing as that sentence replayed in her mind.

Two days to reach Draxix.

All thoughts of Corrupted vanished from her mind. Uriel knew how to get to Draxix.

And he was taking these monsters.

Lo'thec's expression soured. "You're certain that's the best move? Aren't there places we could attack with less... defenses against my dragons?"

Uriel's calm demeanor finally cracked as he snarled at Lo'thec. "Your dragons?" Power crackled at his hands, shadow tendrils snaking around his feet. "*Your* dragons?" he repeated, advancing on Lo'thec as the darkness around him grew.

The auer shrank back, lifting his hands. "That's not what I meant."

Uriel snatched the auer's hand, wrenching it to the side to reveal the brand of the Shade on his forearm. "You belong to *me*. We attack Draxix. I do not need to justify my plans to *you*."

Rae's eyes widened, her head spinning, but thoughts were impossible beyond her thundering heart.

Lo'thec nodded. "Draxix, then."

Chapter 30

Kin kept his body close to Xykos as they flew, absorbing the warmth radiating from the wyvern. Very little of it permeated his thick clothing, but it helped.

Anything helped.

Winter in Isalica was brutal, but winter in Isalica at a high altitude before dawn?

Practically torture.

Coltin had warned him, had made sure the king wore enough layers, enough wool and furs, but the icy wind still froze his eyes and cheeks.

Almost there.

Kin angled the wyvern to descend, flying beneath the clouds for a time. It was less frigid, but made them more visible to those on the ground. Not ideal, but would have to do for the time being, and the dimness of dawn would aid their stealth for a little longer. Nema's Throne was only a few hours away now, beckoning to him on the horizon with the promise of warmth.

As the first light of day glimmered along the eastern sky, Kin cherished the sight. Pinks and oranges would soon stretch through the clouds, but the grey moments before the color were often his favorite. The promise of beauty to come.

They soared over the lowest regions of the Yandarin Mountains, keeping far enough away not to get swept into the snow swirling around the peaks.

Kin eyed the blizzard, hoping they'd be able to avoid it completely, but narrowed his eyes at the distant shapes dappling the sky near the mountain range. To be visible at this distance, whatever it was had to be huge.

He glanced towards Isalica's capital, the city a dappled shape among the white fields of snow and diamond-like towers of the palace. Debating the promise of respite versus getting a closer look, Kin gazed at the mountain.

He'd only seen Thrallenax at a distance during his hurried flight from the prison to Lungaz, rushing to rescue his wife and daughter. He'd certainly not given it much attention. But this close, the mountain made him feel infinitely small.

The black shapes, gliding along the distant ashen cliffs

and white slopes, were much larger than his wyvern.

Are those dragons?

It made sense, considering how close they were to the supposed portal into Draxix. He didn't know much about its actual location other than it was on the mountain somewhere. But the impression he'd gotten from Matthias was that only a handful of dragons even ventured out of the mountain, and he didn't see the familiar gold or green of the two he'd met. Each of these were black. But they weren't... right. Something about their silhouette and the curve of their spines into their tails, the way they moved, even.

He'd seen movement like that before.

Very, very recently.

Nymaera's breath.

Kin's chest hollowed out.

Those are Corrupted dragons.

They headed straight towards the dragons' domain and there was nothing he could do, not on a single wyvern only a third their size.

Dread clutched him as he looked back to Nema's Throne. There was only one thing he could do. Hope someone in the palace knew a way to contact anyone in Draxix to warn them.

What if Uriel is among them?

"Vah, Xykos!" Kin squeezed with his calves, urging the wyvern to fly faster.

Damn the cold. Damn his frozen fingers. He needed to get to Nema's Throne as fast as possible.

"Vah!"

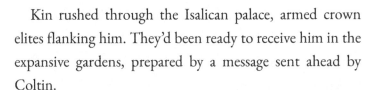

Kin rushed through the Isalican palace, armed crown elites flanking him. They'd been ready to receive him in the expansive gardens, prepared by a message sent ahead by Coltin.

He'd nearly doubled over in relief when the guards told him that Katrin, Dani, and Amarie had arrived at the palace two days earlier, and his skin buzzed at the idea of finally seeing his wife again. It felt far longer than only a month and a half apart.

The crown elites kept a formidable pace, which Kin appreciated given the time sensitive nature of the news he carried. As much as he wanted to shout the warning to every person in the palace, he contained the panic, knowing it would only make things worse if shared with the wrong people. Corrupted dragons... Best to keep that revelation contained to only those he trusted most.

They rounded a corner, and the guards stopped by open double doors, dipping their chins to encourage Kin to enter the room.

"Kin?" Amarie's voice echoed from inside, and a breath later, her face appeared, wide-eyed. She bolted for him, so much relief etched into her features that he wondered what hell she'd been through. She hesitated for a moment, eyes snagging on Sephysis before her stride continued with less vigor.

There was so much to tell her. The dragons. Ahria. But all of the words vanished as she collided with his chest and his arms wrapped around her. He eagerly breathed her in, using the sensation to ease the tension and cold still lingering in his limbs.

Amarie pulled back from the embrace, but kept her arms around his neck. "Coltin's message was vague. What happened? Is everyone all right?"

Dani and Katrin stood at the far side of the room, talking quietly to each other, but they paused to listen for his answer.

"I'm not sure. Conrad sent word two weeks ago that they were heading here. Ahria hasn't been well, and it seems to be Art related. But we have bigger problems." He looked over to the Isalican queen and Dtrüa. "I think Draxix might be in danger."

Dani glanced at Katrin, then back at Kin. "Why? Did you see something?"

"Uriel has himself a new summoner. A powerful one. Corrupted dragons. I didn't get terribly close, but they looked and maneuvered like Corrupted. And they were flying near Thrallenax. Their movement looked deliberate, like they were searching for something."

The Dtrüa let out a colorful curse. "First Eralas, now Draxix?" She angled her cloudy gaze at Katrin.

"Eralas?" Kin looked at Amarie as his wife nodded, expression grave.

"Eralas fell three days ago."

"Nymaera's breath."

"Jarrod hadn't known detailed information about the culprits. He only said dragons... but if they're Corrupted..." Katrin reached for Dani, touching her arm. "Do you think Uriel discovered the entrance to Draxix?"

"It's possible. He's had plenty of time and Shades to sacrifice to the cause. And he stole all Melyza's journals. Who knows what knowledge they held." Dani strode towards them, clicking her tongue. "We need to leave immediately. Liam is there. Matthias and Damien are there." She halted at the doorway, where the crown elites still waited. "Signal Zedren and Zanmea to land, Zaniken can stay here to protect the city. Prepare their saddles. I want to be airborne in less than an hour."

"Right away, General." They departed immediately, steps hurried.

"I couldn't tell if Uriel was with them." Kin had hoped that Damien and Matthias's journey might have been slow enough to keep them away. But now they would be in the center of whatever destruction the Corrupted intended, along with Dani's husband.

Dani faced him. "If Uriel flies with them, then the laws of travel do not apply to him. He was *just* in Aidensar. And if he can move that fast, Draxix might already be under attack."

"Uriel has access to a shadow realm that allows him to be almost anywhere instantly. You're right, the laws have never applied to him." Kin shuddered.

"We're coming with you to Draxix." Amarie glanced at Kin for his nod of confirmation.

There would be no convincing her out of it, and if all the others would be there... Kin and Amarie could make a difference.

The Isalican queen lifted her brow, and her eyes darted from Amarie to Kin—no, not him—Sephysis. "Are you sure that's wise?"

Dani narrowed her eyes but said nothing.

Amarie stepped away from Kin, pausing before answering, "We don't know if Uriel is even there, and Kin has it under control."

"I'm missing something." Kin placed his hand on the hilt of the bloodstone blade, looking at his wife. The blade pulsed once against his fingertips as if it knew already what they were afraid of.

The Dtrüa leveled her gaze just above his head. "Uriel seeks to cause another Sundering. We must take care to prevent giving him such an opportunity."

Kin's limbs numbed. And the study spun around him in a haze as he repeated the phrase back to himself. "Did you say *Sundering*? That's a far cry different from what he's always sought before. He wants to rule the human kingdoms, but that would destroy them..."

Katrin nodded gravely. "We think he knows he's lost too much ground to recover. Think about what we've accomplished in recent years. What he's lost..."

"He now seeks to destroy that which he cannot have." Dani tilted her head, her shoulders sagging.

"But how..." Kin glanced between the women. "No one knows why the first one even happened."

When he looked at Amarie again, his wife cringed. "That's... not entirely true. Melyza told us how he plans to accomplish it. If Sephysis collides with the Berylian Key, if it cuts me..." Her throat bobbed. "It's all over."

Sephysis thrummed against his thigh, as if confirming what Amarie said. And cold joined the numbness in Kin. His throat swelled, and he looked to his wife, realizing the impending danger his mere presence posed not just to her, but their daughter.

"Maybe you should stay here?" Amarie murmured the words, meeting his gaze.

"No. You're not going to Draxix without me. And Sephysis could be a big help. It's not limited by gravity." Kin kept his hand on the blade now, something in him wanting the extra security to make sure it didn't move without his knowing.

Like when it decided to carve up my desk.

"But can you control it?" Dani blinked in his direction. "If Uriel is there... Can Sephysis be compromised? Melyza warned us it would seek vengeance against Lo'thec, one of the auer elders." Her blind eyes bored into him. "If you have any doubt about your control over the blade..."

"I'm in control." He urged the dagger to stop buzzing on his thigh to prove it to himself, and Sephysis went dormant. "We don't know that Uriel will even be in Draxix. I'm coming with you."

"All right," Katrin murmured, and the others nodded. "We'll open a portal. Meet us at the landing in the garden." She walked off with Dani down the hall, leaving Kin and Amarie alone.

Kin's mind still spun. "Did Dani say that Uriel was in Aidensar? You saw him?" He couldn't help the concern slipping into his tone.

"Yes and no." Amarie slid her touch down his arm, taking his hand. "He killed Melyza after we left. I don't think he knew we were there, though." She tugged on his hand. "Walk with me."

Kin held tight as they strode through the palace, and they filled each other in on their adventures.

As they stood in the armory, Amarie strapped blades to her body and braided her hair. "Do you have any idea what might be wrong with Ahria? Matthias's brother, Seiler, said Micah went to pick them up from the port. She and Conrad should be here in a couple days." Her voice was soft, now, speaking of their daughter, and heavy with worry.

Kin felt only the slightest pang of guilt for being relieved they hadn't made it to Nema's Throne yet. Ahria would likely have insisted on joining them in Draxix as well.

But she'll stay safe here.

"Conrad wasn't very forthcoming about her symptoms, but it's understandable considering the danger of the message being intercepted. Do you think it could be related to the power you gave her?" Kin touched Sephysis at his thigh, the only blade he ever carried now.

A few more wouldn't hurt.

The bloodstone blade already hummed in anticipation of what was to come, some disapproval arising as Kin added a sword to his right hip.

"I don't see how. She has a small portion of it, and the power has never made me sick." Amarie finished latching two swords to her back before slipping a knife into each of her boots. "What if Uriel did something to her?" Quiet fury tainted her tone.

The thought had crossed Kin's mind, but he'd tried not to linger on it. There was no telling what the master of Shades might have done to their daughter in the time he held her. And Ahria, herself, hadn't been able to recall all of it due to the torture she'd endured. The thought made Kin's blood heat, and Sephysis eagerly drank in his anger. "If he did, then Damien should be able to tell. So he better not die in Draxix today."

Chapter 31

MATTHIAS COULD SEE THE TOP. Only minutes now, and they'd be at the summit.

After the news from Zelbrali, they'd intensified their pace, taking less breaks and pushing themselves through their exhaustion. The night before, they'd debated climbing through the night since they were so close, but decided having a full night's rest would be more beneficial than reaching the summit while the Primeval slept.

The king hauled himself up the last of the climb, gaining a glimpse of the barren mountain top before turning to monitor Damien's progress only a few feet below him.

A light mist permeated the air, dampening his clothes and hair. A welcome change to the sun beating on them, had it not made everything slippery.

He'd already jumped twice that day, saving them from a long plummet to their deaths.

As Damien neared the top, Matthias backed up, ready to help if needed, but the Rahn'ka pulled himself to his feet beside him.

The summit was nearly perfectly flat, with sparse vegetation and a lone pedestal at the center.

Matthias looked sidelong at his friend, catching his breath. His pack weighed on his back, but he didn't dare put it down yet. "Not exactly what I imagined we'd find here."

A mountain peak is rather exposed for it to be the actual meeting spot for the Primeval.

"I swear, if this is another step in the fucking trial..." Damien stomped forward, stepping in his usual uneven walk even in his frustration. He approached the pedestal, Matthias close behind.

"What do you suppose this is?" Matthias eyed the small structure. Dark stones piled into a round column as tall as his waist. Nothing rested atop, yet he hesitated to touch it.

"I don't sense anything from it. But I didn't sense the portal hovering over a fiery death either." Damien crossed his arms lightly, studying the pedestal. "Did I miss something else Liam said while I was talking to the flowers? He just said we had to get to the top of the mountain, right?" A tension lingered in the Rahn'ka despite his attempts at humor. It was the news of Eralas, still hovering like a storm cloud. And Rae's presence there.

Matthias shook his head. When they'd stayed the night at Liam's cabin, the man hadn't mentioned any other steps. "No..." He rolled his lips together, breathing normalizing now, and hovered his bare hand over the stone. "Should I touch it?"

Damien shrugged. "What's the worst that could happen? Other than possibly spontaneously exploding?" He sighed. "I don't like that I can't sense any of the Art the dragons use."

"Well, we didn't come this far to climb back down." Matthias sucked in a deep breath and placed his palm against the smooth, warm rock. It immediately started to glow, and he narrowed his eyes. No sensation, heat or cold. He looked at Damien, keeping his hand on the pedestal. "Maybe it needs both of us."

Damien considered for a moment, maybe still trying to reach out and sense something with his Art. He finally sighed and extended his hand to the pedestal. "Either this works, or the dragons are having a nice laugh about how stupid we look up here."

The stone beneath his hand began to glow as Matthias

laughed, and then a deep rumble echoed through the king's head. A voice like Zelbrali's, but somehow more immense, like the mountain itself, spoke directly into his head.

You have passed your trial.

He barely had time to read the recognition in Damien's gaze before everything around him winked out of existence.

The mountaintop. The sky. The thin open air.

All vanished.

Color spread across his sight, reminding him of the first step through one of Dani and Katrin's portals. He kept his breathing steady, unable to see the Rahn'ka as his body tumbled through nothingness.

Then his boots connected with something solid, and the world dimmed.

Matthias's mouth fell slightly open as he took in their stark change of environment. Walls surrounded them, over a hundred feet high, on all sides. Walls that curved at the base, just enough to... No, not walls. Natural rock.

And within the giant space, open to the sky, were eight massive pillars each as wide as a single-residence home. They stretched upward at a height that made Matthias crane his neck to see the top.

What is this place?

Foliage painted the rough ground beneath his feet, vines

spreading like a net cast from several trees growing near a distant rock face. Some of the pillars had moss along the cracks and carvings, while others looked new or barely ravaged by time, each with a decorative capital on top. A distant rumble of thunder drew Matthias's gaze skyward, where he could see the rim of stone creating a circular frame of dark thunderclouds. Like he looked up from the bottom of a massive bowl.

Damien stepped up beside him, his gaze with Matthias's as another thunderclap echoed down into the crater. "Looks like we finished our climb just in time."

Movement brought his attention back to the top of one of the pillars. A shape shifted atop it, like the pristine carved stone moved.

Matthias's eyes widened as he took in the enormous lone dragon perched high above them.

Nymaera's breath.

He'd never seen a dragon as large as this one, its deep violet scales shimmering in the muted light like they were mixed with crushed diamonds. It stared at them, massive claws gripping the edge of the pillar's capital as it peered down. Golden horns curved delicately back from its head, and spikes ran along its jaw.

Ants. They were ants to this being.

Beside him, Damien barely breathed.

"Humans." The dragon's gravelly voice echoed through

the space, easily heard even from so far away. "You have survived the climb to Oias's Peak. And now you dwell in the crown of Omin."

Matthias swallowed, placing his pack on the ground behind him. "We are honored—and humbled—to be in your presence. Thank you for meeting with us. Will..." He glanced at Damien before refocusing on the Primeval present. "Will others be joining us?"

"We are all present," the great dragon answered, bellowing a puff of smoke towards the top of another pillar, where it swirled and rippled off what Matthias had thought a stone capital. But with the stark relief of the smoke, he could make out horns. Teeth.

Skulls. They were dragon skulls. And each of the other pillars bore one of various, massive size. Some looked far older than the others, and he realized the state of the pillar seemed to match that of the skull. And the truth settled.

Oh, gods. Do the other dragons know?

"You are king of the frozen lands humans call Isalica." It was not a question, but Matthias nodded once before the Primeval's attention swung to Damien. "And you are one of three embers of Rahn'ka power remaining in this world. You are the strongest of them, but that is only temporary."

Damien frowned, a vein near his jaw pulsing. "And you're the Primeval." He gave Matthias a sideways glance as he stripped his own pack off. "The only one?" He didn't seem afraid of pointing out the obvious, possibly sensitive subject.

The dragon's chest rumbled, but with what emotion, Matthias couldn't tell. "I am the Fifth Prime. The last remaining Primeval."

"We've come seeking your advice and aid." Matthias had never felt so small, but he dared not show his nerves. "We strive to imprison Uriel, and assistance from the dragons would go a long way."

"While a noble goal..." The dragon's tail curled around the backside of the pillar, neck arching down towards them. "We have already given what aid we can." It shifted, gaze moving to the skulls upon the surrounding pillars, but didn't speak whatever thoughts came with the glance.

Damien stepped forward. "We are grateful for the help with the construction of the prison. And for the dragons that already fight alongside us, but—"

"You cannot have more," the dragon boomed, amethyst eyes reminding Matthias of Amarie. "We have no more to give to your cause. I wish you luck in your endeavor against Zuriellinith."

Matthias bristled, but fought to control his frustration.

Luck?

The king clenched his jaw. "Why? He was once one of you. He now threatens the existence of all those on the mainland continents. And yet you decline our request?" He swallowed and repeated, "Why?"

The dragon's head lowered more, though still only stretched a third of the length of the towering pillar. It blinked, gaze boring into him, but he didn't let himself flinch. "Do you see the strength of the Primeval?"

Matthias opened his mouth to reply, but then closed it. The Primeval were dead, all except one.

"Then can you offer advice at least?" Damien extended his hands in a placating gesture. "We have utilized all sources we might possibly have to learn about Zuriellinith, to discover his weaknesses and purpose. But we've reached the limit of human and Rahn'ka knowledge." He stared up at the dragon, his one eye unflinching. "The Rahn'ka know what it is like to hover near the edge of extinction. And ridding the world of Uriel will only help to protect the dragons that remain."

The Primeval tilted its head, slitted pupil contracting and expanding. "I can offer you insight, if you would like. Insight to why we cannot send our limited remaining numbers into a war against him. To help you understand what you face, should he ever regain the skin of his kin." Its wings flared, blocking out enough of the light to cast a shadow over them both. "But it is not easy to witness, I warn you. It is your choice."

Matthias looked at Damien, heart pounding. "I think we need to know. Whatever it is, if there's a chance it could help..."

The Rahn'ka nodded. "Whatever it takes."

"So be it." The Primeval nearly whispered, "Close your eyes. Clear your mind. And brace yourself."

Matthias did as instructed, eyes shutting out the day, and tried to focus on the sound of his own breathing. He had no idea what he was about to see. *When* he was about to see. But if it was related to Uriel, when Uriel was a dragon...

Something pressed against his senses, bidding him to open his eyes, but when he did, he saw only blackness. He could feel Damien with him, even if he couldn't see the Rahn'ka. He could smell the rainforest, the fresh mist that heralded the coming storm. But the scent faded as a blackness deeper than the back of his eyelids settled.

Despite knowing, panic rose at the back of his throat. A gross familiarity with the worst time of his life. The worst thing he'd ever endured. His heart thundered.

It's not the same. I'm still in control.

The dragon's voice echoed through his head like a guide, deep and consuming, and Matthias let it.

Long ago, before the Sundering shattered the world, Zuriellinith flew as one of us. But he lacked a strong connection to the Art, and became an outcast among dragons. During this time, the world was known as Mentithe.

The world brightened ahead of him. He soared as if on the back of a dragon, but it was different. The colors were more vivid, new depths he'd never known before. Like an entirely new spectrum existed humans couldn't see. It dawned on him that he saw through the eyes of the dragon rather than riding atop it, and excitement bloomed.

He thought for a moment he was over Aidensar, the massive trees with trunks larger than houses, but a string of mountains ahead didn't belong. A deep canyon cut through the land where an ocean should have been. As the view shifted to the right, the canyon lands spread out to encompass a massive city. Its spires were like nothing he'd ever seen. They grew like cave crystals, glittering in a prismatic display. Banking left, something shone in the sun between the distant canyon cliffs, glimmering copper that became clear as they grew closer. A massive gate, with chains the size of ships clanking along the gears as it parted to allow a caravan in the canyon below to pass through.

The auer ruled Mentithe, with humans as their slaves.

And sure enough, humans worked the massive gears, sweating under the sun to turn the cranks as the gate began to close.

Zuriellinith, like all of our kin, was born with a link to the Art, but it never fully manifested. Unlike the others, he never found his place. Never found his other half, his élanvital, if he even had one. He refused to contribute to our way of life, and in turn, was rewarded with torment.

The vision before Matthias swirled, an odd sense of nausea coursing through his body, wherever it was. Massive flakes of snow fell from the sky, already coating the mountain behind. He almost didn't see the dragon before him, the scales blending into the mountainside. Its chest swelled with breath, heaving quicker than Matthias had ever seen Zelbrali do, as the dragon turned to expose its pale belly. A smear of deep maroon stood stark against the snow, the flakes sizzling as it touched the torn flesh. He lumbered towards the injured dragon, taking in the plethora of scrapes and shallow cuts that marred the crystalline scales. The dragon recoiled, wrapping its ridged tail against itself as it backed against the cliffside, leaving a smear of blood on the fresh packed snow.

Zuriellinith was taunted, provoked, often to a level of brutality that left our healers scrambling to save his life. Perhaps it is our fault, for letting it go on as long as we did, but dragons can be merciless.

A fresh layer of snow began to coat the dragon's scales, his golden eyes closing as he tucked his head beneath an outstretched wing.

With no functional level of the Art, he was defenseless against the others. Until eventually, he damned his kin and vanished into the wilds of Mentithe for a hundred years.

Matthias's vision took to the open air, showing the familiar mountainside of Thrallenax against the cloudless sky. There were some peaks beside the mountain that seemed out of place. It also looked smaller, somehow, as if portions of the cliffs hadn't yet erupted from the land. A dark shadow loomed beneath one of the larger cliffs, a massive opening into the mountain itself. The black walls of the cavern were purposeful, the stone melted and smooth. It shone like obsidian with small colorful shapes taking to the air from its edge.

During that time, we nearly forgot about him. The torment he'd endured. We couldn't have predicted what it had forged him into. What he became.

As he flew closer, the shapes became dragons, still small compared to the opening in the mountain. A clear gateway to their more sacred of places. There had been no reason to hide, then.

He returned to Thrallenax, and he was something else entirely. He'd stolen the Art of the Rahn'ka and reformed it into a monstrosity, corrupting its intended purpose—to borrow life essence with permission. But what he became... What he inflicted on those he should only borrow from—no, he only stole—he took by force and gave nothing back. Left nothing for the life energies to regenerate. To survive.

The dragons within the gate to Thrallenax began to dwindle, drawing back into the mountain as the now larger white dragon approached.

Zuriellinith stood stark against the obsidian floor as Matthias dove towards him. The black of the walls around them shone in his depthless eyes, a clawed hand lifting to the golden dragon that'd sailed in behind Matthias. White mist formed around the creature, though white wasn't the right color. Matthias realized it was something he'd never seen before with his human eyes. It swirled through the air, racing from the gold dragon towards Zuriellinith. The strings of the Art shuddered in his vision, dancing through the air as Zuriellinith consumed.

The gold scales tarnished as the dragon collapsed to the ground, wings twitching and drying like a plant left without water. Bones emerged beneath the dull scales, flesh shriveling as the dragon's mouth fell open in a soundless roar. A kernel of white ebbed from the dragon's mouth, and no matter how Zuriellinith pulled at that bright energy, it didn't come. It fell through space and time, Matthias's vision morphing into a mess of darkness as the final sliver of the dragon's life energy found a new resting place. The lightless realm devoured it, leaving strange fractures along the thin mesh of the fabric coating the world in the Art.

In doing so, he created a new hell. And the creatures that now dwell there, summoned to this world by ungodly Art, you know as Corrupted.

His vision shifted back to the land of living, and he tried not to think too long on the fact that he'd just witnessed the first Corrupted being born.

Two dragons, larger than Matthias had ever seen, landed within Thrallenax, the orange glow of the inner mountain shining on vibrant scales. They advanced, but Zuriellinith snarled. He lunged, his body dipping into the shadow at the walls. The white vanished into a pool of oil, which soared over the obsidian floors and surged past the two dragons, who danced to avoid lashes of tendrils.

Matthias lurched forward, narrowly dodging a lash of shadow as it latched onto one of the larger dragons. They screamed, flesh steaming as the shadow drew a grey line of decay through their emerald scales. He dove off the inner edge of the gateway, falling into the hot air of Thrallenax's central chamber. The dim shape of Zuriellinith banked hard against the outer edge of the chamber, his head pointed towards the shadow of another dragon and small stone ovals placed in perfect lines upon the rocky edge closest to the magma pool.

He unleashed his power, destroyed an entire clutch of eggs, and then turned on the dragons who'd guarded them.

Drained their life as if it were a river, leaving a husk of scales behind.

The destruction described played out before Matthias, the shadows licking up the walls of the main chamber towards him. His heart sped as the tendrils lashed out, the vision of the dragon he inhabited fading into blackness.

The Primeval rallied together, driving him away from Thrallenax and permanently exiling him, for the damage to our hatching grounds had been catastrophic. The lives he'd taken and prevented from ever beginning was unforgivable.

And for time, we thought it had worked. That exile was enough. Zuriellinith was gone, but he'd left something behind in the stone. Part of his blight, we soon learned, as over the following decades, eggs failed to hatch. And the ones who did, rarely survived their tenth year. It was chaos, a time of grief and mourning, but also incredible rage. Calls were made to hunt him down, end his life. Force him to reverse what he'd done. But none of that came to pass as he remained unchecked, hiding in the auer's land.

As our numbers decreased, our desire for retribution flourished.

We couldn't allow him to destroy our future anymore than he already had. And the Rahn'ka sought vengeance for what he'd done to their power. So for the first time, dragons and Rahn'ka worked together to create a prison designed to strip Zuriellinith of his draconi flesh and trap his soul inside.

It was our only option, as anyone who ventured to kill him failed.

Brightness filled his vision again, and he glided near a giant stone structure. Stones stacked in a pyramid stood above the swath of dense trees, their leaves brilliant shades of oranges and yellows. A swirl of blue mist hovered over the stone, as if the entire structure glowed with Rahn'ka power.

For a time, the prison contained him. Peace spread through the dragons. Our numbers climbed. We'd nearly recovered entirely from him, but...

When the Berylian Keystone was destroyed, the ley lines ruptured, changing the land, killing tens of thousands, and spreading the Art in a fine mesh. Humans rose against their oppressors with their newly acquired access to the Art, and the auer fled to Eralas after a united rebellion killed more of their already-decimated population.

The image wavered, cracked, suddenly descending into stark, rolling grey hills. The broken land fell into the waves of the ocean as they swelled into a maelstrom where moments ago the prison had stood.

But the Sundering also unleashed Zuriellinith from his prison, unbeknownst to us at first. He overtook the body of another dragon, much as he'd done to you, Isalican king, and he returned to Thrallenax to finish what he'd started.

The damage he'd done to our breeding grounds the first

time paled in comparison to how he razed them the second time. He didn't stop with the young. Once finished with the hatchlings, he moved against the Primeval.

Matthias blinked and dragons fell from the sky above Thrallenax, its face now different. Storm clouds rolled in, dark and brooding, as thunder clapped over the land. Shadow whirled through the sky, wrapping around the onyx scales of a dragon with curved horns. Water poured over the craggy cliffs, the snow melting as fire roared from dragons' jaws against the waves of darkness.

Rain fell, and the vision altered. Zuriellinith disappeared from the sky, the snow shifting to a tropical mist. It was where he truly stood, but at a different time.

The eight pillars stood before him, four bearing the weight of a Primeval rather than only one.

With half of our Primeval remaining, we fled to a new land where he could never find us. But we were not yet safe.

Time seemed to move faster, like the opposite of his own power. The vines around him grew, the foliage thickened. The saplings at the back of the crater grew into trees. The dragons on the pillars faded into only their skulls.

Primeval are not born. They are not sired. It is not a bloodline that decides which dragon becomes a Primeval. To be a Primeval is to be connected to the fabric of the Art directly, giving us access to wonders you can only imagine. Once a dragon reaches its zenith, sometime between one and two thousand years of life, a dragon can evolve. Depending on the nature and strength of their Art. Their connection. These evolutions are impossible to predict.

Because of Zuriellinith's blight, our hatchlings rarely saw adulthood, let alone lived long enough to see the potential of becoming a Primeval. And so, the Primevals have slowly faded into history, lifespans not enough to sustain the loss of our young. Our population.

A sudden shift to the vision came as a shock, and Matthias flew through the air near the peak of Oias. The scent of smoke tangled with the vision of a plume of fire as it erupted from his mouth, targeting a strange black shape.

Something felt different about this vision though, a strange hue at the edges that suggested this wasn't a memory.

A distant roar echoed, and Matthias realized it was his own ears that heard it as the Primeval released him from the vision.

Matthias staggered backward, sucking in a sharp inhale as colors returned to normal, as smells lost their depth. But the smoke remained, another distant cry, but one unlike a dragon's. "What the hells..." He turned to Damien, who looked to the eastern rim of the Primevals' sanctum.

Lifting his gaze, Matthias examined the wafts of smoke in the distance, just high enough to be visible above the rock face.

"That last vision. It was different."

"Because it happens now. You saw through the eyes of one of my kin." The Primeval shifted on top of the pedestal, neck stretching as it also examined the horizon.

"That black dragon looked like..." Matthias met Damien's gaze, hoping the Rahn'ka would contradict him.

Damien grimaced. "Corrupted. With a Hollow One for a rider."

"We must fight." The Primeval's eyes flashed with a bright white light that rippled through its body, followed abruptly by a blaring noise. The alarm rose from the ground itself, vibrating through Matthias's boots. "Zuriellinith has come."

Chapter 32

THE WOOD SAW THUNKED TO the porch as Liam nearly jumped out of his skin. The sound echoing through the valley was unlike anything he'd ever heard. A deep bellowing, woven with high-pitched chimes and bells.

Zelbrali's head lifted from where he'd been napping near the tree line, and the dragon got to his feet in an instant, wings flapping.

"What the hells is that?" Liam hurried down the front stairs, jogging to the side of the cabin where he could look out on the valley. He blinked into the late morning sun as a flock of birds took to the sky from their roosts, noisily protesting the sound.

"There's been a breach." Zelbrali moved close to him, gracefully lowering himself to the ground. "No time for harnesses. I need to get to the access portal and see what's going on. Then get to the roosts."

"I need a minute." He ignored Zelbrali's disapproval before he launched himself back to the cabin. There may not be time for harnesses, but he still needed to be armed. And he hadn't thought to wear his swords while working on repairing his porch. If there was a breach, that meant anything could be in Draxix.

Anyone.

The front door banged against the wall of the cabin, and he snagged his swords from where they sat just inside. Throwing the straps over his shoulders, he lashed them into place as he ran back to Zelbrali. With practiced ease, Liam braced his foot on Zelbrali's elbow, throwing himself up onto the dragon's back without stopping. The dragon took off, wings thrumming in the air as dark shapes manifested in the northern sky.

"Why has this alarm never activated before?" Liam narrowed his eyes on the dragons in the distance, their matte scales twisting something in his gut.

They turned west, towards the lake where the portal hovered, invisible. But the air remained clear, with no signs of the shimmering tear in the fabric activating.

"It has, but not while you've been present. We increased the sensitivity of the alarm, since it failed to notify us when you and your friends accidentally arrived here. It is for

inhabitants of the island, triggered by the Primeval."
Zelbrali banked, satisfied that the portal now lay dormant,
and altered north to follow the intruders.

Liam scanned the water, but his vision snagged on a
dark form on the beach's pale sand.

Something that didn't belong there.

His heart caught only for a moment. "Wait. We need to
go to the lake." The other dragons would be focused on the
invaders, making him and Zelbrali the only ones anywhere
near the portal.

*And whatever is down there could be a threat. Sneaking
in while everyone else is distracted.*

Zelbrali huffed, shaking beneath Liam in disagreement.
He didn't turn, continuing towards the winged fleet
headed for Oias.

*Hopefully Damien and Matthias made it to the top by
now.*

"There's something down there." Liam tapped his heel
hard against Zelbrali's side. "The others can handle the
attackers."

Zelbrali finally tilted his head, gazing at the beach with
slitted eyes. "That's—" The dragon turned without
warning, forcing Liam to grip tighter to his scales as he
propelled them even faster towards the figure on the beach.

The dragon's abrupt change of heart made Liam's chest
squeeze, his adrenaline rising. He drew one sword, unable

to see the target anymore with Zelbrali's head in the way.

"You don't need that." The dragon flew lower, not slowing.

The trees rushed by beneath Liam, and he contemplated ignoring Zelbrali's words before stowing the sword. As the dragon threw out his wings, Liam clutched a rough spine on Zelbrali's back to compensate for the mid-flight stop so he didn't launch clear over his head and straight into the lake. "Warning would be nice before you do that. No saddle, remember?"

"Go." Zelbrali landed, crouching. He ignored Liam's complaint. "Help her."

The dragon turned just as Liam shifted to slide down his side, spying the figure he'd seen from above now at his feet. Soaked, loose strands of her dark hair stuck to her cheek, half-coated in sand.

"By the gods. Rae?" Liam landed next to her, turning her over gently by the shoulder. "Hey, you with me?" He patted her face, fear sparking through him at the woman's blue lips and fingers.

The Mira'wyld's eyes flickered open, dark circles framing them. She rasped through chapped lips, "Uriel is here. In the body of an auer elder." She cringed, shivering despite the warmth of Draxix. "Did Damien... Is Damien..."

"He's here with Matthias, arrived a week ago." Dread pooled in Liam's gut, growing more intense as her eyes slid closed. "We need to get you somewhere warm." Reaching beneath her knees and shoulders, he lifted her from the sand. Zelbrali crouched lower as Liam carried her onto the dragon, and she roused enough to help pull herself onto the dragon's spine.

Rae slumped forward, panting at the effort.

Liam settled behind her, wishing he had a waterskin to give her. "Gentle, this time, all right Zel? Gentle but fast. Take us to the cabin."

"You got it." Zelbrali lifted into the air as Liam kept his arms around Rae. Something bright gold glittered in the corner of his eye and he noted the earring she wore, thicker than the others and ornately carved.

"You've got that thing on." He remembered it from when she'd given it to Ryen to suppress his Shade connection. His heart twisted, jaw flexing. "Where's the key?"

Rae leaned heavily on him, touching a small buttoned pocket just above her breast with a shaky hand. "I can't..."

Liam understood, then. She'd needed to be invisible, somehow managing to come through with the invaders. Uriel must not have been aware of her presence, but with the Isalican cold and how long she could have been in the air...

"You're lucky you didn't drown." He wanted to reach into her pocket and unlock that damn earring right then, but he couldn't risk dropping it.

"I'm part alcan. I can breathe in water," Rae whispered.

Liam snorted. "Of course you are." He should have known better than to second guess one of the women in their assembled group. Every single one of them seemed to have numerous tricks up their sleeves. "You're a mess though, so you'll be sitting this one out." He looked up as Zelbrali crested the cliffside to the cabin, widening his turn towards the clearing to make the bank more gradual.

"I just need Damien," Rae murmured. "I'm weak, but mostly uninjured. And there are things he needs to know."

"I'll tell him about Uriel. It's too dangerous to take you where he is right now." Liam looked at Oias in the distance.

The black forms of the intruders circled the peak, interrupted by various colored shapes of dragons battling them. Streams of the Art flowed visibly in the air between them, but seemed to have little effect on the dark dragons.

They're trying to find the Primeval.

"It's not just Uriel." Rae looked at him, eyes pleading. "There's more. I need Damien."

Zelbrali landed gently in the clearing, and Liam dropped to the ground before reaching up for Rae.

"Then I'll bring him to you."

She slid off the dragon's back, practically falling, and he caught her upright. She swayed, but he looped his arm under her knees again and lifted her off the ground. Her head rested against his chest. "They're Corrupted dragons," she whispered, as if trying to get out all the information she could while he was there to hear her. "Lo'thec... An auer elder is loyal to Uriel. He's the summoner. And hollow ones are here, too. You need to be careful."

He carried her inside, striding quickly for the first bedroom and setting her down on the soft mattress. "We will be careful." Retrieving the key from her pocket, he inserted it into the earring keeping her Art at bay.

"Hurry!" Zelbrali's voice reverberated through the cabin, an answering boom sounding somewhere in the distance.

As soon as the earring clicked and fell into his palm, Rae sucked in a deep breath, and a little color returned to her face. "Get Damien." She stared at him. "Send him here."

Liam set the earring, key still within it, on his desk. "I will." He hurried to the kitchen, grabbing a pitcher of water and the bread basket before returning to Rae. He put everything down within arm's reach of her, eyeing her soaked clothing. "You need to get dry."

"I'll worry about that." Rae reached for the water glass he poured her. "Go. I'm fine."

Turning to the door, Liam could see Zelbrali anxiously pacing out the cabin's front windows. He took one glance back at Rae, assuring himself that the cabin was far enough away from the conflict.

Rushing out the door, Liam hurtled himself onto the dragon's back.

Zelbrali didn't wait for him to be fully seated before he rushed off the cliff face in front of them.

They dove towards the canopy before Zelbrali banked in a different direction than Liam expected. He angled himself away from Oias, where battle between dragons and Corrupted raged, aiming for a vaguely cone-shaped mountain to the west beyond the lake.

"Where are we going?"

"You need to find Damien, and he's with the Primeval, hopefully." Zelbrali's voice rumbled as he beat his wings harder. "The Primeval will forgive the slight of a direct approach given the circumstances. Probably."

"More gambles than I'm used to you being willing to take."

"From what I recall, you once gambled quite a bit yourself." Zelbrali's tone held the undercurrent of a smile, like he knew he had him there.

Liam's face heated. "Not my proudest days. But for both our sakes, I hope you're right on this one."

As they neared the access portal, a familiar popping sound and rainbow-like ripple formed in the air above the water. Liam held his breath as he braced for more Corrupted to appear directly in front of them.

Zelbrali angled his head, eyeing the portal as it formed. Two forms shot out of it, one green and one dark grey. "Looks like we have more help."

Relief poured through him as he looked down at Dani atop Zedren.

Zelbrali opened his maw in a roar towards his fellow dragons, who banked along the tree line at the edge of the lake, turning towards him.

Zedren rose up to fly beside, and Liam looked over at his wife, perfectly at home in the saddle on the neck of the dragon. Below, he could make out Kin and Amarie on Zanmea. And their presence still brought an odd comfort to know they'd come to help.

He'd ask how the hells they knew about the attack on Draxix later.

Liam roughly patted Zelbrali's neck. "I hope you're right about Damien and Matthias being with the Primeval."

"If not..." Zelbrali glanced at the two dragons now flying with them. "We will still need to remain to protect the Primeval. So for everyone's sake, I hope they are there."

Chapter 33

DAMIEN DELVED INTO THE KÁ of Draxix as he looked out on the horizon. His stomach still roiled from instinctual fear when the Primeval had swooped down from her pedestal without warning, plucking the two humans up in her talons like a hawk grabbing its dinner.

But even with her giant talons around him, her ká radiated with something similar to a mother's care, and it imbued trust within him.

The Primeval eyed him for only a moment before her attention shifted back to the view of Draxix. Below, the lake with the entrance portal shimmered in the sunlight. The serenity it conveyed didn't match the chaos that unfolded to the northeast. Oias's summit was just visible beneath a layer of smoke, the trees along its face unfortunate collateral damage to the battle that raged. Six black shapes circled the peak, blasting flame at three dragons who maneuvered expertly around the mountain.

Defending, but also distracting.

Uriel doesn't know where the Primeval is.

Another thought darted through him.

Unless he's after the hatchlings again.

Two shapes appeared above the lake, the air behind them rippling as the portal faded. Zelbrali joined them a moment later, coasting along the water's edge. Turning upward, he skimmed the trees before ascending the mountain Matthias and he now stood upon. As they grew closer, he could make out the shapes of riders on each of them.

Matthias stood next to Damien, staring at Oias. "How did he get Corrupted dragons?" he whispered, throat bobbing. "And do you think he came here himself?"

"He is here." The Primeval's voice boomed. "He rides on one of his abominations." She tilted her head to look at them. "Your friends have come on the backs of my kin. Do you intend to fight with us?"

A pivotal question.

Damien fought the rising dread of facing Uriel. His knee, the one practically destroyed in the fight in the bunker, ached. And a headache bloomed directly behind his missing left eye. He breathed in, accepting the energy offered by the stones and trees of the Primevals' sanctum, using it to banish the pain and terror. "Yes."

"Yes," Matthias echoed at the same time, and the dragon's chest rumbled.

A few moments of strained silence passed before Zelbrali crested the summit, Liam on his neck without a saddle. Beside him, Zedren appeared with Dani, and Zanmea with Kin and Amarie. The three dragons landed on the edge of the mountain, a formidable wall of scales and muscle and power.

It was strange, for a breath, to see them all together in one place after so long. But a piece of that puzzle was missing. The worry for his wife resurfaced. Had these same Corrupted been part of the destruction in Eralas? If it'd been dragons, he could only begin to imagine the devastation.

Rae would find a way to survive.

As if reading his mind, Liam shouted, "Rae came through with the Corrupted!"

Kin and Amarie looked at Liam, but Dani only gazed at the Primeval with cloudy eyes.

"She needs you," Liam continued before Damien could summon the words to reply. "She's in rough shape. But she told me to find you and tell you, Uriel is here in the body of one of Eralas's elders, and Lo'thec is with him."

A rumbling growl started in the chest of the Primeval,

echoed by the other three dragons, and it sounded as if he were suddenly in the middle of a rockslide.

Damien had so many questions about how Rae knew of Uriel, or how she'd even gotten to Draxix, but they were all swallowed by the sudden jolt of fear for her condition. "Where is she?"

"Back at the cabin." Liam slid off of Zelbrali as the golden dragon shifted in anticipation. "You and Matthias go. If this is going to be a full out battle, Zelbrali will need his gear and it's back there, too."

The dragon snorted in annoyance. "I don't need it, *you* need it."

Matthias chuckled despite the tension and started for Zelbrali. "I can take care of that while you see to Rae."

"What about us?" Kin maintained a stoic expression in Zanmea's saddle, but the former Shade couldn't hide the protests of his ká with Damien's senses open. Interestingly, a piece of him felt solid, and it was the connection drawn between him and the dagger that faintly glowed red at his thigh.

The Primeval swung her head to the Feyorian king. "Go with your comrades and defer to Zedren for instruction."

The charcoal dragon Kin and Amarie sat upon bowed her head low before the Primeval, who was easily twice her size. Damien realized right then how small the other dragons seemed beside their ancient leader.

Liam climbed onto Zedren, the only dragon who came anywhere close to the size of the Primeval, sitting behind Dani.

Zedren bowed his head towards the Primeval, eyeing his riders before focusing on Zanmea. "We'll fly to the hatchlings. They're our greatest priority."

Zanmea ensured Kin and Amarie were still secured before she took her cue, launching back into the air towards the mountain under siege.

Matthias rushed for Zelbrali, Damien right behind him, and they climbed onto his golden neck.

"Be ready to use that power of yours." Damien braced himself as Zelbrali turned towards the cliff. Without the leathers of a saddle to hold onto, the distance to the ground below seemed to double.

"Always am. But I won't need to. Zel won't drop you." Matthias patted the dragon's neck. "Let's go, my friend."

The flight to the cabin passed in a blur of thoughts and fears, all a mess in Damien's mind until they landed. He had no idea what state he'd find Rae in. Liam had been painfully vague, but he had to believe the man wouldn't have left her alone if it had been dire.

As his feet hit the grass outside the cabin, Damien hurriedly soaked in all he could from the foliage around. The ká tangled in his senses as he stored the energy in every muscle, making it feel as if he floated instead of ran.

"Do you want my help inside? Tacking Zel will take me a good twenty minutes." Matthias called after him.

Distant booms vibrated the ground as a piece of Oias's cliff face broke free and fell. A plume of debris rose from the trees as they disappeared beneath the crumbling rock.

"Just get Zelbrali ready." Damien called back as he pushed through the front door, not allowing himself to get caught up in the escalating battle. "We'll be out soon."

He'd only spent a little time in the Talansiet family cabin, but rushed through the front room towards the hallway to the various bedrooms. "Rae?" he called out at the same time his senses pinpointed which room she was in. He passed the study to go to the second door on the right, pushing it open hard enough that it bounced off the wall with a thunk.

"Damien?" Her raspy whisper answered him from within. She was barely visible, buried under a thick blanket that had been haphazardly pulled up from the base of the bed. Her leathers lay in a soaked heap on the floor. As he approached, she drew a bit of blanket back from her face, her eyes gaunt. Her body shook with tremors, lips blue. "Damien," she sighed. "You're here?"

Damien's knees hit the wood floor hard as he dropped beside her. He took her hand, and the connection between their ká forged instantaneously. The comfort the connection shot through his body only made it easier for the Art in him to speak to hers in a silent exchange. He didn't speak before his power began to mend her body, sharing the energy he'd accepted from the life all around the cabin.

She groaned as he warmed her muscles, easing the shivers until they stopped. "Uriel is here," she whispered. "He destroyed Eralas."

"I know." Damien squeezed her hand, brushing his other over her hair. With each stroke, he urged her to warm further, and gradually the moisture from her braids faded. "When I heard about Eralas, I was so afraid something might have happened to you. But I see in your usual fashion, you found a way to survive. And... get here, somehow."

Rae cringed. "I strapped myself to the belly of a Corrupted dragon."

"Of course you did." Damien couldn't help the smile, tracing a line down her cheek as her eyes slowly returned to normal.

"It wasn't the best choice I ever made," she admitted, lips losing their blue tint.

"Just another story for the grandkids."

"Damien," Rae murmured, taking his hand and pushing the blanket back a little more. Beneath, she was utterly naked. "There's something else."

If there wasn't a battle raging outside, Damien might

have taken more time to admire her body, but he turned his attention to her leathers. He heated his ká, forcing them to dry. "What is it?"

In an unusual bout of hesitation, Rae paused.

"Are the kids all right?" He met her eyes, forgoing his attention on the leathers. They were practically dry anyway.

"Yes. They're fine."

"Then what is it?" Her hesitation told him something dire had happened, but his mind couldn't process anything beyond the current attack.

She inhaled a staggered breath. "On the way here, they... they destroyed the prison, Damien. I watched it sink."

Even the voices in his mind stilled.

Damien stopped breathing as his head rushed to comprehend what exactly she was saying. Images of Mirimé stretched out on top of the monoliths, critiquing his form as he worked to mend the ruins. Each stone he had carefully placed to appease the guardian so they might allow access to the massive undertaking of the dragons. The only place in the world that would possibly contain the greatest evil any of them had known.

It's gone?

The concept just couldn't settle. How had Uriel found it? How had the Corrupted managed such a feat? With the actual prison so far below ground, could it actually be gone?

But it'd sank. Rae had said sank. Even if it was still there, it was deep below the sea now, flooded and inaccessible. No matter what power being a Rahn'ka granted, he and the others couldn't breathe underwater. They wouldn't be able to carry out the spell that would seal Uriel within it.

Decades of work. Of negotiations. Of scheming.

Gone.

"Damien." Rae's gentle whisper, less raspy now, brought him back as she touched his face with a cool hand. "I didn't know if you were still at the prison."

Damien tried to shake the despair from his mind. There wasn't time now to focus on the prison. "Matthias and I left a week ago. I sent you Rin." He didn't allow himself to imagine what might have happened if Matthias and he had still been there.

"Rin never made it back to me." Rae slipped her hand from his face to the back of his neck and pulled him to her in a tight embrace. He didn't resist as she wrapped her arms around him, still laying on the bed. She didn't speak, her mouth pressed against his neck as she slowly breathed in and out.

Feeling Rae against him, Damien used her to recenter himself. She'd always had a profound effect on him, and the relief of her being safe and in his arms again gradually allowed him to relax into her. The feeling of her bare skin against his hands wonderfully threatened to banish all thoughts of what went on around them. He felt only the elation she usually caused in him. Peace, despite the news.

He kissed the side of her head, drawing in her scent as his ká remained tangled with hers. The intimacy of the action made each touch feel like sparks coursing through his veins.

Rae tilted her head, dragging her mouth over his jaw until she claimed his. Her inhale through her nose was deeper, quicker, fingers running through his hair.

He questioned the sudden desires rising in him, knowing that she felt it, too.

Now isn't the time.

Yet, Rae's tongue played against his, and it sent fire down his spine.

Matthias needs time to saddle Zelbrali, anyway.

With the prison gone, and the destruction of Eralas, everything felt more desperate. Lost. But in Rae's arms, hope remained. And reminding her of how much he loved her felt imperative. Of taking a moment together, which they hadn't had in months. He'd almost lost her, again. And she'd almost lost him.

"I need you, Lieutenant," she murmured against his lips.

He ran his hand back over her hair as he positioned himself above her. He renewed a deep kiss, savoring her lower lip as her body arched up against his. "I'm yours, Dice." Damien ran a hand down her bare hip. "Always."

Their mouths collided again, fierce and needy, and he worked with one hand to unfasten his breeches. His leathers provided an unwanted barrier between his chest and her naked one, but removing clothing felt like a luxury they didn't have time for.

He just needed her, no matter what form that took. And as he finished unfastening his breeches, he indulged himself to run his fingers along the inside of Rae's thigh to the soft folds of her sex. The warmth and wetness only confirmed she didn't need the luxury either.

Her hips twitched, a soft moan escaping her throat as she wrapped her legs around him.

He guided himself towards her entrance, barely aware of anything but where they touched. Where they kissed and pulled and held each other. She lifted her body against his as he played with the hard tip of his erection against the bundle of nerves of her womanhood.

A whimper choked from Rae's lips, and she tilted her head back as he kissed her neck, finally easing his length into her. She shuddered in tandem with her ká tightening against his. The invisible grip encouraged him to press deeper into her, eliciting a warm gasp near his ear. His lips moved along her skin in rhythm with his thrusts, each more desperate than the last.

Her nails bit into the bare skin of his hips, just barely exposed above where his breeches still covered his thighs.

The bed groaned against the wooden floor, bumping the wall as their tempo increased.

Rae met each of his movements, her inner muscles sweeping waves of pleasure through him. It made every inch of him tingle, the pressure in him mounting as he drew up to look at her. She held her breath, legs quivering at the promise of her own release.

Reaching a hand between them, Damien continued the fast pace as he drew his thumb in circles over that bundle of nerves, and Rae erupted. Her body arched off the bed, a cry leaving her lips as the zenith of their passion unfurled within him as well. It scorched his insides, and he rode out each wave of their ecstasy with slowing pulses.

Panting, Rae opened her eyes and gave him a soft smile. "You've brought me back to life, Lieutenant."

Damien smiled down at her before leaning forward, their bodies still interlocked. He drew a long kiss from her mouth, brushing the loose strands of her hair behind her ear. "And you remind me what really matters." He kissed her again. "I love you, Dice."

"I love you." She quirked an eyebrow and flexed those inner muscles again, making his hips buck at the jolt. It only broadened her smile. "I think we need to go kill some Corrupted now."

"Always adding even more romance to the moment," Damien teased. He rocked his hips once more, growling at the glazed look in her eyes, before easing from her. Ushering his ká out from the cabin, he checked on Matthias, satisfied to sense he was still working to finish tacking the dragon. "If Matthias asks, you were in *really* bad shape, and I had to heal you for a while." He pulled his breeches up, refastening them.

Rae laughed, sitting up and inspecting her now-dry leathers before getting dressed. She left her cloak draped over the bed, no longer needing it with Draxix's temperate climate. "I don't think Matthias is going to believe that."

Damien shrugged, focusing on his lingering elation from their affection. There was no point in being dragged down by the news she'd brought. He needed to remain focused on the now.

There's nothing I can do about what has already happened.

"Do you know what Uriel looks like? The body he's taken?"

Rae nodded. "Uriel took Elder Tyranius's body. He is working with Lo'thec, who is responsible for the Corrupted dragons." She finished tying her leather tunic in place, running hands over her braids to ensure they were secured.

"How he managed to get enough energy to summon dragons is a question for later." Damien glanced at the window, unable to see the battle through it, but he could imagine it well enough. "We need to do what we can to limit the dragon losses in this. They're way worse off than we thought." He moved to Rae, gently tugging the ends of her braids out from the collar of her leathers as she fastened the last button of her breeches.

"What do you mean?" Rae pulled on her boots. "Did you meet with the Primeval?"

"Yes. The one that remains. Their numbers aren't good. Uriel destroyed a huge portion of their population before he was imprisoned the first time, and they still haven't recovered. It's why they've been so hesitant to help."

"Shit." Rae started for the door, still wide open, and walked into the hallway. "Oh." She paused, turning to him. "Lo'thec is having trouble keeping his dragons in line. He estimated he will lose control over them today or tomorrow. I know that doesn't help us much right now, but we need to send them back where they came from before they are let loose on Pantracia."

"I always thought Lo'thec was the shady one of the elders." Damien followed her into the hall, walking towards the front door beside her. "Are other elders working with Uriel? I'd guess Kreshiida."

Rae took his hand. "Kreshiida tried to stop him. He killed her. He killed them all, except Lo'thec, Olsaeth, and Ekatrina."

Damien winced. "Three elders on his side. No wonder

Uriel was able to get into Eralas. What about Erdeaseq?" He'd always liked the arch judgment, though hadn't interacted with him in years.

"I think he's dead, too. His wounds were serious, and he lost consciousness, but I had to leave him. Maith and Kalstacia were with me that day, but I lost track of them after the attack began." Rae's throat bobbed, and he could see the effort it took for her to keep it together with all she'd seen and suffered. "Uriel said he needed to stop in Aidensar before coming here. Do you know if Corin is all right? Amarie, Katrin, and Dani, too?"

"Amarie and Dani are here. So I assume the others are all right. But we'll find out when this is over. We'll need to stay focused to make sure all of us get out of here. We don't need more setbacks." Damien had been unsure how he felt seeing all of them together in one place, but now the anxiety grew. Five of the six needed for the imprisonment spell were here, all in danger with Uriel present. And if they'd already lost the prison...

Don't think about that right now. Save the dragons and stay alive.

Rae led him into the fresh air that now smelled of rain. Clouds gathered above, threatening their onslaught.

Matthias and Zelbrali waited in the clearing, the king leaning on the dragon's flank with crossed arms that he relaxed upon seeing them. He looked Rae up and down. "All good?"

"All good." Damien nodded, moving towards him at a slightly faster pace now that he could see Zelbrali fully saddled.

The dragon turned his head to look at them, and Damien could have sworn he rolled his eyes.

The Isalican gave him a knowing smile. "Just good?"

Rae offered Matthias a chipper smile. "Utterly fantastic."

Damien choked on a laugh as Matthias clapped him on the back and said, "Glad to hear it. I only finished prepping Zel a minute ago."

"No more delays." Zelbrali grumbled, turning his attention to Oias. "We're needed against the Corrupted."

Damien reached for Rae's hand, entwining their fingers. Their wedding bands pinched together, and it made him smile. "You think today is the day to see if all that training for the last ten years actually works in a real fight?"

Rae smirked as she climbed onto Zelbrali, taking the third seat on his neck. "Today is definitely the day."

Matthias took the front position on the saddle. "Whatever you're talking about, I hope I get to see it."

"I'm fairly certain it'll be hard to miss." Damien settled into the saddle, feeling more confident in the sky now that Rae was at his back. Her Art could protect him in the air, even if his failed. "Just get us close, then you won't need to worry about me and Rae anymore."

Zelbrali took two steps before launching into the air, barely waiting for them to buckle in their legs. Though Damien only buckled the first set of straps, like Rae had.

Everyone fell silent as the golden dragon soared towards the battle. One of the Corrupted dragons had fallen, now skewered by a sharp stone rise, its black blood oozing down the stone as its body began to melt away. One of the dragons who fought against the invaders bled from the neck but remained airborne.

They rose higher, Damien's connection to the ká below growing more tenuous. But he'd been collecting energy every moment he could since leaving the Primeval, and his ká felt close to bursting. His skin buzzed as Rae's Art surfaced in her own preparation, and the Rahn'ka focused his gaze on the Corrupted closest to the peak of Oias.

"Take us as high as you can." He spoke loud enough for Zelbrali to hear over the wind ripping around them. "We'll get off up there. No need to land." He touched the loose buckles of the saddle holding him in place, readying his power in his fingertips. A light pulse of light blinked to life around him, but he doubted the others could see it. His own ká swelling with whispers of what he'd absorbed.

"No need to land?" Matthias looked back at them. "What happened to your fear of heights?"

"We've been... working on that." Rae smiled, but it didn't reach her eyes.

"I'm better with her around."

Zelbrali's body rumbled beneath them. "I'll try not to be insulted." He adjusted his pitch, pointing his head skyward as they climbed higher.

Rae huffed a laugh, patting the dragon's neck.

They flew higher and higher, the air thinning and cooling as they rose. Above Oias's peak, Zelbrali's head twisted towards a different Corrupted dragon altering course to fly southwest.

Towards the Primeval.

Even at a distance, Damien could make out the shine of purple scales still positioned at the rim of the dormant volcano. As he watched, the great dragon moved to the edge of the cliff, dropping off of it with a spread of monstrous wings. There wasn't time to see where the Primeval headed.

"Guess this is our stop." Damien removed the buckles at his legs, holding himself in the saddle with one hand gripping the edge of leather. He glanced back at his wife.

Rae released herself from her own harness, perching in a crouch on the seat as she met his gaze. "Ready?"

Damien took a steadying breath as he summoned more power to the surface, imagining his tattoos glowing beneath the thick leathers.

Just like we practiced.

He only had to forget how many hundreds of feet they were above the ground, unlike the mere twenty they averaged when in the secluded Helgathian training grounds.

He nodded. "I've got you."

"I've got you," she echoed, and as Zelbrali banked to pursue the Corrupted that flew towards the Primeval, Rae jumped from the saddle. But her feet didn't fall far, colliding with the shield Damien threw up in perfectly rehearsed timing, creating a solid landing for her to run towards the Corrupted attacking the dragons defending Oias.

Damien hurtled himself after her, blue light bursting around his feet with each step as they left the safety of Zelbrali behind.

Just the two of them, in open air, and he didn't dare look down.

Wind swelled beneath his boots, lifting him and the concave shields higher towards the Corrupted attacker. The tail swept towards them, forcing Rae to roll beneath it and Damien to shirk back as the pointed tip skimmed past his waist.

The Corrupted swooped around, lancing more fire at the summit of Oias as it did. The Hollow One on its back, however, tracked them as Damien and Rae ran forward.

Arm buzzing, Damien gripped his fist to channel the energy from his tattoo, and when he loosened the grip, the shaft of his spear manifested in a curl of blue light. The steel bracelet around his wrist melted, reforming at the end of the spear as its blade. An addition to his weapon crafted for these particular foes. With a wave, a series of shields grew like stairs before Rae, and she took each one without hesitation, gaining further altitude on the Corrupted as it looped back towards them.

His power wouldn't have much effect on the mottled black hide of the dragon. They'd have to get close enough to use their blades on it. The thing was more monstrous than it'd looked from a distance. As he started up the stairs he'd created, Rae threw herself from the top just as the Corrupted soared beneath.

Wind gathered beneath her, keeping her airborne as she lifted her blade in a grand, sweeping arc along the dragon's neck and belly. Onyx blood spewed from the wound, cascading over the shields in pools of murky ink.

The creature howled, wings spreading as it banked suddenly to curl back over them, gliding over their heads and forcing Damien to throw himself down onto his shields to avoid its claws.

As Rae fell, he funneled his ká to the open air beneath her. She landed in a crouch on a last-second shield and spun to face the dragon.

Blue light sparked as armored boots hit the manifested pathway between him and Rae, the sound lost in the flurry of wing beats as the Corrupted turned again towards Rae.

Damien looked up at the plated armor surrounding the Hollow One, its glowing red eyes barely visible in the slit of its helmet. Darkness clung to every part of the thing as it withdrew its axe from the holster on its back, unrestricted by its bulky armor.

Damien scrambled back, taking in his opponent while his wife launched again with her sword. The blade must have struck bone, because her momentum jolted to a stop, her sword embedded in the Corrupted dragon's neck. Rae let go of the blade, landing roughly on the shields behind the Hollow One.

The Corrupted dropped, passing beneath them and their platform as the Hollow One took a daunting step forward, raising its axe.

The soulless figure towered over him, at least seven feet tall, and swung its double-edged axe in a figure eight maneuver, slicing the air with brutal force.

Extending his hand to the warm shield, Damien sent a pulse of power into the pathway ahead of him. Blue motes danced up around the Hollow One's boots, jolting the creature briefly before the shield dissolved. Then the Corrupted humanoid was suddenly gone, and Damien looked down to see its dark shape plummeting towards the distant canopy.

His stomach did a little flip, finally acknowledging how high they were and at the image of the Hollow One striking the ground below. With the Corrupted dragon gone for the moment, he looked at Rae's amused smirk to recenter himself.

"So nice of you to let him finish his flourish first." She watched him reconstruct the shield between them, her chest heaving.

"It felt rude to interrupt." Damien carefully got back to his feet, placing the butt of his spear against the makeshift ground for balance. "This is a bit harder without vision on my left side."

Rae's jaw twitched. "Good. Fights were a little too easy for you before." She winked at him.

Damien huffed, quickly looking for the Corrupted still focused on Oias's summit, but could only see the one circling back towards Zelbrali and Matthias. The Corrupted they'd fought had vanished, likely behind the stone cliffs to prepare for another attack against them.

Where are the other three? Have they all gone after the hatchlings?

Panic twisted his stomach. "Have you seen Uriel yet?"

Rae shook her head, spinning at the sound of leathery wings behind them.

The smell of sulfur was their only warning.

Rae leapt for Damien, throwing out her hands as she countered the dragon's coming inferno with a gust of icy wind.

The fire lanced from the Corrupted's mouth, whipping his hair back in a wave of heat.

Flames curled in the air around them, forced around the wave of Rae's cold wind protecting their flesh from melting off their bones. But the heat grew more intense as the Corrupted hovered above them, and she cried out at the demand on her abilities.

Despite all instinct, Damien untangled the weave of ká beneath them and the shields vanished. They fell through the air, granted sudden reprieve from the fire in the cold gusts of wind rushing past them. Turning himself during their free-fall, he thrust his spear down in front, summoning power into its tip that thickened the air before they slammed into a new shield, taking them both to their knees.

Rae groaned, panting, and scanned the sky for their opponent. She faced Damien and looked up, eyes widening. She reached for another blade...

The Corrupted snatched her clear off the shields right in front of him. Black blood splattered the manifested surface and his wife as it continued to leak from the gaping wound she'd made on the beast's neck. A breath later, the dragon released her, and the momentum left her plummeting through the air towards Oias.

Desperately, he locked onto the familiar feel of her ká, and even at a distance, he summoned it towards the surface of her skin. A faint shimmer filled the air around her, and she collided with the mountain a half-second later.

The dragon circled, coming back for him. It slowed as it neared, and once again, the scent of sulfur filled his nose as it reared its head back in preparation.

Without his wife, he would be charred in seconds.

Rae's blade glittered within the black mess of its butchered neck, still protruding from the bone.

His muscles ached as he pushed everything he could into them, no time to focus on a shield as he lifted his spear over his shoulder. He aimed for the glimmer of her sword, and as he launched his spear, the ká he'd accepted from Draxix hurtled it forward harder than he could have managed on his own. Light exploded from the head of the spear as it made contact, but the blade—not the Art—severed bone.

The Corrupted choked on its own flames, barely bubbling over its wolf-like lips before its body went slack in the air. It fell, and Damien hurriedly reached out to his spear, tugging it back through the air with his Art as the creature crumpled in against itself and hit the canopy below in a crash of thunder.

Leaning on his spear, Damien heaved a steadying breath

as he looked back to the cliffs of Oias, searching desperately for Rae. He found her, carefully balanced on a ledge and, overall, looking whole.

Thank the gods.

With each step towards her, he conjured a new shield to place his hurried steps on.

She watched him, slowly rising to her feet on the narrow ledge of rock, leaning against the cliff. Her attention shifted from him, chest rising faster as she yelled, "Damien, look!"

He spun, horror lurching through his chest at the vision of Zelbrali, high in the sky, locked in a death spiral. A free-fall towards the unforgiving ground. Matthias, still buckled in the saddle, shouted inaudible words to the golden dragon.

They weren't close enough to help. The distance was too great for them to run even with Rae's wind to lift his shields. Even if they had full strength.

And none of the other dragons and riders were in view. Too far away, likely protecting the roosts and hatchlings.

Protecting their last Primeval.

Matthias and Zelbrali plummeted, a tangle of claws and bursts of flame. Black, charred scales entwined with radiant gold.

Chapter 34

"THAT IS NOT WISE!" ZELBRALI growled the warning backward at Matthias as they kept flying—kept *falling*.

But the Isalican king ignored the dragon, unlatching his other leg. "I'm no good to you where I am!" he shouted back, wind occasionally tainted with flame blasting by his head, and he gripped his friend's golden scales.

Zelbrali snarled, Corrupted claws lashing out at his flank, but the dragon managed to wedge his hind leg between, pushing back. The Corrupted's tail had twisted around them, pulling tight on Zelbrali's left wing and preventing them from fixing the deadly free fall.

Matthias climbed up Zelbrali's body, heading for that problematic tail, axe in hand. The two giant beasts jerked sideways, and he shouted, grip slipping on a scale before he corrected. His heart thundered in his chest, drumming through his ears in place of the missing wing beats.

This is not how this ends.

He couldn't jump—not yet.

Though the ground fast approached, he had another minute. Half a minute. And if he hadn't already spent so much energy jumping the last two times Zelbrali got locked into a death spiral, he would have tried again by now. But he needed to give Zelbrali every second he could to free them from this madness first, because it seemed like the dragon just needed more time to figure out how to counter the Corrupted's tactic.

But there'd never been enough time.

Crawling along the dragon's spine, Matthias neared his shoulders, where the Corrupted dragon's tail ended. It wasn't enough to strike there. He needed to sever it closer to its body so it would free more of the golden dragon.

He looked over his shoulder.

The ground was too close, and they were moving too fast.

He'd never be able to sever a thick tail in time, even if he had it within reach.

Matthias could see the leaves on the trees as the ground grew closer. Closer. He swore, desperation souring his tongue. "I'm taking you with me this time!"

Zelbrali didn't answer, and the king had no idea if he'd

even heard him, but his veins heated. The Art swirled through him as he clutched the dragon's scales, channeling it into his draconi friend, as well. It burned and chilled at the same time as it surrounded the dragon's consciousness with vastly more effort than it took him to take another human.

Muscles taut, Matthias yanked time into reverse.

Time stuttered, bouncing backward in uneven blips of memory, as far as Matthias could take them. Sweat beaded on his brow as he pulled, trying to give Zelbrali every inch he could.

And it wasn't much.

As time jolted back into motion, Zelbrali roared. Old wounds still oozed along his scales, even as the Corrupted's claws raked to open them again.

Matthias's body jerked in the saddle, the straps again securing his legs. He wouldn't release them, not now that he knew it would do no good. "I got nothing left, my friend," he panted, trying to catch his breath.

Zelbrali twisted the opposite way he had before, freeing one of his front legs. He swiped beneath his belly, and Matthias looked back to see the Corrupted's tail loosen just enough from Zelbrali's wing for it to snap out. Their spin quickened with the extension of Zelbrali's wing, though the descent slowed minutely.

The Corrupted dragon howled, black blood spraying through the air as Zelbrali landed a hit Matthias couldn't see. A grotesque tearing sound broke through the whipping wind.

He looked down, his stomach clenching at the once-more impending impact. If they hit, it would kill them both instantly. The Corrupted would be dead, too, but that wasn't enough.

"Come on, Zel," Matthias whispered, sure the dragon wouldn't hear him even if he shouted.

Closer. Closer.

"Damn it." The Isalican king's breath came faster. "Zel!" He rallied his power, but nothing gathered. Nothing responded more than a whisper. It wasn't enough. It couldn't save them.

He suddenly lurched in the saddle as Zelbrali's second wing snapped open to catch the air, spinning them on top of the Corrupted, granting Matthias a perfect view of the encroaching canopy. Zelbrali's roars mingled with the growls of the Corrupted, a lance of fire escaping its mouth in a plume that Zelbrali twisted his head to narrowly avoid, sparing Matthias.

Snatching his axe off his back, Matthias hurtled it at the Corrupted dragon's neck. Every other time, it had bounced off. But this time, Zelbrali had gouged through the scales already, giving him a soft spot to aim for.

The axe sank into the dragon's neck, and the tail unwrapped. Zelbrali swiped again. The grip faltered.

Closer.

Zelbrali jerked, his hind legs kicking hard against the belly of the Corrupted, and gravity crushed Matthias against the saddle as their plummet abruptly ceased. The Corrupted crashed into the trees below, and Zelbrali leveled out to soar parallel to the tree line, tree tops scratching his belly.

Matthias could finally breathe, touching his friend's scales as Zelbrali's flight wavered. "Land," he instructed gently, glancing to where he'd last seen Damien and Rae. "As close to Oias as you can."

Chapter 35

SOMEHOW, THE LAST TIME AMARIE had flown on the back of a dragon, it hadn't been quite as impressive. Granted, the circumstances of fleeing Lungaz had distracted her from the experience. Kin sat in front of her, lightly gripping the handles at the front of the saddle.

The beautiful grey draconi carrying them already bled from her right wing, with other minor wounds dappling her sides.

Tight leather straps held her and Kin in their seats, but it didn't stop her heart from dropping out every time the dragon made sharp adjustments to their trajectory.

Amarie breathed faster than normal, her power hot in her blood as she held it at the ready.

Zanmea dove under a Corrupted dragon, blasting fire at its underbelly. She twisted, drawing a short squeak out of Amarie as they were briefly upside down.

As the dragon righted, claws splayed in attack, Amarie's knuckles whitened on the leather saddle's handles. "Oh, this takes some getting used to." She ducked as another Corrupted flew over them, tail lashing inches from her head.

A blur of red streaked up from them as it did, Sephysis eliciting a roar from the Corrupted before the bloodstone blade returned in a swoop towards them. It landed in Kin's extended hand, his fist quivering beneath the pulsing weapon, knuckles as white as hers.

Two more Corrupted banked over the treetops ahead, Zedren descending to cut between them. The Corrupted behind, which bore two riders, spread its wings wide to slow as Zedren slashed at the riderless one in front. The riders leaned into the movement as the Corrupted soared upward, turning towards Zanmea and them.

The dagger ripped free from Kin's grip, and his jaw flexed.

"Kin, what's—" Her gaze drifted, locking on the two riders as the dragons found the same altitude.

The riders stared at them, and Amarie recognized them both.

Time eddied and slowed, Lo'thec and Tyranius sending

a thread of fear through her. Lo'thec sneered in the same way he always did, but the usually passive Tyranius... *smiled* at her.

Uriel is here in the body of one of Eralas's elders.

Liam's warning echoed through her. He'd taken Tyranius, and Lo'thec worked with the master of Shades.

Wind pushed against her face as the dragons banked to avoid each other, but she could have sworn Uriel's laugh murmured in the air.

Instead of taking another dive at the hatchling roost, placed in the middle of a hollowed-out mountain formation, the Corrupted dragons' attention altered to them. Below, smaller, differently-colored dragons worked tirelessly to evacuate the young draconi, picking them up two at a time and flying them somewhere safe.

"I think we just moved up on the priority list," Amarie warned before shrieking at a sudden descent. "Where is Seph?"

Kin looked back at her, his dark hair whipping around his face. "It's not listening very well." He extended his right hand, the spiderwebbed scar over his Shade tattoo straining as he beckoned to the dagger with his open hand. A blur of red arced up from beneath Zanmea, but where Sephysis had been the moment before was impossible to determine. It appeared to make its way towards Kin's hand before it whirled away to the other side of the dragon, where Uriel and Lo'thec had circled back towards.

As long as it doesn't turn on me.

"Seph wants vengeance." Amarie watched the blade whip past their opponents, and Lo'thec had the good sense to cast it a wary glance. "Seph wants to kill Lo'thec." She narrowed her eyes on the empty saddle in front of the elder. "Where did Uriel go?"

Amarie looked behind them, doing a double-take before what she saw registered. "Zanmea!" She tapped her boot against the grey scales. "Your Primeval needs help!"

The grey dragon altered course immediately.

The giant violet dragon battled with two Corrupted, but it was the tidal wave of shadow passing through the jungle like a deathly mist that made her heart leap. The Primeval fought from the ground, her gnarled wing pinned by a Corrupted.

With a blast of fire, Zedren caught the attention of one of the Corrupted who whirled to meet him in an aerial slashing of claws and teeth. But the other seemed focused on keeping the Primeval grounded while the darkness crept closer.

The tendrils lashed out at branches and leaves, decaying to ash in their wake. Purple scales glimmered in the bright blasts of fire exchanged between the Corrupted and

Primeval. The massive dragon's head spun in surprise, the lance of fire from her jaws catching the dead foliage aflame.

Black tar bubbled up over the draconi leader, but she persisted.

Zanmea descended, clutching the other Corrupted dragon and ripping it off the Primeval. It turned, wolf-like snout closing on Zanmea's left flank, and tore itself free. Zanmea wavered as the Corrupted's wings pounded in the air, launching itself behind them towards the dragons lifting the hatchlings.

The Primeval bellowed, "Defend the hatchlings!"

Zanmea altered course, abandoning her dive towards Uriel and the Primeval.

"We can't just leave!" Amarie shouted as their mount carried them back towards the hollow mountain, to the one Corrupted dragon left attacking those who sought to defend the young.

"I must follow her orders." Zanmea spread her wings wide, colliding midair with the black creature. Wings and claws flurried around them, before a snarl was cut short by a snap of jaws. The grey dragon let go of the Corrupted, and it fell towards the decimated jungle.

A roar vibrated through the air, and the three of them looked back.

The Primeval had returned to the air, but shadow roped around her, the leathery edges of her wings greying as Uriel siphoned her energy. Uriel no longer even looked like the auer he'd inhabited, his body morphing larger as it hovered over the Primeval.

A stone hardened in Amarie's stomach at the sight of the magnificent being wasting away beneath Uriel's power. With each dimming scale, the Primeval's wings faltered until they failed entirely. Her body jerked backward, slamming into the side of a cliff. Shadow rippled around her, diving into the stone to hold her in place. Unrelenting.

Zanmea's powerful wings shot them forward again, back to the leader she was devoted to protect.

Wings erupted from Uriel's mass, inky and veined with purple.

"Gods," Amarie whispered as a tail unfurled from within his darkness, dragging wisps of misty shadow with it.

"Zanmea, don't!" Kin yelled over the wind tearing past them as muscles grew and bulged from the cocoon of power Uriel shaped. "You can't face him alone!" Kin looked paler than usual, one hand still outstretched, trying to control the dagger that was nowhere to be seen.

Zedren, closer to the Primeval than Zanmea, darted through the air towards her. Liam and Dani still sat atop his neck, but they didn't see the Corrupted beneath them launch skyward. The Corrupted that Zanmea had taken down only moments ago. It latched onto Zedren's legs and pulled him and his riders straight out of the sky. They all crashed into the desiccated jungle, sending up a plume of dust around them.

Amarie looked back towards where the hatchlings had been for any sign of help. An array of different colors dotted the horizon, but they were too far out.

Kin shouted, his body tensing as a flurry of red flew from somewhere behind them. Sephysis cut through the air, rushing past as a deafening roar filled the air, sending a chill down Amarie's spine.

An enormous dragon erupted from Uriel's ball of shadow, skeletal wings lined with sinuous tangles of pure darkness caught in the air. His snout, slightly shorter than other dragons, gaped as purple flames lanced towards the Primeval, still pinned to the cliff. Uriel's black scales absorbed even the sunlight, reflecting nothing back.

Zanmea ignored Kin's shouts, barreling through the sky with the blur of Sephysis only just ahead of her. A streak of crimson danced through the air as the dagger drew a line along Uriel's exposed flank. Shadow expanded on the edges of the cut, and as quickly as it had appeared, it sealed again as Uriel's giant head spun towards them. His eyes were fathomless pools of ink speckled with gold. He didn't seem to care as Sephysis whirled back again, ripping through the webbing of his wings that re-knit moments later. The master of Shades didn't relent, still bearing down on the Primeval, onyx claws tearing through the stone cliffside.

At the last moment, Amarie realized what Zanmea intended to do. She braced herself against the saddle as the grey dragon collided with Uriel's side. The impact—despite Zanmea's smaller size—jerked Uriel free from the cliff and the Primeval.

A flurry of shadows and claws moved in a blur beneath Amarie, the leather straps holding her in place biting into her thighs at the pressure. The world spun in a swirl of red and purple as Sephysis soared at any exposed movement Uriel made to dislodge the smaller dragon.

Zanmea roared, her fire melting the rocks behind Uriel as the shadow dragon snapped at her throat, aiming for Kin and Amarie as much as for a killing blow on his opponent. But she'd maneuvered just enough that his teeth sank into her chest rather than her neck, but his wild swipe caught her already-injured right wing.

A black shape filled her peripheral vision, and Amarie turned her head just in time to see a Corrupted dragon slam into their mount.

Everything shook in the sudden thunder as Zanmea rolled, crashing her ridged back into the cliff. Amarie shielded her head and neck as stone rained down on her and Kin, Sephysis suddenly there in a whirl around them that cut at stone instead of their attacker.

Something hot and sticky sprayed her cheeks, but she wasn't sure whose blood it was. Claws and teeth gnashed beneath them, the Corrupted howling as Zanmea must have landed a blow.

A new color blurred within the cloud of debris from the mountainside, blue scales shining as a dragon's wings cut through the dust. Zanmea fell from the cliffside, her wings beating wildly to keep herself airborne, and rolled so Amarie could see the blue dragon wrestling the Corrupted towards the ground.

Trees cracked beneath them, the Corrupted twisting and shattering more foliage as it fought to free itself.

Uriel dove after them, latching onto the blue dragon's back and tearing it clear off the Corrupted draconi.

Amarie held her breath, glancing at Zanmea's bleeding wing and the Corrupted that now rose again, red eyes locked on the grey dragon. "Shit," she muttered, fear rippling through her that their mount wouldn't survive another attack.

A deafening crack split the air, drawing her and Kin's gaze to the blue dragon in Uriel's clutches. But its azure form slipped from Uriel's grip, lifeless, cascading to the dead jungle below.

"Fly up," Amarie whispered, and then repeated it louder to Zanmea. "Fly straight up! As fast as you can, Zanmea!"

Kin twisted to look at her as the dragon followed her request and inclined her body. "What are you thinking?" Concern shone in his eyes, but she couldn't just sit there. He had his dagger, but what did she have?

Nothing that would help from such a distance.

"I need to get closer to that Corrupted." Amarie's heart thundered harder as she unbuckled one leg, the vertical incline flipping her stomach. The two swords strapped to her back weighed with promise. She opened the channels of her power, siphoning it into her muscles and blades until sparks crackled at her fingers.

Kin's frown deepened. He looked away for only a moment as Sephysis blurred past them, arcing back to circle around Zanmea like it did around Kin when she saw him practice. "What are you going to do? They're resistant to any Art."

Amarie looked down, the Corrupted dragon in pursuit barely behind Zanmea's tail. "I know." She lifted her gaze to him, vision tinted with rays of amethyst. She unclipped one of her swords, but didn't draw it. "But the Berylian Key can fuel my body and my blades." Her mouth twitched in a failed attempt at a smile. "Try to catch me after, will you?" Her heart squeezed at the look on his face, but she had no choice.

If Zanmea fell, they'd both die with her. So she had to do what she could, even if it meant jumping.

"Always." His eyes spoke so many more words there wasn't time for.

Amarie's head moved in short, fast nods. She couldn't form a response, unlatching her other leg. Clinging to the handle, she crouched on the spot she'd sat, gazing straight down at the monster closing in on them.

Dropping a deep breath into her lungs, she sent a quiet prayer to Nymaera and waited until Zanmea's flow of movement put her directly above the Corrupted.

And let go.

The fall was faster than she expected, with the Corrupted soaring towards her. She drew her sword mid-fall, smacking it against the Corrupted's face to deflect herself over its snout rather than into its mouth. The blade sank into the scales behind its horns, her blow empowered by her Art. Her muscles responded to the power too, tightening her grip on the hilt of the sword as her body jerked to a stop, anchored in place by her blade. Just as she'd hoped. She gripped an onyx scale with her free hand.

The Corrupted howled, shaking its neck, but she clung tight, stabbing her second sword repeatedly into its neck. Violet power darted from her hands, spilling over her skin as she drew more and more. Her muscles burned as the power of the Berylian Key cycled into them, the strength as palpable in her awareness as the colors erupting from her.

But the Corrupted jerked, too hard for her to counter the movement, and dislodged the sword from its neck.

Amarie fell, shrieking, and lost her grip on her second sword as she slid over its scales, scrambling to find anything to grab onto. She dragged her remaining blade along its hide, pulling the dagger from her thigh and slamming it into the dull scales as they rushed by. She clenched her jaw, breath coming in short gasps until her free fall jolted to a stop when her sword found purchase.

The Corrupted's roar was distant beneath the pounding of her heart.

She took a moment, trying to catch her breath. "Not dead. Not dead," she breathed, looking around to regain her bearings. Her gaze snagged on a disruption within the Corrupted's scales near its flank, twenty feet back up its body. A burned symbol, one vertical line crossed by two arched horizontal curves and surrounded by a circle.

The summoner's mark.

Grunting, she slammed her dagger higher into the dragon's hide and started the slow process of climbing up the soaring monster. Her muscles shook, flooded with power, as she alternated using her sword and dagger to scale the Corrupted.

Finally reaching the mark, she ignored the sound of the Corrupted's jaws snapping at Zanmea's tail. Burying her sword into its side, she used her dagger to carve around the outside of that mark. Cut after cut.

"Come on..." she muttered, slicing as fast as she could through the thick hide. With a final swipe, the chunk of flesh with the summoner's mark on it ripped free, tumbling through the air towards Draxix.

The Corrupted altered course, twisting upon itself to turn its jaws on her. Teeth neared her face in an instant, and she let go of her sword.

Her scream dissipated on the air as she fell. Something flashed in her vision, then pain radiated through her skull in a sudden blow, and the world went black.

Chapter 36

KIN COULDN'T TAKE A FULL breath the entire time he strained to watch Amarie.

Zanmea's maneuvers to avoid the Corrupted as it turned back on her made it impossible to keep his eyes on his wife, and every time the Corrupted came back into view, he'd have to find her again. The glow of the Berylian Key's power erupting from her skin made it easier, though.

Sephysis's insistence to pursue Lo'thec hadn't helped matters, and they had to do something to stop the Corrupted from killing Zanmea. The dragon already suffered too many injuries to face off with the Corrupted dragon again.

The glow in her eyes spoke of her conviction, and Kin knew he never could have talked her out of the dangerous maneuver to help Zanmea.

He'd never seen Amarie's power affect her body as much as it did now. Cracks had appeared like veins against her fair complexion, little rivers of purple and pink light that flowed across her features. Even before she started unbuckling the harnesses. But where she clung to the side of the Corrupted, her power blazed along her skin.

Zanmea snapped at the Corrupted's tail as it whipped past them, Amarie a blur as she fell down the length of the creature's dark body. She caught herself, just as Kin readied to yell for Zanmea to dive.

Sephysis tugged on Kin's awareness, demanding he allow it to attack as it desired. It'd obliged him in adhering to his commands only after growing frustrated with its failed attempts against the auer. The desire to kill Lo'thec reigned supreme, but the dagger had failed to penetrate whatever wards the traitorous elder had around himself.

And now it wanted to try again, sensing the auer growing closer.

Kin growled, fighting the invisible bond between him and the dagger, more discernible in combat. Red tainted the edges of his vision, the same shade that blurred past him as he forced Sephysis in another protective pass around Zanmea as they spun back towards the Corrupted.

Amarie had made her way back up the thing's body, hacking at something on its flank. Blood blended into the Corrupted's scales as it poured down its side, and as something fell away, the creature turned on Kin's wife.

A breath later, Amarie was falling again, and Kin's heart seized.

"Zanmea!" he screamed over the wind, panic causing him to forgo his continued war with Sephysis.

The dragon carrying him spun and dove, and he half expected the Corrupted to match their movement, but the creature didn't even look at them. Its tail whipped sideways as it turned away, slamming into Amarie and sending her body spinning through the air.

Her dagger slipped from her fingers as she tumbled in a free fall towards the jungle far below, limbs limp.

With the Corrupted no longer pursuing, Zanmea pointed her nose directly at Amarie and Kin held his breath.

It exploded from his chest as he and Zanmea suddenly jerked upward, his body pushed hard against the front of the saddle. Zanmea roared, the pitch different from her usual defiant call, and Kin looked down into the gold-tainted pools of black in Uriel's eyes. His teeth stained dark red with Zanmea's blood, he let go of her back leg and clawed along her belly, working his way above them. He whirled as Kin yanked on the bond to Sephysis, and the dagger blurred as it retaliated before Uriel could get another grip on Zanmea.

Heart wrenching, Kin looked down again for his wife, searching the sky. She couldn't have hit the ground yet...

A Corrupted dragon, bearing Lo'thec on its neck, soared where he'd last seen her. And there, at the front of the saddle with Lo'thec—Amarie. Sprawled, and unnervingly still.

"No," Kin whispered.

Uriel rose beside them, shadow pulsing at the tips of his wings as Zanmea wavered.

He knew it was the end, but pushed all he could into Sephysis as the blade fought against him. It tore free from his control, lancing after Lo'thec and his Corrupted before Kin even had a chance to turn it back on Uriel.

Sephysis was openly defying him to pursue Lo'thec, but with the elder's proximity to Amarie...

Zanmea screeched, and the Corrupted dragon Amarie must have freed from Lo'thec's control spun back around in the air, flying straight for them along with two other jewel-colored dragons. The Corrupted collided with Uriel, roaring as if it understood Zanmea's soul wasn't unlike its own.

Uriel's form jolted in the air as the three dragons crashed into him. Teeth gnashing and claws slashing, he allowed gravity to briefly pull him down. Powerful wings, laced with tendrils of black, lifted him again, and Uriel's jaw closed on the renegade Corrupted's neck.

Black sprayed through the air as his teeth cut clean through flesh and bone. With a whip of his neck, he threw the thing's body towards one of the other attacking dragons, an orange draconi nearly the size of Zedren. It slowed his attacker only slightly before the Corrupted body fell towards the ground.

Zanmea faltered, dropping from Uriel as the orange dragon, partnered with a red, pushed him back towards the cliff side.

Zedren roared his return, Dani and Liam still in the saddle. The larger dragon looked at Zanmea. "Fall back," he instructed. "Go to the hatchlings. You've lost too much blood to keep fighting here." Without waiting for a response, Zedren rushed past them and let out an inferno at Uriel.

Zanmea banked towards the crumbling cliffside and away from the altercation with Uriel.

"No! I can't leave." He touched Zanmea's scales, knowing full well the dragon needed to obey Zedren's command, her wing growing weaker with each movement. "Leave me here."

Zanmea twisted to look at him. "You plan to fight from the ground?"

"I'll fight whatever way I need to." Searching desperately for Sephysis, Kin followed the tether between him and the dagger, trying again to pull it back. He turned in the saddle towards where he could sense Sephysis, watching it and Lo'thec. The Corrupted he rode on snapped at the weaves of red rushing around them, and maneuvered more wildly than before.

"The slave appears displeased with its summoner," Zanmea growled, disgust in her tone as she landed in a large clearing that had already been drained, decimated by Uriel's power. She lowered her head, allowing Kin to drop to the ground, dead foliage crunching beneath his boots. Rather than immediately taking off, she eyed him. "I regret I am unable to assist in the rescue of your wife."

Kin's stomach churned. "You've done enough. Thank you."

Zanmea huffed a purring sound. "Good luck, my friend." With a strained flap of her wings, she took to the sky, soaring away from the chaos.

Kin watched her for only a breath before scanning the sky for Lo'thec. Finding the auer's Corrupted, which appeared to be the last remaining, he narrowed his eyes as the hell-raised draconi shook its neck against Lo'thec's control. Teeth snapped back at the auer, who kept one fist clenched around Amarie's wrist.

Rage simmered hotter in Kin's chest, bubbling together with Sephysis's continued assault against the auer. The Corrupted didn't seem to know which it was more annoyed with, the rider attached to its neck, or the dagger scraping along its scales. The creature banked sharply and it descended.

Kin hurtled himself over the desiccated ground, each step unstable with the layers of plant life compacted in death below his feet. Through the skeletal trees, he could make out the horizon. It granted him the view of Lo'thec's Corrupted landing, sending up a wave of dust with the impact. Little swirls appeared in the floating debris as the creature spun, still snapping at Sephysis, now just a red glow passing through the cloud.

A breath later, the Corrupted launched back into the air, riderless.

Lo'thec still has Amarie.

Whether the auer intended to use her as a bargaining chip or give her to Uriel, Kin didn't want to find out.

Branches and brush, all dead, smacked his legs as he ran through the jungle, aiming for the spot the Corrupted had landed. The trees in that space, crushed flat in some impact during the battle between dragons, created a new clearing, and Kin slowed as he approached the edge of it.

Lo'thec stood in the middle, spinning in different directions as he kept his eyes on Sephysis. He held Amarie in front of him, tight to his chest. "You won't get me, you cursed piece of tin!" Something shiny poked out from behind Amarie, a large medallion Lo'thec wore. It bore a symbol—

That symbol.

A vertical line crossed by two horizontal arches. Surrounded by a circle. What Sephysis had carved into the desk.

Damn dagger tried to tell me.

The bloodstone blade circled them, deterred by a faint yellow bubble surrounding Lo'thec. Each time Sephysis skimmed its surface, bits of the red stained the shield momentarily before fading.

He has some kind of protective barrier against Seph.

Amarie snarled, struggling against him, and Kin praised the gods she was alive. Her movements were slow, though, evidently still disoriented. She tried to spin on him, but he threw a wicked punch into her ribs, adjusting his grip to her throat.

"You're not making this any easier, sov'jet," Lo'thec hissed, squeezing.

She choked, hands flying to her throat. A gold bracelet shimmered on her wrist, one that hadn't been there before. Not a thread of her power colored her irises.

He did something to her.

Kin debated his options, as few as they were. Sephysis

still wasn't listening, though he pressed harder in his mind against the dagger. It was acting out of pure rage, unable to see the futility of continuing to skim along Lo'thec's shield.

He had to get Amarie away from Lo'thec, but he doubted he could outmatch the auer in combat. He prepared to move forward, anyway, feet shifting to—

In a blink, Lo'thec dropped the flickering golden shield.

Sephysis circled once more, as if aware it could be a trap.

The dagger's intention shuddered through Kin in an instant. A horrifying instant.

It didn't care about Amarie. It would go straight through her heart and into Lo'thec's.

Kin's heart stopped as he bore down on his efforts against the Art-infused dagger.

Don't you fucking dare.

Sephysis didn't obey. The dagger surged forward, and Amarie's eyes flew wide, her scream trapped beneath Lo'thec's grip. Her panicked expression tripled inside Kin, and in a flurry, he mutated it to further empower the press of his will against Sephysis's tether.

A roar erupted, and for a moment he didn't realize it was his own voice. Kin pushed every ounce of himself into the bond with Sephysis. The command. Including his love for the woman it was about to destroy. The connection went taut, like Kin's own hand extended across the distance to seize the dagger's hilt. His muscles ached and shook, and

Sephysis froze, mere inches from Amarie's chest.

She gaped at it, eyes flicking to Kin.

Sephysis vibrated, trying to enforce its own will back against its wielder. But Kin didn't give in, or it might have pierced Amarie. And with the action, wrought far greater destruction.

I told her I had control.

Kin could hardly breathe. So close. Sephysis had come so close to not only killing Amarie, but to causing a second Sundering.

And I told her I had control.

The tension radiating off Sephysis eased, finally, and it retreated from Amarie by a few feet.

Lo'thec snarled and his shield snapped back into place. He yanked a short knife from his coat. "I guess I may as well just take—"

A monstrous black form crashed into the clearing. A wave of shadow collided with Lo'thec and Amarie, sending Sephysis flying through the air.

Kin lifted an arm to shield his eyes as debris sprayed, Uriel's dragon form tangled with the orange dragon. The dragon snapped at Uriel with bloodied jaws, its neck torn beneath its jaw.

Uriel curled around, clamping his jaws on the dragon's neck and twisting. He slammed the dragon onto the ground, and a crack broke through the air. Uriel bellowed his victory, only to be cut short.

Sephysis whipped across his face, cutting a line from the side of his snout to his eye, and the triumph in Uriel's tone altered to fury.

Kin urged Sephysis back again, slicing down Uriel's neck and narrowly avoiding a tendril of shadow that lanced from his wings.

Brush crackled beside Kin, and he spun, reaching for the sword at his hip he had yet to touch. But Dani emerged, Liam next to her, and he eased his twitching hand away. Both of them panted, taking in the chaos before them.

Dani clicked her tongue then looked at Kin with wide eyes. "Where is Amarie?"

"We came to help, we saw what Lo'thec—" Liam's words were cut off by the swoop of Uriel's tail that forced them all to drop to their knees to avoid being hit. The red dragon had joined the fray, knocking the master of Shades back from them.

"I lost sight of Amarie." Kin grimaced, sweat dripping down his temples at the effort of keeping Sephysis engaged with Uriel.

The Dtrüa transformed, white fur spreading over her body as her face lengthened with feline features. Four giant paws hit the dusty ground before the pure white panther looked up at him with her usual cloudy eyes.

Kin gaped at her, having heard of her ability but not witnessed it himself. For a moment, he didn't understand why she'd shifted, but then she took off into the clearing.

She'll find Amarie.

Relief poured through him, and he launched after her. Lo'thec hadn't reappeared after Uriel's crash on top of them, either, and Sephysis kept harassing Uriel even when Kin loosened his demand on the bond. He couldn't confidently continue focusing on the dagger and run without falling on his face.

Dani, a good distance ahead of him, moved gracefully through the ashen debris, grey coating the white fur on her legs. She maneuvered around the lifeless orange dragon, paused, and then darted for where its limp tail had downed several dead trees.

Kin skidded to a stop near the bloodied head of the dragon, losing sight of Dani. Maroon ran in tiny streams away from the pool gathering from the orange-scaled neck, torn to expose the white bone within.

Crashes echoed behind them as Uriel and the red dragon snarled and scorched each other. Their tails whipped through the ever-growing cloud of ash and dust. He wondered why neither took back to the air. Perhaps Sephysis played a part in that, lashing across Uriel's wings and cutting through the black tendrils that formed the membrane.

"Over here!" Dani yelled, and Liam rushed alongside Kin to the orange-scaled tail that curled around on the other side of the dragon's head.

Amarie lay under it, her legs trapped beneath the heavy weight. Ash coated her face, dried blood on her cheek and neck. "I can't move," she rasped, hardly even able to struggle with her hips stuck.

"I'll get this side." Liam gestured with his chin to send Kin to the other side of the tail.

He gripped at the orange scales, finding purchase between them, and heaved. Foot slipping in the muck of blood and ash beneath the dragon, he steadied himself again as Liam grunted.

Dani grabbed hold of Amarie's wrists, pulling her out from beneath the heavy weight before the men dropped it again with a grunt.

Ignoring the roar of the warring dragons behind him, Kin rounded the dragon's tail towards his wife. Touching her, his heart finally began to slow. His thumb smeared the grime on her cheek as she looked at him before pressing hard against his chest in an embrace.

Amarie shook against him, clutching his arms. "I have no power." She let go of him, straining to get the gold cuff off her wrist, but the thin metal was too tight to fit over her hand. "Lo'thec put this *thing* on me..." Her voice wavered, eyes bright with emotion as the battle waged behind them.

Kin touched her wrist, examining the bracelet. "We'll get it off." He moved his hand down to hers, entwining their fingers. "But we should get out of here. Uriel and Lo'thec are obviously willing to adjust their plans to still get what they ultimately want."

Us.

He didn't say it out loud, but it had always been that way. Uriel hunting them. Anyone else would only be a bonus.

Gazing west at Oias, he could just make out shimmers of blue within the air and Zelbrali's golden scales reflecting a ray of sun that broke through the clouds. The far dragon untangled himself from a Corrupted, sending it crashing into the ground.

"Kin!" Amarie gasped, and he whipped his vision around to where she looked—towards where Uriel had been fighting the red dragon—and there he was.

Uriel charged at them, still grounded, his jaws wide as he lunged.

Liam jerked Dani away, and Kin pulled Amarie closer. There was no escape, not from that.

The master of Shade's bellow shook the ground, impending death nearing.

The ground began to rumble—too fast to be Uriel's lumbering steps—and bright light suddenly blinded them all, cascading over the jungle in waves of green and silver.

Uriel balked, his charge ending abruptly as he shrank away from the light as if it burned him.

A dragon roared, loud and triumphant, as the light faded.

Zedren descended from the cliffside, his green scales incandescent under the cloudy sky as he landed between them and Uriel. The Art rippled off him like heat waves in a desert, altering the very terrain. Life bloomed within the decay, green sprouts bursting through the dust. Leaves unfurled on branches, and Zedren roared again with unabated fury, his head turned towards Uriel.

Flora continued to spread from Zedren as he widened his stance, his claws blooming more greenery instead of breaking into the earth. Green motes exploded up from the new flowers, drifting into the air around the dragon in an ebb of energy so unlike the shadow beast he faced.

Uriel roared defiantly at Zedren, who answered in kind. As the green dragon took a step forward, the very air around him vibrated.

With the advance, the master of Shades stumbled. They all watched in stunned silence as the black wings crumbled, black ash floating away in the breeze like snow. Uriel's horns dropped to the growing grass, wisping into dust amid fresh wildflowers.

Zedren's muscles rippled beneath his scales as he unleashed an inferno onto Uriel. The shadow dragon's wings wrapped around himself in a cocoon as the fire raged against each vein of darkness.

Kin shielded Amarie from the heat, finally reaching out with his mind to find Sephysis.

He squinted through the bright light of the fire to try to make out Uriel beneath it, but the black shape vanished among the waves of orange and white.

The fire abated as Zedren growled. But as the smoke cleared, Uriel was nowhere in sight. Whatever black mass had been there before had vanished, leaving the ground barren as Zedren's Art continued to expand, spreading new life where Uriel had stolen it.

Sephysis responded to Kin a breath later, as if snapping back into its own awareness. It darted back to him with ease, leisurely floating through the air as it grew closer to Kin's waiting hand.

Lo'thec must be gone.

Amarie started upon seeing Seph, tensing and pulling away from Kin.

He didn't blame her, not with what the dagger had attempted, and took a step further back as he caught the bloodstone blade. He tried to express his disappointment in the blade through the bond, only feeling a vague response. The Art that bound them was exhausted, too, especially with the struggle that had ensued between them. Kin pushed Sephysis to his thigh, buckling the straps to hold it there.

Eyeing the blade another moment, Amarie let out a slow breath. Blood still oozed from a gash on her head, and she turned to Zedren.

But it was Dani who spoke. "Is it over?"

The massive green dragon lowered himself before them, his chest rumbling. "Zuriellinith is no longer within Draxix. Nor is his ally." His deep voice vibrated through Kin's body. "It is over." No joy touched his tone, only sorrow and grief.

Amarie returned to Kin, and Dani let out a sigh.

"Damien should have a look at you," Kin muttered, wrapping an arm around his wife's shoulders, grateful she could trust being near Sephysis. His heart ached, and touching her was the only comfort. They were alive, and Uriel was gone.

Chapter 37

"USUALLY THERE'S A LOCK SOMEWHERE..." Rae muttered, examining the gold bangle locked around Amarie's wrist.

"I think a couple of my ribs might be broken." Amarie laid perfectly still in the clearing Zedren brought back to life.

Rae had hardly believed it when she and Damien watched green spread over the decayed jungle, reviving it like no other power she'd ever seen. She wondered what it meant, if anything, but her questions would need to wait.

Zedren had disappeared along with the injured Primeval shortly after confirming none of them were about to die. Though Amarie was in the roughest shape, none of her injuries were life-threatening.

Zelbrali stayed behind with them, though even he seemed distracted.

Liam, Dani, and Matthias all hovered near the golden dragon, allowing Amarie space while Damien and Rae inspected her.

"Should we stitch that gash on her head?" Rae absently asked Damien, who sat on the ground next to where Kin held Amarie's head in his lap.

"Probably." The Rahn'ka frowned and spoke to Kin. "You should still monitor her for a day or so, make sure nothing gets worse."

"Can't you try healing her anyway?" Kin looked at Damien as he started to pull away. "If the bracelet is stopping her Art, would it still be able to stop you from healing her?"

Rae glanced up, meeting Damien's gaze as they paused. "He has a point."

"Wouldn't the bracelet stop your healing Art, too, then?" Amarie looked at Damien.

"No, it doesn't. It's creating a barrier between your access, not mine's ability to affect your ká." Damien looked at the bracelet for another moment, as if considering that it might hold other hidden dangers.

"Exactly. When Kynis took me from Helgath all those years ago, the auer healed me while I wore the Art-blocking earring." Rae lifted the bottom of Amarie's shirt to check the bruising on her ribs and cringed. "It's worth a try."

"All right," Amarie agreed, and Kin nodded too.

Damien hesitated only another moment before he shrugged. "Can't hurt." He reached back out, placing his hand on the side of Amarie's head. He closed his eye as Rae sensed his Art build in his fingertips. Barely visible motes passed from his fingers into Amarie's scalp and for a moment nothing happened. But beneath the stain of blood and strands of her auburn hair... the skin shifted to mend together.

Amarie shuddered, groaning through clenched teeth.

The wound puckered with a scab, then a scar, before fading as if it'd never been at all.

Damien sucked in a steady breath as he took his hand away. "I took care of your ribs, too." He smiled lightly at Amarie. "I'll need to take another look at them tomorrow, though. My energy is pretty drained and I can't do more." He looked to Kin, who sagged with relief as he ran his fingers idly over Amarie's braids.

"Thank you," Amarie breathed. "That was a very foreign feeling. I suppose that means I need to keep this thing on?" She lifted her wrist, slowly sitting up. "Not that we know how to get it off..."

"I'm just glad it worked." Damien sat back on his heels. "And yes, until I have time to patch you up entirely, it's probably best to keep it on. But we'll find a way to remove it. It'll be easier once we're back in Nema's Throne."

The Berylian Key nodded, rising to her feet with Kin's assistance, but she seemed steady.

Rae stood with Damien, watching Amarie give Sephysis a wary look, even though the dagger sat dormant in its sheath at Kin's thigh. The former Shade twisted his hip and kept his wife on his opposite side.

Damien didn't miss it, either, as he stood. "Did something happen?"

A muscle twitched in Amarie's jaw, but she said nothing.

"We had a close call," Kin supplied. "Sephysis wanted to go through Amarie to kill Lo'thec. But I stopped it."

Rae started. "It *what*?"

"You don't understand," Amarie whispered, staring at the ground.

"Make us understand." Damien's tone sounded close to how it did when he gave an order, but Amarie didn't balk.

Her throat bobbed. She quickly recounted the story about Sephysis that Melyza had shared, and the dagger's need for vengeance against their family. "And she told us why Uriel wants the dagger. Uriel must have gotten the truth out of her or her journals, because Lo'thec knew to hold me in front of him. Because if Sephysis pierces the

Berylian Key, it will cause another Sundering and all Art will be wiped off the face of Pantracia."

Rae's mouth dried. "You're telling me that we only avoided a second Sundering because Kin regained control of Sephysis?" She turned wide eyes on Damien, who'd gone a few shades paler at the news.

"A Sundering. That's what Uriel is attempting." Damien rubbed the back of his neck.

"And he thought it would be easier if he took out Draxix first," Rae added. "Summon the Corrupted dragons, destroy the two adversaries most likely to stand against him, and then shatter the world."

"He just got lucky that both Amarie and the dagger were here so Lo'thec could make an attempt." Damien looked at Oias's still-smoldering peak in the distance. "And we got lucky that he didn't succeed in destroying the dragons, or in using the dagger." He turned his attention to Kin, who frowned.

"I have control of the blade now." His tone hardened. "It won't be a problem again."

A hint of hot anger touched Rae's throat. "But you knew. You both knew this was Uriel's goal, and you came here, anyway. Together. Why would you do that?"

Amarie's gaze shot to Rae. "Because Kin has control of Sephysis, and Draxix needed us. More dragons would likely be dead if we hadn't been here. You didn't see that part of the battle, so you don't know all the good Sephysis did, too."

Rae opened her mouth to argue, but Damien placed a gentle hand on her shoulder.

"I think we need some space to regroup," he said with a softer tone. "We're stuck here for a couple days at least, until we figure out how to get back to Isalica without portals since the one to Thrallenax has been closed. So let's take the afternoon and talk again with clearer heads."

Amarie gave a subtle nod, keeping her gaze on Rae for another moment before looking at Damien. "Thank you again for healing me." She turned with Kin, and they strode together to where the others stood by Zelbrali.

Rae whirled on Damien as soon as they were out of earshot. "They knew and still brought her *and* the dagger right to Uriel!"

Damien touched her wrist. "I doubt they realized Uriel would be here, let alone Lo'thec. It was bad luck. Besides..." He gave her a little squeeze. "We've done a few irresponsible things in all of this, too."

Frowning, Rae rolled her shoulders before letting out a breath. "Maybe." She sighed. "Is this how everyone else feels when we do things without telling them first?" Regret pooled in her gut.

I should apologize to her later.

Silence surrounded them for a minute before Rae tackled the topic she desired least to discuss. "What are we going to do about the prison?" She kept her voice low, so even the Dtrüa wouldn't hear.

Damien's gaze became distant as he pursed his lips. He was silent for a while before heaving a sigh. "I don't know. Which means that even if I would like to keep the secret and not worry everyone... we need to tell them. Maybe between all of us, we can come up with something."

Rae nodded. "Tomorrow. We've all endured enough today. Let's tell them tomorrow."

Chapter 38

A DENSE BANK OF SNOW-HEAVY clouds had drifted into the valley of Nema's Throne, and large cotton ball-like flakes were falling by the time the carriage pulled up through the front courtyard.

Katrin waited patiently, though her stomach churned. Not only because she had no idea what state Ahria would be in with her mysterious illness, but because her husband still fought in Draxix.

Micah led the escort on his familiar grey stallion, looking rather travel worn and in desperate need of a bath. "My queen," he greeted, a smile spreading over his handsome face as he brought his horse to a stop before her. "You made it home safe."

Her expression hardened and his smile faded. "I did, and with my companions, however they were immediately pulled away by more conflict." She locked eyes with her old friend as he dismounted, knowing Micah would want to know the danger Matthias and the others were likely in. She touched his arm, gripping hard through the thick fur of his coat. "It's Draxix."

Micah's brow furrowed, snowflakes catching in his short beard. "Matthias is still there? What happened?"

Behind him, the guards dismounted and lowered the carriage stairs.

"As far as I'm aware, yes, he's there. Kin spied Corrupted flying towards the portal, but I don't know much else. There's nothing we can do from here but trust in our friends and pray to the goddesses." She'd already spent the morning in the temple of the palace, beseeching any god that would listen. "We can discuss it later. Probably best to avoid extra stress for Ahria right now."

A muscle in Micah's jaw feathered. "I want to know everything you do as soon as possible," he murmured, gently giving her upper arm a squeeze.

She nodded, meeting his strong gaze. "Of course. I'd like to get Ahria to a comfortable place and examine her. I'd rather it be private, so I'd appreciate it if you could distract Conrad." She looked towards the carriage as Conrad stepped out, reaching back to offer assistance to Ahria. She moved slowly, and the look on Conrad's face confirmed he'd need ample distraction to leave her side.

"I'll see what I can do." Micah leaned into Katrin and kissed her cheek. "I'm still glad to see you home safe."

She smiled, looking up at him. "It was my first adventure in a while. But I'm relieved to be home, too. I don't think I'll need another outing like that for a long while. Maybe after Zael is grown. Maybe."

Micah chuckled, patting her shoulder. "Maybe," he echoed, a knowing look on his face, before striding towards Conrad.

Katrin followed, waving off the bows of the guards as she stepped past them. Her attention shifted to note every movement Ahria made, her complexion, and how exhausted she looked. Her heart softened, and she approached the woman's other side to assist. "I have a room set up for her. I can take her."

"I'm not a child," Ahria mumbled, but gave Katrin a slight smile. "But I really hope you can help." Her jaw twitched, her eyes a little glassy.

And Katrin understood. She'd seen that look countless times. Hesitant hope bordering on desperation.

"We'll figure it out." Katrin slipped her hand within the thick cloak on Ahria's shoulders, finding her hand and squeezing it. "No matter what it takes. You've been ill long enough."

Ahria's throat bobbed, but she only nodded.

"Take their things to the west wing, please. The Olliander Suites." Katrin didn't look at the guards as she gave the order, and they immediately started moving in her peripheral vision. "It's a bit of a walk, but I felt it would be better to have you near my chambers. However, I'll take you directly to my personal infirmary, first."

"Come, let's get out of the snow." Micah gestured towards the front doors.

Ahria whispered something to Conrad, and he removed his arm from around her, offering it to her to hold instead.

As they walked through the palace, people waited off to the side while they passed, giving quiet, polite greetings to their queen and king regent.

Katrin wished it hadn't been such a trek by the time they reached her infirmary, just down the hall from the royal chambers. Ahria had become even paler after the long walk.

Micah nudged Conrad, who still held onto her. "I can show you to your suite so you can get cleaned up while Katrin has a look at Ahria."

Conrad exchanged a look with her, and he must have read something in her determined expression. "That sounds good." He reluctantly detached himself from her.

Katrin couldn't blame him. He hardly knew her, but more importantly, he probably hadn't let Ahria out of his sight in weeks.

"It's all right," Micah encouraged. "She's in good hands. Would you like to meet your great aunt? Or your cousins?"

Conrad frowned, confusion in his expression. "My what?"

"I'm fairly certain they were pronounced dead during the military coup, and neither Seiler nor Kelsara seemed interested in correcting that rumor." Katrin spied a twitch in Conrad's expression that suggested he recognized the name Kelsara. Which implied he'd been forced to learn some of his royal genealogy.

"Seiler, as you probably know, is Matthias's brother. He and Kelsara live here with their children, who would be your cousins. Kelsara being your grandmother's sister." Micah exchanged an amused look with Katrin before nodding in the direction of the hallway. "I'll take you to meet them after you get cleaned up."

Conrad looked to Ahria, who seemed just as amused by the look on his face as the rest of them.

"Go." She shoved his shoulder lightly. "I'm fine. You should meet your family."

Conrad took a visible deep breath, leaning in to give Ahria a quick kiss on her temple. "I'll come check in later."

Micah nodded at Katrin, and she returned the gesture in thanks. The men disappeared down the hallway a few moments later, leaving Ahria alone with Katrin.

The young woman's shoulders drooped as she let out a shallow breath. "Thank you," she whispered. "Conrad has been amazing, but I just... I just can't."

"Come," Katrin said gently, touching her arm to guide her inside the private infirmary. "Make yourself comfortable." She closed the door behind them as Ahria wandered towards the pillowy bed, removing her cloak as she went.

Where Matthias had his study to keep just as he wanted, this was Katrin's space. Smaller in size, but that was the way she liked it. A large window dominated the far wall, which served as the backdrop for the bed Ahria now tested the softness of.

Katrin stripped off her cloak, hanging it and Ahria's on a set of hooks behind the door, then made her way to one of the walls of shelves. Without needing to think about which container was which, she plucked it from the shelf before pausing. "Tell me what you've been feeling. Which symptoms have been the worst."

Ahria laid on her side, pulling a thin blanket over herself. "I'm tired. I have no energy. No appetite. It gets worse when I tap into my... my Art."

Katrin replaced the initial tin she had retrieved and switched to another. "Have you noticed a difference depending on how much you tap into? Or is it the same reaction regardless of how much energy you use for your Art?" After learning about the situation with Uriel from Damien, Katrin had researched the Berylian Key. And a slight anxious excitement to actually work with the power mingled guiltily in her gut. But the greater priority was to help Ahria feel better. The poor thing had been showing symptoms since her father's coronation, which was over six weeks ago.

"It's bad after using it at all, but I think it's worse when I use more of it or for longer periods of time. Then I'm nauseous, vomiting, dizzy, and I lose consciousness." Ahria closed her eyes. "And I usually have a headache."

Katrin considered the mix of herbs as she spooned it into the steaming tea pot the palace staff had diligently delivered while she greeted the arriving carriage. She watched the dried herbs swirl in the water for a moment as she contemplated what Ahria told her.

Art related, most certainly. Though that suggested something purposely done to Ahria rather than a common stomach illness. Her father had enemies in Feyor now who may target her maliciously, but considering everything else going on in their lives, it felt irresponsible to dismiss the greater threat.

She was held in by Uriel for weeks, and then taken to Lungaz.

Katrin swooped another tin off the shelf, taking half a scoop of the herbs inside to add to the tea pot.

On top of all of it, Ahria was still dealing with how to control her power. Katrin had heard bits of the ordeal from Matthias, who'd heard from Kin. Third hand information that wouldn't help.

"Tell me what it's like to control your power. Have you still been struggling? Does this illness seem to make it harder to control, or easier?"

Ahria didn't answer right away, thinking. "It doesn't overwhelm me like it used to, but I assume that's because my mother only gave me a small amount to work with. But even then, it doesn't feel as powerful as it did that first day she trained with me."

Katrin moved to the opposite side of the room, to a wall of bookshelves she'd populated with her favorites and some she hadn't had an opportunity to read yet. She ran her fingertip along the spines until she found the tome she'd thought of. *The Art of Energy.*

"There are rare circumstances of spells that can essentially drain the energy from the target of the malevolent Art. But there's specific circumstances." She flipped through the book, seeking the information she remembered skimming. "It requires you to still be ingesting the same thing daily, which might have been possible if something was being slipped into your meals while in Ziona... but the symptoms have endured on the ship and in Isalica, correct?"

"It's been the same, no matter where I am, and the people around me have kept changing the whole time. The only person always with me is Conrad." Ahria shook her head. "He makes my tea, gets me food."

Katrin considered but dismissed the idea. The prince's concern appeared genuine, and he wouldn't have brought Ahria to her to be found out.

She eyed the book and shook her head. "These ingredients are practically extinct at this point, anyway." She crossed back to the steeping tea, filling a small cup. "This won't taste good, I'm afraid. And I can't offer sugar or it'd change the effects." She crossed the room, gingerly handing the tea cup to Ahria. "Best to down it all quickly. It's not too hot."

Ahria's nose wrinkled as she smelled the tea. Exhaling, she shuddered and then drank the contents, face distorted in displeasure. When she set the cup down, a small burp escaped her lips, and she cringed. "Gods, that was awful."

Katrin smiled. "But it'll help with the nausea. Give you a boost of energy, hopefully. And open up your energies to my prodding. I assume the healers in Ziona ruled out the most basic of diagnoses. You're not pregnant?" She had to ask, the symptoms and timeline matched.

Groaning, Ahria rolled onto her side, scratching the back of her head. "Not pregnant."

Katrin narrowed her eyes, hyper aware of every movement the woman made. She spied a spot of red at her hairline, where Ahria had clearly scratched before. "Have you noticed rashes or other irritations?"

"Not really."

"But what about that spot on the back of your neck you just itched?"

Ahria shrugged. "I don't know. My scalp gets itchy sometimes."

Katrin stepped up onto the built in platform around the bed that allowed her to get closer. "May I touch you?"

"Of course. Want me to sit up?" Ahria propped herself up on an elbow.

"Maybe roll onto your stomach a little more? I want to look at this spot near your hairline." Something seemed off about the way her hair laid, and the shadows on her scalp beneath it.

"All right," Ahria murmured, rolling onto her stomach as requested and propping the pillow under her chin.

Katrin pushed up the sleeves of her teal dress, touching Ahria's neck and pulling down her collar. She brushed her hair upward, examining her spine. A strange black line etched from just within her hairline up onto her scalp along the back of her head, around six inches long. Katrin brushed Ahria's hair away from it, barely caressing the tattoo-like mark.

"What is it?" Ahria held perfectly still, quiet dread in her tone.

"A mark of some kind." She parted Ahria's hair directly along it. "I don't know what it is, but it's far too straight to be a birthmark. I need to check more directly to see if it's tied to all this." Katrin shifted, squaring her stance to allow herself to delve into her own power without losing her balance. "I'm going to merge my aura with yours temporarily. You might not even notice, but don't fight it, all right?"

Ahria gave a subtle nod, keeping her breathing even.

With a thought, Katrin urged her own power to well up through her fingertips and closed her eyes. It swelled into Ahria where she touched near the strange mark, Katrin's vision changing in the blackness of her eyelids as her senses reordered themselves. Golden waves of her energy mingled with the beryl and blue glow of Ahria's, but something else flashed. Bruised darkness, purples and black vines tangling possessively around the energy of the Berylian Key. They lashed out at Katrin, and she flinched as pain slashed through her.

The darkness retreated back to Ahria, squeezing possessively as Katrin heard the woman whimper, her breath growing more ragged. The Isalican queen drew back in a flash, her golden light blinding her real vision, leaving spots as she blinked.

Ahria had curled into a fetal position, her face pale with agony as she moaned.

"I'm sorry." Katrin touched Ahria's forehead, brushing the beads of sweat. "That should not have happened like that, but whatever it is..." Her mind whirled as she tried to consider what she'd seen. A hollow had formed in the pit of her stomach, the darkness claiming Ahria terrifyingly familiar. But she didn't want to say it out loud.

Gazing up at her with bright, worried eyes, Ahria breathed fast and shallow. "Tell me. Tell me what's wrong with me."

Katrin pursed her lips. She couldn't lie. "I need to do more research to know for certain. I haven't encountered anything like this before. But... I do suspect it may be related to Uriel."

Ahria shook her head, her gaze boring into the healer. "How? What did he do to me?"

"I'm not sure." Katrin chewed her lip as she stepped back down to the floor. "I haven't directly interacted with Uriel very much. Matthias protected me from it pretty vehemently. But do you recall anything from when he imprisoned you? Anything that might have caused this?"

Sitting up, Ahria clutched the blanket around herself. "He didn't let me sleep. I was hallucinating. Days blurred together. He never stopped asking me questions, but I don't remember them all. I don't remember what I said. What he said. I don't know. I don't—" Her throat bobbed as she clenched her jaw shut, hands shaking. "I thought maybe the memories would return over time, but they haven't," she whispered, her mouth contorting in disgust as her voice cracked. "I don't know what he did to me."

Katrin reached out to her, taking her hand. She gripped it firmly. "I won't stop until we figure this out." She left no doubt or question in her tone. "You're safe here. But it's probably best if you lock down your Art as best you can, just as your mother taught you. Damien will be here in a few days, I'm sure, and he may have some ideas, too." As Katrin said it, she wanted desperately to believe it. That Damien would come back to Nema's Throne from Draxix with the rest of them.

Please, Aedonai, bring them home soon.

Chapter 39

DANI'S NOSE TWITCHED, THE SCENTED colors wafting around her a mix of violet, sage, and a shimmering gold she'd never experienced before. Though the purple and green, according to her husband, matched the color of the dragons' scales. Liam had described the space to her a few moments before—a rocky flat-bottomed crater with vertical cliff sides, open to the sky. Within, there were eight giant pillars standing sixty or seventy feet tall.

On each sat a horned dragon skull.

For that, Dani wished Katrin had been there to grant her a glimpse of the sight surely no other humans had seen. But she exhaled the feeling, embracing the smell of that glittery gold with enjoyment. It reminded her of mango and a touch of almond.

The Fifth Prime, as the amethyst Primeval referred to herself, sat on one of the pillars. Zedren occupied another. And the golden scent drifted from them both.

"Zedren has changed... significantly," Dani whispered to Liam.

"That is because he has ascended and taken the place of First Prime." The Fifth Prime's voice echoed through the open area in a way that nearly made Dani cringe at the volume.

The others stood next to them and whispered among themselves at the statement.

"You returned life to what Uriel drained. How is that possible?" Damien addressed the green dragon.

"The ascension of a dragon is an unique expansion of power that affects a lot more than just the forest. We are connected to the fabric in a way I cannot explain." Zedren sounded the same, but a hint of pride touched his tone that made Dani smile. "We've summoned you all here today to thank you for your aid in defending Draxix. And we acknowledge that the outcome would have been very different had you not been present."

"We couldn't sit aside. Not with all the dragons have done for us." Matthias's blurry shape shifted towards the pillars. "We only regret being unable to prevent any loss."

The violet Primeval rumbled her agreement. "But the loss could have been much greater. We lost three of our kin, but not a single hatchling." She paused, and silence settled for a few breaths before she continued. "Having witnessed the monstrosities crafted from the souls of our ancestors, we have decided to offer you a gift."

Dani looked towards Liam, the scent of surprise emanating from a few of the others.

"A gift to use against Uriel?" Amarie asked, the Key's power coloring her scent even though she kept it tucked away. After her second healing session with Damien the day before, Zelbrali had offered to remove the gold device blocking her power. It had taken seconds.

"A gift to use against his soldiers. The Corrupted." Zedren shifted atop the pillar, claws scraping stone. "It is a realm lock, and it has the power to seal the hell from which the Corrupted are borne."

Silence fell for a moment before Damien joined Matthias, his boots quiet on the hard ground.

Dani elbowed her husband in the ribs. "What's happening?" she whispered.

Liam leaned closer, murmuring, "Something is floating down from the Fifth Primeval. A little ball or something. Looks pretty plain to me. It's floating towards Damien and Matthias. Damien just caught it and is holding it like it's about to explode or something."

"How does this work?" Matthias's voice.

"You must attach it to a being who you then drain with Uriel's power, because it must go to the realm you wish to close, and there is no other way to access the place where the Corrupted dwell," Zedren explained. "But the timing will be paramount, as Uriel's power holds the potential to reopen the realm again, should you fail in your other quest."

"Thank you." Damien's voice. "We appreciate your trust in ridding our world of Corrupted. We'll find a way to accomplish this."

"We need to get back to the mainland," Kin spoke as if he'd been holding in the words the entire time. "Will you be reopening the portal to Thrallenax?"

"We cannot," the Fifth Prime answered. "The portals to Draxix will remain inactive until you have defeated Uriel. But you have an élanvital with you who can craft a portal."

Dani straightened. "I cannot forge a portal without Katrin."

"You can forge a portal with a Prime." Zedren's tone held pride again, but this time, it was pride for her. "I will create one with you and you may all return to Nema's Throne."

Chapter 40

JARROD STARED AT THE MESSENGER, his wildly pounding heart matching Neco's at his feet. "Where are they?"

The Ashen Hawk dipped her chin. "Just entering the courtyard, your majesty."

Snatching his cloak off the back of his chair, the Helgathian king bolted from the room and nearly collided with Corin halfway down the hallway when the master of war strode around a corner.

"Whoa, where's the fire?" His husband's gaze tracked him, but he didn't stop.

Neco already rounded the end of the hall, headed for the stairs.

Jarrod met Corin's gaze for a second, grateful the wolf was keeping his thoughts to himself for the time being. "Maithalik is back."

Corin hurried to catch up. "Is Rae with him?"

"No. But Erdeaseq is."

"Shit." Corin matched Jarrod's pace at his side, remaining quiet.

For the past five days, refugees from Eralas had been popping up on Helgath's east coast. They'd arranged for supplies and temporary accommodations for them in Degura and Edrikston, but no one questioned had any information about Rae. Just that massive black dragons had attacked their cities, with smaller Corrupted running rampant and terrorizing the civilians.

Corin had been relocating the Helgathian forces for the past week, and most of them were assembled in Rylorn ready to board with the armada. Without knowing exactly what was going on, though, they couldn't risk sending them.

It took everything in him not to head for Eralas himself to look for Rae.

They arrived at the front steps a few minutes later, breathless even before they took in Maith and Erdeaseq's appearance. Grim. Dried blood and soot marred their skin, leaving his chief vizier hardly recognizable with the arch judgment beside him.

"Do you need a healer?" Jarrod rushed the question as he descended the stairs towards them, forcing himself not to ask about Rae until they'd answered.

Maith shook his head. "No, Kalstacia aided us in Eralas and a healer in Degura finished the job." As the king opened his mouth, the auer lifted a hand and continued, already knowing the next question. "Rae isn't in Eralas anymore. She got out."

Jarrod exchanged a look with Corin. "How?"

The chief vizier's gaze dropped, throat working. "She hitched a ride on one of the Corrupted dragons."

"*She what?*" Jarrod's blood heated, but he tamped it down.

She must have had a good reason.

"Let's get inside." Corin nudged him. "It's freezing out here, and you must be exhausted."

Maith nodded and strode past, Erdeaseq pausing on the same step as Jarrod. "Eralas needs your help. I know it will take time..."

"Our military is ready," Jarrod assured, noting the uncharacteristic desperation on the auer's face. "We have an alliance, and I intend to honor it."

The arch judgment's face sagged with relief, and he followed Maithalik inside.

Neco whined, and Jarrod put a hand on his head, idly scratching. His thoughts ran wild.

Where did Rae end up? Is she alive? Why hasn't she sent word?

The hawk would be slow, of course, but if Rae had made it to an ally capital, she could have found a member of the Sixth Eye to convey her message. He still employed Auster, though the man was minutes away from retirement, and he had acted as their faction liaison for years.

"I'm sure she's fine," Corin murmured, touching his shoulder. "Stowing away on a Corrupted is the most Rae thing she could have done."

Jarrod clenched his jaw. "I'm not sure if that makes it better or worse." He sighed, trying not to look at the smoke clouding the eastern horizon before turning and ascending the stairs. They needed to talk with Erdeaseq and Maithalik in a private room as soon as possible.

Reaching one of the more secluded studies near the palace's library, Jarrod dismissed the two guards, who had taken to following them, before they could rush ahead and open the doors.

They threw a suspicious look at Erdeaseq before departing, but the auer elder didn't seem to notice. His honey-colored eyes were more sunken than usual, and his expression never changed from a grimace.

Maith bowed his head slightly to the arch judgment as he held the study door open for him. The auer hesitated for only a moment before stepping into the darkened room.

Corin moved ahead to retrieve a firestarter and began lighting the sconces in the study. No one moved to open the window curtains, and he looked between the two auer. "What happened? Did anyone else from the elders' council survive?"

Erdeaseq settled into a seat, shaking his head. "My people need your help. But he—" The auer cut himself off, his brow furrowing before he looked again at Maith. "Are you sure? Are you sure speaking his name isn't dangerous?"

Jarrod remained silent, understanding the two auer must have already discussed parts of the events on their way here.

"I'm sure." Maith nodded, tone gentle. "Uriel is no god."

Erdeaseq exhaled slowly, rolling his shoulders. "Then... *Uriel*," he whispered the name, "has swayed several on our council against us. He killed the rest, save for Tyranius, whom he took as his new host, and Lo'thec seems to be Uriel's new right hand. Eralas has no true leader looking out for its people. Olsaeth and Ekatrina, who remain in Quel'Nian, are corrupt and serving... him."

Jarrod nodded, and Erdeaseq met his gaze.

"Raeynna climbed onto one of their soulless mounts, and they flew north with Lo'thec. But he... but Uriel went somewhere else." The arch judgment thanked Maith when the chief vizier handed him a glass of water then took one for himself. "Corrupted are loose throughout our island, killing and harassing people relentlessly."

Corin met Jarrod's gaze from the other side of the study, where he'd finished with the sconces. His eyes held the unspoken question of how much they could openly discuss around Erdeaseq.

The king nodded to Corin, trusting the arch judgment was on their side. "Our army will take care of the Corrupted. We will finish preparations tonight and depart at first light." He leaned forward, studying the shaken auer elder. "We will need you, though. If the two remaining elders are corrupt, we have no hope of restoring order without you present."

Erdeaseq nodded. "I agree."

"We should send word to Isalica," Corin suggested. "If the Corrupted were headed north..."

Jarrod hummed. "Aye. Auster can relay it. But that was days ago, and I suspect whatever was planned for the north... has likely already happened." He hated the feeling that weighed like a rock in his gut. Helplessness. From here, he could do nothing for their allies in Isalica.

"Is there anything else we should know?" Jarrod kept his tone as gentle as he could.

Erdeaseq shook his head, looking so little like the powerful auer he'd first encountered in the Sanctum of Law so many years ago.

"All right." Jarrod sighed. "Get cleaned up. Get some rest. You're going to need it for tomorrow." He looked at Maith. "I'll need you to stay in Veralian."

"Understood."

Neco barked, and the wolf's voice drifted through Jarrod's mind. *I'm not staying here this time.*

Jarrod scowled but relented. "Fine. But only because I know how much you enjoy the taste of Corrupted blood."

The black wolf sneezed and then bared his teeth.

"I'll send word to Rylorn to set sail first thing tomorrow. Do you want a ship to stay behind for us?" Corin tilted his head.

"No." Jarrod looked at Neco. "Send them all. I'd like us to approach in a less obvious fashion."

Corin smirked. "The Herald it is, then. I'll get a message to Andi."

Chapter 41

AHRIA GROANED AS CONRAD GENTLY roused her. "Are they here?" she mumbled, the same question she asked each time she saw him. She wanted to see them, her parents, but she wished she could see Talon, too. Even though he would be so disappointed in what Uriel had done to her.

Katrin hadn't been able to confirm, but a dark voice in the back of her head told her exactly what she'd agreed to during Uriel's questioning.

What she couldn't even remember.

His hand stroked through her hair, then trailed down her cheek. "They're here. And based on the glance I got through the windows of the portal in the garden, they look all in one piece." Hope and relief colored his tone for the first time in weeks. "Katrin's gone to meet them, and I'm sure they'll be up to see you soon." He placed a gentle kiss on her forehead before offering to help her sit up. "Who do you want to see first? I can play guard at the door for you."

She swallowed, accepting his hands and sitting up in bed. "I'd like to see my parents first, no one else. Except you, of course." Exhaustion still pervaded her muscles, her appetite lackluster given the spread of food available. Her body ached constantly, not receiving what it needed to thrive. Nothing Katrin had given her had helped much, but she suspected—and desperately hoped—her mother would be able to relieve the agony she'd endured for weeks.

Conrad nodded, slipping away from the bed and crossing to the door. He paused, looking back at her. "This will be over soon, one way or another."

Ahria nodded back, then looked at the floor. This was her own fault, and she deserved the consequences, but if it could ruin their plans to imprison Uriel...

She sat in silence once Conrad stepped outside the door to their sitting room, shutting the bedroom door behind him. She stared at it, imagining the looks on Kin and Amarie's faces when she told them.

What will Kin think of me?

Desire for Talon to sit with her, tell her it would be all right, ached so deeply in her chest that she wondered if her heart struggled to beat. He would have known the perfect thing to say, and he'd know what to do.

"Gods, I miss you," she whispered into the empty air as her eyes burned. "I miss you so much." Wiping the wetness from her cheeks, she drew in a shaky breath and tried to center herself.

Voices murmured outside her door, and she recognized Conrad's firm response before a door beyond the bedroom clicked shut. Sniffing, she straightened the blankets and her thick, soft sleep shirt, and looked up when the bedroom door swung open.

Kin and Amarie stepped inside, Conrad behind them, and her mother rushed to the bed.

"Take it back," Ahria whispered, and Amarie nodded, placing a tender hand on her arm. The Berylian Key's energy seeped from her soul into her mother, finally allowing her shoulders to relax. The pain eased, and a whimper escaped her throat at the physical relief.

Amarie wrapped her arms around Ahria, who gratefully returned the embrace. "Is that any better?"

Ahria nodded, not letting go. She could breathe easier already, the nausea subsiding. "Much."

Conrad let out a breath, standing by the door.

Kin approached as Amarie loosened her grip. He settled onto the edge of the bed near her. "Katrin wasn't able to figure out what was affecting you?" Despite where they'd just come from, Kin looked remarkably put together. Not as refined as he'd been for the coronation in Feyor, and still in the riding leathers he'd likely battled in.

Bowing her head, Ahria swallowed. "Not definitively," she murmured. "But judging by the evidence, I think I know what happened." She could barely get the words out, like her lungs were running out of air.

Amarie glanced at Kin, then back at her. "Whatever it is, you can tell us."

Her father squeezed her calf in silent agreement.

Ahria looked at Conrad, who nodded once, and she went back to staring at the sheets in her lap. She'd only spoken the words out loud once before to Conrad, and her hands shook at the thought of saying them again, but she breathed in slowly. "I think I'm a Shade."

Kin's touch twitched through the covers of the bed, but didn't recoil like she expected.

Amarie sucked in a slow breath, her grip on Ahria's arm tightening just a little. "What makes you think that?"

Ahria rolled her lips together. "Uriel wouldn't let me sleep, and I don't remember everything that happened, but I remember lots of questions. Constant questions, and I remember saying *yes* at one point, but not knowing what he was asking... and..." She forced a breath. "Katrin found a black line tattooed on the back of my head, hidden in my hair."

Amarie looked at Kin, tension in her face. "Do you mind if we look?"

Ahria shook her head, angling her chin away from Kin.

Her father's gentle hands parted her hair, and a growl rumbled through his chest. He must have looked at her mother, not speaking anything aloud, as he let her hair fall back into place. He reached for his daughter's hand, squeezing it. "This isn't your fault." His tone had deepened, the anger evident, though not directed at her.

"I agreed," she whimpered, throat tightening again.

Kin's grip tightened. "You agreed under torture. Something Uriel has had thousands of years to perfect. You weren't aware of what you were agreeing to. He manipulated you, Bug. It's not your fault."

Amarie wrapped one arm around her, pulling her close. "Kin is right. It's not your fault. In no world is this your fault." She looked at Kin. "Why would Uriel make her a Shade? To what end? This doesn't benefit him, especially if she can draw power from him."

Kin shook his head. "Only if he allows it. At this first rank, there's not much granted to the Shade, and he still controls all use of power. He very well could be giving her nothing but still be able to track through the mark."

Ahria stiffened. "You think he's using this to keep tabs on where I am?"

"It would make sense, but that seems extreme just to gain your location." Amarie frowned.

"I don't understand why it was making you so sick, though. I only suffered these symptoms during my withdrawal from the addiction to the power, but you have never accessed it. Only your own..."

Amarie's gaze shot to him. "Kin..." She pulled Ahria closer. "Can Uriel use the bond in reverse? Can he... Can he take *her* power?"

Ahria looked up at her, mouth dry. "My symptoms were unbearable whenever I tried to use the Art."

Kin stiffened, his head rapidly shaking back and forth. "I don't know. I never heard of a case where Uriel put the mark on someone with their own Art. Not even Alana..." He chewed on his lip as he looked towards Conrad, who stood perfectly still near the doorway. "We need Damien to look at this. He arguably knows more than I do about the Shade tattoo and connection. He can block it."

A tremor worked through Ahria's muscles. "Will that work?"

"We will figure it out." Amarie stroked her hair. "Damien helped Kin. He will help you, too."

Chapter 42

"CAN YOU GET A READ at all?" Rae whispered to Damien, the door to Ahria's bedchamber still shut with only her parents and Conrad inside. She sat on a plush chair across from him, braids fresh from that morning's shower.

"Not without completely invading their privacy. Just... the surface anxieties." Damien leaned forward, resting his elbows on his knees. "Katrin was vague, though. But I could tell she was pretty worried, too."

Matthias, Liam, and Dani accompanied Katrin to discuss events somewhere else in the palace, leaving only the two of them waiting to see Ahria.

"Hopefully it's nothing too serious," she murmured. "I can't imagine if it were Sarra in there."

The thought of his daughter made Damien's chest ache. It'd been months since he'd been home, and even if all had been well when Rae was there, he worried about Sarra. She'd surely start hearing voices soon, and he only wished he could be there like he'd been with Bellamy.

The door to the inner bedroom chamber swung open, and Kin stood there, silently looking at Damien. He nodded once, and the Rahn'ka stood.

"I'll wait here." Rae leaned back, giving her husband a nod of understanding as her voice flowed through his mind. *I'll stay here in case you need a discreet second opinion.*

Damien gave a shallow nod in response as he made his way towards Kin. The former Shade's eyes were darker than usual, and he held the door open for the Rahn'ka.

The room inside was dim, the curtains drawn over the window. Conrad and Amarie sat on either side of Ahria, tucked in among the blankets of the four-poster bed.

The younger Berylian Key's eyes were glassy as she looked at Damien, and her ká swam with guilt. "I did something really stupid," she blurted, earning a quick look from Amarie.

"That is *not* how I would put it," her mother assured, tone gentle. "It is not your fault."

Conrad looked only at her, barely acknowledging Damien's entrance as Ahria bowed her head. "Damien won't think it's your fault, either."

Damien didn't miss the undertone of warning in the prince's voice. "You all seem to already have an opinion about what's wrong. But you still want me to take a look?"

Kin shut the door softly behind them as he crossed towards the bed.

The four of them fell silent, but it was a supportive silence, giving Ahria the time she needed to say the words.

"Uriel deprived me of sleep. He asked countless questions..." Ahria sighed, scratching the back of her head. "He turned me into one of his Shades."

Damien stiffened, but encouraged his feet to continue forward, mind whirling with implications.

Is that what's been making her so sick? That doesn't make sense.

Amarie stood, moving away from Ahria to make space for Damien.

"Can you sever the bond, like you did for me?" Kin hovered near the foot of the bed, looking hopefully at the Rahn'ka.

"In theory, as long as it's genuinely the same. It'll be different with her being the Berylian Key." He glanced back at Amarie. "Do you hold all of the power right now?" His mind continued to mull over the concept presented to him.

"I do." Amarie stood. "She felt a lot better once I took it back."

"Do you have a mark?" Damien glanced down her bare arms, but nothing marred her skin.

Ahria turned towards Conrad, parting her hair with one hand. "He hid it on the back of my head."

Leaning closer, Damien inspected the straight black line of ink tattooed down the back of her skull. "Do you mind if I touch it?"

"Go ahead," she whispered.

Damien swallowed before reaching, and the second his fingertips brushed the tattoo, a jolt of familiar darkness shot through him. A Shade. Uriel had made a Shade out of one half of the Berylian Key.

He held in his curse.

His mind stretched to Rae's. *Dice. I need you to go get Matthias.*

He felt his wife's affirmation of his request in emotion rather than words, though a question drifted through their bond. *Can I tell him why you need him?*

Ahria's a Shade. I think I can break the connection, but I need to talk to him about what this means.

Shit. I'll be back soon.

As Ahria let her hair fall back into place, Damien breathed control into his own ká, protecting it from the corrosive energies permeating hers. This wouldn't be the same as separating Kin. He'd been one of many Shades, more easily forgotten. Uriel would be paying attention to what happened with Ahria. He'd know the moment Damien began to cut the bond, most likely, and there was no telling what he might do to stop him. They had no idea where Uriel had gone after the battle in Draxix.

"You've never used the power of a Shade to your knowledge, right?" Damien tried to block out the stare he could feel from Kin.

Ahria shook her head. "I've never even *felt* his power, let alone used it. Just my own."

"And that's when you felt worse? When you accessed your own?"

She nodded. "A lot worse."

Damien sorted through the information as he extended his hand towards Ahria. "I'm going to take a closer look. See if I can tell what's happening, preferably without alerting Uriel."

Ahria gave another shallow nod before placing her hand in his.

As he closed his grip around hers, Damien hardened his barriers. He placed every protection he could on his own energies, his skin warming from the process. As he closed his eye, a faint blue shimmered on the back of his eyelid, etching the runes that would hopefully hide him from Uriel's awareness.

Ahria's ká was familiar, yet strange at the same time. Pieces of her parents, he recognized, but arranged into something completely different. There were also pieces of another, not tied to her blood, that shaped her ká. Weaves that supported the foundation of her soul, imprinted by someone he'd never personally met.

Talon.

He admired the structure for a moment, looking from a distance, before he spied the dark veins infiltrating from the outside edges. Bruise-colored tendrils that burrowed into the natural flows of her ká. They weren't as deep as those he'd dug out of Kin's soul, but these were lined with barbs that would make separation that much more difficult. And they seemed far more concentrated in particular areas. Areas connected with the flow of the Art.

The energy undulated, hungrily devouring bits of Ahria's ká.

That's what he's really after.

The flow had gone the other way with Kin. Pushing power into Kin's ká for him to use. This connection *stole*.

The darkness of his eyelids flashed with images of a massive beast rushing across the water between Helgath and Eralas. The monster that'd been powered by the Berylian Key so many years ago. What had plunged Eralas into darkness for weeks. It then morphed into a massive onyx dragon, flecks of shadow dancing from his wings as he soared over the desiccated jungle of Draxix.

Damien's eyes snapped open to banish the images, and he slipped his hand from Ahria's.

"What is it?" Amarie stood in front of her daughter, Kin at her side, both eyeing him.

Damien sucked in a steadying breath, forcing his barriers to remain in place. "This Shade connection isn't the same as the usual ones. He's been using it to take power instead of give it."

Kin's upper lip twitched. "We had suspected that possibility. Can you sever it?"

"It'll take time. At least as long as it took me to separate you." Damien turned from Kin to look at Ahria. "And it'll hurt, but the symptoms you've been feeling should go away as soon as I'm done."

The young woman nodded. "All right."

"What would he be using her power for?" Conrad asked, still holding Ahria's other hand.

Damien paused, the thoughts bubbling into a mild ache in his head. He glanced at Amarie. "Last time he used the Key's power..."

"He became that *thing*," she whispered, eyes darkening.

"Is that why he was able to take on that dragon form in Draxix?" Kin's jaw tightened.

Amarie shook her head. "He pulled power from the Primeval to do that."

The realization struck Damien like a stone. "The Corrupted dragons. Lo'thec, even as an elder, wouldn't have had enough energy to summon six of the things. Uriel must have fed him the power to do it."

"You're saying Uriel stole our power to summon the Corrupted dragons that destroyed Eralas and Draxix?" Amarie's voice was barely above a whisper, but rage lingered beneath her tone.

Ahria's throat bobbed, and a fresh wave of guilt tainted her ká.

Conrad's grip on her hand tightened. "It isn't your fault," he whispered.

"He's right." Damien turned his attention back to Ahria. "But we better break this bond before he's able to take more."

Ahria sucked in a deeper breath. "Do it."

"I'll need to touch the tattoo."

She angled away again, turning her head to give him access to the mark.

Conrad shifted, too, facing her so she could lean forward onto him.

Amarie murmured something in a dangerous tone to Kin, but Damien kept his focus on Ahria as he positioned his hand against the nape of her neck.

"Remember to breathe." The Rahn'ka closed his eyes again, focusing on the runes of his power. He'd have to work as quickly as possible to finish before Uriel could react to what he did.

The bedroom door burst open, and everyone's attention shot to Matthias, Rae behind him.

"Have you severed the bond?" The king breathed harder than usual, as did the Mira'wyld.

Damien narrowed his eyes. "I was about to start."

Matthias sighed. "Good. Don't. Don't sever it."

Kin started, taking a step towards the man. "What? Why?" Anger radiated through the former Shade, and he looked as if he might punch Matthias if he suggested it again. A glimmer of red shone at his thigh, along Sephysis's hilt protruding from its sheath.

"Hear me out," the Isalican king held up a hand, pausing before he continued without taking his eyes off Kin. "We might be able to use the bond between Ahria and Uriel to our advantage. Yes, he can use it to track her, but perhaps we can use it to track *him*." Only when a bit of tension eased from Kin's shoulders did Matthias look at Damien. "And knowing where he is might be rather useful, no?"

Amarie exchanged a look with her husband, but said nothing.

Ahria's eyes brightened, though, and she looked at the Rahn'ka. "Can you?"

Damien narrowed his eye at Matthias before facing the hopeful look from Ahria. "Would you want that? It would mean you'll keep feeling the way you are right now."

She nodded without hesitation. "If there is some way we can use this against him..." She huffed. "I would *love* that."

"But she will need to use the Key's power to imprison Uriel, right?" Amarie watched Damien. "What would stop him from stealing her power in that moment?"

"Stealing her power?" Matthias straightened.

"You missed that part." Damien met Matthias's gaze. "He's reversed the usual exchange of energy. It explains how they had enough energy to summon those Corrupted." He looked down at the rumpled covers, sorting through the maneuvers he'd have to make in Ahria's ká without speaking it aloud. "I think I could build in a limit, though. Create a bottle-neck, in a way, to severely limit what power Uriel can take without completely breaking the bond."

"Will I still be able to perform my role in Taeg'nok?" Ahria blinked at him.

Damien paused and nodded. "He won't be able to take more than a trickle, even if you hold half the power. So yes."

"I don't like it." Kin frowned, crossing his arms. "Uriel will still be able to track her."

"Then we use it to our advantage." Damien didn't give in to Kin's glare.

"Because he won't *know* that we know." Ahria looked pleadingly at Kin. "I want to do this. I want this to be useful to us."

Kin's frown deepened, but after a moment, his shoulders relaxed. "It's your choice, Bug."

"See if you can find his location," Ahria said to Damien, then offered her father a soft smile. "If this can help us, I need to do it."

Amarie touched her shoulder. "We will support you."

"There's something else." Matthias drew their gazes again. "I received word through our Sixth Eye friends from King Martox. Arch Judgment Erdeaseq has sought refuge in Helgath. Jarrod is sending his armies to fight in Eralas against the Corrupted swarming their streets. Erdeaseq will also return to the island with the army to reclaim control from the elders who have sided with Uriel."

"Was Maith with Erdeaseq?" Rae looked up at Matthias.

"I was told your chief vizier escorted him."

Rae's shoulders sagged with relief, despite her words. "Another war, raging in Eralas."

"This will all be over soon, though." Conrad looked around the room, still holding Ahria.

Damien controlled his instinctive flinch. It was supposed to be over soon...

But that was before the prison sank to the bottom of the ocean.

Rae met his gaze, and he didn't have to explore her ká to know she was thinking the same thing.

"We have another complication." Damien controlled his guilt. There hadn't been another time to tell them. He steadied himself against their stares, their ká's subconsciously leaping out at his for answers before he even had a chance to voice it. "It involves the prison."

Chapter 43

MATTHIAS STARED AT HIS COFFEE, darker than the mahogany table it rested on. The others in the room—Damien, Rae, and Katrin—murmured among themselves while waiting for the rest.

Everything, all the holes in their plan, whirled in his mind.

The prison had sunk. And that was best-case scenario. Worst-case, it could be totally destroyed. Without the lock they'd retrieved from the maelstrom, they'd never be able to make another.

All their other problems related to the plan, and Uriel wouldn't matter without the prison.

The only small victory was Damien had successfully used Uriel's connection to Ahria to find the master of

Shade's location. Currently, he resided in Aidensar, but the day prior, he'd been on the border of Feyor and Delkest.

Matthias knew that location far better than he wished. That decrepit temple that still, on rare nights, haunted his dreams.

Ahria entered the room, face flush with more color than when he'd last seen her. Conrad walked right behind her, the tension eased from his face.

A few breaths later, Kin and Amarie strode through the double doors, finding seats next to their daughter, and the room's staff poured coffee and tea for those who wanted it.

Dani and Liam joined, too, though Micah wasn't with them as Matthias had expected.

Liam looked his way. "Micah is occupied with palace politics at the moment. I'll fill him in after."

Matthias nodded, and Liam turned his attention to the lingering staff and whispered discreetly to them. A moment later, they cleared the room, making certain to leave the table appropriately filled with breakfast pastries.

Ahria was the first to reach for a pastry, and Matthias's mouth twitched to contain his smile, much like Conrad's. He met the man's gaze and gave a subtle nod that the prince returned.

Quiet settled over the room, eyes gradually turning to the Isalican king.

"I know we have a rather daunting issue to discuss, but before we get to the prison, there are other things I'd like to touch on." Matthias drummed his fingers on the table, taking a deeper breath. "Helgath has mobilized its army to aid Eralas. Jarrod, Corin, and Erdeaseq are departing the capital today to travel to Rylorn, where they will board a ship to join their armies in Eralas and fight the Corrupted overwhelming the island."

A few people nodded, though no one spoke to interject.

"I'd also like to discuss the device given to us on behalf of the Primeval." Matthias looked at Damien, who produced the small Art-laden mechanical device and set it on the table. It was dome shaped, bearing barbed hooks on the flat side that looked like they could do some damage.

Damien glanced at his wife. "Rae and I—"

Someone knocked on the meeting room door, and everyone fell silent for a breath.

"Enter," Matthias called.

The door swung open, and a crown elite poked her head in. "I have the Locksmith here to see you all. He says it's important."

Matthias looked at Amarie, who straightened, before nodding. "Send him in."

Muffled voices and footsteps followed the order before Deylan strode into the meeting room, thanking the guard and shutting the door behind him.

"What brings you so far north?" Matthias asked while Ahria rose from her seat to approach her uncle.

The two embraced, and Amarie smiled.

"Well, I heard about Ahria's health, and I wanted to see how she was doing." Deylan pulled back from her, giving her a once over, and she murmured something to him. As she returned to her seat, he continued, "But on the way here, I received some troubling news. Is it true that your prison is below the sea?"

Damien's single eye narrowed, his hand extending to the device on the table as if to hide it, but then stopped himself, setting his fist down beside his coffee cup. "I thought the faction's viewing chambers were destroyed. How did you hear?"

Deylan's mouth cracked into a smirk that made Matthias furrow his brow.

What could possibly be amusing about this?

"I *heard*," Deylan drawled. "From our water-dwelling allies. They found this for you, too." He retrieved a copper compass from his pocket and tossed it to Rae, who caught it with a frown.

"This is my..."

"Yes. The alcans found it. They also have your prison, and they're keeping it safe in Luminatrias."

Rae's chair scraped across the floor as she abruptly stood. "What did you just say?"

"Luminatrias. It's mostly a rumor for those of us up here on land, but it's down there. It has another name too, though, the—"

"The City of Light," she whispered, and all gazes shifted to her.

"How do you know it?" Matthias looked from Deylan to her and back again.

"My grandfather lives there." Rae blinked, shaking her head as she slowly sat. "Andi... my mother gave me a key of sorts. To enter the city if I decided to search for it and find him."

"But you don't know where it is? It must be close to Orvalinon if they've found the prison, but with the currents..." Katrin looked ready to dive face-first into the library, and Matthias chuckled under his breath.

Rae shook her head again, pocketing the faction device, but Deylan huffed a response. "That's all right, because I know where it is. It's just east of Orvalinon, between it and the island."

Silence hovered in the room for a moment while everyone exchanged glances.

"The prison wasn't destroyed then, when the Corrupted sank the sanctum?" Damien focused back on the Locksmith.

Deylan crossed his arms. "Nope."

The air in the room suddenly became taut.

"We need to make the most of this. Uriel thinks it's gone," Amarie breathed, looking at Rae, who nodded shallowly with disbelief.

Kin cleared his throat. "Will the prison even function without the sanctum, though?"

"The energy of the Art isn't two-dimensional. Sanctums aren't the source of the power, but are built where the Art is the strongest. If it was strong on the surface, it should be strong beneath it," Damien reasoned. "We'd just have to ensure the prison was in a location where we can breathe rather than accessible only to alcans."

"I can go," Rae whispered. "I can enter the alcan city and find out what's going on."

Matthias's gaze snagged on Ahria, who only stared at Conrad with a look of silent conviction.

The crown prince had gone green, his eyes focused on the dark grain of the table rather than anyone else in the room. His chin jerked to Ahria as she placed a hand on his. She whispered something to him. He shook his head minutely, sliding his hand out from beneath hers to fiddle with something hidden beneath the collar of his shirt.

Deylan faced Rae. "Can I see your key?"

The Mira'wyld pulled a small box from an inner pocket of her cloak and opened it to reveal a spherical glass object, carved with runes on all sides. She placed it in Deylan's hand, who turned it over.

"This *is* an access key to Luminatrias, but you'd need another." Deylan gave it back to her. "The keys to enter the city are rarely given, so few exist on land. But you need two, so that when used together, they may open a doorway through the wards."

"Do you have one, then?" Rae tilted her head.

Deylan's expression finally dimmed. "No."

"Can you get one?" Damien seemed to be controlling the hope in his tone.

"Perhaps. But it will take time. The alcan city is tightly controlled and we've never been granted access before." Deylan let out a breath. "But I can reach out to our allies and inquire."

Conrad shifted in his seat, causing the legs to briefly squeak on the wooden floor. "There's no need." His expression was grim as he pulled a silver chain out from around his neck. The pendant that hung from it, wrapped in thin wire, shone in the sunlight pouring from the window behind him. The seafoam-colored glass chimed as it touched the table top, and he pushed it towards Rae. "You can use mine."

Rae stared at it, as did Matthias, in disbelief.

"It doesn't work that way," Deylan muttered, lifting his gaze to the Zionan prince. "Each must be held by one with Alcan blood to be used, as far as we know."

Everyone fell silent again, watching Conrad.

"Are you...?" Matthias held his breath.

Conrad stiffened as he met the Isalican king's gaze. He slowly reached across the table, taking the glass key back into his grip. "My father left it for me before I could even walk. I guess it was in case I ever wanted to see his homeland. Didn't know I'd need two." He sucked in a deep breath and met Rae's bewildered gaze. "I'm sorry I didn't tell you. I... wasn't ready."

Rae didn't move, an array of emotions passing over her expression before she clenched her jaw and averted her gaze to the table.

Kin stared at Conrad, but his tone was gentle. "But you're ready now? Obviously you just told us about your heritage, but are you ready to embrace it and go to Luminatrias with Rae for us?"

Conrad eyed the necklace curled in his palm. His body was so tense, it looked like he hardly breathed. "You need me to be. Waiting for the Sixth Eye to negotiate will take time, and Amarie said it. We need to move fast to take Uriel by surprise." He closed his grip around the key and nodded. "I'll go to Luminatrias with Rae."

Matthias felt a small swell of pride, even though he'd known the young prince for such a short time. "Then the two of you will go." He spoke slowly, still studying Rae. "If everyone is in agreement."

The Mira'wyld only nodded, muscles in her jaw still feathering.

Conrad nodded too, looking a little greener than before.

"Assuming all goes well with the alcans, and the prison becomes usable again... what's next?" Kin looked to Damien, whose attention remained on Rae.

Matthias wondered if he was communicating privately with his wife. "Damien?"

The Rahn'ka looked up, his expression confirming he'd been pulled from another conversation. "If we are able to complete Taeg'nok, it tightens our timeline for when we can use that." He gestured to the dragons' device on the table. "Uriel cannot be imprisoned yet when it's used, because we need a Shade to destroy someone or something we can attach the device to. But I believe we need to stay focused on Taeg'nok as our higher priority. Hopefully an opportunity will present itself to use the lock and seal away Corrupted."

"I'd still love to hear how you plan to kill something with Shade power with the proper timing to use it." Kin looked skeptically at the device.

Damien's lips pursed briefly. "There could be an opportunity." He looked hard at Kin, making the former Shade lean back in his chair.

"I think it's time you take us all through our roles in Taeg'nok." Amarie's tone softened. "If it's getting as close as it feels, we need to know what to do, and who knows when we'll all be together again?"

Damien glanced at his wife before nodding. "Now is probably the best time."

Chapter 44

CONRAD'S SKIN TINGLED AS THE air around him warped in an array of rainbow colors. He held his breath unintentionally, and the next deep inhale came with the taste of the nearby ocean.

Seagulls' cries echoed across the rocky beach, the sky glowing orange as the sun broke over the horizon. And a very confused looking fisherman stared with wide eyes as he pulled his small rowboat up onto the shore.

He faced the eastern horizon, taking in the shadow of an island in the distance. Two tall crags of stone, twin sentinels above the gap between them where the sanctum had once sat. The rock looked discolored in places, where foliage might have once bloomed, but now it was charred black. Destroyed and dead.

Rocks crunched under Rae's boot as she stepped through the portal next, taking a deep breath of fresh, salty air. She nodded politely at the fisherman, avoiding Conrad's gaze as she strode to the small waves lapping at the shore.

Katrin appeared a moment later with Dani, and the portal vanished. "We will wait at the tavern closest to the docks."

Dani nodded her agreement. "Good luck."

"Thanks." Rae lifted a hand in farewell. "Don't get into too much trouble." Though her words were spoken in jest, her tone lacked any mirth.

She's still mad.

Katrin smiled warmly as she lifted the lantern she carried at her side. She twisted her hand in the air in front of the housing, and a pale light wrapped around the glass. "This will continue to work underwater, but only for a few hours. Hopefully you're successful before then."

Conrad gratefully took it, his clammy hands squeezing the metal handle. "Here's hoping."

Isalica's queen turned, giving the still-stunned fisherman a gentle smile before following Dani towards Orvalinon.

The fisherman finally remembered to bow once her back was turned, drawing a short chuckle from Conrad.

Rae faced the sea, the water flowing part way up her boots. She'd braided her hair against her head, hands clenched into fists before relaxing again.

He followed to the surf, looking down at his boots. He knelt, his fingers brushing the froth of the waves as it crested the rocky sand before he loosened his laces.

"Have you breathed in water before?" She watched the waves, her expression difficult to read.

"Yes. But it's been a while." The skill had come in handy a few times while serving on ships, though after becoming captain, he rarely ended up in the water. "Do you know what it's going to be like down there?"

"No," she breathed. "Other than cold and dark." Bending, she pulled off her boots, tying their laces together before securing them to her belt.

Stepping out of his own boots, he did the same. The dense grains of sand stabbed into the bottoms of his feet, and the cold water sent a shiver down his spine as it touched the tips of his toes. He urged himself to remember that the feeling of cold would pass as his body adjusted to the water like it always did, but Isalica's frigid ocean was far different from the water he'd swam in before.

Definitely missing the Dul'Idur Sea in summer right about now.

He'd been looking for purpose in all of this, and now, standing alone with Rae ready to dive into the sea, he longed to be back in the palace with Ahria. Wished the responsibility he'd once wanted hadn't come.

I'm such a hypocrite.

Rae finally looked at him, one eye green and one yellow. "Are you ready?"

He nodded, even though his stomach roiled. He wiggled his toes, the alcan webbing already forming between them in response to the water. His hands would change, too, once submerged. "Right behind you."

"Stay close," she warned. Stepping further into the water, she waded in until it reached her thighs, not once balking at the frigid temperature. Pushing out an exhale, she dove into the surf, and he followed.

The icy water knocked the breath from him, but he quickly remembered to let it in. To draw in the water like air and let it fuel his blood. The salt only stung for the first breath, but as he let out a final exhale of bubbles, it filled more naturally into his lungs. He swam close to her, aided by the new growth between his toes. Lifting the lantern to spy the rocky drop-off on the ocean floor ahead, he frowned when the beams of light couldn't penetrate what lay beyond.

Rae angled downward, disappearing from his view below the shelf before he kicked harder to catch up.

A sudden current tugged at Conrad, her power encouraging the surrounding ocean to flow stronger, propelling them faster through the azure expanse. Down and down they swam, and soon, Conrad's lantern was the only source of light.

The pressure in his head built to an uncomfortable level before his ears finally popped, adjusting to the descent.

Time passed slowly as they reached depths he'd never attempted before. The lantern's light only spread a few feet from the housing in the open water, leaving everything beyond in twilight darkness. They'd moved away from the rocky underwater cliffs of the island, swimming into the open water Deylan had directed them to.

As they reached the darker depths, Rae reached out, grasping the glowing ward key in her fist. Damien had secured it with a thin leather cord to reduce the risk of dropping it. She slowed, as did the current, and faced him. "Your key with mine will help guide us." The words flowed strangely underwater, slower and with less sharpness.

I've never spoken underwater before.

He opened his mouth to respond, but it felt odd, the water forming bubbles along his vocal cords instead of words. He coughed, a fine mist of bubbles coming from his lips.

"Open your mouth wider," Rae instructed. "Form the words around the water. Speak slowly."

He tried again, certain to take a steady breath of sea water. "All right." His own voice sounded strange. Refusing to linger on it, he reached to his neck, producing the silver chain with his father's gift on it. It was pure luck he'd even had it on when the need for it arose. Though, after the conversation about his father before departing for Nema's Throne, he'd felt the inclination to keep it close.

The small glass marble glowed within the wire housing, and Conrad held the necklace in front of him.

Rae's gaze lingered on his hands, where the webbing had formed between his fingers up until his middle knuckle. If he'd been full alcan, it would have spanned the entire length of his fingers. But her hands hadn't changed.

He looked into the empty twilight darkness of the water ahead of them. "Do you think these will work anywhere along the ward?" He eyed the glimmering glass, its pale green glow brightening as he extended his arm forward.

"Deylan said they should." Rae looked around. "But we need to make sure we're close enough." Her lips had taken on a blueish tint, and she wrapped the cord of her key around her wrist.

Conrad nodded as he swam forward, watching the trinket in his hand. Deylan had been vague as to how they would find the protective barrier around Luminatrias. Of course, he probably didn't really know.

The glow of the glass grew more vibrant, casting an aura of light beyond that of the lantern. Movement to his left made Conrad's heart leap before he realized it was a pair of fish fleeing his proximity. Their scales reflected the key's light as they glided through the water, before they abruptly dimmed, the light no longer touching them like they'd passed through a wall.

The ward.

Holding the key out in front of him, he followed the path of the fish.

The water felt strange, more dense, directly in front of him, and the floating glass key swayed unnaturally forward as Conrad stopped. Still holding the end of the chain, he narrowed his eyes as the little orb snapped into place against an invisible wall, and his heart jumped with relief.

Rae mirrored his movement, her own key drifting ahead of her like his had. It touched Conrad's, and a hum gently rippled through the water, both glowing as brightly as the lantern.

Conrad exchanged a glance with Rae before they both reached forward to touch their respective keys. Following Deylan's advice, they pulled them about three feet apart and down, drawing a glowing line through the open water. The hum intensified as they drew the keys further apart. It buzzed up through his fingers and into his entire body, and for the first time it felt like he could sense whatever Art was at work. The vibration in his core brought a calm he hadn't expected, considering where he was.

Like the flap of a tent, what they cut away wavered. Light sparkled within, but he kept his eyes locked on his own glowing key.

The narrow opening took shape, and the hum ceased. The keys snapped out from whatever held them, drifting naturally down to hang from their chain and cord.

Conrad swam through, Rae close behind, and the water warmed. Both of them turned, guiding the keys back to the opening. They pulsed with light as they touched the outer edges of the opening, snapping back into place. The chain wrapped between Conrad's fingers tugged as the keys suddenly pulled together like lodestones. They hovered as the water they'd just swam through flickered, the ward reforming with a chime from the keys.

He and Rae both caught their keys as they dropped from the ward, the light in them falling dormant.

As they faced the city, Conrad's heart leapt. He'd imagined the alcans having grand sea-inspired architecture, but nothing like this.

The ocean floor was no longer barren ahead of them, thousands of lights emanating from Luminatrias, illuminating the entire city. Buildings taller than the palace in New Kingston dominated the city, stone archways and sea-grass covered homes sprawling for at least a mile along the ocean floor. Small fish swam in shimmering schools, reflecting light like clusters of stars.

Near the center of the city, the buildings were the tallest and most elaborate. Domed-stone ceilings and tiered gazebos covered in salt-water ivy and barnacles. The city was rife with life, teams of sea creatures pulling wheelless wagons, and alcans everywhere.

All too far away to notice them.

Save for the armored group swimming straight towards them, spears in hand.

A knot formed in Conrad's chest. This could all end very quickly if the alcans were as unwelcoming as the tales about them suggested. He lifted a hand in greeting as he tucked away the key and hoped the approaching guards would see the alcan webbing between his fingers.

Rae tucked her key, the leather still wrapped around her wrist, into her sleeve before lifting her hands. "We are allies," she announced once they were close enough to hear.

But the alcan guards didn't pause, circling them, though one did say something to another in a language he didn't understand. The words flowed as clicks and trills more than words the way they knew them, though some vocalization blended with the sounds.

Their armor appeared light weight, but covered more of their bodies than the simply clad alcans he'd caught sight of in the faction headquarters. Considering the drag of the water on his clothes, he understood the need for the tight fitting attire.

In the glow from his lantern, their skin was navy-tinted, dappled with smears of lighter blue to create camouflage amid the water. The faction-loyal alcans had been in the air of the bunker, and their skin had appeared the same shade as his own then. Just another part of them that changed in salt water, and he looked at his arms to confirm he hadn't inherited the trait.

"We need to speak to someone in charge. About the island that sank just east of here." Conrad didn't know if they understood him at all, unable to read anything in their expressions.

The guards behind them poked them gently in the back with the tip of their spears, all while they still spoke. To each other or to him and Rae, Conrad had no idea. They poked again, a little harder.

"All right. All right." Rae shot the one behind her a glare. "We're moving." She looked at Conrad, falling silent as they all started the swim into the city.

The guards led them above the city proper, towards one of the taller towers near the center.

This is going to be a long swim...

Below, the openings between buildings flowed almost like streets on the mainland, though doors opened on both the lowest and highest levels of the buildings. Large glowing orbs of light, contained by braided bits of seaweed, hovered at the edges of rooftops. Their illumination shimmered on the buildings of the city, more pearlescent now that they were closer. Each structure's outer walls shone like the inner surface of a seashell, glimmering in an array of color.

I wish Ahria could see this.

The beauty prevailed even as the guards ushered them downward with more prods from the spears. They swam to arches that encircled one of the inner domed buildings, open to the sea around it. He realized, now that they were closer, just how massive the structure was. He could have fit at least ten Dawn Chasers inside.

As they grew closer, his muscles ached with fatigue.

"Do you speak Common?" Rae tried again, but none of them answered her.

Conrad frowned. "We're not dead, so maybe they do." He fought against the mounting turmoil in the pit of his stomach, forcing his expression to remain calm. He needed to portray the stern captain. The stoic prince.

They swam past intricately carved pillars as they entered the structure, the guards escorting them spreading out. Their graceful movements around the pillars made Conrad feel clumsy every time he had to adjust to avoid hitting something. They made their way towards the center, where a denser line of pillars suggested an inner chamber.

The guards slowed, one extending his spear out to stop Rae and Conrad from crossing through an opening between pillars. He didn't speak, but his frown conveyed the direction to them just fine. One of the females behind them peeled away from the group, disappearing into the chamber ahead.

Conrad eyed the spear the guard held parallel to the ground, knowing another was held the same way behind them. The craftsmanship of the weapon was unlike anything he'd seen before, but that stood to reason. Very little was known about alcans on the mainland, other than the occasional visits they rarely made. In reality, it was remarkable that Conrad had ever met another person that shared alcan blood, let alone two.

Of course, they're mother and daughter, so does that really count?

Looking at the guard before him, he noted the subtle differences between the alcans and humans. The more he studied them, the more the image he'd constructed of his father in his mind changed, and he wondered what he'd really looked like. The guard's eyes were the most apparent difference, large sea-colored irises and a crescent pupil. He hadn't inherited that trait, unlike Andi, making it easier for him to blend in on the mainland.

Coarse hair, like Conrad's, donned their heads in closely-shaved styles, most taking on a short mohawk appearance. One of the guards had grown out a section of hair, forming dreadlocks down the back of her head. Each of their noses was slightly flatter, all pierced with hoops on the nostrils, some with multiple.

The webbing at their hands and bare feet was far more impressive than Conrad's. Their movement here had taken what seemed like half the effort, the webbing extending past their toes just enough to more efficiently catch the water.

Rae glanced at the guard holding the spear to her back with narrowed eyes, her braids floating sideways with the motion. "I know you can understand me. We need to speak to whoever your leader is."

The alcan only poked her with the spear again, and she begrudgingly faced forward. But a breath later, the guard hissed, "Be patient."

Casting Conrad a pointed look, Rae raised her eyebrows. "So they *do* understand."

"Now we just have to hope they'll listen." Conrad looked at the doorway the guard had disappeared through. She emerged a moment later, tapping the base of the doorway with the bottom of her spear. She nodded her head at the lead guard, clicking her tongue.

The lead guard lifted his spear, tapping it on the ground like she had and gestured towards the doorway.

Water caught in Conrad's throat as he considered what lay beyond. Hopefully it wasn't a cell. So much relied on him and Rae successfully negotiating with the alcans, that failure wasn't an option.

The prison would be lost down here.

Lifting his chin, he exchanged a quick look at Rae before swimming forward as directed.

Inside the chamber, the ground dropped to form deep, wide steps like an amphitheater. Each level boasted a stone railing at the front, thick enough to be more like a desk. Strange crystalline objects sat on them in no particular order, along with neatly stacked piles of thin slate that appeared to have something carved onto them.

Only the upper levels were empty, the rest... Conrad quickly tried to count how many alcans were there. Eighteen, not including the alcans who stood apart from the rest on a unique shelf at the opposite side.

His skin tingled under their stares as the guards led Rae and Conrad to the bottom of the chamber, where all alcans could look down on them.

"You feel outnumbered?" Rae murmured. "Because I suddenly feel very outnumbered."

He didn't answer, glancing up as the guards finally pulled away from them. Two remained nearby, but moved towards the outer walls of the chamber.

"Your blood is partly of our world." A female alcan to the left stared at Conrad. "Who are you, and who are you descended from?" The Common language rolled off her tongue like she'd spoken it since birth.

Rae pursed her lips, looking at Conrad.

He straightened, not allowing any doubt to show on his face. His father was loyal to Luminatrias, he had to be since he'd had the key to the city, and had every right to gift it to his son.

He did leave us to go fight in some war.

"My father was Ernesjan, hailing from the House of Spears. My name is Conrad Pendaverin."

The female paused, then spoke to a male in their strange language.

Rae kept her mouth shut, either unwilling to provide her heritage or not wishing to speak out of turn. Of course, they hadn't asked her, and perhaps the less questions the better.

A male alcan with beads adorning his short mohawk spoke. "Your father gave his life to defend our people. I, Trinithian, acknowledge you as a descendant of my House in your father's absence."

Pain subtly bloomed in Conrad's chest. He knew based on all his mother had said that his father was likely dead, but realized suddenly that he'd been hoping. Hoping that there was a chance he was still out there and just unable to return to his family.

Conrad bowed his head to the alcan he presumed led the House of Spears. "Thank you."

Another male, this one with a completely shaved head, unlike the rest, addressed Rae. "You breathe as we do, yet I see no other signs of alcan lineage. You create water currents, but even a Mira'wyld cannot breathe water."

Rae rolled her lips together. "My grandfather was alcan. I do not know of which House, but his name is Adamonicus. My name is Rae Lanoret."

More murmuring rose between the group, though the same male spoke again. "Adamonicus is a loyal citizen. I, Bethenicium, acknowledge you as his descendant."

Rae dipped her chin but said nothing.

"Why have you come?" The female alcan addressed them both, her face impossible to read.

They must be aware of the prison if they told the faction about it.

"We come on behalf of a group seeking to protect Pantracia." Conrad glanced at Rae, and she gave a subtle gesture for him to continue. "Against a force I'm certain your people have heard about. His name is Uriel, and he's the one responsible for the recent attack on Eralas, the destruction of the nearby Rahn'ka sanctum, as well as Draxix, where the dragons now live." He tried not to think about how Rae should have been the one telling them all this, but hesitation would destroy any hope of gaining the alcans' trust. "We're trying to imprison him." Saying 'we' felt strange, but he urged himself to continue. "Before Uriel can enact the next part of his attack, which will affect everyone in Pantracia, including your people. But we need your help."

The alcan leaders stood stiff, backs straight as they floated in place. A few spoke among themselves, but one of the other females responded to Conrad. "What aid do you seek from us?"

"The prison we built for him." Rae circled her hands in the water at her sides, keeping herself in place. "We believe it could be near here. Uriel sank it a week ago, but we've heard that it survives among your people."

"You've heard?" A male tilted his head. "From whom did you hear such information?"

Rae didn't hesitate, either. "Our allies in the Sixth Eye."

More chatter. Clicking tongues and low trills, as the alcans discussed. A language impossible for an outsider to learn.

"What threat does this Uriel have against our people?" A female who hadn't spoken before interrupted the murmuring.

"He seeks to cause another Sundering." Rae lifted her chin. "A Sundering that will destroy the fabric of the Art and remove it from this world."

The chamber grew eerily silent, the alcans exchanging looks instead of words. Finally, one spoke clearly in their own language, and the others offered subtle nods.

"We will consider your request," the first female said. "Our guards will escort you to an air chamber where you may wait."

Conrad sucked in a breath, looking at Rae as the guards moved forward. They'd said all that they could for now, and he suspected the alcans would do their own looking into the events they spoke of.

We just have to pray they don't keep us waiting too long.

The guards swam to them, gesturing upward with their hands rather than their spears. The one that had spoken under his breath to Rae before nodded to them both. "This way, please."

They left the council chamber, swimming to the far end of the domed structure. Outside of it, a row of more rectangular buildings sat nestled among coral and tall sea grass. The doorways looked different, pulsing like the surface of the ocean.

"Watch your step." The guard swam to stand near the doorway, looking back at them. "The shift to air can be disorienting."

Conrad eyed the doorway, wondering why the alcans would have chambers like this when they could so readily breathe underwater.

I guess they must tire of swimming sometimes, too.

Using his hands, he positioned himself as best he could in the doorway like he was simply walking on the ocean floor. He pushed his foot forward first, breaking through the Art-laden barrier that held the water at bay. The next move was more of a stumble than a step as his upper body passed through, and he barely managed to catch himself as he practically fell through the doorway. His lungs contracted as he sought a dry breath, and what water remained in his lungs came out with a forceful exhale, sputtering onto the floor.

Rae crossed the barrier in a similar fashion, grasping the wall to keep upright as her knees wobbled. She coughed, remnants of water spraying from her mouth as she bent over. Clearing her throat, she gasped for another breath. "Gods, I'll never get used to that."

"Me neither." His voice rasped, still not fully back to what he was used to it sounding like. He looked around the room, the distorted shapes of the guards in the water moving away. The room they stood in seemed to only be the entryway, plainly decorated with an intricate arch that led to the rest of the structure. Another thin sheen of Art hung in the air of the next doorway, almost like a curtain.

A cushioned bench adorned the wall on the other side, and Rae staggered towards it. She paused only briefly at the sheen, passing through without nearly as much concern as he would have felt. But she looked at her hands on the other side, then patted her legs. "Huh. That's a neat trick." She continued to the bench, plopping onto it with an exhale and another cough.

Conrad followed, and the wave of heat that passed over him as he walked through the doorway almost made him lose his balance again. His clothes instantly stopped clinging to his skin, fabric drying in an instant. He touched his hair and felt no moisture in the tight curls against his scalp. "I guess that makes sense, if the alcans live both in and out of the water. They wouldn't want to walk around soaking wet all the time." He lifted his hands, watching the slow disappearance of the webs between his fingers.

"Hmm," Rae agreed, staring at her own hands with an unreadable expression.

He glanced in her direction, tension still lingering between them. In all the years he'd watched her come and go off Andi's ship, he never thought they'd end up working together. And in the destroyed faction headquarters, they'd grown closer, but that familiarity seemed gone now.

The words Conrad sought in that moment were difficult to find. He was entitled to his own secrets as much as she was. And gods knew she and Damien had plenty.

"We don't need to talk," she murmured, still not looking at him.

He stiffened. "But we should. I should. I owe you an explanation."

Rae met his gaze. "You owe me nothing. I misunderstood." Her two-tone eyes no longer unnerved him like they did when he was younger, her Art no longer a strange, intimidating force.

Wonder when that changed.

"I'm... trying to get better about opening up. It's not exactly a strong suit of mine." He crossed his arms, seeking the vague comfort the action brought. "So if you could pretend I *do* owe you an explanation for why I kept my heritage quiet, it might be helpful."

"A little ironic that in trying to be open, you close yourself off," Rae pointed out, gesturing to his crossed arms.

Looking down at them, he frowned and forced them back to his sides even if it felt awkward.

Rae's lips twitched in a half formed smile. "But no, I can't pretend that. Your heritage will never be anyone else's business, and you never have to share that with anyone you don't want to. I've kept more than my fair share of secrets, and I'm not in a position to judge you. I just thought..." Her voice trailed off, throat bobbing as she looked at her hands again. "When I realized you were connected to all this, I thought about all the times I saw you as a kid, and I was excited to have you as a part of this group. You were always so patient with Bellamy, even though he's a few years younger than you. I don't know. I think I'm just a little sad, as stupid as that is. I thought there was more trust between us."

"It doesn't really have to do with trust. I do trust you. It's just... not something I talk about." Conrad looked at the back of his hand, now completely human, like he was used to. "I never knew my father, not really, and I was so used to denying that part of me." He huffed a small laugh. "You'd think sailors would be more accepting of alcans on ships, but it's actually the opposite. They think it's an unfair advantage, and that we don't really belong there, let alone in a captain's seat." He met Rae's eyes, wondering if her mother had ever told her that before. Told her what Andi had faced to achieve her position on the Herald.

"Andi knew, then, of course," Rae muttered thoughtfully. "Did she advise you to keep it to yourself?"

He chewed his lower lip. "She said it would make things easier. I'd stowed away naively thinking I'd be accepted on a ship with my alcan blood. She set me straight in that fairly quickly. Then it just became... habit. My own crew didn't know. Still don't."

Rae nodded. "I didn't even know I was part alcan until after I married Damien." She laced her fingers together over her thighs. "You could have told me, you know. But I understand why you didn't. And I'm grateful you're with us. I think you're better at staying calm and controlled than the rest of us."

Conrad quirked his brow up. "Hardly. I think I'm just better at hiding the sheer panic." He smiled when she let out a light laugh. "And I hardly belong with all of you, anyway. Ahria is the only reason I'm around."

Her brow furrowed for only a second. "Then I guess we're all grateful to Ahria." Her lips slowly spread into a wider smile. "Because we have the half-alcan Zionan prince in the alcan city negotiating for the retrieval of the prison on our behalf."

Conrad shrugged. "We'll see if that ends up helping or hurting, I suppose. But..." He made his way to the bench, settling beside her. "I'm glad to know the truth about my father. That he did die out here serving the city. That's better than the dark thought that he was just avoiding me and my mum."

"I'm sorry about that, by the way. It must be hard to have grown up without him."

He shook his head. "Like I said, he was gone before I could even form memories." He subconsciously reached for the necklace tucked in his pocket, thumbing the glass bead. "I think it'd have been worse to remember him and then not have him anymore."

Rae nodded, touching her own ward key still bound to her wrist.

He lifted his chin towards her motion. "Are you going to ask more about your grandfather? I'm surprised Andi isn't down here herself looking for him."

The Mira'wyld shrugged. "She found her family and no longer needed to search for him, she said. But, no, probably not. He might not even acknowledge me, let alone my mother. Maybe it's best not to form memories."

Conrad turned to her. "I think you misunderstood me. If I had a chance to have those memories, even if it meant more pain, I would take it. I might have said it was easier, but that doesn't mean that's how I'd actually want it to be. I wish I could have just one day with him, even if that was all I'd get."

Rae looked at him again, nodding. "Maybe next time. I'm not just here to find the prison with you. I need to look for something else lost with the sanctum. I won't have time to search for my grandfather, too."

"What else are you looking for?" Conrad didn't remember anything being discussed with the group, and a small part of him wondered if this was another Damien and Rae secret. He didn't know much about the Rahn'ka or their sanctums, other than the prison needed to be built in one.

"There is a guardian at every sanctum." Rae lowered her voice. "I need to find their soul, more or less, so they may survive."

Conrad winced. "I hadn't thought about what else might have been destroyed in the attack, other than the prison." He wondered what the guardian looked like. "You think you'll be able to find it?"

"I don't know. Damien altered my Rahn'ka tattoo to react to similar power, so I'm hoping that helps me track it through the water. But I need all the time I can get." Rae opened her mouth to continue, but her gaze shot to the watery doorway, where two alcan guards now waited. "That was fast. I think it's time to return."

Chapter 45

RAE WATCHED THE ALCANS MANEUVER the prison through the city's wards, Conrad supervising its transport. They'd run thick ropes of seaweed around the object, securing harnesses to a pod of small orcas who aided in lifting it from the rubble. She almost hadn't recognized it, the once-shiny solid black cube faded into a dull grey.

With the right energy source, it will come back to life.

She swallowed, dragging her eyes from the transport—growing farther and farther away—to assess the sanctum ruins scattered around the ocean floor. She'd caught a glimpse of the destruction under the powerful underwater lights the alcans had used to find the prison. Some of the lights remained, left to float above the ruins, bobbing with an invisible current but staying in place.

The sanctum lay in shambles across a large swath of the ocean floor. The debris had cut into the sea grasses and corals, the Rahn'ka monoliths toppled and broken. Already, some sea life had claimed the surface of the stone, fish weaving through their newly formed habitat.

At least the alcans are helping.

She held onto that victory, and reminded herself that finding the guardian's essence would be a bonus. Though she could read her husband's expression when he made the request. He desperately hoped she'd be successful, even if he told her it wasn't a priority.

Taking a deep, salty breath of ocean, Rae pushed up her sleeve. Stone lay crumbled in all directions, and the fountain Damien had asked her to look for could be anywhere. Her tattoo barely glowed, and she traced her finger over the skin.

"It will be in the fountain," Damien had told her. "Their power stems from there. You remember the three-tiered one Sindré had? Where I had to go any time I needed to heal myself?"

Rae had nodded as he laid his palms over her forearm, heating the ink. "What will it look like?"

"I have no idea. But this should guide you to it. The focus object for the guardian's ká will still radiate Rahn'ka energies for this to react to." His power wove through her, bonding to the tattoo he'd given her years ago. "It should be obvious."

"Obvious," Rae repeated to herself, voice quieter within the water. Looking down at her arm, she started swimming.

From her original spot, she swam north, then east, then south, making her way out and then back in, keeping an eye on her tattoo for any sign that she'd neared the essence. Nothing, each time, and her fingers ached with the cold.

Without the guide, her task would have been impossible in the half mile of debris. Though it'd been hours and she'd still found nothing.

Rae swam west next, and when her navy-blue ink brightened, she exhaled her relief.

Following the increasing glow, she kicked through the water, heart picking up speed when she spotted a larger chunk of stone, separated into two tiers.

"There you are," she murmured, the two intact tiers of the fountain illuminated by the pale blue light emanating from her arm. The bottom was missing, but as she moved closer, the intensity of her tattoo grew.

It must still be inside the stone.

Rae spun, floating in circles until she found a good sized piece of broken stone to use. Dragging it closer to the fountain, she dropped it on the spout, but the water slowed the impact enough that nothing broke.

Frowning, Rae tugged her power to the surface of her skin and tried again while adding a current. The water flowed faster, and she heaved the rock at the fountain. Again and again, each time invigorated by the small pieces breaking from the main structure.

Finally, her next hit caused a crack to stretch across the front and side, and one more hit broke the fountain in two.

Behind the spout, where the water used to flow from, lay no pipes or paths or openings for water. It was solid stone, but a shimmering object sat within. A skull.

Rae swam closer, running her fingers over the strangely smooth relic, which was far from human. Fox, based on what Damien had told her about Mirimé. Grasping it, she jerked it free from the debris, admiring the hue that matched Damien's power. It blended into the ocean deep, so transparent it nearly disappeared even as she held it.

"I've got you," she whispered, unsure if the guardian would hear. Success bloomed through her, satisfaction quickly following.

With her task complete, she needed to find Conrad.

Though their group had thought the ward keys needed to be held by two individuals, the alcans had assured her that wasn't the case. So Conrad had left her his key, and she used it and her own to return within the warmer water, closing the opening behind her.

She turned towards the eastern edge of the city, which curved in an arch towards distant undersea cliffs. At the base of the destroyed island, the structures were intact and protected by Luminatrias's ward that had deflected the sanctum ruins to where they now lay. The alcan council had stated there was a sacred place there, among the cliffs, that held the same potent flow of Art required for Taeg'nok. A cavern that would enable their non-alcan friends to breathe.

They must be finished by now.

Conrad was supposed to meet her there, so she swam, the fox skull safely tucked into a kelp-woven backpack provided by the alcans.

As she grew closer, fewer buildings adorned the ocean floor near the opening of a slot canyon, its edge rimmed with Art-infused lamps. It was lined with natural sea life clinging to the stone. Ahead, she could make out another opening, with two alcan guards stationed on either side.

Her muscles screamed for rest, but she mustered a little more strength. Once the guards nodded to her, floating aside to let her pass, Rae swam inside the cavern. After a short distance, the natural formation led her up. Surprise helped expel the salt water from her lungs, and she sucked in a breath of humid cavern air, but it caught in her chest.

"By the gods," she whispered as her mouth fell agape.

My father's cavern.

As she swam for the edge of the water, in the back of her mind, she wondered if Andi had been the one to show her father that cave under the lake in Delkest they'd often visited. The cave she'd shown Damien so many years ago. But this one was far, far more monstrous.

I wish he could see this.

Stretching a hundred feet over her head, and deep into the giant cavern, were thousands of colorful crystals glittering with raw energy. Some as large as her body or even larger, creating the illusion that she stood within a geode.

The crystal hanging on the cord around her neck, the gift from Damien when she had showed him her father's cavern, reacted as if it also acknowledged where they stood, brightening. She touched it absently as she climbed from the water onto the rocky shore.

There was no need for lanterns here, the Art-laden crystals illuminating the space almost as if it were day. Her gaze traveled around the cavern, feet meandering further inside, until she spotted the glossy black cube in the center.

Conrad stood before it, turning to face her.

A question clouded his expression, and she nodded, patting the kelp backpack. "I found it." Her words came out breathless, the cavern's power ebbing against her skin in a way she wished her husband could experience.

But he will soon enough.

She eyed the prison, stepping closer to it.

"It changed as soon as we entered the cave." Conrad looked at two alcans who still sat near the water's edge, chatting in clicks and soft tones. "So I guess Damien was right. It doesn't need the sanctum." He looked up towards the ceiling. "But I guess it's possible we're under where the sanctum was."

"We must be. Sanctums are built at the intersection of ley line power," she whispered. "Even though the ley lines were broken during the Sundering, some of the bigger ones still remain at places the Art flows more easily."

Conrad gave an impressed huff. "We're lucky that this happened to be here, too, then. Uriel won't find it before we're ready."

"Yes." Rae pressed her palm to the side of the prison, her heart thundering at the implications.

The prison was whole. The prison would function.

And Uriel thought it was destroyed.

All the ways they could, should, or might use it to their advantage reeled through her mind at breakneck speed.

"We need to tell the others as soon as possible," she breathed, looking at him. "We need to get Dani and Katrin down here."

Conrad gestured his head towards the two alcans. "That's what they're here for." He stepped closer, lowering his voice so it wouldn't echo through the cavern. "Do you think we need to worry... with how helpful the alcans are being?"

Rae focused on him, and gave herself a moment to think before answering. "The alcans depend on the Art. A second Sundering would wipe them off the face of Pantracia. They also informed Deylan when the prison sank, so I think we can trust they are on our side."

He nodded. "That's good, we needed this string of luck." He looked towards the water, its surface glimmering with the reflection of crystals. "Things are about to get serious, aren't they? The prison was all we were missing and now..." He looked back to the obsidian-like object, its massive shape somehow dwarfed by the cavern around it.

"Now we move fast." Rae started for the waiting alcans. "Once Dani and Katrin can portal in and out of here, we can—"

Conrad caught her arm. "One thing, before we go. I asked about your grandfather for you. Adamonicus."

Something hardened in Rae's gut, but she paused. "And?"

"He's not here and won't be for another week. He's serving as a liaison between alcan clans and is traveling in the southern seas. But then he'll return here to Luminatrias."

"Oh." She rolled her lips together. "Thank you." A part of her regretted not being able to meet him, but other matters were more pressing. "Too bad we can't stick around."

"You could write him a letter. The representative of the council I spoke to sounded like they would be willing to ensure he received it. Then, maybe when all of this is done..."

Rae narrowed her eyes at him before slowly nodding. "All right. I'll leave a letter for him."

Chapter 46

IS THIS EVEN THE RIGHT WAY?

The halls of the Isalican palace wove and turned in ways that made it easy for Kin to get lost. He doubted he'd be able to find his way around even after months there.

Hopefully it won't be months, but...

They hadn't heard anything from the others who had made their way to Orvalinon to meet with the alcans. And the tension among those still in Nema's Throne was palpable when they met for lunch.

It's only been half a day since they left. Who knows how long it'll take.

Kin had selfishly kept Amarie to himself that morning, but now, she wanted to take time to be with Ahria. It made sense, with Conrad gone, that the pair could get some quality mother-daughter time. He wished he could have joined, but they planned to have dinner with just the three of them that evening, and he had to talk to Matthias.

He and the Isalican king hadn't had any time to catch up since the battle at Draxix. And now with Damien finally being upfront with the requirements of the spell to imprison Uriel, Kin's anxiety had spiked. Only Matthias would understand.

I have to find his study first, though.

Hopefully, the pair of guards that gave Kin a respectful bow as he passed through an archway indicated he was going the right direction.

The rich tapestries and carpet of the king's chamber hallways began to look familiar, and Kin approached the door he felt fairly certain was the study. There were no guards there, but Kin had noticed Matthias dismissed them as often as he did.

Touching the iron handle, Kin paused when voices carried through the dense wood.

"It won't matter if they die. Not if everything else goes to plan." Damien sounded almost tired, and Kin could imagine him rubbing the back of his neck.

"That's putting a lot of trust in everything else going according to plan." Matthias was curt, an undercurrent of something else in his tone. "And what if..." The man's voice faded, and Kin felt the king's attention on the door.

Kin winced. Of course one or both of them would have realized he stood there. And he doubted they'd be forthcoming with whatever they'd been discussing if he asked. He sighed, knocking once before pushing the door open. "Am I interrupting?"

Matthias shook his head. "Not at all. We were just discussing the logistics of tracking Uriel and capturing him."

Pretty sure you're leaving out some important details there.

Kin didn't push. It wouldn't get far with Damien and Matthias. He nodded, stepping into the study and carefully closing the door behind him. The curtains on the large window at the back of the room were open, granting a view of the snow-covered mountains and palace rooftops. The sky glowed with the oranges and pinks of sunset, which happened so much earlier here in the frigid north. The dinner bells would be ringing soon, most likely.

"Still nothing from Katrin or Rae?" With their wives gone to Orvalinon, it made sense that Damien and Matthias had sought each other out. They were the two natural leaders of the group, and both had the bad habit of taking all responsibility onto their own shoulders.

"Not yet," Damien sighed. "But we're trying to take that as a good sign. If they'd been unsuccessful, they'd probably be back by now."

A muscle feathered in Matthias's jaw, but he didn't contradict the Rahn'ka. "If they're successful, we need to be prepared to move quickly to capitalize on the advantage. We just can't think of a good way to lure Uriel to a location that will work to grab him. He can vanish into shadow at the drop of a hat, so Damien would need to be there, but also at a spot our portal-makers know. Right now, he's still just hiding in Aidensar, but his exact location changes every few minutes."

"It's smart of him. He isn't sure what exactly we know, and is probably being cautious. It has to be something he really wants to get him to show up in person, and there's a fairly obvious answer here to what that is." Kin lowered his hand to his left thigh, patting Sephysis, which was buckled into its sheath. "He'll come for me, so we use me as bait."

Damien frowned, fiddling with the strap of his eyepatch where it latched at the back of his head. "It may just have to come to that, even with all the danger. Amarie shouldn't be anywhere near you, though. We don't want to give him another opportunity to get what he wants." The Rahn'ka discreetly glanced at Matthias, but Kin couldn't read the meaning behind it.

"The question still remains as to where and how to get Uriel's attention. It still needs to be a location Katrin and Dani know." Matthias moved to his desk, flipping over a crystal glass before pouring amber liquid from a decanter.

"If Melyza was still alive, we could have used her cabin, since they all know it. But with her dead..."

"She doesn't need to be alive for us to use the cabin. Based on what Amarie told me, Uriel probably thinks *we* don't know she's dead. We can use that to our advantage." Kin had formulated the plan throughout his time alone with Amarie that morning while they went over the details of her time in Aidensar together.

Matthias narrowed his eyes at the former Shade. "So... we, what? We pretend we think she's alive?"

"Yes, and I send her a letter requesting a meeting to discuss her knowledge of Sephysis. Uriel saw me struggling to control the dagger in Draxix. It makes sense that I would seek more help. And Melyza is a logical place to go. One we could have realistically found through our various connections to Eralas." Kin looked at Damien, who still frowned.

The Rahn'ka took a deep breath. "This all depends on Uriel not being aware of our previous visits to Melyza. But he knows we were in the area, because of the Shade that was in the library with Katrin."

Matthias still watched Kin. "The Shade only knew they were looking for Melyza, not that they successfully found her or her body." He scratched his beard before smoothing it out. "I think it's worth a shot. Deylan will have a faction contact in Aidensar who can forge the letter, then we use

Ahria to monitor Uriel's location to see if he'll take the bait. I doubt he could resist the temptation of Sephysis coming right to him. But he will probably have Lo'thec with him, too, so we should be prepared for that."

"I think those are all reasonable risks. If it gets Uriel to the prison, it'll be worth it, right?" Kin looked between the two, wishing they'd explain without him having to ask what they'd been discussing when he arrived.

More secrets I'm sure they think are worth it.

Damien watched Matthias as the king took a slow drink of his whisky, some silent conversation passing between them.

"Are you sure you're ready?" Damien turned his attention to Kin, making the former Shade's stomach flip. Even with only one of his eyes, he had an uncanny ability to make Kin question everything.

"I understand what I need to do. I may not like it, but if it's what needs to be done to trap Uriel forever, I'm going to do it." Kin unconsciously scratched at the webbed scar on his right arm, hidden beneath the sleeve of his tunic.

Matthias nodded. "I don't like it, either, if it makes you feel any better."

"I'm not talking about that." Damien's eyes flicked down to Kin's side. "I'm talking about the dagger. We can't have what almost happened in Draxix, happen again. We have to assume Lo'thec will be there. It'd be better if you left Sephysis behind."

Kin's jaw tightened as the dagger gave a protesting vibration in its sheath.

"The dagger has no hiding aura," Matthias gestured with his chin to the weapon. "Uriel can sense energy sources, just like you can. If Kin shows up in Aidensar without the dagger, he might realize it's a trap. Hells, he could even sense you."

Damien shook his head. "I have plenty of practice hiding my power from him. He won't know I'm there, and I could easily encompass Kin and the dagger, too, if necessary"

Kin ran a hand through his hair. "I should arrive separately, so he can sense me coming. If I just appear out from within your barrier, that's going to give it away, too. I can walk there from Kiek."

The Rahn'ka didn't look convinced. "Having Sephysis anywhere near Amarie risks giving Uriel exactly what he wants."

"Amarie won't come to Aidensar." Kin had already discussed that aspect with her, and she'd heartily agreed.

Damien sighed. "How would I even know when to join you?"

"If you give me the other faction communication device, I will approach the cabin as soon as I get a signal from

Conrad that you've arrived behind the cabin. And bringing the dagger to Aidensar gives me an opportunity to leave it there. I'll make sure it doesn't come back through the portal with us to the prison."

"But then it will be loose in Aidensar," Matthias pointed out.

"I don't think so." Kin ran his thumb along the hilt of the bloodstone blade. "I don't think the connection has a range. Naturally, it'll seek me out, and it'll take Sephysis time to make its way from Aidensar back to Isalica. Plenty of time to imprison Uriel."

"That's a lot of conjecture." Damien leaned against Matthias's desk. "We're talking about another Sundering."

"We've already said it, though. Assuming Rae and Conrad are successful, we have to move fast. There isn't time to sort out all the details. It's better to catch Uriel unaware. If he didn't believe the prison was destroyed, he might not dare show himself even with Sephysis as bait." Kin looked between the two of them.

"It feels sloppy," Matthias muttered. "Anything could go wrong with this."

"Good thing you should be able to give us a few extra chances, right?" Kin met the king's eyes. He hadn't seen Matthias's power in action himself, but had heard about how it'd been used in Draxix when they'd recounted each other's sides of the battle.

"The chances become fewer the more people I need to take back with me, and we get no extra chances if I'm dead." Matthias rolled his shoulders. "What if Sephysis won't listen and refuses to stay in Aidensar?"

Kin glowered. "I'm in control. It'll stay in Aidensar. But even if something goes wrong, I'd never allow Sephysis to hurt my wife or daughter." No matter what happened, he'd make sure that statement remained true. His family wouldn't be in danger because of him.

Matthias slowly nodded, glancing at Damien before nodding again. "All right. Then we better get Deylan to set this up."

Damien's attention turned to the study door, relief sagging his shoulders. "They're back."

Silence fell, tension straining through the room as everyone held their breath.

A few moments later, soft footsteps echoed from the hallway and the study door swung open.

Katrin and Rae stood there, the latter looking utterly exhausted. A strange seaweed-woven backpack slung over her shoulder, and both women offered tentative smiles.

"The prison is restored." Rae turned her bright eyes on her husband. "The alcans helped us relocate it."

"Dani and I are prepared to open a portal for all of us to get to its new location." Katrin strode to Matthias, who wrapped his arm around her shoulders.

"Where is it?" Damien straightened off the desk, approaching Rae.

"In a cavern beneath where the sanctum was before." She shuddered when the Rahn'ka touched her arm, and a little color returned to her face.

Matthias looked at Kin. "Go find Deylan and get the letter sent. Make sure he notes the exact words you'd use. This is our chance."

Kin nodded, his heart suddenly beating faster.

This is really it.

Rae passed the bag she carried over to Damien, and the Rahn'ka took it gingerly before wrapping his arm around his wife and kissing her forehead. It made him suddenly miss Amarie, and he wondered if both of them would make it out of the coming battle alive.

With whatever Matthias and Damien were talking about...

He banished the thoughts from his head. There couldn't be doubt. He wanted to believe that first and foremost, they'd become friends and they'd tell him if it was imperative.

I trust them.

"When should I set the trap for? Probably need a few days for the message to make it to Melyza's cabin."

"Three days, then." Damien nodded. "Set the meeting for three days from now."

Chapter 47

Smoke filled the sky, hovering above the once-luscious tree line of Eralas. The great beech tree of Ny'Thalus still hung out over the ports, but the branches were skeletal and charred. The docks beneath it broken and covered in ash and debris. No ships remained in the harbor.

Where did they all go?

Corin scanned Helgath's coast behind them, looking for the spider-web-like sails of the Eralasian ships, but couldn't make out anything. In fact, all ships, except for those they'd brought with them from Rylorn, had fled the area.

Neco growled as he stuck his snout through the Herald's railing posts, his amber eyes focused on the auer coastline.

"What do you see, buddy?" Corin gently touched the raised hair between Neco's shoulder blades. He followed the wolf's gaze, but couldn't make out anything distinct. Just that Ny'Thalus looked very abandoned. The balconies and windows cut into the cliffside were quiet, the Art-laden orbs that usually made them sparkle were all extinguished. The long, slanted road that led from the docks up to the land above the sea cliffs was empty, save for a few smashed carts.

Jarrod approached the railing, stopping on Neco's other side. "You think they're still just *defending* Quel'Nian?"

Last they'd heard, the fighting centered around the capital, since most had fled upon the order of the capital to consolidate the area their army needed to defend. According to the Hawks that had managed to infiltrate the auer line, Uriel's elders had been spreading an array of propaganda.

"The rumors they're spreading... *I'd* still be defending the capital from our troops. Unfortunately, we have centuries of bad reputation to battle through. Can't really blame the people for thinking the Corrupted came from Helgath rather than their own people. It's the more believable story." He stroked Neco without thinking about it before looking over to his husband. "Any good news come with that hawk?"

Jarrod lifted an unopened slip of paper between two fingers. "It's marked for my master of war. You know I don't read your messages." He gave a slight smile as he passed the paper over Neco.

Corin scoffed. "I'm just going to tell you what it is, anyway." He broke the seal and skimmed over the coded message, translating it in his head. He let out a relieved sigh. "They managed to talk to one of the auer commanders on the southern border of Quel'Nian. I guess she realized we didn't actually send the Corrupted when one of their scout groups saw our troops killing them in a skirmish outside Maelei. She's agreed to meet. But only with you."

"Good thing I'm almost there, then." Jarrod looked Corin over. "Ironic that it was addressed to you if they'll only meet with me. Plus, they don't know who else is accompanying us."

They'd kept Erdeaseq's name out of all correspondence, in case Uriel caught wind the arch judgment lived. The last thing they needed was an assassin targeting the rightful leader of the auer council and the only loyal elder still living.

"Well, it's got some other stuff in it about troop maneuvers and reassignments. But I thought the other part was more interesting for you." He turned towards the helm of the Herald, catching the eye of her captain.

Andi narrowed her gaze as Corin gave a quick gesture to her. She flipped her braid over her shoulder, scowling. She kept her hand on the hilt of her rapier as she walked down the stairs from the aft deck. "What?" Her sharp tone confirmed her agitation at being beckoned on her own ship.

"We need to dock in Maelei instead of here."

She gave a suspicious look at the water beyond. "Are there Corrupted under the water down there that will put holes in my ship?"

Jarrod shook his head. "Last report confirmed those particular beasties were around the northern islands, engaging in their fake attacks against the auer fleet. Should be safe enough."

Andi gave him a dubious look. "You're providing hazard pay for this little excursion, right your majesty?" Her lips twitched, as if she fought back a smile. "This old girl could use some new sails. Or a new hull, depending on the next few hours."

Helgath's king smirked at her. "Don't I *always* provide hazard pay?" He scoffed. "Send your bill to the palace, and it will be paid."

The smile broke on Andi's face. "Your continued generosity is always appreciated, majesty." She gave him a courtly bow.

"Mhmm," Jarrod drawled. "You know, you remind me so much of your daughter sometimes."

Andi lifted her eyebrows. "Can't help it if the girl's got natural good sense." She turned her back on them, letting out a sharp whistle. The helmsmen looked at her, and she gave a few quick gestures with her hand and pointed south. He nodded before spinning the helm of the Herald sharply starboard. "It's honestly been positively quiet considering a Lanoret is on board. I guess the risk of some potential action is to be expected. I get antsy otherwise."

Corin chuckled. "Come now, I'm not nearly as much trouble as my brother."

Andi shrugged. "Anything else, your majesties? Or you wanting full service with a bottle of whisky while I'm here?" Her eyes darted back to the island, giving away her continued suspicion. The captain had demanded answers from Jarrod as soon as they boarded the ship in Rylorn, though Eralas hadn't been her concern. Thankfully, he'd received a message through Auster that Rae was safe and sound in Isalica after her reckless ride on the Corrupted dragon. The news had brought Andi enough relief that the woman had retired to her cabin for a few hours.

She cares so much more than she lets on.

"Nah, we need to be sharp." Jarrod glanced at Corin, who nodded his agreement. "Though a selection of cheeses would be lovely." He grinned, adding, "Maybe some fruit. A little chocolate, even, if you have some."

Corin pursed his lips to keep the laugh contained, but Neco whined.

Jarrod dared continue, "Neco would like something a little meatier."

Andi wrinkled her nose. "I'll see what Cookey can dredge up for you." She spun away, making her way to the stairs that led below deck.

"Better go make sure she grabs a bone for you, too, boy." Corin thumped his hand against Neco's side.

The wolf sneezed as he trotted after her, casting a final wary glance towards the island before he loped down the stairs.

Corin leaned against the ship's banister. A new pillar of smoke rose from somewhere further inland, but it only added to the general haze that covered the island. The darkness of it made him shiver, recalling the weeks of black they'd been trapped within when Uriel first attacked the island.

But this is likely all just a distraction. To pull the others away from what they're doing.

"Do you think this will all be over soon?" Corin glanced at Jarrod, studying the concerned lines of his face.

Staring at the island, Jarrod whispered, "Aye. But I don't know if that's a good or bad thing." He reached for his husband's hand, squeezing. "I wish I knew what was happening with the others, so we might better prepare for whatever outcome. But perhaps it's better we not know until it's done, since we can't do a thing to help them."

He nodded, chewing the side of his lip. "I know Damien and Rae have been working on this for so long. It's crazy to consider it could go wrong." Corin rubbed his thumb along Jarrod's. "I just hope we're all able to see the other side of this."

The king's throat bobbed. "Me, too."

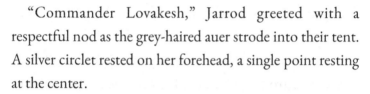

"Commander Lovakesh," Jarrod greeted with a respectful nod as the grey-haired auer strode into their tent. A silver circlet rested on her forehead, a single point resting at the center.

"King Martox," she drawled, her hand settling near the chakram blade at her hip, but Corin trusted it was in habit rather than threat. Her ruby eyes unnerved him, reminding him of Corrupted.

"Won't you sit?" Jarrod invited, political formality in his tone.

"Don't patronize me," she sneered, before quickly correcting her expression. "I'm not interested in politics. You claim—" Her eyes widened as her gaze snagged on the cloaked figure standing behind Helgath's kings. "Arch Judgment Erdeaseq," she breathed, bowing her head low as she raised and lowered three fingers from her forehead.

"They told us you perished."

"I live only because of our Helgathian allies." Erdeaseq stepped beside Jarrod, giving them both a subtle, grateful smile. "And what they say is true. An unprecedented evil has infiltrated the elder council. Those who remain do not act in Eralas's best interests and are the ones responsible for the Corrupted attacks. We must stop them and reclaim our capital. Our homeland."

Lovakesh hesitated, eyeing the arch judgment up and down. She spoke something quickly in Aueric, which Corin suddenly regretted not studying seriously.

Erdeaseq responded matter of factly before he held his hand out towards the Commander. On one of his fingers there was a woven wood band.

Lovakesh stepped forward, smoothly releasing the strap holding her chakram in place. She uttered something that sounded like an apology before she cut a quick line across Erdeaseq's palm.

The auer elder didn't even flinch, his blood pooling briefly before it swirled on its own accord. It gathered, slithering to the ring on his middle finger. The blood vanished, but the ring glimmered with golden light. And the wound across his palm knitted together in the shine, healing as if it was never there.

It must have meant something to Lovakesh because she nodded, stepped back, and bowed again, more deeply this time, with three fingers to her forehead. "What is your command, Arch Judgment?"

Erdeaseq touched the ring with his other hand, the Art still glowing around it. "Send word to your fellow commanders telling them the truth. We must ally ourselves with Helgath and turn our attention inward."

"Yes, of course." Lovakesh looked at Jarrod, her gaze now lacking its previous disdain. "If what you have said is true, I expect we will encounter some resistance."

"Ekatrina and Olsaeth will not surrender easily, and they are most likely the summoners responsible for the hordes of Corrupted on our island. It's imperative we get to them directly without loss of any further civilian life." Erdeaseq's honey-colored eyes hardened.

"Yes, sir." Lovakesh nodded. "I'll assemble a small task force immediately. Perhaps we can finish this quickly and quietly if my soldiers are able to infiltrate the Sanctum of Law."

"Do we have your permission to move further inland to continue our assault against the Corrupted?" Corin already knew the answer, but politics still dictated his need to ask.

Lovakesh nodded again, touching three fingers to her forehead, but this time directed towards the Helgathian kings. She then gave a subtle gesture to the auer guard standing at the back of the tent, and the man vanished silently through the tent flap. "The order is already given."

Chapter 48

THE ENORMITY OF THE CRYSTAL cavern, and the energies each swirling shard emanated, could have distracted Damien for months.

Years.

But the looming danger, the fear of what came next...

He rolled his shoulders, silently familiarizing himself as quickly as possible with the powers that surrounded their gathered group, asking for their willingness to share.

And as the cavern accepted him, he gratefully took in the ká.

Damien had used Ahria's bond with Uriel to track him every five minutes since they'd sent Kin through to Kiek. The former shade had his and Rae's communication device, plus Sephysis at his side. Each time Damien checked, Uriel remained at Melyza's cabin.

The alcans had sealed the area, warded it so strongly that not even any of them could exit the cave into Luminatrias if they tried. Though Damien preferred to think it was a barrier to ward against Uriel rather than him and his companions. The pool of water on the far side of the cavern, which Rae had described as the beginning of a wide underwater tunnel, looked black beneath the glimmering surface.

The glow from the crystals illuminated the cavern, but they'd also diligently added stakes with lanterns attached throughout the space, lit with oil and fire rather than the Art-created orbs the alcans offered.

Rae withdrew the map rolled beneath her arm, laying it flat on the ground in front of the Rahn'ka, pinning the corners with small crystals.

"Just received word from Kin," Conrad announced. "He's close."

Ahria crouched beside Damien, offering her hand with a deep breath. "What if Uriel is already moving on Kin?"

"Then there's no time to waste." Matthias looked at Katrin and Dani, the pair ready to create a portal to Melyza's cabin. "Everyone knows what to do."

Amarie nodded at her daughter, standing with the others in a semi-circle around the map.

Everyone donned their fighting leathers, their blades, hair bound and as prepared as possible.

Liam murmured something quietly to Dani, but Damien kept his attention on Ahria. "Ready?"

Ahria nodded as he took her hand. Her throat bobbed. "Do it."

The Rahn'ka extended his power into her body, swirling through her veins until it found the connection between her and the master of Shades. The action came easily after doing it in Nema's Throne, and he could tell now that Uriel definitely hadn't noticed. His mind traced the familiar lines of Pantracia's energy across the oceans and over the lands. And Uriel remained in the same forests he'd been before.

"Still in Aidensar." Damien couldn't help the grin as he looked down at the map without opening his eye. Faint blue lines, more defined where his left eye had once been, painted the shape and drawings of the map. But in the darkness, his power created a bright spot in the forest below Kiek. "And still right where we want him to be."

Opening his eye, Damien found Matthias's hard stare first. He recognized the look in the king's face. The mounting tension. The knowledge of what would probably happen next.

And he'll see all of it. Even if the rest of us don't remember every outcome he fixes.

The Isalican king would preserve his power, though. Try to see more than one error before attempting to fix it. They only had so many tries. And if what they feared actually happened...

A collective stillness hovered across the group as they all stared at Damien. Even Dani's cloudy eyes bored into him.

If I got any piece of this wrong, their blood will be on my hands.

Rae caught his gaze. "We got this."

"It's time to move." Amarie's knuckles were almost white as she gripped her hands in fists. She'd been tense since the moment Kin had walked through the portal to Kiek.

"You'll have ninety seconds." Dani faced Katrin. "And then we'll open the portal for you to come back. Stay alive until then."

Damien fought down the rising butterflies. "With the energy I've gathered from this cavern, I shouldn't have any trouble holding down my end of the plan until we get everyone back through." He nodded at Conrad. "Tell Kin the clock starts now."

The prince nodded, opening the device in his palm and spinning the dials.

Dani and Katrin pulled apart, tearing a hole in the fabric of the Art that would lead him to a garden bed behind Melyza's cabin in Aidensar. Where Uriel waited to ambush them. The power rippled before snapping into place, the surface like that of a lake.

"Ninety seconds," Dani whispered again, voice calm despite the situation.

"Goddess be with you." Katrin bowed her head to him, her lips still moving as she whispered a prayer.

Damien nodded once at the Isalican queen before looking at Dani.

The Dtrüa smirked and motioned with her head to her élanvital. "What she said."

He exhaled at the subtle humor, focusing on the hardening of his own ká. His barrier snapped into place with ease, then he stepped into the portal.

Colors swam around him, blurring his existence until the scent of pine and swamp hit his senses. The portal promptly vanished behind him.

Ninety.

Damien let his senses loose, connecting with the plant life outside of Melyza's cabin, rapidly interrogating their ká to the recent visitors and events. He crouched, even though he was still well hidden from the interior where Uriel waited to ambush Kin.

The Rahn'ka nodded to himself as he found Kin's nervous ká approaching, his blood racing as his heart quickened its pace. He heard wet footsteps on stone, the former Shade approaching as planned from the front of the cabin. Damien didn't dare reach out to Lo'thec's ká directly to confirm his presence, but he could sense the effect of the auer's footsteps across a patch of moss beside the cabin, which was enough to tell Damien he was there.

Eighty.

Damien rounded a corner, and his eyes found Kin, but the man didn't even look at him. Sephysis, strapped to his thigh, hummed as Kin gripped the hilt, drawing the bloodstone blade from the sheath. With a simple wave, the dagger took to the air, hovering just off Kin's shoulder. A crimson aura gleamed around the blade, which appeared to vibrate. For a moment, Damien expected it to tear away from Kin and rush into the cabin after its old master, but it remained.

He really does have it under control.

Keeping to a crouch, Damien slid around to the front of the cabin, staying below the window sills. The front door was closed, and as Kin approached it, Damien silently said a prayer.

"Melyza?" Kin called through the door, his voice surprisingly steady as he knocked. No answer came, and he didn't risk a glance at Damien.

Sixty.

Kin thumped his fist on the door once more, and the door creaked as it opened a few inches. Darkness pervaded inside, and the former Shade strode in. "Melyza?"

Damien felt his own pulse thudding in his neck, holding the breath hovering in his lungs as he inched as close as possible to the doorway. He tentatively sought the energies of anything inside, but nothing responded. Uriel's power had destroyed it all entirely when he'd killed Melyza. But he needed to figure out where Uriel actually was before he could act.

Kin only needs to survive a minute.

Kin halted in the threshold of the doorway, letting the Rahn'ka keep his eye on the Feyorian king's profile, and the man's eyes widened in a convincing display of surprise. "Uriel," he whispered, and goosebumps gathered over Damien's arms.

"Won't you sit with me?" Uriel's voice—the voice that once belonged to Elder Tyranius—echoed with eerie sweetness. "I was hoping we might speak before things... devolve into bloodier affairs."

Kin's shoulders tightened. "What could we possibly have to talk about?"

"Plenty. You served me loyally for ten years. And you were always one of my favorites."

Damien tried to imagine the layout of the cabin as Amarie had described it to him. Tried to pinpoint the exact position Uriel maintained based on his voice. He flexed his hand, forcing the muscles in his whole arm to respond to the call for power.

Keep him talking. Get him outside.

"That's funny, because all I remember is the way the whip felt on my back."

Uriel tutted. "I was merely trying to correct your course. You'd begun to stray."

A chair ground on the wooden floorboards.

Kin twitched, his ká giving away the fear even if he managed to keep it from his voice. He glanced at where Sephysis hovered beside him, and his ká calmed ever so slightly.

Thirty seconds.

"I know what you're trying to do." Kin backed up as footsteps sounded inside, moving closer.

Uriel's low chuckle sent a shiver down Damien's back. "This can go two ways, Kinronsilis. And I hope you know I prefer the way that does not result in you bleeding out."

Damien pressed his back against the cabin, keeping his breath shallow and slow.

"You left me bleeding out once before, do you have regrets?" The mocking tone almost made Damien smile. "Oh, of course you do. I'm sure you wished you'd stuck around to finish the job. That would have saved you from losing your *entire kingdom*."

Ten seconds.

Uriel snarled, advancing towards Kin. He cleared the doorway, and Damien held in his sigh of relief. "That could have been *our* kingdom. We could have ruled *Pantracia* together."

Kin's brow twitched. "Together? I doubt that. You'd tire of me, just like you did with Alana."

Any second now, that portal would open.

Damien still held his breath, watching Uriel's back as he pursued Kin into the front garden. He looked at the master of Shade's boots, where little sprigs of green turned brown and withered as he passed.

Where's Lo'thec?

"You've been like a son to me, Kinronsilis. I only ever wanted what was best for you." Uriel's hands flexed at his sides, fingers poised as if they'd morph into claws.

"I'm not yours." Kin's eyes remained on Uriel, even as the air beside Damien rippled to life. The portal formed silently, tearing through the empty front doorway in an array of color.

"Behind you!" Lo'thec's warning ripped from inside the cabin, and Damien wasted no time.

His ká answered in a rush, and he extended his hand towards Uriel's back. Power lanced from him, attaching itself in a dense layer to Uriel's own ká. It spread over him in a faint shimmer of blue, sparking with pale color matching the energy he'd collected from the crystal cavern.

Uriel spun, wild-eyed, and locked his gaze on the Rahn'ka. His body trembled with rage as he growled,

"Fucking cockroach. You should be dead." The curl of claws erupted from his knuckles, back hunching as the auer host grew taller, horns sprouting from the sides of his head. A black, distorted maw with long, jagged teeth, belonging to a beast he'd only seen in drawings created of Matthias's memories.

Damien's power jerked against his control as he rushed to accommodate the sudden swell of his shield. It grew brighter as shadow lanced from Uriel's flesh against the barrier. It bubbled and writhed where the Rahn'ka fought to hold in the beast's attempts to draw more power.

Kin charged at Uriel, a roar erupting from his lips. Sephysis remained, hovering in the air with only the slightest vibration giving away the blade's internal struggle. Uriel's body jerked as Kin's shoulder collided with his gut, and the pair fell backward into the doorway and through the portal.

Damien stumbled before he could throw himself through, too. The ground beneath his feet fractured, crumbling as if a hollow cave lay beneath him.

I need to get through that portal.

He shirked sideways, able to sense the barrier containing Uriel fading quickly on the other side of the portal, but—

Red eyes blinked at him, giving him only a breath to register what they belonged to before the Corrupted launched at him in a flurry of claws and teeth from the fresh hole in the ground. It collided with Damien's chest, heavier than a dog, and sent him flying backward.

Lifting his arm to block the snarling maw, he gasped as pain seared through him. Blood dripped onto his face as he shoved his left hand against the cavity of the Corrupted's gut, and his spear rang in the air as it erupted from his closed fist. The Corrupted went slack, its spine severed with his spear's head coated in black blood.

Damien shoved the creature off him, scrambling to his feet.

Sephysis shook in the air, red sparks dancing off the blade as if it fought some invisible force. A breath later, it shot into the portal and vanished within, Lo'thec right behind.

"No!" Damien bolted for the portal, and the world whirled in a spectrum of color.

Chapter 49

"WHY AREN'T YOU OPENING THE portal?" Ahria wrung her hands together, palms clammy. "It's been ninety seconds."

"It has been seventy-three seconds," Dani breathed in that calm, airy tone of hers. "Seventy-four."

Ahria sucked in a shaky breath through her teeth, and Conrad squeezed her shoulder. "This is so much worse than being on the other side."

Amarie approached, giving Conrad a slight smile before sighing. "I wish I was with them, too."

But we can't be near Sephysis.

Despite all her desperation not to lose yet *another* father, Ahria understood. Because if that dagger found its mark in her or her mother, everything as they knew it would end. Pantracia would end. And whatever was left... Ahria couldn't imagine it.

She looked at Dani, but the Dtrüa shook her head.

"Best get into position." Rae gestured towards the black shape of the prison, beckoning Ahria. She moved cautiously over the uneven cavern ground, looking far too calm for where her husband was and what might be happening to him.

Ahria nodded, finally leaving Conrad's side to join Rae. She needed to focus on her role, her part to play in imprisoning the monster who branded the back of her skull. Half of the Berylian Key's power swirled in her veins, gifted back to her that morning by her mother. There was no need for a hiding aura, which allowed her to focus solely on her role. With Damien's block on the Shade connection, she didn't feel any of her previous illness.

She stepped behind Rae, watching Conrad draw his copper sword and wait near Katrin and Dani. "How are you so calm?"

The Mira'wyld looked at her, nearly the same height. "I've fought many battles before. Panic will kill us. You remember what we practiced?"

Ahria nodded, touching Rae's wrist and sending a short pulse of energy into her just as Amarie had taught her to do. Except when the time came, Rae would need a lot more than a drop, given in a steady, tolerable pace.

"Try not to kill me," Rae whispered, but her mouth quirked in a smirk.

"Now," Katrin called, garnering everyone's attention as she once more used her power in tandem with Dani's. They channeled energy, slowly pulling apart the air to form the portal that would bring not just Kin and Damien back, but Uriel himself. And likely Lo'thec.

Matthias stood with Liam, blades ready on both of them, while Amarie hovered near the portal opening, ready to provide Damien with the energy he would need to maintain his shield around Uriel.

Conrad stuck with Liam, too, though his gaze kept returning to Ahria.

Gods, keep him safe.

The portal snapped open, and everyone collectively held their breath.

When no one immediately came through, Ahria's heart beat harder. "Where are they?" She stepped towards the portal, but Rae grabbed her.

"They may not be ready." Matthias held up a hand. "We wait. Ten minutes."

It took a moment for the time count Matthias spoke to make sense, but Ahria recalled the conversations about the Isalican king's Art. His ability to jump backward in time and provide them all another opportunity, even if they weren't aware of it.

He would have told us if this wasn't the first time we've been through this moment.

The watery surface of the portal broke, and a black beast tumbled through.

Ahria gasped, fear tightening its hold as she beheld the monster rising to its clawed feet. Long, charred limbs attached to a tall, hunched body. It growled, breath coming in deep, raspy snarls through a jagged maw.

Uriel.

She froze, body unable to respond to her need to move as Uriel's gaze passed quickly over all of them, snagging only briefly on the prison. The curled horns on his head angled down as he spun back to the portal and charged for it.

Katrin stepped in front of him, blocking his path, and Matthias shouted, launching towards them.

But the Isalican queen thrust out her arms, and a howl of wind echoed through the chamber. Strands of her hair, loose from her bun, blasted back with the sudden burst of air, and her Art slammed into Uriel, throwing him into a patch of crystals with a crash.

Rae acted next, calling the flame from one of their many lanterns into her palm before lancing it at Uriel in an inferno that heated the cavern like a dragon's breath.

Another form staggered out of the portal, and Ahria choked on her breath as Kin appeared, Sephysis at his...

What the hells?

Panic scorched through her. He was supposed to leave the blade behind.

Uriel rose from within Rae's blaze and let out a roar that vibrated Ahria's bones. And with the roar, the pale sheen of Rahn'ka energy that had lingered around his body broke apart.

Sephysis lanced through the air in a flash of red, aimed at Uriel. But a wave of shadow grew from the ground and encased the bloodstone blade. A terrible, high-pitched ring emanated from the block of darkness. It vibrated, motes of red sparking along the edges as the dagger attempted to escape. The master of Shades lumbered over the broken crystal, advancing back towards the portal.

Lo'thec emerged next, the ground of the cavern cracking as his boots touched it. The stone shone red hot as it parted, and black creatures erupted from the fissures. The water bubbled as more dark shapes emerged, advancing towards their summoner to form a protective circle.

Liam, Matthias, and Conrad faced the Corrupted, their blades shining as they blocked their advance deeper into the cavern.

The portal still rippled in the air, beckoning the last of their party to break through. Amarie waited for Damien.

Her sole purpose—to power him—needed to remain her priority, but Ahria could see her desire to leap into battle against Uriel.

Uriel charged at Kin, lip curling to reveal jagged, yellow teeth.

The former Shade managed only one step sideways before Uriel collided with him.

The cavern descended into chaos. Corrupted screams and the sounds of shattering crystal.

An outline appeared in the obsidian surface of the prison, Rae's hands twitching with power as she carefully manipulated what Ahria gifted her. The spot where Ahria kept her hand on the Mira'wyld's back heated as the Berylian Key's energy flowed. From Rae's palm crackled a stream of lightning, mixed with bursts of flame and the flow of water. All the elements, mingling together, air and life amid the rest. It would have been stunning were they not all seconds from world-sundering consequences.

Kin's yell broke over the din of battle.

Ahria stole a glance and choked again, mouth agape as she struggled to get a breath down.

Kin lay prone beneath Uriel, Sephysis still trapped in the shadow prison Uriel had created.

Her father's skin looked paler, as if Uriel drained energy from him as he loomed, his lines of sharp fangs hovering so close to Kin's throat.

Kin kicked up at the nightmare's concave gut, but Uriel didn't move.

Conrad and Liam were cut off by Corrupted, Matthias beside them, none able to reach her father.

Where the hells is Damien?

Uriel's claws flashed, and Kin cried out as blood splattered across the cavern ground.

Amarie screamed as Kin's body jerked, then ceased to move entirely.

Ahria's father lay motionless, throat split open. His blood coated Uriel's claws, and the wicked beast chuffed what sounded like a laugh as he stood.

Damien, finally, emerged from the portal, and the two who'd created it immediately collapsed it.

But it's over.

Ahria couldn't breathe. Kin was... Kin was dead. They couldn't imprison Uriel without him.

Why isn't Matthias jumping us back?

A dire thought struck her.

What if he already has and this is the final outcome?

Damien's power exploded to life, Amarie at his side, and a light blue barrier encased Uriel.

The Nightmare, as Matthias had called that form of Uriel's, moved to charge them, but his feet were rooted to the ground.

Liam let out a cry of pain, and Ahria felt utterly helpless as Sephysis tore through his chest.

Sephysis.

She looked at Lo'thec, who held some sort of sheath. With Kin dead, he'd stolen control of the blade, and Ahria watched in horror as a streak of red light ripped through Conrad's arm, his thigh, and he dropped to the ground.

Matthias took down Corrupted after Corrupted, killing his way towards the Rahn'ka who still hovered near the portal's original location. His hand gripped tight on Amarie's wrist as if helping to hold her in place, too.

"No!" Ahria's eyes burned, hot tears streaking her cheeks. The dagger angled for her, and everyone shifted, everything moving in slow motion for a second before the bloodstone blade bolted for its target.

But Rae was faster, yanking Ahria out of the way and putting herself between her and the inevitable Sundering. Fire and water flashed in front of her, the focus from the lock shifting to a makeshift shield.

Sephysis didn't hesitate and tore through the elemental shield like paper, and punched through Rae's chest before circling back towards Ahria.

The Mira'wyld's knees folded as she looked down at the hole in her chest.

Ahria covered her mouth as she staggered backward, Damien's anguish echoing through the chamber in a bellow of rage. Her back collided with something solid, and she touched the groove Rae's power had begun to carve into the prison. It faded, flattened, turning back into the smooth prison surface.

We've failed.

Amarie abandoned Damien with a shout, charging at Lo'thec as the dagger altered course for her, instead of her daughter. She only made it a few steps towards the elder before Sephysis found her back. It sank into her flesh, between her shoulder blades, and she crashed to her knees.

Oh, gods.

Matthias didn't stop, hacking through body after body between him and Damien.

The ground beneath them started to shake, crystals falling from the cavern ceiling. Rumbling far, far beneath their feet rose to a deafening level, crevices snaking across the cavern floor. Cracks of power broke across Amarie's skin, beryl light streaming from within. The streams of power arced towards Sephysis's hilt, still protruding from her back as Damien slid along the ground and caught her.

The Rahn'ka grabbed the dagger's hilt, and veins swelled in his arms as he pulled. He screamed as he tried and failed to remove the blade from the Key.

Ahria fell to her knees.

It's over.

Chapter 50

BLACK BLOOD SPRAYED ACROSS JARROD'S face, coating his senses in the decayed stench of Corrupted. But he didn't let go of the connection, looking at his own body through Neco's eyes. He'd used the wolf to invade further into Quel'Nian, where he'd found one of the remaining wicked elders.

He could still taste Ekatrina's blood on his tongue.

Corin fought at his side, defending his human body relentlessly in the absence of his mind.

It's not over yet, keep fighting. Jarrod sent the thought to Neco before releasing the wolf and returning to his own body. One elder likely still lived, but the number of Corrupted emerging from dust and dirt had greatly decreased, and half those in existence had fled, their leashes severed.

Neco shook, then bolted back into the fray of battle.

Jarrod stood, drawing his sword. "Thank you, Husband. Always nice to come back to a breathing body."

"My pleasure," Corin drawled. "I've always preferred your head still attached to your shoulders."

Jarrod chuckled, stepping into an attacking Corrupted to sever its spine in a smooth, sweeping motion. "Do you think we'll—"

The ground beneath their feet groaned and rumbled before starting to shake. Even the Corrupted paused their assault as cracks broke through the muddy ground, splitting the rock.

Neco, to me.

When the wolf didn't reply, Jarrod scanned the battlefield.

He was just here.

A tree crashed to the ground, shouts and cries echoing from all around them.

He sought his connection to the wolf, but found nothing. An emptiness filled him, one he hadn't known for decades, as his soul recognized the loss.

"Jarrod," Corin whispered, barely audible over the noise.

The king followed his gaze, dread pooling in his gut. "No."

A mass of black fur lay on the ground, unmoving.

Jarrod bolted for Neco, steps unsteady over the shaking ground. He dropped to his knees next to the wolf, looking for any sign of injury. Nothing. No blood. No wounds. "What's happening?" He looked up at Corin, then back to Neco's face.

White fur had suddenly sprung up around his snout and eyebrows, which hadn't been there before. The signs of age he'd always expected to see in the wolf well past his typical lifespan. And now...

All around them, Corrupted melted into the mud, and auer screamed.

"The Sundering," Corin gasped, clutching Jarrod's shoulder. "By the gods."

Jarrod breathed, finding none of the colored scents around him anymore. "It can't be. That means..."

Rae. Damien. All the others. They failed.

He looked up at his husband and took his hand, his other still buried in Neco's fur.

Corin squeezed, meeting his gaze, and shook his head. His eyes turned glassy, and he sank to the splitting ground beside Jarrod.

Chapter 51

MATTHIAS NEEDED TO TAKE DAMIEN back with him, needed the Rahn'ka to remember this. Something had gone wrong on the other side of the portal, and he needed to fix it. He plowed through the Corrupted, swinging his axe as fast as he could.

Kin was dead. Taking him back wasn't an option. Liam, Conrad. Sephysis could turn on him, too, at any moment, but he needed the Rahn'ka. Jumping without him would risk the same thing happening all over again and Matthias could be too weak to jump far enough a second time. A third. Each time risked everything.

Sephysis circled Lo'thec before jolting towards Ahria.

Rae went down defending the young Berylian Key, and Damien's scream rippled through the air and the Art within it.

Ahria recoiled towards the prison, and Katrin ran towards them only to be cut off by a Corrupted.

Dani charged in a blur of white fur, tackling the Corrupted before it struck Katrin, and a whisper of gratitude flowed through the Isalican king.

Amarie moved for Lo'thec, and Matthias growled as he brought his axe down on the neck of another Corrupted, sending up a stream of black liquid.

He understood. He understood what Amarie wanted to accomplish, or rather, to stop. Stopping Lo'thec was their only chance of stopping the Sundering, but if he could just make it to Damien...

Sephysis hurtled for Amarie's back.

Jump. I need to jump.

Despite the thought, Matthias gritted his teeth and gained another step towards the Rahn'ka.

If I can get to Damien even after the Sundering starts, we can still recover. And he can test his theory about stopping it.

Shouting his frustration, Matthias took out another Corrupted. A sickening sound of metal hitting flesh drew his gaze back to Amarie, who dropped to her knees with Sephysis embedded in her back.

His mouth dried, and beneath them, the ground rumbled. The cavern shook, crystals breaking and falling, chunks of stone rolling from walls.

Damien moved closer to him, but stopped to catch Amarie. He grabbed the bloodstone blade, but couldn't pull it from her back.

Amarie cried out in pain as he struggled, still alive despite the blood coating her.

"Fuck," he breathed, leaping over a fallen Corrupted and clamping a hand onto Damien's shoulder. He summoned his power, letting it flood his—

Nothing.

Nothing happened. Nothing responded.

Panic reeled through him. The Sundering negated the Art, which meant the only source of power was...

His gaze landed on Amarie, lines like lightning erupting from her skin and flowing into Sephysis. It drained everything she had, and he didn't have time to consider the possible consequences of his next action.

Grabbing Amarie, he met her gaze. "Sorry," he murmured, but something in her eyes told him she understood, and the next second, power exploded within him. Her last gift to him, granting him the power he so desperately needed.

Uriel roared, his nightmare form expanding larger and larger. He focused on Matthias, dropping to all fours to launch at his prior host.

With one hand on Damien and the other on Amarie, Matthias forced time to reverse.

Matthias tried to go back further, but he couldn't control his own Art. It carried *him* through time, further and further, to before they'd even arrived in the cavern. For a brief moment, Isalica's cold air hit his face, but then everything spiraled forward again.

The Key is controlling it.

Time and space whipped around them, jolting to a stop once more in the cavern. Amarie's power still seared his insides, his breath coming in short gasps as Liam caught him under the arm. Flashes of beryl and blue sparked in the corners of his vision, his whole body alight with the power.

Amarie.

He whipped his gaze up, finding her on the ground, blood pooling around her.

"Mom!" Ahria shouted, and everyone reacted at once, darting for her.

Katrin moved the swiftest, dropping to the cavern floor beside Amarie in seconds. She looked at Matthias, though. "Where is it?"

"Stab wound. Her upper back," Matthias managed, counting those present and realizing Kin and Damien were already in Aidensar. He looked at Dani. "How many seconds have passed?"

"Twenty-seven."

"Conrad, get a message to Kin that Sephysis is going to come through the portal." Matthias shot a look at the prince, who already worked the dials of the device with Liam looking over his shoulder.

"Heal her. You need to heal her." Ahria helped roll her mother onto her side, where Katrin inspected the wound. She flattened her palm on the back of Amarie's neck and murmured, "Give me the power."

Conrad crouched beside Ahria, helping to stabilize Amarie as her daughter twitched under the sudden assault of the full force of the Berylian Key's power.

Hopefully that dampener Damien put in place holds up and Uriel doesn't notice.

"Can you help her?" Matthias eyed his wife, guilt turning his stomach at what he'd let happen to Amarie.

"I don't have much time if we're still sticking to the schedule." Katrin met Matthias's gaze for only a moment before she pushed up her sleeves. "But I can stop the bleeding at least."

"Do what you can."

Liam eyed him. "What happened?"

Matthias swallowed. "Sephysis came through with Kin, and Damien was delayed. Uriel killed Kin, and... and everything went wrong after that."

"Why the hells did Kin bring that thing through with him?" Liam crossed his arms, expression darkening.

"He must not have had a choice." Matthias rubbed his face, the shock of death still raw against his nerves. "I brought Damien back, too, so hopefully he can fix whatever went wrong on the other side."

"What attempt is this?" Dani tapped her finger tip against her hip, still keeping count for when they should open the portal.

"Second attempt. But when the Sundering started, we couldn't stop it. And my Art no longer worked. I only made it back here because of her." Matthias motioned with his chin to Amarie.

The Berylian Key cried out in pain as Katrin cut the back of her tunic open wider with the little knife from her boot. His wife pushed her hand against the gaping injury, blood quickly coating her own skin.

Rae knelt beside them, holding her hand.

"Sixty-eight seconds," Dani murmured.

Amarie yelled again, body jerking in agony at Katrin's rapid attempts to stop the bleeding.

"Can I help you?" Ahria put a hand on Katrin's shoulder.

Katrin shook her head as she pulled her hands away. "I've done everything I can. It doesn't seem anything vital was hit inside, but I'll need to take a closer... longer look when this is done." She picked up the edge of her skirt, the hem already tucked into her belt, and wiped Amarie's blood on it. "I'm sorry I didn't have time to manage the pain."

"Can you stand?" When Amarie nodded, Conrad wrapped his arm beneath hers and helped her to her feet.

"I need some power back." Amarie's voice was still rough, her skin pallid.

Ahria complied, and a little color returned to her mother's cheeks, but not much.

"Was Lo'thec with him?" Conrad moved away from Amarie, his hand brushing the pouch secured to his thigh that held the dragons' device they still hoped they'd have an opportunity to use.

"Yes. There will be a lot of Corrupted."

"Sounds like a good time." Liam drew the dual swords from his back.

Matthias met Liam's gaze before shaking his head, unable to find humor with the vision of his friend's lifeless eyes still haunting him. So many of them dead.

"We need to open the portal," Dani warned, taking her spot. "Are you ready?"

Katrin nodded, moving to stand in front of Dani and touch her hands. Smears of Amarie's blood still clung to parts of her skin.

"Best get into position." Rae gestured towards the black shape of the prison, beckoning Ahria.

The portal came to life, and Matthias hardened his focus. Shook his hands. Drew his axe. Uriel wouldn't remember. Neither would Lo'thec. They had that advantage, and as long as Damien fixed his end of things...

Chapter 52

KIN STARED AT URIEL, CAREFULLY backing away from the doorway of Melyza's cabin.

Sephysis hovered in his peripheral vision, and Kin still tried to understand the hasty message Conrad had sent him. He'd read it, secretly looking at the letters while keeping the device hidden within his pocket.

Seph comes back with you.

The Rahn'ka had nearly fallen over while he snuck around the cabin, making his way to the front door. Blood oozed over his arm from a wound, but nothing had happened yet. The frantic look in Damien's eye told Kin they'd already failed and he'd seen it.

They were already counting the seconds until Dani and Katrin reopened the portal, and he didn't have time to ask questions. Didn't have the luxury of speaking to Damien at all. He just had to trust.

The grass sprouting between the stones of the path in front of the doorway withered as Uriel's power devoured it. "You've been like a son to me, Kinronsilis. I only ever wanted what was best for you." Uriel's hands flexed at his sides, fingers poised as if they'd morph into claws.

"I'm not yours." Kin tightened his control of Sephysis as the dagger quivered in the air beside him. It's desire to strike aligned with Kin's anger. His growing rage.

He hadn't intended on using Sephysis, but with the news of the dagger's unavoidable involvement...

A figure shifted inside the cabin, near the back wall, and Kin recognized Lo'thec, still partially hidden. Sephysis reacted, but only with a tiny jerk forward before Kin wrestled control.

Your revenge is coming. Be patient and trust me.

Sephysis relented, and Kin controlled his smile. As a reward, he allowed the dagger just what it wanted.

In a flurry, the bloodstone blade launched forward.

Uriel balked, stepping to the side even though Sephysis had never been aimed at him.

The dagger flew through the open doorway of the cabin, to where Lo'thec had given away his position.

Uriel snarled, looking back to where the dagger had gone, just as the air in the doorway rippled, shining like the surface of a bubble.

The Rahn'ka's power slammed into Uriel, a blue aura hardening around the auer's limbs. Almost as suddenly as that'd occurred, Uriel's body shifted. His arms elongated, skin darkening like the shadows he controlled. Horns grew into curls at the sides of his head as massive fangs took the place of his teeth.

Matthias's rendered drawing had been terrifying, but nothing compared to the jolt of fear that lanced through Kin as Uriel's darkness pushed against Damien's barrier, a creature trying to burst from a cocoon.

"Go!" Damien screamed, but Kin was already moving. He charged, slamming his shoulder into Uriel's gut and shoving his old master backward.

Sephysis giddily struck at Lo'thec again, ricocheting off the auer's wards. Kin half expected it to ignore the call, but his awareness of the blade shifted as Sephysis whirled back through the main living space of the cabin, lancing towards the portal just as Kin felt the spark of its power on his skin.

Colors fractured in the portal, the gap between places, and he saw it. Every other time he'd crossed through a portal, Sephysis had been in its sheath at his thigh. But entering this portal just a second apart... He saw the tether. The Art-bound connection that must not have allowed him to pass through without the bloodstone blade the previous time.

A second later, they tumbled out of the portal, rolling across the cavern floor. The light-blue barrier still clung to Uriel, containing him, as the others in the cavern jumped into action.

Rae began to charge the prison lock, while Liam, Conrad, and Matthias held their blades ready for battle.

Damien broke through the portal right behind them, and Amarie—

Gods, what happened to her?

His heart nearly stopped at the sight. Blood soaked her tunic, her face wan. Her bright eyes met his, and a muscle in her jaw flexed. She slapped her hand onto Damien's shoulder, baring her teeth as she pushed enough power into him that his tattoos glowed incandescent.

The blue shield around Uriel brightened, the runes etched along its surface now visible. The Nightmare began to rise, but his knees buckled, pushing him back to the ground as the Rahn'ka's power tightened. A draconi-like roar broke from Uriel's mutated jaw, claws digging into the cavern ground.

Before Kin could warn anyone, Lo'thec emerged from the portal, limping, with blood staining his leg. Corrupted burst from the ground at his feet, too many, too fast, and Liam went down.

Conrad was there a breath later, copper sword flashing as he thrust it into the Corrupted's flank. It screeched, reeling back and lashing towards him. Liam kicked the thing off before he rolled towards it. His dual blades sang as they came together, severing the thing's head.

Kin hastily shoved up his sleeve to expose his scar-webbed tattoo. He sought his connection to the bloodstone blade and ordered it away. As far away as possible.

The dagger reminded him of his one request. The revenge he'd been promised.

I will get it for you.

Matthias darted towards Kin, his axe at his side. Black flashed in his peripheral vision when he was halfway across the cavern, but he didn't turn fast enough. A Corrupted collided with the Isalican king's leg, fangs sinking into his thigh. He shouted, slashing with his axe.

The thing dodged, slinking to the ground like a feral cat. He swung again, catching air as it moved again, too fast. As it danced around him, a high-pitched whine escaped its mouth when an arrow thunked into the side of its neck. Another, an instant later, pinned its head to the cavern floor.

Kin followed the trajectory, spying Katrin as she nocked another arrow into her bow while perched between two massive crystals on the far side of the cavern. And as soon as her husband started forward again, she turned her attention towards the water, where something serpentine emerged from the depths.

"Ready?" Matthias panted, pulling Kin's attention back to where they stood. The Isalican king glanced at Damien and Amarie as they walked away from the portal towards Uriel. Towards where Rae and Ahria worked on the prison's surface, Rae's lightning etching deeper lines into the rim of the doorway.

"Almost." Kin sent his demand to Sephysis, and the blade vibrated in its distaste. But it obeyed.

Sephysis threw itself at the water's surface in the corner of the cavern, vanishing within. As Kin debated how far to send Sephysis away, a different idea suddenly struck him as he looked at Lo'thec. Uriel wasn't a threat while contained by Damien and Amarie. He could focus on the auer and the device they'd been given by the dragons. The device that would close the Corrupted hell by using Lo'thec to do it. This was the opportunity. But a second possibility occurred to him.

He reached mentally for the dagger. *Stay in the tunnel. I'll need you.*

Kin felt a weight lighten on his shoulders, Sephysis's frustration turning to giddy anticipation, as he turned his scarred arm to Matthias. "Do it."

Matthias only needed to tap the blade of his axe against his forearm to split his skin. Tucking the axe under his other arm, he dipped his finger into the wound and took Kin's arm. Using his own blood, the Isalican king traced the line first, then each circle, square, diamond, and triangle in the order Kin had received them, even though they were no longer visible beneath the scars. How he'd remembered those details, Kin had no idea, but the man didn't hesitate.

With each new shape, a familiar sensation flooded Kin's senses. It felt incredible, which was the part that scared him the most. The energy. The power. The embrace of shadows. It flowed into him without pause. It felt more raw than it ever had before, and the impulse to flick the darkness pulsing at his feet made his head buzz with toxic satisfaction. He eagerly delved into his restored Art, feeding the onyx tendrils at his feet and pulsing them outward to test the control. They answered his will, trembling as if excited, too.

He breathed, fighting to remember his purpose and not be consumed by the greed for more.

Each lash of shadow, each subtle use of his Shade power, pulled on Uriel. The bond forged by the tattoo—ignited and intensified by Matthias's blood—now empowered him beyond the master's control.

I just need to use it. Drain Uriel of his energy by using all his power myself.

"You got this," Matthias murmured, tone deadly. "And I gave you a few extra marks for good measure." He gestured at Kin's arm. "It should help with what we need to happen to that one."

But it wouldn't be the geometric shapes on his arm granting him the ability to drain life from a sapient source. That particular ability was unique to Taeg'nok and the connection forged using Matthias's blood as the abandoned host. The extra shapes only made it easier.

They looked together towards Lo'thec. The auer elder stood near the water, a massive bear-like Corrupted crawling from the cracked ground beside him. Liam, Dani, and Conrad all stood as a defensive wall to protect the others, still focused on their required roles near the prison.

Kin's eyes flicked from Ahria, powering Rae, to Amarie.

Please don't see me as a monster.

He couldn't stop now, and the Shade reached deeper into the shadows.

Uriel screamed, and Kin looked at his old master as his shape flickered at the edges. But Damien's barrier only tightened further, the Rahn'ka wholly focused on the master of Shades and keeping him contained. Amarie kept her hand on his shoulder, granting him the strength.

Amarie met Kin's gaze, her eyes flicking only briefly to the shadows rolling at his feet. To the small coursing waves of tendrils he maintained. They held no purpose other than to exist, for now. And then his wife smiled. Brief and subtle, but he saw it.

He couldn't help but give her a half smile back before he turned.

Conrad and Liam worked in tandem to take down the hulking Corrupted, its bear-like bulk bearing down on them before Dani leapt onto its back. With her white maw already stained black, she tore into the Corrupted's spine.

Lo'thec's face paled as he looked across the cavern to Uriel, desperation taking hold. He drew his hands up, preparing a muddled cloud of bruisy-purple Art, and flung it at Conrad and Liam, who'd backed away from the Corrupted as it died.

The Zionan prince threw himself in front of the crown elite, whipping his copper sword up. The blade slashed through the purple cloud as if it'd been something solid, and the runes on the weapon glowed as the power shattered.

Lo'thec turned, bolting for the water, but Kin seized his opportunity. He reached through his connection to the bloodstone blade. *Come back.*

Shadows snaked across the cavern floor like dark lightning, grappling the auer by the ankles and sending him sprawling on the ground.

Lo'thec whirled back around, and Kin felt the auer elder attempt to control the shadows, too. Kin could sense it as the power flowed from Uriel into Lo'thec's Shade tattoo, and Uriel howled. But Lo'thec's attempt was futile.

Kin's grasp upon the shadows held firm, and they dug deep into his flesh. Then he found the new link within his power granted by Matthias's blood. The shadows around Lo'thec burrowed into him, breaking past his flesh to touch his soul. And with Kin's thought, they devoured the new source of energy.

The auer elder gasped, rolling onto his back as his eyes darkened. Blacker and blacker. A new wave of power filled Kin's muscles, bringing an almost drunken euphoria. He stepped closer to Lo'thec as his body arched against the ground.

Conrad approached in the corner of his eye.

Kin glowered down at Lo'thec as he cried out again, shadow tendrils wrapping around his throat. "Don't worry, you piece of shit, your life will have meaning." He looked for the Zionan prince, who already held the device the dragons gave. "Do it."

"No! No, have mercy!" Lo'thec kicked, but the shadows held fast.

Conrad looked pale as he approached but slammed the sharp blades of the device into the auer's chest.

Lo'thec screamed, body arching as the mechanism clamped down into his sternum, his ribs.

Kin let the Art flow freely, then. Unrestrained, it drained the life from Lo'thec at a horrifying pace, shriveling his skin until his eyes were nothing but blackness.

He sent a thought to Sephysis. *Go with him.*

The bloodstone blade answered his call without pause, bursting from the water and soaring for Lo'thec. It slowed as it approached, as if taunting the writhing auer. It hovered near his head, the tip of its blade pressed to the underside of his chin. But at Kin's command, it didn't attack. It only stayed close, centered on its prize.

He needs to die by Uriel's power.

The Art ebbed through Kin's veins, and he pushed it down into the writhing shadows at his feet. Let them consume what he took from the auer like greedy piranhas.

A hum began in the dome of the device, a swell of orange light pluming out of it and coursing over Lo'thec's body. The warm light fell to the ground beneath him, cutting into the stone like lines of lava. A swell of nothingness opened beneath the auer, hundreds of red eyes glowing deep within the blackness.

The auer gave a raspy scream, his throat narrowing and withering like the rest of his body as the Shade power consumed. His bones cracked and crumbled as he ceased his struggle, his mouth frozen in the scream before he and the device fell into the open pit.

Sephysis fell with him, released by Kin. The blade cut into the dead flesh of the auer, happily tumbling into the chasm with him.

In a flash, the gate to the deepest hell vanished as if it had never been.

Chapter 53

CORIN'S SWORD CUT CLEAN THROUGH the neck of the lizard-lion Corrupted that flung itself at Jarrod. His husband knelt in the undergrowth of the Eralasian forest, eyes closed. Certainly not a position he should be in, in the midst of battle as Corrupted wove through the trees around them.

But what Jarrod hoped to accomplish had been successful. A number of Corrupted had abruptly changed their minds and fled, heading towards the coast somewhere far behind them. Loose, now that their summoner had been killed.

Neco bounded towards him, but it was Jarrod who saw through those amber eyes. A blink, and then Jarrod rolled the shoulders of his human body.

Neco shook, then bolted back into battle.

Jarrod stood, drawing his sword. "Thank you, Husband. Always nice to come back to a breathing body."

"My pleasure." Corin smirked at him. "I've always preferred your head still attached to your shoulders."

Jarrod chuckled, severing the spine of an attacking Corrupted in a smooth, sweeping motion. "Do you think we'll know if they succeed?"

"Gods, I hope so." Corin looked to the line of Helgathian soldiers mingled with their new auer allies.

A mangled mass of black lunged at them from the underbrush.

Corin lifted his blade in time to catch its jaw, pushing it back as Jarrod circled. He prepared for it to lunge, but the creature froze. It quivered, its fur shaking with the motion before it collapsed in a heap, the shine of its red eyes winking out. Its body began to shed the black, like those they'd killed before. It melted, crumbling at a more rapid rate than normal into the ground.

Quickly looking at his troops, Corin saw the confusion on his soldiers' faces as they cautiously approached multiple mounds of black, all fading fast.

"Well... shit." Corin couldn't help the smile as he looked back at his husband.

Jarrod touched Neco's head as the wolf ran to sit beside him, panting. "Shit, indeed."

Chapter 54

AMARIE GAPED AT KIN, FLASHES of him defending her from Ormon resurfacing in her mind. The way he manipulated the Art as if it were second nature. She wondered if it felt right to use it again.

Will he miss it?

But in the moment, she only marveled at him. He'd sent Sephysis into the hell as well, which hadn't been part of the plan, but she didn't need to ask to understand why.

"It's almost open!" Rae shouted, shaking with effort as she bored into the prison, creating the door. "I won't be able to hold it for long!"

Ahria stood beside her, funneling energy into the Mira'wyld just as she'd taught her.

Amarie maintained the flow of power to Damien, but her body felt weak. Exhausted. Her back had reopened at some point, and warm blood trickled down her spine. "I don't have a lot left," she panted. Though her power felt nearly endless, her body could only sustain so much.

"Drain him faster, Kin!" Damien shouted and Uriel roared from within his temporary prison. His claws dragged over the barrier, but he couldn't move. His nightmare form had shrunk back to the size of his auer host, the shape trying to remain.

Amarie looked back as Kin manipulated great waves of shadow, pushing tendrils of power up onto the walls, writhing like snakes. They blocked out the light of the crystals, sweeping them all into dusk, the only remaining light coming from the lanterns and Rae's power.

"You can't do this!" Uriel shouted, his face now auer once more. "I created you! I *saved* you!"

"I guess that was your mistake." Kin smiled, and chitinous plates of armor erupted over his skin, coating his body in a way she'd only seen once before from the Shade who'd killed her.

Amarie's heart skipped a beat, a flash of terror sweeping through her before she focused on his eyes.

It's all right. It's Kin.

Uriel bellowed, and Damien grunted as he inched Uriel closer to the prison.

The black wall finally cracked, and Rae gasped as she pried it open with her power. "Now!"

Before any of them could respond, Uriel roared. A wave of shadow lanced up, coursing over his body. The Nightmare returned and cracks formed in the pale barrier surrounding him.

Damien screamed, his muscles shaking with effort as he extended his hands towards Uriel, whose claws tore at the shield, leaving a trail of blue sparks. "I need more, Amarie!"

Amarie dove as deep as she could into her well of power. The vast ocean had receded, but she dragged the remnants from the depths of her soul. Drawing it into a tidal wave, she thrust it into Damien, her knees threatening to give way.

The Rahn'ka breathed deeply in recognition before he took a strong step forward. With the movement, a wave passed over the shield around Uriel, repairing the tears. It pulsed with pale light before it constricted, and Uriel howled as the force pushed him back. Clawed feet dragged along the ground before his form melted away to be elder Tyranius again. Uriel's eyes flew wide as his body struck the doorway of the prison, colliding with a fine mesh Amarie hadn't noticed before.

As the master of Shades passed through the opening, Damien's shield vanished. Uriel's cry turned into a distant echo as a weave of blackness erupted from its host's back, passing through the mesh while Tyranius convulsed against it. He crumpled to the ground, paler and gaunter than she'd ever seen him.

Rae's Art buzzed in Amarie's senses, somewhat dulled by how little power remained within her. But the Mira'wyld's hands flashed with all the elements, slamming a heavy slab of obsidian-like stone into place.

The prison pulsed, a sheen of white radiating across its entire surface before it resumed exactly how it had always looked.

Kin's shadows vanished in a blink, light taking over the cavern as silence fell.

Amarie's grip on Damien's shoulder waned, and she staggered. She tried to stay upright, but...

The Rahn'ka held her, slowly lowering her to the ground. "It's all right. You're going to be all right."

Chapter 55

RAE WIPED THE BACK OF her hand over her forehead, grateful for the last push of power Ahria had sent her after the prison door sealed shut.

With Uriel inside.

Doubt raged through her, keeping adrenaline coursing through her veins, but as she stared and stared at that door... Disbelief hung on her heart, preventing immediate celebration. But it was true. He was gone.

They'd done it.

Damien's comforting tone drew her attention, and her breath caught when she saw Amarie in his arms, the back of her shirt stained dark.

Rae rushed over, but Kin was faster. She knelt beside the former Shade, glancing at his now-powerless hands before meeting her husband's gaze. "Did her wound reopen?"

Amarie's eyelids fluttered, but she remained conscious, breathing faster than normal. "I couldn't stop. He needed the Key."

"Mom!" Ahria raced over, sliding to the ground on Kin's other side. She softened her voice, "Mom. Give it to me."

Matthias hung back with Liam and Dani, shoulders tight and eyes dark. He murmured something to them, but Rae couldn't make it out.

"What even happened? I didn't see..." Kin looked to Damien, but the Rahn'ka didn't answer, his attention focused on Amarie as Ahria reached to take her hand.

"Sephysis." Matthias stepped closer to Kin. "Our first attempt, Lo'thec stole control. The Sundering had started when I jumped..."

Rae winced, recognizing the heaviness of guilt in his tone.

Amarie closed her eyes as Ahria squeezed her hand, and Rae felt the transfer of energy between them as the entirety of the Key's power passed to Ahria.

"Give her some space." Katrin moved calmly towards Amarie's head, giving Rae and Kin a poignant look before eyeing Damien. "I can see to the pain while you heal her. If I remember right, your power packs a bit of a punch when mending."

Damien nodded, pressing his palm to Amarie's sternum. He didn't wait for Katrin before his eye closed, familiar focus tightening his bearded jaw. But the Isalican queen quickly settled at Amarie's head, pressing her hands against the Key's temples. She entered a trance as quickly as Damien had, her power golden against Amarie's auburn hair.

"Is she going to be all right?" Ahria turned bright amethyst eyes on Damien.

Damien's head twitched slightly to the side, but he didn't answer as his ká radiated at his fingertips, passing into Amarie's. Rae could sense the way his energy flowed, still enriched by the power of the Berylian Key, just as hers was. And before he opened his mouth, she already knew, and a sigh of relief escaped her lips.

Damien withdrew his hand. "She'll be fine. But you really should take it easy for a few days. Plenty of bedrest." He looked at Amarie as she opened her eyes, brighter and more aware than before.

Katrin withdrew her hands from Amarie's head as Kin held out his hand to Amarie, relief coating his expression.

Matthias closed his eyes, though his body had yet to relax.

Kin's wife accepted his offer, sitting up slowly and nodding to Damien. "Rest sounds tolerable." She smirked, unaware of the Isalican king's struggle.

Rae stood, touching her friend's shoulder before joining Matthias. In a low tone, she murmured, "It's not your fault."

"Debatable."

She huffed. "All right. It *is* your fault. It's your fault we're all alive and Uriel's in that box."

Matthias gave her a dry look. "I should have jumped sooner. I couldn't get to Damien, and I thought if he didn't come back with me, he might—"

"You jumped at precisely the right time." Damien shifted his attention to Matthias, still sitting on the ground. "If you hadn't jumped at that moment, a number of things would have been different. The portal was late, I assume because Katrin was busy healing Amarie. Which enabled Kin the extra moment required to distract Lo'thec so I could get through the portal." Damien looked back at Amarie as Kin wrapped his arms around her. "She's alive. We're all alive. It was the right timing."

Matthias's gaze softened, straying to Amarie, who gave him a gentle smile.

"I agree with Damien, even if that dagger fucking hurt." She leaned against Kin before scanning him, her brow furrowing.

"Speaking of that thing, where is it?" Damien started to stand before Katrin snatched his arm, and he winced. The

Isalican queen didn't even ask before she hovered her hand over his injured arm, her golden power going to work..

An oddly relaxed look crossed Kin's face. "Gone."

"Gone where?" Rae glanced around the cavern, half expecting the bloodstone blade to come flying out of the water.

"I gave the blade what it wanted. Lo'thec. And it followed him right into the Corrupted hell before it was sealed. It can't threaten our world again now. Or my family." Kin looked to Ahria, who now stood beside Conrad, their hands entwined.

Amarie's mouth twitched. "Good." She let out a breath and looked at the black cube. "Without Sephysis the prison can't be broken by another Sundering."

The realization hovered between them all, the cavern drawing comfortingly quiet.

Amarie broke it with a soft inhale. "I can't believe it's all over."

Something buzzed from two places, and Rae nearly jumped, looking for the source of the sound.

Ahria looked at Conrad. "Is that...?"

The Zionan prince reached into his pocket, along with Kin, both withdrawing the faction's communicators.

The Zionan prince popped it open first, his face contorted in focus as the buzz turned into a soft whir.

Rae tried to look over his shoulder at the spinning dials, but only caught a few words.

"Eralas has been reclaimed by Erdeaseq. Helgath's kings are returning home." Conrad released Ahria to put both hands on the device. "Apparently the mysterious destruction of the Corrupted turned the battle pretty quickly."

Rae grinned, the last of the tension within her finally easing off. They'd all made it. She looked at Damien, sending him a thought. *We did it, Lieutenant.*

Damien's smile was broader than she'd seen in a very long time. *That we did, Dice.*

Chapter 56

KIN THREW HIMSELF ONTO THE sofa with a grunt, causing it to slide along the elaborate carpet of the sitting chambers. But the relief of the cushions—and finally being able to put up his feet—alleviated any embarrassment. Along with the fact that he could just enjoy the comfort without distraction.

Amarie quirked an eyebrow at him before taking the spot to his right with exaggerated grace. Her complexion looked better now that they'd all had a proper meal, but exhaustion still dimmed her eyes.

"It feels surreal," Ahria murmured to Conrad, standing on the other side of the room while removing her boots. "Are you sure it's gone?"

The prince had checked the back of her head twice already, Amarie and Kin both confirming, too. She no longer bore the mark of a Shade.

But Kin understood her reluctance to believe it, for he, too, kept looking at the unmarred skin stretching over his forearm. Not only the tattoo, but the scar... gone.

Gone forever.

He hadn't noticed before that even with Damien blocking his connection to Uriel, there'd still been a heavy weight on his shoulders. On his *soul*. Becoming a Shade had always kept a piece of him locked away in a dark corner and, for the first time, it was able to emerge once more.

And without Sephysis...

It brought a tremendous peace that he'd never thought possible. Relaxing back into the crook of the sofa, Amarie nestling in beside him... It was perfection. Something he'd never thought he'd have.

There were political worries for tomorrow, perhaps, but not today.

He idly ran his hand up Amarie's arm, toying with a strand of her hair before rubbing the base of her neck. Glancing across the room, he saw his daughter, waiting for Conrad as he carefully leaned his copper sword against the wall.

Ahria joined them, sitting on the armrest of an overstuffed chair across from them.

A second later, Conrad took the seat of the same chair, and she leaned against him.

His family. All in one place. All safe.

I hope Talon can see this.

A soft smile twitched Amarie's lips. "How are you feeling, Ree?"

Their daughter nodded. "Like I did before Uriel took me. I feel good. Damn tired, though, and a little hungry." She tilted her head, concern still etched in her features. "How's your back?"

"It's... not great, but it will get there. Damien is going to have another look tomorrow before we leave for Feyor." Amarie looked up at Kin through dark eyelashes. "Someone needs to sit on a fancy chair awhile longer."

Kin sighed dramatically. "I guess we can't keep avoiding it, can we?" He leaned towards the low table between their seats, forcing Amarie to adjust. Indulgence felt appropriate for the moment, and he quickly poured himself a glass of Isalican whisky that Matthias had sent to all their chambers as soon as they arrived back in Nema's Throne.

For proper celebration.

"Actually, I was thinking..." Ahria glanced at Conrad, who nodded at her, before she chewed her lip and continued, "There might be somewhere else for you to go first. But it'd definitely delay your return to Feyor."

"Well, *I'm* already all right with this idea." Kin smiled as he poured his glass, wordlessly asking the others if they wanted some, too, and ultimately filling all four glasses.

Amarie huffed a laugh under her breath, taking the glass from him and sipping. "Of course you are." She eyed Ahria, though. "What is it you're thinking?"

"I know you haven't met Riot yet, but I know how much Viento meant to you, and it would mean a lot to *me* if you, you know... wanted him." Ahria smiled, but Amarie had gone still as stone under Kin's arm.

Silence prevailed before Amarie whispered, "Riot." She swallowed, shifting a little. "Did you name him?" Emotion ran thick under her tone, despite her efforts to hide it.

"I did." Ahria shrugged. "I was ten."

Amarie laughed, nodding as she sat straight, lowering her glass. "If you're sure, I would... I would really love to have him." Her eyes shone, lower lids brimming, though no tears fell. "Leaving Viento was hard, but you must know it was nothing compared to leaving you."

The smile on Ahria's face vanished, and their daughter rose from the armrest to kneel before her mother. Taking Amarie's hands, she shook her head. "You made the best choices you could given everything else. I had a good childhood. And you're here now. I don't feel it needs to be said, but in case you need to hear it... I forgive you, Mom. I forgave you a long time ago."

Gods, Amarie still hasn't forgiven herself.

Kin tightened his arm around Amarie's shoulder, placing a kiss on the side of her head. "It was the right choice. Along with not telling me. You did what was best."

Conrad slowly stood, drawing their attention. "I should give you all a moment..."

"No," Amarie interrupted. "Please stay." She swiped a tear from her cheek, still holding Ahria's hands. "You're part of our family, too. As messy as it is."

Ahria looked back at Conrad and nodded her agreement. "You're stuck with us now."

Conrad chuckled, the smile lingering as picked up a filled glass and sat back in his chair. "I think it's the other way around."

Rising, Ahria kissed Amarie on the forehead. "I love you, Mom. And I'm sure. I want you to go to Olsa and get Riot. He's young enough to sire more offspring if you wish, too."

Amarie looked at Kin, but didn't wait for his answer before nodding again. "I think that's a great idea."

Letting go of her mother, Ahria moved to Kin and kissed his cheek before murmuring, "Just so you don't feel left out, Dad. Love you."

Warmth spread through Kin's insides, greater than what the whisky could cause. He caught Ahria's hand before she could pull entirely away, squeezing it hard. "Love you, too, Bug."

Three weeks later...

Amarie hadn't spoken since arriving in her small hometown village, and Kin didn't press. He only paid to stable their horse while she strode down the dirt road. Deep grooves showed where carts had sunk into the mud during the winter months. There hadn't been snow in the region for at least a couple weeks, judging by the dryness, though the trees were still barren. It'd still be a while before the first buds dared make their appearance.

Children played down a side street, tossing marbles within a drawn circle in the dirt, undeterred by the chill. Smoke huffed from chimneys while the distant clang of a blacksmith's hammer echoed over the air.

Scents changed with each building they passed, from baked goods to horses, to leather tanning and the muddy smell of pottery.

Above it all, Kin only felt peace. A quaint village, with no murmurs of malcontent or crime. No evidence of violence or even a whiff of suspicion.

A warmth spread through his chest, knowing his daughter had grown up here.

Loved. Cared for.

Amarie meandered through the streets, and he would have thought her directionless had she not turned twice already. Her steps slowed as she approached a squat home with a narrow porch and dusty windows. Her throat worked as she walked closer, stepping onto the wood and peering inside the front window.

No noise came from within, the front door nailed shut with a two by four.

With a shaky inhale, she looked at Kin. "Lorin lived here with his wife and son when I met him," she explained, touching the railing where thick roots wrapped around a missing plank in repair. "Talon would have arrived a few months after I left." Her voice was barely a whisper, her breath clouding in cold mist before her mouth.

Kin surveyed the house, glancing beyond the low fence beside it, thick with hibernating vines. An oak stood in the back, the branches donning a treehouse within. The smooth curve of the branches themselves formed the walls and roof, further evidence of Talon's presence in the homestead.

Amarie gripped his hand tighter. "I was so angry. And hurt. Even my memories of those days are... tainted."

"You had every right to feel the way you did." Kin faced her. "And you did the best you could, all things considered."

"People keep saying that." Her shoulders slumped. "I don't know if I'll ever agree. But at least she was happy here. At least she had a family. Stability. I never had that."

Kin moved into her, brushing his hand along her jaw. "And our daughter had something good because of the sacrifice you made." He brushed his lips against hers. "But I am sorry you had to make it. And for my part in all of that."

Amarie sighed, turning away from the window and leaning into him. "I wish we could have done it all together."

He wrapped his arms around her waist, nestling her head back against the crook of his shoulder. "Me too. Though of all the people to end up raising her, I'm glad it was Talon. I mean..." He leaned his face down against her temple. "Just look at that treehouse."

Glancing over his shoulder, Amarie gave a subtle smile. "It's true. I'm glad it was him, too." She nudged him into motion, and they returned to the street. "When I was here, I stayed with Deylan and his family. His wife and daughter have relocated since then, but..." She cringed, though a smile hid beneath it. "I wasn't really fond of her. The wife, that is. His daughter was adorable. But I imagine it's not easy being married to someone in the faction."

"Or just married to Deylan." Kin gave her a teasing smile, earning a laugh.

"I thought you two were friends now?" Amarie gazed up at him, the bright, cloudy sky reflecting in her irises.

Kin shrugged. "Don't know if we've really been around each other enough to say that. But he's a decent enough guy. For someone who's punched me in the face."

"I punched Talon, too, if that helps." Deylan's voice drew their gazes up to where the man leaned on a post on his front porch.

Two rocking chairs adorned the far side, a small table between them.

"Is punching people a regular occurrence for you?" Amarie tilted her head, letting go of Kin to greet her brother. "Because it sounds like you might have a bit of a problem."

They embraced, Deylan chuckling. "I have a problem with people treating my little sister poorly." He gave Kin a pointed look, though his smile softened the would-be threat. He released her, offering Kin his hand.

He took it, gripping Deylan back perhaps a little harder than he deserved. "Didn't expect to see you here. Not since you just up and vanished from Nema's Throne before we returned from imprisoning Uriel. Nervous we weren't going to get it done?"

Deylan grinned, returning the tighter grip. "On the contrary, I went back to helping the Sixth Eye's recovery efforts with complete faith in your little group of magnificent people." He let go, gesturing with his head for them to come inside. "I kept something of yours. Want to come take a look?"

Amarie glanced at Kin before nodding. "What is it?" An undercurrent of dread laced her tone, and he wondered what she would possibly have left behind that would be unwelcome to see.

But Kin followed her inside, taking in the warm living space with fondness. It felt like a home, despite the absence of people.

"Where is your mother?" Amarie's question was tentative.

Deylan shrugged. "Off doing her things. I think today is pottery day."

"Does she visit Roslyn and Ilia? They're in Jacoby, now, right?"

Her brother nodded. "She stays with them a week every month or so." He led them to a desk in a small office at the back of the house. Sliding open shallow wooden drawers, he retrieved a sheet of parchment. "I didn't keep everything, because, well..."

"I know why," Amarie murmured.

"Mmm. But I kept this one, and now I'm rather glad I did." Deylan faced them, holding the parchment so only he could see what was on it. "Even if we aren't *friends.*"

Kin glanced curiously at the paper, looking at Amarie for answers, but couldn't read any in her guarded expression. He didn't know all that had happened when she came to the village to give birth to their daughter, but she certainly viewed the time with trepidation.

"I drew a lot while I stayed here," she explained. "Though my... artwork got rather dark along the way."

"I didn't know you liked to draw..." Doubt in his understanding of her blossomed for only a moment before he forced it back down.

I don't need to know everything because now there's plenty of time to learn it.

"She's got a bit of a knack for it, too." Deylan turned the parchment around, and anything else Kin may have said vanished from his mind.

Amarie squeezed his hand again at seeing the drawing— a lifelike charcoal depiction of his own face at a three-quarter angle, chin slightly downturned.

Kin stared at it, at each detail that rendered his face. The scar along his temple, the stubble along his jaw. "I think you captured my likeness better than that royal portrait painter back in Feyor." It sent a flutter through his stomach for some reason, to consider that she'd drawn it during that time with Ahria.

A hint of color touched his wife's cheeks as she shrugged. "I can't believe it's still in good condition after all these years."

"Do you want to take it with you?" Deylan's tone had softened. "I have a cylinder I could roll it into."

Amarie hesitated, looking at Kin again. "Do you want it?"

"Yes," he blurted. Swallowing, he cleared his throat. "Of course I do. It's a piece of you and... of me. Part of our story."

She smiled and nodded at her brother. "That would be really great, thank you."

Deylan gave her a gentle smile, unspoken words lingering behind his gaze. "I'll have it ready for you after you retrieve Riot. Ahria mentioned you'd be coming for him."

Amarie chewed her lower lip. "Where is he?"

"Stable on the south road, near the blacksmith." He laid the drawing on the desk. "His tack is in the closet next to his stall, you can't miss it."

Three weeks later...

"WE HAVE A SERIOUS PROBLEM." Ahria paced through their sitting room towards Conrad, breakfast platter in hand as she lifted it under his chin. "The last almond croissant disappeared, and it's making me rather... sad." She grinned despite her own claim.

He chuckled, pushing the silver rim of the platter down before returning to latching the buckles of his vest. "You'll just have to go down to the kitchens and get more then." He leaned over the tray, kissing her forehead.

Forcing her mouth to frown, she wrinkled her nose. "I thought there might be perks to being with the prince," she muttered dryly. "Can you come with me?"

"I'm already running late for the judiciary sessions today. *Someone* wouldn't let me get out of the bath this morning." He tugged on the laces of his boots, quickly tucking them into the top rather than tying them.

"Are you complaining?" Ahria skipped around him, blocking his way to the door. "And I thought you didn't have hearings today? Talia told me yesterday they were painting in that room and you'd have the day off."

Conrad paused, making a face as he crouched to stuff in the laces already coming loose again. "I don't remember hearing that."

"Well the *queen* said you had the day off. So will you please come to the kitchens with me?" Ahria batted her eyelashes, grateful for the change in her body the past weeks.

Ever since they completed Taeg'nok, and her mark disappeared, her appetite and energy had returned in full force. She could hardly get enough. Food, adventure, time alone with Conrad...

He sighed dramatically, standing. "You better not be getting me in trouble again." But a smile touched the corner of his lips.

"When have I ever done that?" She gripped the front of his uniform, tugging him close to her and lifting her chin. "More importantly, when have you ever disapproved of said trouble?"

"I've gotten better. More responsible." He moved into her, wrapping his arms around her waist and pulling her against him, stirring warmth in her chest. "More worthy of that stuffy title you hope to abuse."

Ahria slid a hand over his short hair, running her nails on his scalp. "You helped save the world. You've more than earned all the titles." She brushed her lips against his, tempting even herself away from her goal. "Need I repeat? You have the day *off*, Captain."

He hummed against her lips as he kissed her. "All right. Then I suppose I better take my mouse down to the kitchens so she can properly indulge in more almond croissants."

Smiling her victory, Ahria kissed him once more before dragging him towards the door. "And after that, I want to go to the—" A knock on their door cut her off, and she scowled with a groan. "Everyone is against me eating today."

"You already had a croissant *and* a fruit plate *and* two eggs," Conrad pointed out, quirking a brow.

The voice of a guard echoed from the other side of the door. "Deylan Salte has arrived and is requesting an audience with your highness."

Ahria blinked. "Why is my uncle here?" She let go of the prince and rushed to the door, flinging it open.

Deylan hardly had time to brace himself for her hug, staggering backward a step with the enthusiastic embrace.

"Ree, how are you?" Two swords created an 'x' on his back, as if he were ready to leap into battle.

"So much better," she murmured, letting go of him. "Come to visit me already?"

"Actually..." Her uncle's eyes slid to Conrad. "I'm here to speak to him."

Ahria followed his gaze, furrowing her brow, but saying nothing.

"Come in," Conrad offered, and Ahria followed her uncle back inside their sitting room.

We're never going to get out of here.

She tried to keep the tension from her face, reminding herself it could wait. It could wait all day if it had to, and would be just as perfect.

The guards shut the door to their chambers, leaving the three of them alone.

Conrad gestured to the set of lavish purple couches at the center of the room, casually picking up the other trays left in Ahria's wake after their breakfast. He placed them on a table by the door before giving her a knowing glance that she happily smirked at.

Deylan's curious expression passed quickly as he settled into one of the seats. "Your mother came by Gallisville and got Riot, by the way. I think she loves him already."

Ahria's shoulders relaxed at that, satisfaction warming her heart as she perched on the armrest of the couch. "I'm glad."

Conrad opened the armoire near the doorway to their bedroom chambers, and he brought out the now familiar copper sword. Its hilt shone, as did the inlaid metal runes on the leather sheath. He'd diligently cleaned it after returning from alcan territory, along with all the faction contraptions he'd been loaned. All tucked carefully inside a new leather pouch he also picked up.

"I assume you're here for these?" He crossed the room, offering them. "I appreciate the loan, they did come in handy."

Deylan lifted a palm towards the prince. "Not exactly." When the prince lowered the items, he continued, "I came here to offer you a position within the Sixth Eye."

Ahria's gaze shot to Conrad, but she clamped her lips together.

The Zionan prince hesitated, spine going rigid. Surprise shone in his eyes, along with something else. "I'm..." He stopped, chewing on his lower lip for a moment. "I'm flattered, but... my loyalties... I'm not sure I can give the Sixth Eye what they'd be looking for. Ziona..."

Deylan waved his hand and shook his head. "The Vanguard fully understands and expects you to put your duties as crown prince first. We'd never ask you to put anything before Ziona or its people. Though... we also feel you're in a unique situation given your relationship to the Key." He motioned to his niece. "And we'd like to keep you equipped to handle any threats that may arise in the future."

Ahria lifted her brow in surprise. "I guess the fact that I'm still in this room means the faction is changing their rules on whether I can know who serves the Sixth Eye."

Deylan nodded. "As are the rules about familial bonds, should the relationship between you two ever..." He waved a hand again. "Evolve." His gaze centered on Conrad again, who looked slightly paler. "On the same note, if it were to end, we would dismiss you from your obligations."

Ahria swallowed, sneaking a peek at her prince's face.

Conrad's face had hardened in its usual unreadable way, but she could see the defiance in his eyes against Deylan's last implication. "My responsibilities would be only related to the Key? And the Sixth Eye wouldn't involve me in any of their other ventures, then?"

Deylan shrugged. "Probably not. And if we wanted to, it'd be your choice. But as the potential future father of the continued Berylian Key bloodline, I persuaded the Vanguard you were a good recruit. It helps that you were part of the team who defeated Uriel."

Silence settled for a breath, and Ahria kept her focus on Deylan. She and Conrad hadn't discussed things like children, or even marriage, aside from the five minutes they'd spent wondering if she was pregnant. And he *had* said he'd be excited...

We probably shouldn't mention mom and Damien's plan to separate us from the Key's power again. Not yet, anyway.

The prince remained stiff, but moved towards her. As he did, he secured the leather sheath of the copper sword to his belt. Placing his hands on Ahria's shoulders, he smirked at Deylan. "Tricky. Because you already know I would absolutely put Ahria before anything, so my whole speech about my loyalties to Ziona is kind of a moot point."

Deylan's mouth curved upward. "I may have assumed such."

Ahria's cheeks heated, and she looked straight up at him before smiling and leaning the back of her head against his stomach.

"Does that mean you accept?" Deylan stood, tilting his head.

"I put the sword on, didn't I?" Conrad smiled more broadly. "Does this mean I have to call you Boss now?"

Her uncle chuckled. "Sure does. But only when we're with other members." He unbuckled a dagger from his side, handing it to Conrad. "You get this one, too."

He took it, but placed it along the backside of the couch. "Anything I should know that I don't already?"

Deylan shook his head, starting for the door. "I'll be in touch in the next few weeks once I relay your acceptance to the Vanguard. From there, we'll get you anything else you need. Keep your communication device handy."

"Are you leaving Ziona?" Ahria jolted from the couch, not ready for her uncle to go, even if she'd been perturbed by the delay in getting Conrad out of their rooms.

He paused, opening his mouth to answer, before relaxing. "I don't need to leave right away, if you'd like me to stay. The faction's new headquarters are coming along nicely, and the viewing chambers are nearly operational. I need to return, but I can spare a few days for my niece."

Ahria grinned, nodding. "Please do. I can show you all my progress." She'd been practicing daily with her half of the power.

Deylan smiled warmly at her. "I'd love that."

"But first..." Ahria whispered to Conrad.

"Yes, croissants." The prince beamed back at her. "Let's go get you one. Or two. Maybe even three."

"I need to make a stop at the docks, first." Ahria pulled on his hand. "And I'm out of patience. Come on!"

Deylan laughed and resumed his stride to the door. "I'll see you both later."

Ahria lifted a hand in farewell, grateful they'd get to spend a few days together before his work took him away again.

"Can I actually tie my boots first?" Conrad spun with her to the door, but pulled his hand away to crouch. "You've never had patience."

Ahria held in her groan. "You've tied them three times."

"I've *tucked them in* three times, because of aforementioned patience." He secured them quickly, but she made certain to sigh loudly in protest anyway.

"Seems you would have saved us some time, had you tied them, rather than tucked, in the first place?" She blinked at him, plastering an exaggerated smile on her face. "Oh, nevermind. Are you ready?"

Judging by the narrowing of his eyes, she was certain he had started to become suspicious.

"Either you're really hungry, or you've got something up your sleeve." He stood, fiddling with the creases of his clothing in his typical unnecessary scrutiny.

Damn it.

Ahria rolled her lips together, shrugging. "Maybe I just can't wait to see the city. All I've seen are these palace walls for days."

"The city? Why are we going into the city?"

Chuckling, she opened the door to the hallway. "The docks. I mentioned the docks, remember?"

"I thought you meant the royal docks." Conrad's look grew more skeptical as they walked past the two guards stationed at their chambers. He didn't tense at their salutes anymore, but his hand still twitched to wave them off.

"But then we wouldn't get to walk through the city." Ahria prayed he would let it go. Lying wasn't her strong suit, no matter the circumstances. No matter how badly she wanted this to be a surprise. "I've heard there's this bakery by the city docks that has *really* good honey lavender cookies."

"And there's the truth of it." He slipped his hand into hers, lifting it to his lips, and nipped at her knuckles. "I should have known it had to do with cookies."

Refraining from letting out her sigh of relief, she smiled and squeezed his hand. "I'll eat all my vegetables at dinner, don't worry."

Entering the front courtyard of the palace, Ahria welcomed the warm sun on her face, grateful they didn't need cloaks on the sunny days anymore. Her long sleeve wool tunic was enough, and she smiled as the gentle breeze pushed her hair back from her face.

Everything felt lighter since imprisoning Uriel, and not just because of that damned mark he'd placed on the back of her head. She still missed her fathers, Talon especially, but those gaping wounds had healed to something more manageable. With her blood parents safe and happy and Conrad by her side...

Nothing could dampen her happiness, and her heart swelled to know how delighted Talon would be if he knew.

Wherever you are, Dad, I hope you know that we're all right.

Her heart picked up speed with each step towards the docks, and she hoped Conrad would react as expected to what she'd arranged for him.

She looked ahead, down the hill of New Kingston and over the rooftops of the bustling city's homes and businesses. The Astarian river curled into the city like a lazy serpent, artificially widened by the city's inhabitants hundreds of years before to accommodate the capital city's docks. The ships looked like barren trees, their sails, like leaves, not yet unfurled either. But she looked to the low slung warehouses beside the dock, where she could just make out the tilted masts of the dry dock.

And a few minutes later, they passed the bakery, the one with the delicious honey lavender cookies, and she silently promised herself they'd get one—or two—before returning to the palace.

Conrad tugged on her hand, pulling her back. In her excitement, she hadn't realized she'd gotten ahead of him and was practically pulling him down the street towards the dry dock. "I thought you wanted cookies?"

"I do." Ahria leaned forward, forcing him to continue on with her. She tried to ignore the whispers around them from those who recognized their prince. If he could do it, so could she. "This is just more important."

She led him around the last of the buildings, and her eyes landed on the dry dock.

"What could you possibly think is more important than..." His words trailed off as he followed her gaze.

Dawn Chaser sat among the other ships, ashore and lifted the same as the rest. The ship's sails had been removed, along with several planks of her hull.

Conrad wriggled his hand in hers. "How'd you find out that she was getting fixed up this season when I didn't even know?" He frowned a little, looking at his old ship. "Going to need to give Leiura an ear full for not visiting."

"You know she doesn't like the palace and its *stuffy* halls." Ahria watched a moment as dock workers maneuvered around the ship, the sound of hammers and saws echoing between the brick walls of the nearby warehouses. "But don't blame her. I'm the one who convinced her to bring Dawn Chaser here."

Conrad faced her, confusion blooming stronger in his expression. "You did? I didn't know you two were sending letters back and forth."

"We kept in touch," Ahria murmured.

He chuckled, shaking his head. "Kind of a sorry state for her to be in, but it's still nice to see her." He faced the ship again, taking a few steps forward to peer up at the figurehead. An osprey, wings outstretched, holding an orb of shimmering orange sea glass in its talons with carved rays behind it. Like the bird carried the sun the ship perpetually chased.

"Warren has your hat, though. Might need to get that back." She smiled at him. "If you're up for it, Captain."

He laughed, shaking his head. Sadness lurked in his eyes as he looked back at her. "Doubt I have much time for that nowadays. Unfortunately. I'll have to leave that quest to Leiura."

Ahria stepped closer to him, rolling her lips together as she searched his face. "But what if you did? Have time?"

"I would say it's a dream. No way I can leave the courts to run themselves... and my mum..."

"...already said it's all right." Heart beating wildly in her chest, Ahria sucked in a breath at his furrowed brow. "I spoke with her weeks ago, and we both agreed that the sea needs to remain a part of your life. So... if you accept, you'll captain Dawn Chaser for the duration of Spring every year. Three months. Leiura was thrilled, too. Something about not wanting to deal with all that trade shit. We would leave in a month." She chewed the inside of her cheek. "What do you think?" She'd blurted it all out before she could stop herself, despite the variety of emotions that cascaded across his face through it all.

But the final emotion, culminating in a wide smile, made her heart leap.

"You're serious?" He looked back at Dawn Chaser, then back to her. "You really arranged it?"

Ahria nodded, squeezing his hand. "For a quarter of every year, she's all yours."

Somehow, his grin got even bigger. His sudden movement into her made Ahria gasp in delight as he picked her up off the ground and spun her. As they slowed, his hand tangled into her hair and he pulled her mouth to his in a feverish kiss. Without letting her go entirely, he looked back up at Dawn Chaser, light in his eyes. "Hope you've got your sea legs ready, Mouse. I'm not going without you."

"Of course." She caught her breath, unable to tear her eyes from the stars in his eyes. "Gotta get that hat back."

Chapter 58

MATTHIAS,

It's truly over. The Primeval have confirmed that the prison is holding strong and Uriel is no longer connected to the fabric of Pantracia. The Corrupted are gone, too.

It worked.

However, Zedren expressed that the dragons still want to be cautious and will remain in Draxix for the foreseeable future. Dani and I are going to stay here for now, but we will return to the palace for the new year.

Give my love to my sister, Liam

A knock on the door to his study took Matthias's attention. "Enter."

His crown elites' armor caught the lantern light before Micah slipped through the open door, offering his friend a smile and a wave of the whisky bottle in his hand.

The Isalican king smiled and leaned back in his chair, stacks of paperwork piled on one side of his desk. He set down the letter from Liam. "Micah. I thought you were in that meeting with Arch Priestess Colleen?"

"I was. It ended an hour ago." Micah sat and thunked the whisky bottle on the desk with narrowed eyes. "Did you miss lunch?"

Groaning, Matthias sighed. "I must have lost track of time. All these years later, and I still don't understand how my father managed to run an entire kingdom and still do all the other things he did." Guilt curled in his stomach, reminding him of Katrin's plans to give the kids another archery lesson that afternoon.

I'll join if I can, he'd said.

"What can I do for you?" Matthias focused his attention on his friend, shoving away the internal distraction.

Micah lifted his chin towards the letter still in front of Matthias. "Looks like Liam's handwriting. What's the word?"

"Taeg'nok worked. Uriel is no longer a threat. Neither are the Corrupted." And, yet, a weight still hung on his shoulders. Heavier than he expected, given their success, but he smiled anyway.

The cork popped as Micah leaned forward, and he turned over two glasses on the setting at the desk's corner. "Then there's time for this. And time for you to finally start loosening up. So you can do all those things your dad used to do with you." He took up his own glass, leaving the other for Matthias as he settled back into the chair.

Matthias sipped the whisky, studied it, then placed it down. "I don't know how. There's always so much gods' damned paperwork." He glared at the pile of it. Reports, requests, updates, going on forever.

"You do realize you're king, right? You get to delegate. Tell Jildarin to do it. He's practically drooling for an opportunity to impress you. A life stuck in here isn't a life."

The king scoffed. "He *is* a little eager, isn't he?" He hummed. "But you're one to talk, you know. What are you even still doing here?"

Micah balked. "I brought you whisky."

"No, here. Isalica." Matthias folded his arms on his desk, tapping the glass with a finger. "Last I heard you were rather smitten with the queen of Ziona. Does she not feel the same?"

Micah looked down at his glass, a hint of color rising in his cheeks, which Matthias hadn't seen in a long time. "Talia and I are both aware of the limitations of our...

relationship. You need me here."

Matthias's instinct to agree with his closest friend faltered, and he frowned. "You're my brother, and I'll always need you here, but..." He shook his head, a bittersweet realization forming in his chest. "You're never going to leave me, are you?"

"Never." Micah didn't even hesitate. "I'm the only one you trust to share any of the load you carry, and I know that."

"No. No, that shouldn't be true. You've given everything to this kingdom. To me. I think it's time you do something for you." Matthias's gaze flickered to the crown elite insignia pinned to the General's coat, his rank medal beside it. "I think it's time for you to retire."

"Oh, come on, I'm not that old." Micah shook his head as he took a long gulp of his whisky.

"It's not about age." The king lowered his voice. "It's about life, about you being happy."

"I *am* happy." Micah looked more serious as he met Matthias's gaze.

"But you could be happier. I've never heard you speak of a woman the way you speak of Talia. Is there not a part of you that longs to be with her? Truly, in all senses, in Ziona? Is there anything holding you back beyond your duty to me?" Matthias couldn't bear the thought that Micah would give up a life with the woman he loved merely to serve at his side.

His friend fell silent, his greying beard twitching with his tensing jaw. "Honestly?"

"Of course," Matthias whispered.

"Duty is a big part of it, but there's also what we have. Like you said, you're my brother. I love you. I can't abandon you to—"

"Court a queen?" Matthias chuckled, but an unexpected sadness lingered beneath it. "To be happy? To build a life with her?" He shook his head. "I want those things for you. You'll always have a home here, and although we won't see each other every day, we have portals, remember?" When Micah remained quiet, he added, "I want you to go."

"Is that an order?" Micah smirked, his eyes lightening.

A smile broke across Matthias's face. "If you'd like to consider it as such, but it's more of a request."

"Nah." Micah reached to his shoulder, and carefully undid the pins.

Matthias held out a hand to halt his friend. "You're not giving those to me. Those are yours, and you will retain your rank whenever you're here."

"Oh, our foreign policies advisor is going to love that."

The king shrugged. "It'll be informal." He finished his glass of whisky, happiness filling his heart more than the ache.

"If I do this... then I have something to ask of you, Brother." Micah still nursed his glass, resting it on the arm of his chair.

"Anything. Name it."

"Trust the advisors. Delegate. There's no more Shades, no more Uriel. Those still here have more than proven their worth. If you want me to go live my life, you need to do it too."

The truth of Micah's words hit him hard in the stomach, but he nodded. "Deal."

Micah nodded, satisfied, before downing the rest of his whisky. "I saw Katrin and the kids on their way to the archery range on my way up here." He stood, turning towards the door. He glanced back over his shoulder, smiling. "I need to go do some packing."

Matthias returned the smile, watching his friend walk into the hallway. "I'd better be invited to the wedding!" he called after Micah, earning a loud laugh.

Alone again in his study, the king looked at the pile of paperwork and scoffed. He stood, leaving the room just as one of his attendants approached.

"Your majesty. The meeting with Justice Antony is in the Cobalt room in five minutes. Shall I set up any refreshments?" He jotted notes on a slip of parchment.

"Give them a full spread in case anyone missed lunch." Matthias paused. "But I won't be attending. Advisor Jildarin is well prepared to handle the meeting. Please express my apologies, but they do not need me."

The attendant bowed his head. "Of course, your majesty." He hurried away, leaving Matthias with a strange lightness in his chest.

Without another thought, the king headed for the archery range.

Chapter 59

RAE LOUNGED IN THE SOFT-PADDED garden chaise, watching Damien coach Sarra through creating barriers. Their daughter had started the ascent into her Rahn'ka power a few weeks prior, and she'd excelled.

Where Damien and Bellamy had both struggled, Sarra found her footing, and pride swelled in Rae's chest. The girl had always been good at multitasking, and now it benefitted her greatly.

Rae sipped her water, still recovering from Jarrod and Corin's anniversary party the night before. They'd been married for twenty-two years, and the celebration had been just as elaborate as the year before.

As if summoned by her thoughts, the Helgathian kings emerged within the garden courtyard, looking far better than she felt was fair.

Neco loped beside Jarrod, amber eyes bright as he yipped a greeting and approached Rae for ear scratches.

"Still showing your father how it's done?" Corin grinned at Sarra, and his niece laughed.

Her golden hair shone as she jerked her head back to her father, who must have thrown something at her assembled barrier. The hue of their hair matched perfectly, though Sarra's sported braids similar to her mother's. And although she'd also inherited her father's strong jaw, people always said she looked just like Rae.

"I think it will be a while before that happens," Sarra murmured, always the humble student. She respected her father's power, though that cocky attitude still hovered beneath, waiting with quick wit and sarcasm for the right moment.

"You know... I was a Rahn'ka once." Corin eyed Rae with a teasing smile.

Jarrod laughed as Sarra sighed.

Even Neco sneezed.

"They might be getting tired of that story," Rae pointed out.

Corin gave an exaggerated frown. "It's a good story. I was an awful Rahn'ka."

"Which is why we're all grateful the guardians pulled their heads out of their asses and gave the power back to me." Damien relaxed, patting his daughter on the shoulder. "I'll let up for a bit, but keep practicing against the garden. Their voices will only get stronger as spring gets closer."

Sarra nodded, determined. "It's not as bad as Bell made it out to be."

Rae chuckled. "Men tend to be dramatic."

"We are not." Bellamy's voice stole Rae's attention, and she whipped her head to see her son approaching beside Jarrod and Corin.

"Bell!" Rae leapt out of her seat, embracing him tightly. As she pulled away to look at him, she shook her head. "I thought you were arriving tomorrow?"

Damien and Sarra joined them, sharing hugs among their family.

"Weather was better than expected," Bellamy explained, running a hand through his dark chestnut hair. Tattoos ran the length of his arm, similar to Damien's. "But Sindré doesn't seem impressed by our plan."

"Of course they aren't," Damien scoffed. "It requires them to share their sanctum."

Rae smirked, imagining Sindré and Mirimé bickering over whether the bowl on the podium was sitting just right. "They'll both be all right. Besides, it's temporary until we can get Mirimé somewhere permanent."

"Did you bring what I asked?" Damien looked to Bellamy, but their son wasn't carrying any bags. They'd asked Bellamy, in his stop at Sindré's sanctum, to retrieve certain texts, as well as formally inform her of the plan to transport Mirimé there.

Bellamy frowned. "In my room. But you can get them yourself next time. Sindré was furious I was taking books out of the sanctum, too. Have you heard them scream at you before? It's awful."

Damien chuckled. "Plenty. You forget we took over Sindré's sanctum for nearly a year." He glanced at Neco, who'd settled in the grass just beside the garden's stone pathway.

The wolf's amber eyes opened only a slit to look pointedly back, before he closed them again to bask in the sunlight.

"Well, I don't want to ever hear it again." Bellamy crossed his arms. "What are you doing with them?"

Damien's eyes met Rae's. They'd discussed their plan at length in the evenings, tucked into each other's arms before bed. But had barely spoken about it beyond just them, except for the letters sent to the Isalican queen.

"Damien and Katrin are writing a book." Rae grinned. "Well, Katrin is writing it, and Damien is... consulting?" She tilted her head, glad they'd decided to share some information with the world rather than hide it.

Once complete, the text would be copied, and an edition would be sent to the Great Library of Capul in Delkest, along with any library that would take it.

"A book? About what?" Corin looked suspicious.

"Uriel. Well, more broadly about what we needed to do and everything that happened leading up to it. Don't worry, we're keeping out anything that'd give away who we all are, and it'll be published anonymously. But there's too much knowledge that was too hard to find when it came to what needed to be done. And the secrecy is what gave him so much power for so long. Because no one knew..." Damien looked between them all, but Rae could see the conviction in his face. He'd wanted to keep everything secret for so long before, but now... They both knew the danger of keeping secrets.

"Will Helgath get a copy?" Jarrod asked, leaning against the outer brick of the palace.

Damien laughed, relief in the tone. "We'll make sure to spread the copies out as much as possible. Don't want people to have to gain access to a secret library under the Dul'Idur Sea to get it."

"Have you two titled it, yet?" Rae blinked at her husband, absently squeezing Bellamy's shoulders to relieve the tension always present after a long journey.

"Katrin actually made a suggestion in her last letter." Damien looked at her. "Oath of the Six. It seems fitting."

Rae smiled. "I like it." Her attention flickered briefly to Jarrod as a guard came to whisper in the king's ear.

Jarrod then murmured to Corin before slipping inside.

Neco groaned as he rose to his feet and followed.

"So what are the Rahn'ka books for, then?" Bellamy looked at Sarra. "I thought maybe you wanted them for training."

"Well, yes. But I'm also planning on transcribing part of them to filter what is safe to share with the general public. The Rahn'ka have been far too secretive with knowledge that could help a lot of people. And I think it's time to change that." He gave Rae a knowing look. "While keeping our family safe."

The Mira'wyld nodded, opening her mouth to reply, but the door from the palace swung open again, and Jarrod returned with an unreadable expression. She quirked an eyebrow at him as everyone paused to hear what he had to say.

Jarrod looked only at Rae. "A group of alcans are here. One of them wishes to see you."

Something tightened in her chest, and she glanced between her children and her husband before swallowing. She gave a subtle nod and lowered her voice. "Is he... here?"

The king nodded, gesturing with his chin to the door.

Rae sucked in a deep breath. "All right."

Bellamy moved closer to his father, the expression on his face confirming his silent conversation with Damien. The question in his eyes faded, and he suddenly looked as nervous as Rae felt.

Jarrod studied her for another moment before giving the waiting guard a silent order to open the door.

A tall, broad-shouldered alcan strode into the gardens, his long dark hair dreadlocked and bound behind his head. Tattoos flowed down his neck, disappearing beneath his burgundy tunic and black leather vest. Rings pierced his ears, and his crescent-shaped irises found hers.

Rae didn't even need him to speak to know who he was. To know this was Andi's alcan father. And her own grandfather.

Two other alcans accompanied him, but they waited by the door as he approached. Halting a few feet from Rae, he bowed his head before once more meeting her gaze. "I am Adamonicus. And as I understand it, you are my granddaughter."

Rolling her lips together, Rae glanced at Damien again, who gave her a subtle nod of encouragement.

You got this, Dice, his voice whispered through her mind.

"It would seem so," Rae murmured, still marveling at how much he looked like her mother.

Though, I suppose Andi is the one who looks like him.

Adamonicus smiled, then, displaying slightly pointed white teeth. "I heard you ventured to Luminatrias, so I thought coming to Helgath was only fair."

Rae took a step closer to him, enthralled by his voice, his soft accent, and the peaceful aura surrounding him. She outstretched her hand, and he accepted it. "It is wonderful to meet you. This is my family..." She gestured to the others. "Jarrod and Corin are my brothers, Damien, my husband, and our children, Sarra and Bellamy."

Adamonicus grinned at them. "It is my great pleasure to meet you all." His eyes slid back to Rae. "Thank you for leaving the message you did. It... surprised me to learn I have a daughter above the surface, let alone a granddaughter." He looked at Bellamy and Sarra and whispered, "And great-grandchildren."

"Andi isn't here, unfortunately." Rae hadn't seen her mother in a few weeks, but she was due for a visit for the Ice Festival.

"But you will tell me about her, I hope? And help me reach out so I may meet her?" Vulnerability shone in Adamonicus's expression, something she hadn't expected to see in an alcan.

Rae smiled. "I will. And I'm sure she'd love to meet you, too."

Chapter 60

NOSTALGIA COATED AMARIE'S SKIN LIKE a warm, soft blanket as they rode north along Capul's beach. It didn't feel like over twenty years ago, but even with the years she remembered, she would never forget this place. Never forget the escape through the city, the library's tolling bell, or the way the sand shifted beneath her as she fed Kin cheese.

A lifetime ago, yet not.

This time, Kin rode his own mount, and she missed his warmth at her back.

Riot's hooves thumped through the sand, his black mane tangled in her fingers the way Viento's used to. He'd proven a worthy horse, not that she expected anything less.

Fearless, just like his sire. Full of heart. Ahria had trained him well.

Amarie looked sideways at her husband, riding the dark grey gelding they'd first purchased in Kiek. His gaze found hers, and she offered him a gentle smile.

Wish I knew what he was thinking.

It had taken all her effort not to wish him a blessed birthday that morning, but he didn't mention it, so she forced herself to maintain the ruse that she'd forgotten. But the contents in her pack would make a delicious picnic when they arrived at their destination. The destination she hadn't mentioned to Kin, either.

They hadn't planned to stop before the sun set, but her lower back ached from the long ride and would form the perfect excuse to have an earlier night.

As they worked their way out of the city, they passed the aqueduct they'd escaped through, and she stared at it. Her imagination presented the vision of her and Kin, galloping away on Viento, not a hint of knowledge within either of them of what would come of their meeting. What would change, forever, about their lives.

All because of some books.

Shivers ran down her arms, raising goosebumps along her skin.

When she tore her attention from her replaying memories, she found Kin staring at her.

We've come so far.

He was nothing like the Shade she'd met all those years ago, and yet... he was.

Facing forward, she patted Riot's neck, peace filling her soul.

Everything will be different this time.

Another ten minutes passed before she slowed her horse, nearing the same spot they'd made camp decades earlier. Though, this time, she had no intention of fleeing while he slept.

"What are you up to?" Kin rode closer to her, light-hearted suspicion in his tone.

He knows exactly where we are.

Amarie smiled at him. "I thought we could stop here for the night."

His eyes narrowed only slightly before he gave her a nod. "All right."

She guided Riot further from the ocean, the movements so familiar as she found the exact large driftwood log they'd leaned against before. Still there, despite the years. Still the same gnarled, sea-beaten branches. Her heart fluttered with anticipation, a subtle unease tilting her stomach.

A short distance from the log, a fire pit still remained, lined with rocks. It looked as if someone over the years had even taken the time to improve on it, lining the bottom of the sandy pit with more flat stones. The charcoal remains of an old fire occupied the center, almost like a ghost of their own from years ago.

Dismounting, Amarie tried and failed to keep a straight face while she rummaged through her saddlebags.

Kin landed in the sand beside her, dismounting far more gracefully than he had all those years ago. He patted the gelding's neck as he looked back at Amarie. He started to open his mouth, but it turned into a sideways smile before he shook his head. Untying their bedroll from the back of his saddle, he murmured, "Unfortunately, I don't have a black cloak anymore to spread out beneath us. But I figure this will be more comfortable." He heaved off the bedroll, and started towards the driftwood. He eyed it for a moment before he laid out the bedroll on the sand, exactly where they'd sat that first sunset.

Amarie grinned, gathering a few parchment-wrapped bundles as she watched him. "Not opposed to my sentimentality?" She placed the packages of food on the bedroll before pausing and biting her lower lip.

"Absolutely not. In fact, I'll happily encourage it." Kin looked up at her with eyes of glittering ice. He stood slowly, moving into her. His arms slid around her waist with ease, and he kissed her gently. "Especially if you continue to bite your lip like that. But... we really should see to the horses first if we intend to stay the night here."

Humming, Amarie made a point of biting it again, letting her gaze slip to his mouth before she eased out of his embrace. "If you insist. Why don't you do that while I get food prepared for us?"

He groaned as he moved away, protesting with a smile. "I hope there's rum, too."

Amarie chuckled, shrugging.

With new confidence, he saw to removing the horses' tack, encouraging them both onto the grassy knoll behind the driftwood. He settled the saddles onto the log, piling their packs in the sand beside their bedroll. After giving them water, he looped their reins over a nearby log.

While he worked, she unwrapped the cheeses, meats, and fruits she'd purchased at their previous stop, along with a loaf of crusty bread and lump of soft, salted butter. Lastly, she retrieved a smaller bottle of rum, pushing it into the sand near their packs. He returned to the firepit, bringing a small collection of wood he must have spotted behind the log. Crouching, he arranged it around some dry grass kindling.

"Hungry?" she taunted, flashes of their conversation here returning to her mind. When he gave her a low growl, she laughed and pulled a piece of fireglass from her cloak. Within seconds, the kindling smoked, and moments later, a fire roared to life.

With everything taken care of, Amarie sat on the bedroll and leaned on the driftwood, content to watch him. "I thought a picnic here might be the perfect way to celebrate your birthday."

His poking at the fire paused. Looking back, he gave her a quizzical look. "My birthday?" He thought about it a moment, then chuckled. "I'd honestly forgotten. But I guess it is." Moving to the bedroll, he loosened the ties of his navy cloak and settled it around their shoulders. "This is the perfect celebration."

Amarie chose a piece of cheese and grinned as she offered it to him. "You think so?"

He smiled as he accepted the offering, his lips carefully closing around her fingertips as she fed it to him. Reaching up, he took her hand before she could pull it away and led it back to his mouth. Kissing her knuckles, he whispered, "Absolutely perfect. Because we're here, and now I can call you my wife."

Her intention to wait faltered, and she felt the words rising in her throat. Nerves shook her hands, speeding her heart.

He lowered her hand, rubbing his thumb along hers. "You all right? You've got that look on your face."

"I love you," she murmured, eyes flicking between his.

Kin squeezed her hand, turning more directly towards her. "I love you, too." He touched her jaw before he leaned back, leaving her the cloak briefly while he retrieved the rum from the sand beside their bedroll.

Amarie placed a hand on the top of the bottle. "Wait. I need to tell you something."

His expression grew more serious as he paused, hands beneath hers. "What is it?"

Joy twitched the corners of her mouth, but she kept it restrained as she whispered, "I'm pregnant."

Surprise lifted Kin's brow, his chest rising faster. "Truthfully?"

She nodded. "It's early days, but yes. We're going to have a baby, Kin."

Tossing aside the rum bottle, Kin threw his arms around Amarie and pulled her into him. She settled into his lap as he buried his face in her hair, holding her tight as his breath hitched. A light sob vibrated his chest and the side of her neck before he pulled back, eyes shining. He cradled her face in his hands before he kissed her, harder than before.

Amarie tilted her head, arms around him as she kissed him back with equal fire. Her fingers wove into his hair, and she gently bit his lower lip before pulling away. Love bloomed through her chest, warming her from the inside out. "I keep dreaming it's a boy," she murmured, a tear finding its way down her cheek as she gazed at him.

"It'll be perfect, whatever it is." Kin kissed her cheek where the tear fell, then her forehead. "I'm just happy."

"Yeah?" She chewed her lip again, stroking his face.

"Absolutely. But I can't believe we've been doing all this riding while you've been pregnant." He put his hand protectively over her abdomen. "May need to start having shorter days. And maybe actually stop to sleep at inns instead of camping."

Amarie gave him a playful frown. "I'm pregnant, not a porcelain doll. Though I'm fine with shorter days. And even the occasional bed." She kissed his jaw, his cheek.

"We can certainly afford it." He smiled as he reached for a bit of cheese off the parchment, this time offering it to her. "This does put a timeline on dismantling Feyor's monarchy, though."

She accepted the cheese, savoring the taste. "Does it?"

He nodded, reaching for more. "Gods know you won't appreciate all the fuss if you're still a queen when this baby comes. And I don't want it to be born to that, either."

Amarie chuckled, leaning into him and resting her head against his collarbone. "None of that matters, as long as it's healthy." She peered up at him. "Perfect birthday, my love?"

Kin kissed the top of her hair. "Nothing could ever compare."

Epilogue

Spring, 2634 R.T.
Fourteen months later...

"LOWER THE SAILS!" CONRAD SHOUTED as he hurtled himself towards his ship, heart hammering in his ears. "Get that gangplank up! It's time to get out of here!"

Dawn Chaser's crew roused from their relaxed stupor of sitting in New Haven's dock. The warm spring breeze rushed through the narrow streets, catching the sails the moment they dropped at the top of the mast, forcing the rest of the crew to work faster to disengage the ropes from their moorings.

Ahria laughed, wind whipping her loose hair all around her shoulders, sunlight glinting off the silken strands. She carried the coveted hat box, racing up the gangplank already in motion. "I get to try it on first!"

"You always get it first." Conrad's balance wavered on the moving gangplank, and he grasped the banister before throwing himself onto the deck beside Ahria. His lungs burned pleasantly in the salty air. Looking back to the dock, he grinned.

Warrin had only just made it out of the market streets, his bald head gleaming.

Ahria hollered a victory cry, flinging the door open. "I need a mirror. Need a mirror."

After all, it was considered a higher win if the victor donned the hat in the presence of the one who lost it. And he knew damn well she wanted to rub it in Warrin's face.

Pausing in the doorway, Conrad's hand fumbled to his pocket. For a brief moment, he didn't feel what he sought, and his stomach sank, but then his fingers found the metal.

Barely able to contain herself, Ahria flung the hat box open and put the gaudy thing on her head, peering in the mirror. "I'll never get tired of this," she laughed.

Conrad approached behind her, pumping adrenaline making his ears ring.

The ship eased away from the dock, the sound of the wind in the sails calming all nerves.

Sucking in a breath, he looked at himself briefly in the mirror over Ahria's shoulder.

This is it.

He dropped to one knee, a little hard judging by the

twinge of pain and thunk the action made.

Ahria spun in surprise, and everything about her stilled as she stared at him. At the ring he held in his fingers.

"I'll never get tired of this, either." He smiled, looking up at her. "And hopefully you won't oppose making that official, Mouse." The nerves boiled back up suddenly as he met her eyes. "Marry me?"

Stunned, she blinked at him. But slowly, her mouth broke into a grin, and she nodded feverishly. "Yes. Gods, yes, I'll marry you."

Rising to his feet, he collided with her, mouths meeting in a heated kiss.

The sound of boots on the deck echoed behind them, and Conrad abruptly realized he hadn't bothered to close the door.

"I'm interrupting something, aren't I?" He could hear the eye roll in Leiura's voice. "Just wanted to confirm the heading, Cap."

Conrad pulled away from Ahria only enough to look at his first-mate. "I hear Marxxton is nice this time of year." He looked at Ahria with a grin. "Feel like visiting Helgath? We can go anywhere."

"White sand beaches and crystal blue water?" Ahria wrapped her arms around him. "Yes, please, future husband."

Leiura muttered, "Definitely missed something." She shook her head as she turned back to the deck, shouting the new commands to the crew. "Trim the sails. Take us south, Mr. Forik."

Conrad nestled his face into Ahria's neck, kissing her skin, still slick with sweat. "Future husband. I think I'll rather like that when we can remove the *future* part." He worked his kisses up her neck to her cheek and then lips. Lifting her hand between them, he slid the ring onto her middle finger, next to the delicate obsidian one given to her from Damien. The new vessel for her power, only accessible by her when she chose to wear it. "Then you'll be my wife."

Ahria grinned, looking at the gold ivy-woven ring he'd chosen for the marquise blue topaz gem in the center. She kissed him again, still wearing that ridiculous hat, and whispered, "A beautiful future indeed."

Flour billowed into the air as Katrin flopped the dough onto the counter. She hummed in beat with the pleasant thump each time she threw it onto the surface, stretching and folding it haphazardly. The tune was a new one she'd heard on the streets during the Snowdrop Festival in Nema's Throne. The joyful chaos of being queen at those kinds of events always made moments like this one, in Liam and Dani's cabin, all the better.

Laughter caught her ear, and she glanced through the open window. The lush jungle of Draxix hovered beyond the open area where Jaxx and his dragon Zaniken rested. Geroth and Zael had evidently started a water fight around the dragon's wings with Liam and Matthias.

Dani laid in a bright patch of sun, further away, in her panther form. She had her eyes closed, but Katrin knew better than to assume the Dtrüa wasn't fully aware of the shenanigans not far from her.

A squeak of surprise escaped Katrin's lips as the door burst open a moment later. Her husband rushed in, slamming it with his back as he tried to catch his breath. He held a finger to his lips, shirt and breeches almost entirely soaked.

She scowled playfully, shaping her first loaf as she dutifully ignored him.

Seconds later, Zael poked his head in the window, looking at her. "You seen Dad?"

From where he stood, Matthias shook his head, but Katrin didn't even look his way.

"I can't say if I have." She controlled her smile. "Better go find Uncle Liam instead."

Disappearing from the window, the ten-year-old yelled something incoherent at his uncle and took off again.

Matthias let out a breath. "They are merciless," he scoffed, still smiling as he approached her, side-eyeing the window. "Enjoying your peace and quiet?"

"I was," she murmured, but humor laced her tone. She gave him a once over. "Going to change into dry clothes?"

"Nah, it's a warm day, they'll dry." He slid his arms around her from behind, pressing his wet clothes against her perfectly dry ones.

A small yelp escaped her at the sudden cold, and she struggled, but his grip held firm.

"Maybe I can help you with the bread." His mouth hovered near her ear and, despite the dampness seeping from his clothing to hers, heat sparked through her.

In the time since Uriel's imprisonment, the difference in him was palpable and impossible to ignore. And she could hardly keep up. He spent so much more time with the children, with her, and their lives were so bright. The best times were when she could just sit in her happiness and enjoy it. Like now.

Warmth spread through her faster than she could have predicted. Encouraged by Matthias's wandering hands that made their way over her hips. She ceased her struggle, turning in his grip to place her floured hands squarely on his chest. "Maybe we should make sure Liam can keep the children properly distracted. Or maybe Jaxx can actually start those dragon riding lessons."

"In his defense, he tried, but the little beasts wanted to throw water around instead." Matthias nuzzled the side of her neck, placing a kiss under her ear.

She couldn't stop the breathy moan that buzzed on her lips. "I don't think I'm going to get much more work done on this bread." She ran her hand up into his hair and pulled him back into her for a fiery kiss. Easing away, she ran her finger over his bottom lip. "You're a wonderful father. And an even better husband."

A low growl rumbled in the king's chest. "I'll tell Liam to keep the small humans busy, if that's all right with you, Priestess."

Katrin ran her hands down his back, and firmly gripped his backside to pull him against her and the counter. "I think that's a very good idea."

Damien's muscles burned pleasantly as he focused the energies through them. The stone beneath him moved, answering the requests he made without any hesitation. The surrounding ká all understood what they sought to accomplish. And Sarra had done most of the work establishing the early understanding and acceptance.

His children worked together on the other monolith, slowly drawing it from the ground at what would be the entrance to the sanctum. The final piece that needed to go into place to tap into the energies of the ley lines beneath.

Their monolith glowed with the blue energies of the Rahn'ka, rising far more rapidly than Damien's. Pride swelled in his chest as he realized how his own children were already beginning to surpass him. How they'd taken on the responsibility of the power and flourished.

As the final monolith reached its resting height, Damien carved the grooves of the stone into the proper pattern of runes. He hadn't bothered to check Bellamy and Sarra's work, and when both stones blazed to life, it proved he didn't need to.

A wave of power erupted from the two monoliths, making his skin buzz. It passed over the area in a wave of teal motes, each blade of grass and blooming flower within the sanctum grounds becoming more vibrant, more alive. Each stone in the pathway towards the center altar erupted with light before slowly ebbing back to its normal pallid grey.

The two-story structure on the eastern edge of the sanctum matched the ruins of each of the others, though this one was intact and new. Vines already crept up the walls they'd erected a year before, while other stones looked freshly cut. And to the right of the entrance of the sanctum's main structure, an empty three-tiered fountain sat embedded along the outer wall.

Rae waited by the fountain, sitting next to the crystal blue fox skull that contained Mirimé. She chatted with it, as if it were alive, but Damien had no clue whether the guardian would hear her.

She looked up as the wave of power passed over her, meeting Damien's eyes with a smile. He nodded as he brushed the sweat from his brow and approached her, Bellamy and Sarra at his heels.

"It's ready." Damien nodded towards the fountain and the hole that remained in the wall above the top tier. Where the fountain's spigot would appear. "Hopefully they like it."

"Pretty sure an empty cave would have suited them better than sharing that sanctum with Sindré," Rae chuckled.

Bellamy snorted. "Sindré is still complaining."

Sarra picked up the fox skull, admiring it before looking at her father. "Can I?"

He smiled, that same pride bubbling up in his chest again. "Of course. Think you can seal it up, too?"

"Mhmm." With gentle reverence, Sarra stepped onto the outer rim of the fountain and lifted the skull into the open place. Setting it gently inside, she smiled and backed away.

Light glimmered within the blue crystal, and rock shifted around it. The stone morphed until the skull had vanished within, and a delicate spigot extended from the wall. A breath later, liquid energy flowed out, and they all stood in silence to witness it.

It cascaded gracefully down each tier, and for a moment, Damien wondered if it'd worked. If they'd done something wrong in the construction of the sanctum that didn't allow Mirimé to manifest.

The fountain filled, but no fox appeared.

"Did it work?" Sarra looked at him.

Damien sought the connection to the energies of the sanctum, inviting them into him as he sought to see where the problem was, but all seemed in order. "I'm not sure," he confessed. Stepping to the fountain, he reached to touch the stream of energy, hoping it might reveal something.

Don't do that. A stern voice echoed through his mind, and he turned from the fountain to see the small glowing blue shape of a fox, settled comfortably among the grass behind them.

Sarra, Bellamy, and Rae turned to face the guardian.

"This is nice," Mirimé murmured appreciatively. "Nicer than Sindré's sanctum. Nothing is broken." Their tail flicked, sunlight reflecting within the iridescent fur.

"Sindré likes it in shambles, apparently." Damien frowned. "How long were you sitting there?"

"Since you returned my skull to its resting place." They blinked. "Let's keep this one above the sea, yes?"

"It should be plenty far away from the sea this time around." Damien smirked, looking beyond the altar at the entrance to the sanctum. Through the pine trees beyond, he could just make out the glittering blue surface of the lake. "And it still has a pretty good view. Close to Veralian, too, so it won't be years between visits."

A smile twitched the fox's mouth. "Good." They paused before bowing their head. "Thank you. For not leaving me beneath the water."

"You were trapped long enough." Damien looked to Rae, and then his children. "You guardians are like family. Even if Sindré can be a pain in the ass, and Yondé is a bully."

"And Jalescé is a little weird." Bellamy added.

"Besides, there are more Rahn'ka that need training. More than I can provide. You made that quite evident during my visit before." Damien looked to Sarra. "She's a quicker study than me, too."

"Not surprised." Mirimé rose and loped towards them, sniffing. "Females are usually quicker to adapt, but I think her mixed blood aids that cause, too."

Bellamy chuckled. "Never heard a guardian admit that."

"The other guardians are a little grumpy at auer, still." Mirimé sat. "But it will serve her well."

Rae leaned against Damien, head resting on his shoulder as she looked up at him. "You did good," she murmured under her breath. "You all did."

He wrapped his arms around her, pressing a kiss to her temple. "*You* did good, Dice. Our kids wouldn't be the way they are without you." He kissed her again, longer. "I wouldn't be the way I am without you. I wouldn't be alive without you. I wouldn't be able to see what brilliant kids we made, without everything you did." He nuzzled in against her ear. "Thank you. I'll never be able to tell you that enough."

Rae's eyes shimmered with emotion, and she held him tighter. "It's been my pleasure, Lieutenant."

Kin savored the warmth of the western sun on his face as he stepped out onto the porch, holding his son.

Positioned on a hill by a lake in the northern forest outside New Kingston, the front porch had a perfect view of the western horizon, dense with pine trees and the shimmering water. The horses grazed in the open field they'd carved out of the forest for the purpose, their barn nestled near an outcropping of stone.

Birdsong greeted Kin as he settled into one of the low chairs on the porch, careful to balance the bundle in his arms.

The baby protested only briefly before Kin adjusted the blanket under his chin. Sleepy hands fought to emerge from the folds of fabric, and Kin offered his finger to grip onto.

The sheer joy and comfort in it made his chest hum. There wasn't another place he could imagine himself as he looked back to the horizon again, gently hugging his son. There was only one thing that could have made the moment better.

As if sensing his thoughts, Amarie emerged from the front doorway, a smile on her lips as she approached and leaned over to kiss Nathen on the forehead. "I didn't hear him wake." She kept her voice low, grogginess clinging to her tone. She sat in the other chair, yawning.

"I thought you could use some more sleep." Kin looked over at her, noting she still didn't wear the ornate obsidian ring Damien had made her, a twin to Ahria's.

It had been a long discussion, but Amarie had insisted that it would be best. The Berylian Key would have extended her lifespan far beyond his, beyond their son's, and she wanted to live a normal life. A life with him.

The Rahn'ka had obliged, splitting the Key's power into two rings that would only respond to the original Berylian Key bloodline. And only imbue her with agelessness when it was around her finger.

So, Amarie kept hers on an auer-crafted chain around her neck. Still close, should she ever need the power. The thin gold jewelry had been a gift from Kalstacia after the mender had aided in delivering their child, and it would be practically unbreakable due to Eralas's unique forges.

Kin shifted their son as Nathen's eyes opened, looking curiously up at his father. It made him smile as he wiggled his finger in the baby's grip. "You can go back to bed if you want? I know he's been keeping you up."

"Nah, I can't sleep anymore. I need to feed him before I burst." She gave him a knowing smile. "Then maybe I'll have another nap."

He nodded, but didn't take his eyes away.

His son. His second chance at being the parent he didn't get the opportunity to be for Ahria.

Nathen Talon Parnell.

They'd chosen to keep Parnell rather than Lazorus, as he felt a stronger connection to his adoptive family than he'd ever felt towards the royal name, especially now that Feyor no longer had a monarchy. And their son's middle name... It had hardly been a discussion.

Love overflowed from Kin just looking into those big blue eyes that matched Amarie's. The perfect bow of his lips and fullness of his cheeks. That little boy had Kin wrapped around his finger, and the former Shade wouldn't have it any other way.

"It still hits me, sometimes. The love." Amarie seemed to read his thoughts. "He's so perfect."

Kin smiled as he looked up at her. "I've dreamed of this moment so much. Of him, of you. And Ahria being so close, it's all... wonderful."

He could hardly wait for Ahria to get back from her annual voyage with Conrad, but he understood the escape it granted them from palace life. She'd been over the moon to have a baby brother, and unbelievably helpful in those first days when no one got a wink of sleep other than the newborn.

But these moments, just the three of them, would forever remain in his heart, too.

"It's perfect," Amarie whispered, eyes closed beside him. She reached blindly for him and ran her fingers over his forearm. "It's just... perfect."

The End

Authors' Note

What an incredible journey this has been! It's been such a blessing to share this epic story with you. We feel so privileged to have had the opportunity to write and publish these books on our terms and be met with so much support! The love we have for our characters is boundless, and to have others feel the same way is nothing short of a dream come true. Thank you so much to our families for standing behind us while we embarked on this adventure. Thank you to our friends who have supported and encouraged us. And thank you to our readers, because you make this so very worth it.

May we meet again.
Amanda & Kayla
♥

Made in the USA
Monee, IL
12 March 2024

54373396R00405